TONIGHT, IT'S HUNGRY . . .

The gardenia dress floated out across the threshold of the closet door. The big flower pattern glowed in the diagonal slash of moonlight. But set in the darkness, right above the collar, Melinda saw something. It stood out against the dark background because it was blacker.

"Who's doing that?" she asked.

It came closer.

"Don't you recognize me?"

Melinda shook her head.

"Why, you see me every day."

It came closer and Melinda saw that there were arms and legs. Something twinkled in the face. Twinkled at exactly the spot where an eye would be, if shadows had eyes.

Then the hands reached out.

Only they weren't hands . . .

LET THERE BE DARK

ALLEN LEE HARRIS

JOVE BOOKS, NEW YORK

LET THERE BE DARK

A Jove Book / published by arrangement with
the author

PRINTING HISTORY
Jove edition / November 1994

ISBN: 0-515-11488-X

A JOVE BOOK®
Jove Books are published by The Berkley Publishing Group,
200 Madison Avenue, New York, New York 10016.
JOVE and the "J" design are trademarks
belonging to Jove Publications, Inc.

PRINTED IN THE UNITED STATES OF AMERICA

10 9 8 7 6 5 4 3 2 1

For Andy

PART
ONE

....

1

For years after, this is how Matt explained it:

There was a carnival. Aunt Hester and her brother, Wiley, had gone to it. The sideshow had probably been operated by a legless man in a child's wagon, Mr. Eprin, as Hester called him. And the lurid painting that advertised the show, was it any worse than the one Matt and Tommy had seen at the last carnival to come through Claudell County, two years earlier? The one showing the Frog-Faced Man as he crouched down upon an oversize lily pad, his tongue slithering out no less than eight feet as it deftly zapped a fly? "That one for the Shadowstealer, it was the same thing," Matt insisted. "Just some ol' crazy drawing."

And the contents of Mr. Eprin's mason jar?

Matt figured it was a ghastly concoction of fuel oil and frog eggs, with a few snake tails thrown in—garter snakes, most likely. And the way it had acted? Tommy asked. Why, that was simple, too. When Mr. Eprin poured out the muck before the mesmerized gaze of the two children, it had oozed across the uneven piles of sawdust, much like a shadow that had come to life.

But Tommy persisted, What had followed Wiley through the woods?

This part had always puzzled Matt. Still, there had to be a good explanation for this, too. "Must be, Mr. Eprin hypnotized Wiley. Made him think he was seeing that thing behind him, following."

And the eyes, Tommy asked darkly. Even if everything else could be explained away, how could Matt make sense of that? And they both recalled Wiley's words in Aunt Hester's story.

I give it my eyes.

And Wiley had.

He had scooped them out with a fork taken from his momma's kitchen.

Matt thought a moment. They were having the discussion in Matt's bed, at the usual spooky time, right before they went to sleep. "Could be that the story just drove him crazy. Maybe some stories are like that. They can make you go looney just hearing 'em."

Tommy was staring up at the ceiling. No matter how many times Matt tried to explain it all away, Tommy remained unconvinced. "I don't know," he whispered. "I still keep wondering, What if just telling about that story could make that thing in it come alive? That thing that got Wiley? And what if the more you told it, and the more people heard about it, the more alive it got?"

But Matt as usual dismissed the whole idea with contempt. "It's just a story, s'all. But it sure is a good one."

And Matt rolled over and promptly went to sleep.

But Tommy did not. He lay in bed and stared at the shadow that the moon cast on the door to the room. He watched it, as if at any second it could step out from the wall and slide toward him on noiseless shadow feet, while on and on the words kept whispering through his head:

But what if it's true?

2

It began—for them, at least—on a Saturday night in early June, 1973.

The two boys—Matthew Hardison and Tommy Buford, both then twelve—were walking back from The Rialto, the one movie house in the little North Georgia town of Mt. Jephtha. Their pace was slow, with Tommy—a naturally fast walker—having to stop every few minutes in order for Matt to catch up with him. "Wish you'd slow down," Matt kept telling him, and for a minute or so, Tommy would, out of deference to his friend's involuntary plodding. Not that there was anything intrinsically sluggish about Matt's character: in all other ways, he was speed incarnate. He talked fast, thought fast. His eyes, his hands, moved with a dizzying velocity that even Tommy, at times, found taxing. If Matt walked at a snail's pace, it was assuredly because he had no other choice.

Tommy glanced down at Matt's right foot. "Must be acting up tonight," he observed.

And Matt scowled, "Yep."

Though most of the time Matt's limp was barely noticeable, there were still days when he was unable to get around much at all, days when the two boys would be forced to curtail their normally frenetic level of activity and retreat to Matt's bedroom where they would read or talk or exchange stories. But tonight, Matt's foot was in as bad a shape as Tommy could recall seeing it since the operations began.

"I thought them operations was supposed to make it better," Tommy said.

"They's *supposed* to," Matt concurred. The operations in question—three of them in the last year—had been performed on Matt at Emory Hospital, down in Atlanta, and while they had helped both to improve the appearance of Matt's foot as well as his ability to get around, they were still less than one hundred percent successful. Two more operations were scheduled in the next year, and these, it was claimed, would make Matt's foot good as new. (A claim that, as it turned out, was quite nearly true.)

Many years before, Matt and Tommy had become friends because of the foot. In second grade, their teacher had assigned Tommy to help Matt get around school. At first, Matt was resentful of enforced charity, though no more than Tommy himself. But soon the two boys grew to like each other and, before long, they had become constant companions. One night, after four months of friendship, Matt had asked Tommy, "You want to see it?"

Tommy hesitated, displaying a frown. "If you want me to." And Matt, who was sitting on his bed, pulled off his right shoe and sock, and held up the foot.

"How'd it get thataway?" Tommy asked in bewilderment. He had never seen—or heard of—anything like it. His first thought was, Something had grabbed hold of it and twisted it all to hell, the way you can twist and turn a piece of clay.

"See them?" Matt said, pointing to the indentations in the ankle and the soles.

Tommy nodded, then asked, "What made them scars go in so deep like that?"

Matt shrugged. "Dunno."

"They look like—" But Tommy, out of a sense of delicacy, refrained from completing his thought.

Though Matt, whose sense of delicacy was a little less refined, went ahead with it. "Like something pawed me, you mean." And Matt flashed Tommy a smile. "Maybe I was attacked by a grizzly bear."

It sounded like the makings of a typical Matt story.

"You don't know how you got it?"

"Nope. I don't remember nothing about it. Reckon I was born that way."

How do you get born that way, Tommy caught himself wondering as he stared at what—to his untrained eye—looked suspiciously like the evidence of severe mangling. It reminded him of the deer he had come across while hunting, its paw nearly bit off in the jaws of a steel trap.

And Tommy, without thinking, said, "Maybe it happened in that car wreck."

Matt shot the boy a glance—a glance that made Tommy blush with embarrassment and turn quickly away. He should have known better, he told himself. For while it was permitted to talk with Matt about anything under the sun, there was still one big taboo, one sacrosanct recess of forbidden discourse. The car wreck. The one in which, he would tell you without any visible trace of emotion, his parents had died long ago, the father and mother whose face he had never, to his recollection, set eyes upon.

Matt put his sock back on. "Anyway, I can get around and that's what matters. And one day they're going to operate and fix it up."

And that, for the most part, was the last time the two boys had talked about the mystery of how Matt's foot got messed up.

"Sure is nice not to have to go to school," Tommy remarked as he waited for Matt to come up alongside of him.

Matt nodded and grinned. "Yep, I already got the summer planned."

To which Tommy only rolled his eyes. "I was kinda afraid of that."

Three days before, school had let out, and the two boys were supposed to spend the night together, as they did almost every night during the summer vacation, with Matt sometimes sleeping at Tommy's house, but more often with Tommy staying at the old Lumpkin house with Matt. The Lumpkin house, as it was still called out of respect for the man who had built it a century before, was the largest, and certainly the most conspicuous, house in Mt. Jephtha. And, as was true of most everything in the town, there was a story behind it.

The story went like this: Old Great-grandpa Lumpkin—who had made his fortune in the prosaic manufacture of mason jars after the end of the Civil War—had awakened one morning, jumped out of bed, and told his servant, Elisha, to go fetch paper and pen. When these had been brought to him, he sat down and furiously commenced to sketch sinuous lines and skewed spirals, piling hexagons upon trapezoids. Elisha stared down at the puzzling frenzy and asked what it meant. "I saw it in a dream. And I'm going to build it just like I saw it." And he almost did. His architect—a poetically named Daedalus Hightower, who suffered the torments of the damned in erecting the edifice—tried to explain the utility of straight lines, at least from an engineering point of view. But Leon Lumpkin would not hear of it. "I saw it in a dream. And I want it like I saw it." Here and there, the judgment of the architect prevailed, though this was only to ward off such a mundane disaster as having the roof collapse. But over and over, Hightower's advice went unheeded. "Normally stairways are expected to lead somewheres." But in Great-grandpa Lumpkin's dream, there was a stairway that led right up to the ceiling and stopped. Hallways suffered a similar fate. You would begin down one, on the assumption that it would lead you somewhere, only to find a bare wall at the end of it.

"I may be getting more dreams," Great-grandpa Lumpkin explained testily. But if he did, no one heard about them. The old man died in his sleep, just two days after the house was finished.

Yet, for all its oddity, it was the only house that Matt had known, and it was like a paradise to him. Its strange corners and inexplicable closets were the perfect arena for vast and ongoing games of hide-and-seek, and he and Tommy took full advantage of it. And, best of all, there was no one to call him down. Matt's parents having died when he was a baby—the car wreck was what he told people—he had been brought up by his elderly and eccentric Uncle Leon. And, as anyone in Mt. Jephtha could tell you, Uncle Leon—a childless widower—worshiped the ground Matt walked on. "That boy's been touched by the hand of Fate. He's destined for something," Leon always maintained, though he was never able to say exactly what this might be. But whatever it was, it prompted Leon to violate every canon of proper Mt. Jephtha child-rearing. As when, on Sunday morning, during church service, Uncle Leon would open up the cigar box he brought with him—a box that contained several sheets of drawing paper and a large selection of crayons, all of which Uncle Leon flagrantly put at the boy's disposal, much to the scandal of the nearby church matrons, such as Florence Jenkins.

Florence—who was also Uncle Leon's neighbor—earnestly exhorted him to open his eyes. "Don't you see what's becoming of that boy, Leon? He's going to be a menace, if he ain't already."

"What you want me to do?"

"Show him some discipline."

"Discipline?" Uncle Leon repeated with a frown—the same frown people display upon hearing a long-forgotten name from the remote past. "What for?"

"So's he'll stop living in that little dream world of his."

"Whose dream world do you think he should be living in?" Uncle Leon asked, wide-eyed and—remarkably enough—without a hint of sarcasm.

Though Florence managed to take this in stride. "No wonder he turned out to be the way he is, living in that crazy upside-down old house, with them two." Meaning Uncle Leon and his own even more elderly and eccentric Great-aunt Hester, who, as those who knew of her could vouch for, had not been right for seventy-odd years. All day long, for as far back as anyone could remember, she had sat by herself up in her room, talking her crazy talk, her rocking chair pulled up so close to the window that her knees rubbed the sill. Even if you went in and called her, she still refused to look around at you, though she did sometimes acknowledge your presence.

"If it wasn't for Simmy," Florence Jenkins told people, "no telling what would've happened to that poor child." Simmy being the black woman into whose capable hands Uncle Leon had long before resigned the day-to-day minutiae of his fate. She cooked, cleaned, nursed, washed, mended, listened, and reminded.

"Ain't it 'bout time to change them socks, Mr. Lee," she routinely asked Uncle Leon every Friday. And Mr. Lee— as she had always called him ("Don't know why nobody would name their boy Lee-onnn," Simmy often declared)— routinely obeyed her, once docilely taking a pair of clean socks from Simmy's hands and putting them on right in front of Rev. Taylor during one of the minister's pastoral visits to the Lumpkin house.

Still, Simmy weighing only ninety-three pounds, there were some things beyond even her capacity to set straight. Like the Lumpkin house itself, which Leon occupied in the same way that a squirrel occupies a pecan tree. When somebody—usually Florence Jenkins—troubled to point out a broken window or a board that had come dangerously loose on the porch steps— Leon only sighed and shook his head in philosophical resignation. "Don't know why these things happen," he remarked, in the same tone of voice that another man might use in speaking of a hurricane or earthquake, or any other unforeseeable act of the Almighty. But even his detractors had to admit that Leon invariably accepted such setbacks with fortitude and even a kind of nobility of mind. True, he might stare sadly for a few moments at the broken window or the loose board, but after a few more sighs, he would rise above it all, adjusting himself to whatever inconvenience the catastrophe demanded: putting on an extra sweater in the wintertime, or watching his step when going down into his front yard. And even when Florence continued to pester him, saying: "Don't you know what hardware stores are for?" Leon merely got a far-off look in his eyes and said, "My daddy took me to one once, long ago. A lot of nails and hammers, if I recollect."

But then Uncle Leon had always had his mind on higher things. His life's work was to write the Memoirs of Claudell County, of which Mt. Jephtha was the capital. To this end he went around and sat endless evenings on the porches of his neighbors, talking and listening to recitals of painful gallbladder

operations and near drownings on Lake Hartwell. Everywhere
Leon went he carried with him a spiral notebook—he pre-
ferred blue—and would carefully inscribe what he regarded
as pertinent facts: the date of Ada Buford's cataract surgery,
the list of guests at the wedding of Randy and Martha Taylor,
the street corner at which little Tommy Henderson fell off his
bicycle and had that bad concussion, the blue-ribbon winners
at the 4-H Club Show for the last four decades. Each notebook
had a number fixed at the right-hand top of it. Right before
he died, Leon had been seen carrying Notebook 1768, the last
entry into which was: "Mamie Jenkins, Root Canal Operation,
October 23, 1984. *Painful*."

Though, to give credit where credit is due, Uncle Leon did
occasionally venture forth from his study in order to reprimand
Matthew. Like the time Matt and Tommy had been playing
King Kong, and Matt had somehow managed to knock over
an old armoire in the hallway—it had been designated as the
Empire State Building and Matt had been attempting to scale it,
when, due to his bad foot, he had slipped, bringing the armoire
down with him. "Now, boys," he said, "we mustn't play so
rough. You might disturb Aunt Hester." Though Aunt Hester,
living up on the third floor and being deaf as a post, would
not have noticed the detonation of a thermonuclear device in
the basement of the old house.

As the King Kong incident witnessed, Matt had a passion
for reenacting movies that he and Tommy watched on the
late show. He loved vampires and werewolves, ghosts and
brain-eaters from other galaxies, and was especially fond of
those B movies from the fifties—they had to stay up real late
for them—in which, due to atomic radiation, some otherwise
harmless creature had got swollen up to gigantic proportions:
ants, spiders, locust, octopuses, and houseflies.

And once Matt's imagination had been sparked off by something, there was no stopping him.

It was wonderful to watch Matt in the throes of inspiration.
He was able to direct, script, stage-manage, and act in each of
the improvised dramas—all of which were loosely based on
some movie he had seen or some story he had read. With the
skill of a precocious casting agent, Matt assigned the various
roles to himself and to his friends. Invariably he was the mad
scientist, Tommy the handsome hero; their other friends were

given suitable supporting roles, with Arlene Cunningham—
who had a crush on Tommy—usually offering herself as the
female lead. And there was a kind of fate in Matt's choice:
He *was* the mad scientist, just as Tommy *was* the dashing
hero. Tommy was the kind of kid everybody loved. He was
handsome and athletic, a good companion and a loyal friend.
If you told Tommy a secret, it stayed a secret. But Tommy
also, even at that age, knew his limits. He was not brilliant.
He didn't know things, the way Matt did. He wasn't able
to conjure strange worlds out of nowhere, as Matt could.
But he was solidly planted in the one world he knew for
sure was there: the world of baseball, and classrooms, and
school buses, of neatly combed hair, and clean shirts, and
zipped-up trousers. Matt was not. He couldn't play baseball,
he missed the bus twice a week, his hair was never combed,
his fly was often conspicuously open. But then Matt had other
qualities. Flamboyant and sometimes bossy, Matt was what,
even then, Tommy recognized, without having a name for it,
as a genius. Eccentric, brilliant, and creative, Matt was unable
to rest content with the normal truths of the world around him.
He wanted more. And more came to him. Ideas and projects
hit him the way revelations hit the more demented prophets of
the Old Testament. His eyes huge and glowing feverishly, Matt
would urge, "Let's play *War of the Worlds*" (Uncle Leon had
told him about the panic in the thirties that had been induced
by a radio broadcast of this story, and Matt had always yearned
after a similar triumph) and that's exactly what you did. And
if you didn't, he'd keep at you and at you. Besides, as always
happened, once Matt dragged you, screaming and kicking, into
one of his fantasies, you forgot everything else. The world he
opened up for others defied time and space, it overruled all
other more prosaic activities. He simply told so-and-so who or
what he or she was ("You're a giant spider" or, alternatively,
"You're a girl about to be eaten by a giant spider") and
so-and-so proceeded to do the kinds of things giant spiders
(or girls about to be eaten by them) are accustomed to do.

The year before, emboldened by his amateur theatrics, Matt
had decided to go big-time. He had persuaded his teacher,
Miss Avery, to allow himself and his troupe to put on a
historical pageant entitled "The True Story of the Assassination
of Abraham Lincoln."

It had been the low point of Tommy Buford's short life. Matt had assigned Tommy the role of the President, while Arlene Cunningham played Mrs. Lincoln. Actually, they sat in two chairs at one end of the classroom, with signs around their necks that said, "Mr. Lincoln" and "Mrs. Lincoln." Tubby Bobby Jasper walked back and forth at the other end: He was the play they were watching, and he, too, had no lines. Suddenly an apparition in black strode in from the outside hall, its slight limp barely perceptible. The cape covered his entire body. Fiendish laughter was heard. The cape dropped and revealed a face hideously white, except for the two fangs inserted into the blood-smeared mouth. "I am Count Dracula," it intoned, in a bizarre blend of Transylvanian and North Georgia drawls. "I have come to bite the neck of President Lincoln." A fang fell out, but was quickly refitted. The Count swept down on the remarkably inattentive Mr. Lincoln. He gasped and fell from his chair. The Count disappeared. Mrs. Lincoln cried, "Oh, my, the President is dead." Whereupon Mr. Lincoln jumped up—fangs had been surreptitiously inserted into his mouth while he was on the floor—and declared: "No, I am Undead." John Wilkes Booth entered heroically—though also with a trace of a limp and flecks of white makeup powder adhering to his cheek—and declared: "I must save the country." He produced a stake and promptly pounded it into the writhing form of President Lincoln.

Sixty-four-year-old Miss Avery, while a Southerner at heart, was justifiably disturbed by Matthew's highly revisionistic interpretation of the tragic event and promptly brought the skit—and Matt—to a screeching halt, despite the boy's protestation that they hadn't gotten to the good part yet.

Tonight Matt had his heart set on playing *The Attack of the Giant Crabs*, the movie he had made Tommy watch with him the night before on the late show.

But Tommy wasn't interested. "I don't want to play Giant Crabs. I think it was stupid," Tommy said. "You know there ain't nothing like that. Crabs a hundred feet long."

"How do you know?"

Tommy hated when Matthew said something like that. Of course, he didn't know. There was no way of knowing every last thing that crawled or slithered over the immense surface of the planet. Still, if there were crabs big as semitrucks wandering around somewhere, you would have thought they would have come to people's attention by now.

"Those crabs in the movie, they got under one of those A-bomb tests, then they got all mutated up. Just like that two-headed frog Francis Cummings brought to Mrs. Avery's class."

Somehow, Tommy failed to see the connection. "That was just an old two-headed frog, s'all."

"How you think frogs get to have two heads in the first place?" Matthew asked. "You think God gives 'em two heads, so they can see better?"

"I don't know who gives 'em two heads," Tommy said, feeling as if they were perhaps treading on dangerous ground. "Maybe God does give 'em two heads, you don't know. Maybe He gets tired of looking at all the one-headed frogs."

Matthew groaned. "It's mutation makes 'em that way. Ask anybody." That was one of Matt's favorite phrases. And Tommy had asked, but even the preacher at the Baptist church, when Tommy had mentioned mutations to him—and the monstrous creatures that might spring from them—only had smiled and said, "I don't know 'bout mutations, son. I just know God made everything. So there can't be anything in this world that He hasn't put here Himself, with His own hand. So you forget about giant spiders and such. God didn't mean for them to be, and they won't be."

They walked along in silence, then Tommy, who had been brooding over Rev. Griggs's words, suddenly stopped and said, "God makes everything."

"So? What's that supposed to mean?"

"It means he must make them two-headed frogs, too." Tommy was frowning and looking down at the pavement of the street. And then falling back on Rev. Griggs's argument, he went on, " 'Cause if God don't make 'em, that means there's something got into this world that God didn't intend to be here." He looked up at Matthew. "And that ain't possible. So them things you talk about—like them giant crabs—they wasn't never meant to be."

Matthew looked into his friend's face and he went to say something. But, on reconsideration, he stopped and glanced away uneasily. He wasn't sure how to answer this one. It

was one of those things that sometimes drove him nuts about
Tommy Buford. He had a way of being right, even when
Matthew was being smarter. "I hadn't thought of it," Matthew
said softly. Tommy smiled. Matthew could be a know-it-all
sometimes, but he was a fair-minded know-it-all.

Together the two boys continued to walk down the dark
street, with Tommy now more carefully monitoring his pace.

A little ahead of them was the ravine. At the bottom of
it was the Tallaloona River. Ten miles farther north up the
Appalachia plateau, where the ground was higher, the cut of
the Tallaloona River was impressive enough to be given a
name of its own, Holcombe Gorge. There were places
along the highway where you could pull your car off and stare
across the yawning breech in the earth's surface or peer down
into its wooded depths. It was no Grand Canyon, of course,
but it still took your breath. But here in Mt. Jephtha, the river's
incision was only picturesque. The drop was about fifty feet,
and more sloping than sheer, while the distance from one side
to the other side was only twice that. Still, on a moonlit night,
when there was a wind, it always made chills go up and down
Tommy's spine to stand in the middle of the old swinging
bridge and to look down as the wooden planks beneath his
feet swayed back and forth high above the gleaming riverbed.
The bridge—it had been put up at the turn of the century—
was the only surviving one of its kind in Georgia. Too fragile
for a go-cart, too narrow even for walking two abreast, you
went over it almost on tiptoe, holding your breath, your hand
clutching on to the railings, your eyes fixed warily on the
gossamer cable—the one which, if you crossed the bridge
with that jackass, Clomer Haywood, he was always sure to
say to you, punching you in the ribs, "It's going to snap. Any
second now. Looky, there she goes. It's a-snapping." Clomer
always thought this was just hilarious.

Farther down, about a mile, there was a regular bridge, for
cars and trucks and grown-up people walking on foot. But it
was always the swinging bridge that the two boys used. It
was closer, if you were heading in from town back up to the
Lumpkin house—as they were tonight. But then it was also
spookier, and a hell of a lot more exciting.

Tommy stopped, as he always did, to glance across the
bridge, and up at the cables—he had crossed it once too often

with Clomer to be entirely indifferent to the condition of the cable material.

"What you waiting for?" Matt asked. "Come on."

The two boys walked to the middle of the bridge. Now it was Matt's turn to stop. But this was only as much as Tommy expected. He always liked to stop smack dab in the center of the bridge, and to stare down into the ravine below or to gaze up at the stars or to whisper of mutant creatures hiding in the woods around them, or of ghosts that haunted the bridge itself—sometimes, it was said, you could tell they were walking across it, because on certain windless nights the bridge could be seen to sway back and forth, as if someone were walking endlessly back and forth across it, and yet the bridge—to the human eye—would be absolutely empty. It was also said that if you were bold enough to stand on the bridge at such nights, you could hear an eerie sound coming up from the depths of the ravine. They were some who even claimed to recognize the sound as that of children whimpering and moaning in unspeakable agony.

Behind them, Tommy could see the dark backsides of the stores across from the Rialto. He knew them all, even from the rear. Milton's Feed & Supplies. Joyce's Drugstore. Mt. Jephtha Hardware. The JCPenney's, that was the town's pride. On the far side, it was only woods. A path through it led, about half a mile farther, to the Lumpkin house. Another path led to the water tower, high on the topmost ridge, and beyond that, down the other side of the ridge, to the town's cemetery. Beyond that lay woods. Later, most of this would be cleared. Houses would be built, and the Happy Home Trailer Park would be opened. But that was still some years away. Rising high above the surrounding woods was the town's water tower. It had been put up six years earlier and looked like a big tin can, only set up on a tripod. Matt had used it in his production of *War of the Worlds* the summer before—it was the advance scout for the invading Martian army of stilt-walking saucers. (As, years later, he would use the tower again, in a production of a different sort.) Older kids were always going up onto the platform at night and writing goofy love things on it. Arlene had once told Tommy she hoped he'd write something up there for her one day. Fat chance, Tommy thought at the time. (He did, ten years later.)

Tommy turned to his friend and could tell that he was thinking deep thoughts. His lip slightly stuck out, as if in a pout, his eyes roamed over the darkness of the ravine.

"What about that fire?" Matt asked. "Did God make that, too?"

Tommy glanced down into the ravine. "I don't know."

"If God's supposed to be so good, then how come He had let that revival tent catch on fire?"

It was a question that had haunted Matt for the last two years.

The tragedy had happened only a couple of miles outside town. Tommy's grandmomma, a devout old-time Baptist, had taken the two boys with her in order to hear the celebrated revivalist and faith healer, the Rev. Jessop Odum. It was her idea that they all sit on the first row, on the pretext that she wanted the two boys to see the preacher up-close. Matt was a bit skeptical from the start. He had already heard enough stories about Odum's so-called Miracle of the Flames of Faith, and while he had to admire it as a stunning piece of showmanship, he was convinced it was just a trick. Leaning forward on his folding chair, only ten feet from the portable pulpit, Matt was determined to figure out just how Odum did it, his eyes glued on the can of gasoline that was conspicuously displayed behind the preacher's back.

Normally this was how it went: Odum spoke for an hour about hell, describing it in vivid and memorable terms. Suddenly he stopped in midsentence, looked up to the top of the tent, and declared that the Holy Spirit was upon him. He shouted at his assistant to go and fetch him the can of gasoline, then rolled up his shirtsleeve and doused his outstretched arm. A match was lit, and as Odum held it up, he shouted, "How long is everlasting? How long can a man endure the Fires Eternal?" A stopwatch was produced. Odum yelled "Count!" and before the stupefied eyes of the faithful, he dropped the flaming match on his gas-soaked flesh. Tumult ensued. Women screamed and fainted, men rose to their feet. The fire went on for fifteen seconds, thirty—the time was shouted out by Odum's assistant—a minute, a minute and a half, two minutes. "How long is it?" Three minutes, and still the flames raged about the preacher's arm.

Then, spectacularly, Odum, his arm blazing, would yell

out to the hysterical throng, "Those who need healing, come forth!" Frightened children, with ailments or disabilities, were pushed forward. Old women with arthritis or in wheelchairs were eased toward the pulpit. One by one, Odum lay his left hand—the one that wasn't burning, of course—upon the afflicted, and they would all rise up, healed and whole.

Or so it was said.

When the last one departed, the fire abruptly went out. Triumphantly Odum held his unsinged arm aloft and shouted, "Thus does God's Grace prevail over the Fires Everlasting! Hallelujah!"

But on the evening Matt and Tommy attended, something went wrong. Odum had just ignited his arm and held it up, flaming. Suddenly, without warning, Matt felt Tommy's grandmother's hands upon his shoulders. "Here, Rev. Odum, heal this boy's afflicted foot." Stunned, unable even to register what was happening, Matt found himself being thrust forward by the sturdy old woman. Her hands clutching his shoulder, she guided him up to the platform where Odum was standing. The boy gazed in disbelief at Odum's fiery arm, while the preacher's eyes fixed with disturbing intensity upon him. Tommy's grandmother shoved the confused and benumbed Matt down into a chair behind the pulpit, promptly fell to her knees, and undid Matt's right shoe and sock. She held up the mangled foot.

"Heal this poor child," she prayed. "Heal him in the name of the Lord."

Odum stretched out his healing hand, then stopped. His eyes were riveted to the boy's foot. Matt, who knew something was wrong, stared into the preacher's eyes and saw something dawn in them, something that sent a shiver down the boy's spine.

The preacher shook his head in dismay and took a step back. Matt had always heard the phrase "So-and-so looks like he'd seen a ghost." But up until that moment, he had never witnessed a face about which such a thing could be said. But now he was looking straight into one.

In Odum's eyes there was a horror. A deep, genuine, heart-constricting horror.

The preacher uttered something. At the time, and even long after, Matt figured he must have misunderstood what Odum was whispering. It was too crazy, even for a boy with Matt's imagination, to think otherwise. But what Odum seemed to be saying was this: "You can't be." Then, teetering on the edge of the platform, the preacher whispered the craziest words of all, "I done buried you. I done put you back into darkness, where you were meant to stay."

That was when Odum fell backward from the platform, his flaming arm igniting the sawdust that filled the floor inside the tent. The fire spread upward, quickly engulfing the platform. There was an explosion—it was the remnants of gasoline in the container Odum was accustomed to use in the Miracle of the Flames of Faith. Fire and panic spread through the tent. Matt grabbed his shoe and scrambled out through the back of the tent. He found Tommy, alive and unharmed. He was shouting for his granny. Later, when the charred bodies were pulled from the burnt-out remnant of the tent, they found her, still kneeling. She, along with Odum and thirty-seven others, over half of them children and old ladies, had been burnt to death.

"Why would God let something like that happen?" Matt asked—as he had asked before. And, as usual, Tommy had no answer.

Matt turned back from the ravine and looked into his friend's eyes. "Maybe something snuck into the world that God didn't know about. Came in behind His back." Matt frowned, then looked back at the riverbed. "You want to go listen to Aunt Hester some?"

"What for?"

"Maybe she's telling some more of her story."

Tommy's eyes glanced over at his shadow. It was comfortably next to him, just where it should be. "I don't know."

"Come on. It's not gonna kill you."

Tommy knew what Matt was talking about. They had done it a couple of times before. He wasn't very excited about the idea. Still, he figured it was better than playing Giant Crabs.

3

Back at the Lumpkin house the two boys slipped quietly up to the third floor. Matt put his ear against Aunt Hester's door and heard the old woman's familiar monologue, along with the rapid creaking of Hester's old rocking chair. Matt had observed a general rule, the more rapid and agitated the rocking, the better and spookier the story. And tonight it sounded like Hester was going for the gold medal in Olympic rocking chair competition. Matt glanced at Tommy: "Sounds like she's worked up about something." He opened the door a crack. Aunt Hester was where she had been for as long as he could remember, her rocking chair in front of the window, her nose nearly touching the glass. The two boys crept inside and assumed their usual place in the corner of the room, behind Aunt Hester's old-fashioned and absurdly elevated bed.

Listening to Aunt Hester, Tommy sometimes felt the way he did whenever his momma and daddy took him to the movies. They never bothered to check the time a feature started. Sometimes they'd come in right in the middle of a movie and Tommy would have to use all of his inductive powers to figure out what was going on in the story. But tonight the two boys had lucked out. Aunt Hester had just started. She was talking about her older brother, Wiley, when he was a boy. Wiley—as Tommy had learned from earlier episodes of The Aunt Hester Show—was a born tease and practical joker. God forbid if you were careless enough to let Wiley find out what you were most afraid of. If it was snakes, you'd pull back your covers and find one coiled in the middle of your bed. If it was rats, you'd go to pull on your right shoe and your foot would squish into the belly of a big brown rat that Wiley had caught by the woodpile, and whose skull he had bashed to a pulp. Or if it was something he couldn't so easily lay his hand ahold of—like a ghost—he'd employ all his wits in making you think one was about to get you; he'd sneak beneath the house and scratch eerily on the underside of the floorboards. Or he'd make spooky noises outside your window, or he'd come into your room in the middle of the night and turn every last thing upside down—chairs, tables, calendars, flowerpots, even—in the case of little Jimmy Motes, who was a sound sleeper—the bedstand. Or he'd write across the mirror in squirrel's blood: "I's coming to GIT you TONIGHT." Signed, "GHOST!"

Hester and Wiley had just wandered into the carnival that was passing through town. It had set itself in the clearing on the hill outside of town, right where the water tower would later stand. Even by North Georgia standards, the carnival hadn't been much to boast of. A small merry-go-round and a handful of sideshows. There was the Fat Lady, the Serpent Man, and the Weenie Man. But there was something else, too. A little tent over which was a cheap painting intended to thrill and entice passersby. Aunt Hester's recollection of it was vivid: It showed a thick woods at night, a moon overhead as thin and wan as the paring of a fingernail. A boy was running, his head turned to glance behind him. His face had a look of terror on it, while his bulging eyes were fixed on the pool of blackness that stretched back behind him. It might have been construed as just the boy's shadow except for one thing. If you looked hard at the painting, you saw that all the other shadows—those of the trees and the rocks—fell to the left, in front of the boy. But the boy's shadow stretched out behind him. And if you were sharp enough to notice this, you might also notice something else. The shadow had claws that reached up to clutch at the boy's heels and, hardest of all to detect, a single gleaming eyeball. Over the painting had been written the words "The Shadowstealer." Hester, along with her older brother, Wiley, had paid a nickel to go inside. The tent held only a single bench and a table. Overhead, suspended by a wire, was a solitary kerosene lamp. It illuminated a lone mason jar, set right in the middle of the table. The jar was large enough to hold a small child. Wiley went over to it, knelt down, and stared inside. Even Hester approached a little closer. "What's in it?"

Wiley shook his head. "Looks like tadpole eggs." Hester flinched back with a shudder of revulsion. Some years before, Wiley had taken her to the creek and had shown her the jellylike mass of frog eggs, about the size and shape of a basketball, stuck all through with what looked to her like teeny-weeny eyeballs. Wiley had later dropped a piece of it down the back of her overalls and she had gone screaming home.

"Looky there," Wiley went on, as he walked around the jar. "Them other things. They's like snake tails." Hester saw them, too. They wiggled back and forth across the glass, and were tiny, like the tail of the garter snake Wiley had once chased her around the barn with.

"Oh, that ain't no tadpole eggs. Ain't no snake tails, neither."

Both Wiley and Hester jumped and turned around and saw a man in a child's wagon. He pushed himself forward with his hands, and as he came closer, Hester saw that the man had no legs. He called himself Mr. Eprin. Wiley stared back into the jar. Mr. Eprin rolled himself over to the table and he picked up the jar. He set it on the sawdust-covered ground and he undid the fastener.

"We seen it ooze out," Hester whispered into her window-pane. "At first it was all wiggling and squirming. Them teeny eyeballs, and all them tails a-whizzing. It wiggled closer and closer to Wiley's feet."

"What's it do?"

"Why, it steals shadows," Mr. Eprin whispered. "Watch."

They watched as the oozing thing crept to the place where Wiley's shadow lay upon the sawdust, cast by the kerosene lamp inside the tent. It seemed to expand until it filled the shadow as exactly as water fills a bucket. The only difference was that Wiley's shadow seemed darker now, like pitch.

"Now walk around."

And Wiley took two steps back. The thing moved as the shadow moved. "See there"—Mr. Eprin grinned—"moves and walks and runs just like it was your shadow. Only it ain't. And that is how it does it. It sneaks up behind you at night and steals your shadow when you ain't looking. Then it puts that shadow over itself, like a long black coat, and it commences to follow you. Sometimes when it's behind you, you feel it on your neck, this tingling, and you stop and look back. But it stops, too, and it lays low, hiding snug under the shadow it stole from you, not breathing, not making a sound. And you say to yourself, 'Why I must be crazy. Wasn't nothing following me. 'Cept my own shadow.' And so you turn and you start walking again. And ol' Shadowstealer, it starts a-walking, too."

Wiley asked, "Ain't there no way of telling when it's your shadow, and when it's that other thing?"

"Ain't but one way. Walk over on the other side of that light."

And Wiley did.

"See?" Mr. Eprin grinned. "That shadow's still behind you, ain't it?" And Wiley nodded. There was no shadow in front of him, though from his position relative to the light, that's where it should have been. "Once it's done got inside your shadow, it'll always be behind you, no matter which way you go to turn. And that's how you'll know. All them other shadows—from the trees and such—and they'll be going in front of you. But your shadow, it'll be going behind."

"What does it do to you?"

Mr. Eprin grinned. "Can't do nothing. 'Less you done heard about it somewheres."

Wiley blinked. "Whatchew mean?"

Mr. Eprin was still grinning as he began to roll himself back away from the table, back into the dark corner of the tent. "Ol' Shadowstealer got this rule. It can't git aholta nobody who ain't never heard about it."

"But what if you have?" Wiley asked.

The man's grin got wicked. He stuck out his tongue and wiped his sharp teeth. "Why now, that's a different story," he said, giggling. He pulled back the flap of the tent door.

"Hold on," Wiley said. But Mr. Eprin kept rolling his wagon backward, toward the door flap. "You mean it can git me 'cause I done heard about it?"

"Oh, you ain't got nothing to worry about. All you got to do is remember one little thing." Mr. Eprin's grin now showed every sharp yellow tooth in his head.

"What's that?"

"You can't look back to see if it's a-following you. Can't never look back. 'Cause that's when it gits you."

Wiley's face was pale with anger. "Then why in hell d'you go and tell me for?"

They could only see Mr. Eprin's face as he disappeared into the darkness between the flaps of the tent door. " 'Cause tonight, it's hungry."

Hester continued, "Wiley, he ran outside, fast as he could. And I followed. He looked and he seen his shadow still wasn't in front of him. But then he saw mine wasn't neither. His and mine, they was both behind us. 'Cause that's how the

moonlight was falling. And I told him to turn around and
see if his shadow moved around, too. But Wiley looks at me
and says, 'Don't you remember what he done said? I can't be
looking back, 'cause that's when it gits you.' "

To get home, Wiley and Hester had to go through the
woods. Wiley kept saying, "It was just some trick he done.
Some ol' magic trick. With that light. Making my shadow go
wrong inside a there. But when we get home, it'll be back on
right."

Wiley stopped on the path, once, then twice, then three
times. Each time he said there was a tingling on the back
of his neck, like somebody was tickling him with a feather.
But even so, he kept his eyes looking straight ahead of him.
"I ain't gonna look back. I ain't gonna look back behind me."
And so Wiley kept on, walking and not looking back, until
he came to the very edge of the woods. His house was only
a little ways up ahead, at the end of this dirt road.

That was when Wiley looked down in front of him.

Hester looked, too. Her shadow, it stretched about twenty
feet in front of her, skinny as a rail. And all around hers were
the shadows from the woods.

Only Wiley's shadow wasn't among them.

"My shadow," he gasped, "it ain't where it should be. It
ain't—"

"I yelled, 'Don't look around, Wiley.' 'Cause I'd seen it.
But it was too late. Wiley had already turned and looked. His
shadow was lying flat out behind him. One end was at his
feet, the other end stretched back deep into the woods.

"Only it wasn't no shadow," Hester whispered into the
windowpane above her knees, her rocking chair going back
and forth so fast that the two boys were afraid she might go
flying through the window down into the backyard of the old
house. "It wasn't thin like no shadow, neither. It was fat, like
a big fat black snake, or one of them bloodsuckers, all puffed
up with blood.

"Wiley, he screamed once, and then I watched as it yanked
him back into them woods. He didn't scream no more."

Hester ran back to the house, told her momma and daddy
that Wiley's shadow had gotten hold of him. But they dismissed her panic, saying how Wiley was playing one of his
famous pranks. But Hester knew better. "It wasn't no prank,"

she whispered. All that night Hester didn't sleep a wink. She kept going up to the window. About four o'clock she saw him coming toward the house, walking slow and lifeless.

"Where you been?" Hester asked him—she had run out to the back porch as he was coming up the steps. Wiley's face was empty as the bottom of a bucket that's been turned upside down.

"In them woods."

"What happened?"

"It got holt of me," he said.

"What'd it do to you?"

"Nothing."

"How'd you get loose from it?"

"You got to give it something," Wiley said, his eyes without a glint of fear or agitation or dread, but lusterless and cold as a marble. "Whatever it asks you for."

"Whatchew give it?"

"My eyes."

Hester stared at her brother, her mouth open. "Whatchew talking 'bout, Wiley? They's still right there, on either side of your nose."

Wiley shook his head. "No, they ain't mine no more. They's his now." And without saying another word, Wiley walked to his room and lay down in the bed.

All of a sudden, the rocking stopped. Hester leaned closer to the window, as if it had an ear into which she could confide a whisper.

"Two nights later, I come across Wiley out by the woodpile, alone, his shadow a-trailing off behind him. He had one of Momma's forks in his hand. He was staring down at it. 'I don't want to see 'em no more. Them little nigger kids.' "

"What little nigger kids you talking about?"

"Don't want to see that chopping and cutting. Don't want to see them little hands and feets, them tongues."

Hester looked around her, puzzled. "You done lost your mind? Ain't no nigger kids 'round here."

"There was. Long time ago. Folks done forgot. But that ol' Shadowstealer, he don't let you forget. Once he done got you, you can't never forget no more," Wiley said. He was still looking down at the fork in his hand. "I jus' want to forget 'em, s'all. Jus' want to stop seeing 'em, over and over."

"And I says, 'What you going to do, Wiley?'

" 'Ain't but one thing I can do. Give that ol' Shadowstealer what's his.' And he lifts up that fork he's holding. He holds it right in front of his right eye.

"And I says, 'Wiley, you ain't—' And that's when he commences scooping 'em two eyeballs of his clean out of his head. And I run screaming back to the house.

"When Momma got to him, Wiley was lying against the woodpile. Them sockets of his was empty, the blood was running down his cheeks, and that fork was in his hand. But them eyeballs was gone. Clean gone. They looked for 'em, but they never did find 'em. But there was something else gone—something Momma didn't even see was missing. Wiley, he didn't have no shadow at all no more. Not a speck of it, neither behind him, nor ahead."

Hester stopped, then slowly began to rock back and forth again. "Course, I never said a word to my momma and my daddy about what got Wiley. Never spoke a word about it to nobody. Not Leon, not Simmy, not nobody. 'Cause I knew that's what it wanted. Wanted folks to know all about it, so it could git 'em, way it got Wiley." And again Hester stopped her rocking and leaned closer to the windowpane. Her breath frosted it. "And in all these years, I ain't once looked behind me. 'Cause I know it's always been after me. That's why I don't never turn around, no matter what I hear coming behind me. Like right now I can feel somebody a-sitting behind me, breathing in and out, but I ain't gonna look around. 'Cause I know about its tricks." Matt, startled by Hester's last words, turned to Tommy and whispered, "Let's go."

Out in the hall, the two boys made their way through the darkness to the stairwell. Matt was about to step onto the landing of the second floor when a hard and bony hand grabbed at his neck.

"Matthew Hardison, what you been doing? You ain't been up in Miss Hester's room again, have you?"

"Christ Almighty, Simmy, you nearly scared me to death!"

Tommy—who had seen the pitch-black, rail-thin apparition coming at them—swallowed his own gasp of horror.

"I hope I did," Simmy told him. "I done told you, it ain't right, you two boys sneaking into that poor old woman's room like you do, making fun of her and all."

"We weren't making fun of her. Were we, Tommy?"

Speechless, Tommy shook his head no.

"If I ain't going to believe you, what makes you think I'm going to believe him?"

"We just wanted to listen to her. She told this story. It was real spooky, wasn't it?"

"Spooky story?" Simmy repeated. "I'll spooky story you one night. Now the both of you, go on and git in bed."

Matt protested that they were fixing to play *The Attack of the Giant Crabs*.

"Giant Crabs? Ol' Simmy, she's going to wait till you's a-sleeping and then she's going to come creeping into that room of yours, way you two done with Miss Hester, and she's going to take holta of both your foots, and she's going to yank you out of that bed so fast you's going to think them Giant Crab done got you for sure!"

In Matt's bedroom, Tommy refused to have anything to do with Giant Crabs. Within ten minutes, the lights were off.

Tommy glanced over at the door. The moon was full, and its reflection was working its way up from the floor to the bottom of the door. "You think Simmy's going to do what she was saying?" Tommy asked. " 'Bout sneaking in here to get us?"

"Simmy's not going to do nothing."

"I hope not. Don't feel like having nothing grab me tonight," Tommy said.

Matt sprang up in bed, obviously in the grip of one of his familiar flashes of genius. "I got an idea," Matt said. "You and me and Arlene, we could put it on in school next year. That story Hester told. Arlene could be Hester. You could be Wiley. I could be Mr. Eprin."

"I ain't never going to be in one of them skits of yours again, Matt." Tommy groaned. " 'Sides, won't nobody let us. Not after what you done to Abraham Lincoln."

"What does ol' Miss Avery know anyhow?" Matt said with obvious sensitivity to the issue. Matt continued to stare at the moonlight on the door, his eyes aglow with inspiration, his jaw fixed in the way Tommy had seen so many times before, whenever Matthew was bound and determined to accomplish something he had set out to do. "You'll see," Matt said, "one day I'm going to put it on before the whole school. And everybody will hear about it, and I'll have to put it on for the whole town, and people will come up from Atlanta to see it. And maybe"—here even Matt suspected that he was perhaps getting a little carried away—"who knows, somebody from Hollywood could be driving through, and he'll see it, and want to make a movie all about it."

Accustomed to Matt's daydreaming, Tommy sighed, "Couldn't be no worse than Giant Crabs."

Matt was hardly listening, overwhelmed by this sudden and all-consuming vision of his own destiny. "And when they leave to go home after the movie, they'll all keep stopping, and they'll look behind 'em, to see which way their shadow's going. Won't anybody sleep for weeks," Matt concluded, as if ambition had no higher reward than this.

Tommy looked over. "Ain't you forgetting something? What Mr. Eprin told 'em, how that ol' shadow thing could only get you if you had heard about it somewheres." Tommy hesitated, then asked the Question: "Don't you ever wonder: What if it's true?"

Tommy looked over at his friend for his response. But he didn't get one. Matt's mind was already racing ahead. He was leaning forward and clutching his bad foot—he claimed it often throbbed mercilessly whenever he was in the grip of inspiration. But, despite the pain, there was a grin on Matt's face. A grin of enthralled devilment. "I can just see it now."

And as Tommy looked into his friend's eyes, he could almost believe it.

Shortly after nine o'clock the next morning, Matt sat down at the desk where he did his homework. He had a sheaf of lined notebook paper and a pencil. At the top of the first page he wrote in his cramped, ungraceful hand:

THE SHADOWSTEALER
A Very Scary Story by Matthew Hardison

He smiled down at it, and then began to write, slowly and firmly, pressing down the pencil so hard that you could easily read each word on the blotter beneath.

Fifteen years, and innumerable revisions later, Matt would finish the story.

When Tommy Buford received his copy, he had joked with Matthew. "You sure you ain't worried?"

"About what?"

"Don't you remember?" Tommy went on. "How the Shadowstealer can't get you unless you've heard about it somewheres. Looks like a helluva lot of people's going to be hearing about it now."

Matt, too, grinned. The same devilish grin he had sported on the night when the idea had first seized hold of him many years before. "Yeah, I know."

PART TWO

....

1

Ninety miles north of Atlanta, on the left-hand side of Highway 312, stands a billboard that boldly proclaims: MT. JEPHTHA, HOME OF THE WORLD'S HAPPIEST CHICKENS. Beneath the sign is a weatherworn and tattered painting of a barnyard. A smiling cow sticks her head out of the barn door to watch a group of chickens—the roosters dressed in loud plaid shirts, the hens wearing pleated skirts—as they execute the intricate steps of a square dance, the calls being made by a fiddle-playing hog dressed in overalls and with a red bandanna wrapped around its neck.

"I told you, didn't I?" Matt glanced over at Cathy and smirked. "Maybe you'll start believing me now."

"There really is a fiddle-playing hog," Cathy murmured. In the last two months—due in part to her reading of *The Shadowstealer*, in part to listening to Matt's stories about the town, Mt. Jephtha had begun to assume mythological proportions in Cathy's mind, much like the lost cities of Mu and Atlantis. No doubt, there was a place with that name—she had found it on a map of Georgia, tucked away in the northeastern corner, near the junction of the Tennessee and South Carolina borders. Only she found it difficult to believe that the town could actually have been the way Matt characterized it. The stories he told about it, surely they must have been shaped and embellished by Matt's imaginative gifts. Take the billboard. Probably there was one, she figured. Maybe it even showed chickens square dancing. But a hog with a fiddle and a red bandanna? "Course, down in Cleveland, they may have more chickens, but ours are happier."

"Everything, it's just the way you describe it." Cathy picked up her copy of *The Shadowstealer*—it was conveniently

perched atop the armrest between them. She flipped through
it and found the passage. "Now listen to this. It says, talking
about the town: 'It is here that the steadily rising Appalachia
plateau bursts forth into a series of hillocks sufficiently impressive—at least by North Georgia standards—to be given names
of their own, with the ennobling prefix Mt. attached to it. The
names were all plucked from obscurer narratives of the Old
Testament—Mt. Joab, Mt. Ahab, and Mt. Caleb, the most
imposing of the set and one the town had called itself after.
Although none is more than five thousand feet high, what they
lack in Himalayan grandeur they make up with in picturesque
serenity: intimate, rather than imposing, to be hiked up, not
scaled. No one ever thought of ascending Mt. Caleb because it
was there. Indeed, no one thought much of ascending it at all.
It was simpler to drive up the little gravel road that led to the
summit. The shadow it cast upon the town did not fill the mind
with awe or tempt anyone into metaphysical reveries. It did not
suggest an image of cataclysm and violent upheaval, but rather
a kind of slow and gradual mellowing out of the earth: softly
molded, covered with trees, their hues varying from green to
purple in the spring and summer, then catching fire in autumn
with a thousand shades of yellow and red and orange. Even its
peculiar shape reinforced the image of ripening. Mt. Caleb had
no slopes to the south—which faced the town—but rose up at
a sharp angle, its contours resembling a gigantic gourd that had
been cast into the woods of North Georgia.' " She glanced up
from the book.

"Oh, look," Cathy said as she clapped her hand over her
mouth. "The water tower."

It had just poked up over the horizon, a sight that in rural
Georgia was only a little less common than red clay, the
antiquated water tower for the town of Mt. Jephtha. "It gives
me the creeps, just looking at it."

Cathy was, of course, referring to the chilling final scene of
The Shadowstealer. It takes place at night, high on the platform
of the tower. The hero, transparently modeled on Matt's friend,
Tommy Buford, sits with a gun in his lap and watches the
hideous blackness of the Shadowstealer as it creeps out of the
impenetrable thicket of surrounding woods, slowly undulating
back and forth across the little clearing, inch by inch sliding,
like a vast dark slug, toward the metal ladder that ascends to the

tower. Bereft of hope, fatally resigned to his own destruction, the doomed hero awaits the telltale tingling on the back of his neck, his gun clutched in his sweating palms. Frantically, he whispers the story that his best friend—modeled (no surprise) on Matt—had imparted to him before his horrific death in the previous chapter. A story that it is hoped might somehow cast back into the darkness the creature that an earlier story—that of the Shadowstealer—had called into being. His muscles tense as he hears the scraping of the shadow's claws on the metal rungs of the ladder: It is there. The tingling begins. The gun is lifted to his face. He has chosen to die at his own hands rather than to be consumed by the shadowy ooze. In desperate frenzy, the words of the other story pour forth, and yet closer and closer it comes. The tingling spreads down his spine. He goes rigid as the shadow's claw clutches his shoulder. "Don't look at it," he tells himself, for to see even the smallest particle of the thing means death. In fear and panic, he loses his place in the story. He gasps, then stares down into the black barrel. "Lord God, help us all," he whispers, then—

Matt grinned. "Sometimes a water tower is just a water tower."

"Not that one," Cathy insisted.

"Lord, you're getting to be as bad as the Lady from Toledo." The Lady from Toledo—her name was actually Mrs. Dupree—was Matt's shorthand for the hundreds and hundreds of readers who, after finishing his book, had sent him disturbing, and frequently disturbed, letters that purported to confirm the existence of the Shadowstealer. Mrs. Dupree, the first in the series, had written, "I always knew there was something that was following me. But never till the day I read your book did I know what it was. Thank God I know now not to look back at it or over my shoulder to see if it is there." Other letters angrily denounced him for telling the story at all. "If it's true there is such a thing, and why would you make up something like that if it wasn't, then who are you to go and tell its story, if people wasn't supposed to hear about it?" So a retired Sunday school teacher in Florida had scolded him.

"Good Lord, hon. You did write the damn thing, after all."

To which Matt replied airily, as he always did to all such complaints, "Yes, but nobody made you read it."

2

About the same time that Cathy had her first glimpse of the
water tower, Tommy Buford was sitting on the front porch of
the Lumpkin house.

The years had treated Tommy kindly. Only two weeks
before, at the Stop-and-Go, Tommy had gone in to buy his
nightly six-pack of Budweiser. The cashier was new and had
stared at Tommy suspiciously. "You got some ID to buy that
with?"

"Sure do," Tommy said with a grin and had opened his
wallet.

The cashier had appraised both the date and the face, then
said, "You don't look no twenty-nine to me."

Tommy had been working since four o'clock that morning,
removing the last remnants of accumulated junk out of the
attic. It was presently piled up in the back of Tommy's '79
Ford Bronco—antiquated lampshades, of violent red brocade;
Aunt Hester's dress form, with its waist little more than the
diameter of a Coke can; international souvenirs from the
Chicago World's Fair; a cigar box full of train ticket stubs;
torn lace curtains; a rusted tricycle; a trunk full of ancient
and half-empty bottles of patent medicine. It staggered the
mind. As a child, Tommy had always been mystified by
Uncle Leon's attic, wondering how space that was clearly
finite always had room for one more item. Going on twenty
years Tommy had wanted to clear the place out, and now he
finally had. It had taken him a week of solid work to empty
the attic's content, another week to fix up Matt's study. But,
at least, he had managed to get it done on time.

His work done, Tommy sipped an early Bud. An enormous
cat nestled in his lap, his fur long and glossy, gleaming with
an opalescent array of tabby hues—black, brown, gray, red,
white. The cat stared up at Tommy with his glistening green
eyes. Tigger's face always had the same expression on it,
baleful, harshly judgmental. It was a face that seemed to say,
and sometimes did say, "I ain't taking no shit off nobody."
Twelve years earlier, Tigger had wandered up to the Lumpkin

house and had been taken in—as all of Matt's strays had been taken in. Tigger was the senior cat in the household, and although Matt always denied having a favorite, there were those who, like Tommy, had long doubted the sincerity of Matt's protestation. When pressed to a corner, however, Matt always had the same comeback. "Well, after all, Tigger can talk. So what if I do show him a little partiality?" Tigger had suddenly burst into speech—deep, gruff, even menacing speech—one night when Matt and Tommy were drinking out on the back porch. And he had not been silent since.

"You know who's coming back today, Tigger?" Tommy asked, stroking the cat's impressively leonine ruff.

"Daddy."

"You excited?"

"Oh, yes, Uncle Tommy, I certainly am."

Tommy grinned. "What do you think about having a new mommy, Tigger?"

"I don't know about that, Uncle Tommy. I sure hope she likes kittycats."

"Me, too." Tommy gazed over the porch. There were two cats curled up on the steps. One licked its front paw while perched on the railing. Another stared, hissing, at a huge pissed off–looking crow that waddled through the front yard.

"You think Daddy's told her about me, Uncle Tommy?"

"I reckon so."

"She's probably never seen no talking cat before."

Which Tommy couldn't argue with. Simmy stuck her head around the door. "Who's that talking?" she demanded harshly.

"Nobody," Tommy said.

Simmy stared down suspiciously at Tigger. "You ain't been talking to that ol' worthless cat now, have you?"

"Nope, Miss Simmy."

"Sometimes I think you's worser about that worthless ol' cat than Mr. Matt," Simmy declared. She was about to go back inside, to resume her agitated frenzy of housecleaning, when Tigger said, "Simmy don't think I can talk, does she, Uncle Tommy?"

In point of fact, there was a long-standing controversy in the household concerning the status of Tigger's claim to being the world's only talking cat. Simmy and Peter, for example, were quick to point out the odd coincidence that both Matt's and Tommy's lips moved whenever Tigger began to speak. Also, it was observed that Tigger always talked a little funnier than normal whenever Matt or Tommy had a bit too much to drink.

Simmy stopped and looked back at Tommy. She shook her head. "One day when y'all gone off somewheres, I'm going to take that worthless ol' cat, and you know what I'm a-going to do with it?"

"Oh, Lordy, Uncle Tommy, Simmy's fixing to fry me up in her frying pan."

"No, she's not."

"Don't you be so sure," Simmy said. "Talking cat!"

"There's none so deaf as them who will not hear," Tigger remarked with deep philosophical resignation. To which Tommy nodded his head, and observed, "How true."

"Hmmmpf." Simmy was about to return to her scouring the kitchen floor when she glanced out at the truck. "You'd better take off that last load. You know what Mr. Matt'll do if he comes back and sees it."

Tommy nodded. They had all decided—that is, Simmy, Peter, and himself—that it was best to present Matt with a fait accompli. In the three years since Uncle Leon had passed on to his reward—whatever that might have been—Matt had languidly mentioned cleaning out the century of collected trash that Leon had tucked away in the huge attic of the old house. But, Matt being Matt, the effort never went far.

"Excuse me, Tigger," Tommy said as he set the cat back onto the porch. Tigger meowed—he did that sometimes—a meow that, considering his gruff speaking voice, was startlingly high-pitched and even a bit sissified. Tigger sauntered over to an orange calico and began to lick the other cat's head. Tigger, despite his gruff exterior, had always shown a deep streak of feline altruism.

As Tommy was about to get into the truck, Peter burst through the screen door. "Where you going?"

"To clear this stuff off."

"You coming back?"

"Course."

"You going to bring Jimmy with you?" Jimmy was Tommy's own son, a year older than Peter. Tommy nodded and got into his Bronco.

He stared up at the old Lumpkin house—his second home for as long as he could remember. But that morning he wondered if it would go on being that. He sighed, then repeated slowly to himself, as if it had been a kind of polysyllabic incantation: "mellifluous," "pertinacious," "atrabilious."

"Tigger sure is acting a mite atrabilious today, ain't he?" he said, watching himself in the rearview mirror. But, somehow, it just didn't come out right. He slumped back despondently.

"Sheeeet."

3

Sheriff Wally Clark was sitting at the breakfast table and reading the copy of *The Shadowstealer* he had checked out of the town library the day before. Twice that morning already he had called to his wife and said, "Listen to this." Then he would read to her from the book. In both sections the author referred to the sheriff of the imaginary town of Mt. Caleb. " 'He was a tall, trim, taut-muscled man, his body trigger-quick and cat-agile.' Cat-agile, I like that." Wally grinned. He looked up at his wife. "What you think? You think he was talking about me?"

Matilda, the sweetest-hearted woman in the world, frowned and glanced over at Wally. When he was sitting down you couldn't even see the four-inch brass belt buckle with "Budweiser" embossed on it. She heard him quietly suck his gut in, just the way he did whenever he got around a pretty young girl. "No, hon, I don't think so," Matilda said, who, in addition to being sweet, was also truthful.

"What about the 'cat-agile' part?"

"Well, you do get around real good, I think, for a big man," Matilda said. "How you want your eggs?"

"Like usual," Wally muttered. "You got to remember, he's talking 'bout how things was fifteen years ago. Before I started putting on a little weight," he added defensively.

"That's true," Matilda said. "Maybe so." Though, as she recollected, on the day twenty-five years before, when Wally had gotten down on his knees to propose to her—they were on her daddy's front porch, sitting in the swing—he had started perspiring, less from nerves, she suspected, than from the ordeal of keeping his already large frame balanced on a single kneecap. Not, of course, that it made any difference to Matilda. Despite the fact that she had been driving down to the Weight Watchers Club in Gainesville for the last nine years, Matilda still came in right at two hundred sixty pounds.

"Listen to this," Wally went on, skipping a few paragraphs. " 'His sharp blue eyes pierced through a man's pretensions in a lightning flash of intuition.' What you think of that?" Wally asked grandly.

"That's real nice. Only you got brown eyes, Wally."

"Ain't you never heard of poetic license? He's got to change these here little details, so's people won't know who he's talking 'bout."

"Looks like he done that part real good." Matilda brought her husband his plate of eggs and bacon. "You want some more coffee?"

Wally nodded.

She sat down and stared at the cover of the book her husband was holding to his face. Done in the style of a garish marquee from a carnival sideshow, it showed a terrified boy running from his own shadow. At the boy's feet you could see the claws reaching up out of the shadow. And the tiny, gleaming eyeball. Matilda shivered. Wally had told her about the book. So had some of her friends. Enough for Matilda to set her mind against reading it. As a child, Matilda used to be teased a lot, people saying how she was scared of her own shadow. And she was.

It was puzzling to her why people wanted to read such things. There was already enough in the world to be scared of. Spiders, cockroaches, snakes, wasps—to name just a few. Why go and make up things nobody had ever thought of being scared of before?

But obviously somebody liked it.

In fact, the whole town of Mt. Jephtha had gone crazy over that book. Men, like her husband, who had not read anything more demanding than the Claudell County Telephone Directory in years, had actually visited the library or driven down to the tiny bookstore in Gainesville, Georgia. You could see signs of the obsession everywhere. At the checkout counter of the Piggly Wiggly, at the barbershop, at the bank, at her beautician's. It had even spread to the old ladies of the town.

Matilda could always tell exactly when one of them had finished with the book: that same night, without fail, Wally would get a telephone call at three o'clock in the morning, and sixty-two-year-old Miss Pickens would inform Wally how something black and oozy and long was slinking across their backyard toward her well. "Yeah, I know all about it," Wally would mumble, then roll over and go back to sleep.

Matilda allowed that the book was probably good. But then so were the Bible and *Gone with the Wind*, and Wally had never read either of those. A handful of townfolk might have been animated by "The Local Boy Who Made It Big" sentiment, and these had bought the book out of a disinterested desire simply to read and—it was hoped—to enjoy it. After all, who had ever suspected that Mt. Jephtha could have harbored in its midst a man whom newspaper writers in New York were calling— according to the back of the book, at least—"the compelling and terrifying new voice of the South"? No, Matilda thought, there was something else that was causing this sudden outbreak of literacy. At bottom, she suspected, it was not much different from the urge that prompts teenage boys at a televised football game to jump up and down like crazy fools the moment the camera is turned on them. After all, nearly everybody she talked to was convinced that they were in it someplace. It was just a matter of looking for themselves hard enough. After all, the town of Mt. Caleb, as described in *The Shadowstealer*, did sound suspiciously similar to the town of Mt. Jephtha. So, if he borrowed from the town itself, why couldn't he also have borrowed some of the people in it? Of course, he had changed the names, and maybe—as Wally asserted—some of the little details.

"Oh, hon, that's Reba's new song," Matilda said. She got up and walked over to the radio on the kitchen counter and turned up the volume. Reba McIntyre was her favorite singer in the world. She had been listening out for days to catch her new song, so that Wally could hear it. But now that it was on, he had his nose—of all places—in a book. "Ain't you gonna listen to it?"

But Wally only waved her away with his hand. "I got to an exciting part."

Matilda sighed. She had a passion for C&W, and would get tears in her eyes listening to the tales of infidelity, betrayal, and heartbreak, of women lying awake next to empty pillows, of men drinking themselves into oblivion over the woman they once loved, but had inexplicably wronged. Sometimes, waiting to fall asleep at night, she would stare up at the ceiling, Wally's body nestled next to hers—just as it had been for every single night in their long and hopelessly faithful marriage—and wonder, with a strange kind of longing, what exactly she had missed. She felt she would have had a real flair for heartbreak, if she had only been given the chance.

When the song ended, Matilda sighed. "Reckon I best be waking up Melinda."

Matilda went to the room at the back of the house, where their eight-year-old daughter slept. She was already awake, though still in bed, when Matilda opened the door. "How'd you sleep, hon?" Matilda asked as she pulled back the lace curtains on either side of the bed. Melinda was their only child.

For years, she and Wally had tried to have a child. They had sought professional help, both from respected healers and from shifty-eyed quacks. In either case, there was no success and once again they went back to blaming it on the other one. To Wally, it was simple. "Her organs ain't on right." To Matilda it was also equally simple. "Them times we do it, I always tell him, 'Wally, the house ain't on fire. There ain't no rush.' " Finally, Matilda was advised by a friend that she should attend a Weight Watchers meeting. Somehow it worked, even though the first two months she only lost four pounds. "Reckon it must have been an important four pounds," Wally later remarked.

At any event, Melinda was born. And the fighting and wrangling began again. "What kind of name is that," Wally asked his wife. "You Tarzan, Me Linda?" He wanted to call her Ruby. It was Wally's momma's name. But Matilda set her horns against it. "Over my dead body." An image to give even a brave man pause. And in most cases, Matilda won out, which was why Melinda's room was painted flaming pink, with matching pink curtains and pink bedspread. Pink-framed paintings of inferior motel quality adorned the walls, showing big-eyed little girls holding kittens and puppy dogs. Wally claimed it looked like a kiddie whorehouse.

Still, he doted on the girl even more than his wife did. It was always something of a mystery to him how pretty she was. As folks would always say, on first seeing her, with an ill-concealed gasp of relief, "Why she don't look a thing like neither one of her folks."

Melinda got her bathrobe on and came out to the breakfast table. She put her hand on her daddy's shoulder and was about to say "You still reading that book?" when Wally jumped up, startled, out of his chair, dropping the book to the floor.

"Shit," he said. "I wisht you wouldn't come sneaking up on me thataway."

Melinda picked up the book and handed it to her daddy. She looked at the cover. "It scary as folks say?" she asked. At school she had heard some of the older kids talking about it. They had taken to coming up behind each other in the hallway and hissing—as they grabbed your neck or your back—"The Shadowstealer's got you."

Matilda set a plate of eggs and bacon in front of the girl. Wally went back to his reading, his eyes wide. "Lord," he murmured.

"Ain't they supposed to be making a movie of it?" Melinda asked. There were reports circulating around Mt. Jephtha to that effect.

Wally lowered the book. "I done heard they're trying to get that Robert Redford fellow to play the sheriff. I expect he'll be coming around, asking me for some pointers."

"That'd be real nice, hon," Matilda said.

"Can I go see it?"

"I don't know, hon. It's supposed to be awful scary. I sure know I ain't gonna see nothing like that."

Melinda's eyes were fixed on the cover of the book. "There ain't nothing like that, is there, Daddy?"

"Like what?"

"Like that Shadowstealer thing."

"Naw. A course not, hon. It's just something ol' Matt made up in his head, that's all," Wally assured his daughter. "That boy, he always did have a wildass streak of imagination."

Her eyes lingering on the shadowy claws that reached out to seize the running boy, Melinda frowned. "I sure hope there ain't."

4

Located on the outskirts of town, under the shadow of the water tower, was the Happy Homes Trailer Park. Its owner, Ralph Terman, had named each of the dirt roads that crisscrossed the trailer park after one of his five daughters: Felicity, Joy, Gay, Sunshine, and Consummation. Though the little sign that announced Gay Drive was always being torn down or painted over. The park, which had been cleared in the early seventies, contained about fifty trailers, some of them big and permanent and well kept up, equipped with awnings and flowerpots hanging from macramed chains. The others were tiny, ragged eyesores, with sheets over the windows in place of curtains, and ill-maintained front yards brimming with cans of Bud and discarded wrappers from the local Krystal.

Tommy Buford had lived on Sunshine Lane since his divorce, five years earlier. After emptying his pickup of Uncle Leon's junk, Tommy drove back to his trailer. His son, Jimmy, wasn't there, though that was only to be expected. Tommy got another Bud out of the refrigerator, took off his shirt, and went into the bathroom.

"Transmogrify," he said into the mirror, earnestly raising a single eyebrow.

Two weeks earlier Tommy had bought a book called *Increase Your Word Power in Ten Days*. In the few spare moments between fixing up the attic at the Lumpkin house and doing his regular work—he was a carpenter—he had stood right there, staring at himself, and had repeated fancy and impressive words. But each time, he came away in a mood of despair, muttering, "She's going to see right through me."

At the wedding down in Atlanta, Tommy had been Matt's best man. Matt had told him about Cathy. How she was real pretty, how she was brilliant, how she had been to all the best schools, how her ancestry went back to the dawn of man, how her family had enough money to pay off a good chunk of the national debt. But still Tommy hadn't been prepared. He had been around his share of good-looking women. But he had never met anyone like Cathy. She was dazzling. Slender, with long golden hair and eyes that, when they looked at him, somehow made his knees go weak. But it was more than merely looks. You knew, just being with her, that she had never been ill at ease, had never known any form of social discomfort. "Classy" was one way of describing her. But even that wasn't quite right. After all, Tommy had expected her simply to turn up her nose at him. He could even imagine her telling Matt, "What are you doing hanging around this redneck for?" But she hadn't acted that way at all. She was charming and gracious with him, and had even told him how much she was looking forward to seeing him again, up in Mt. Jephtha.

But Tommy had his doubts. The problem with people like that, people who knew how to behave, was that you never knew what they really felt. It wasn't like that among the folks Tommy had come up with. Like his Uncle Virgil, a hard-drinking roofer. When Virgil met a man and wasn't pleased by what he saw, he'd say so right quick, coming right up into the guy's face and snarling, "I don't like the way you fucking look." But at least, with Virgil, you knew where you stood.

Tommy washed his hands and walked back into the living room of the trailer.

There on the coffee table, where it couldn't be missed, was his copy of *The Shadowstealer*. He had bought two himself, but this one had been given to him by Matt, and it was a constant source of pride to him.

He sat down and stared at it.

It was part of him. Of course, he hadn't actually written a single word, but somehow that made no difference. He had lived through it.

At the wedding Matt had introduced him to Cathy by saying, "He's the guy that kept me going. He stood behind me when there was nobody else."

Tommy had denied it, of course. But in his heart of hearts, he knew it was true.

Like the night of Uncle Leon's funeral, three years before.

For Matt, life had hit bottom. His wife, Emily, had walked out on him the previous year. He had married her when he was eighteen. She had told him she was pregnant, but she wasn't, and knew she wasn't. Though Matt never held that against her: Emily knew only one way to escape from her nightmare of a

family and that was into a premature marriage. Simmy had a
fit when she heard Matt's decision. "You throwing your life
away on some low-life girl." They moved to Atlanta, where
Emily got a job as a secretary in a law firm. She had a short
affair with her boss, but stopped when Matt found out. Still the
marriage went on. She took some self-improvement courses at
a community college and began working in a doctor's office.
This time she married the doctor. Emily, years before, had
given up on the prospect of turning Matt into her idea of the
all-American money-making husband. "You got the brains,"
she told him. "Why don't you do something with 'em that
makes money." She could not understand why Matt wanted
to throw away his life "scribbling that damn story." In the
divorce settlement, Matt asked for one thing: his son, Peter,
who had been born three years earlier. Matt had made it clear
that he was prepared to do anything to keep the boy, and Emily
knew he was as good as his word.

With the death of Uncle Leon, Peter, Simmy, and Tommy
were all that Matthew had left. The night Matt came back from
the funeral home, he had cried, the first tears Tommy had ever
seen in his eyes. Simmy had come up behind him on the porch
and put her arms on his shoulder. "Sometimes life don't work
out way it should," she told him. "But one day I know you
going to do something to make us all proud."

Matt had even asked Tommy what to do. "Should I go on
making a fool of myself," he asked. At that time, Matt had
rewritten his novel eight times, but, at best, had come up only
with polite rejection. Most came back unopened, untouched.

"I don't know," Tommy told him. Inside, he was split. Part
of him wanted to say, "Do something else. Teach, get a good
job." But he couldn't say that. He knew how much it meant
to Matt, knew too Matt's sense of his own destiny. "You'll do
it," he told his friend. "You just have to keep trying."

And Matt did. That night he sat down and once again began
the arduous task of rewriting his book.

He returned to Atlanta two days later. He was working the
all-night shift at a 7-Eleven three days a week. He began
working the same shift at a gas station, on his days off.
The jobs were not high-paying or glamorous, but they let
him bring his typewriter with him, and in between selling
Snickers bars and Marlboros, he was able to continue work on

his book. He and Peter were living in a run-to-seed apartment complex in Clarkston: His neighbors were either Vietnamese refugees or tight-lipped menacing urban rednecks, the bumpers of whose trucks carried stickers that aggressively announced their philosophy of life. Fortunately, Uncle Leon's legacy included three thousand dollars in cash, but this went, for the most part, to pay the property tax on the old house. Simmy, who had lived there since she was nineteen, stayed on. She did cleaning work for some of the elderly women in Mt. Jephtha, and despite her meager income, she not only paid the utility bills on the house, but helped Matt with the taxes. Every other weekend Matt would drive up to Mt. Jephtha with his son. At night, when Tommy came over, and the kids were in bed, Matt would take out the manuscript he was working on, and he would read to Simmy and Tommy out on the back porch. Simmy, in her old cane rocker—it had been left to her by Hester—would chuckle over the humorous passages in the book, and say, "I know that's right." Or Matt would offer a description of the town and its surroundings—like the one Cathy had read from on the way into town earlier—and Simmy would nod her head in recognition, "That's just the way it be." But sometimes Matt would slip into one of the book's frightening episodes, and Simmy would cease her easy rocking. Sitting forward, her eyes fixed on the darkness behind the house, she would suddenly bolt clean out of the chair and clasp her hands to her ears. "Simmy ain't going to listen to no more of that now. I won't be sleeping tonight nohow." Then, alone, just the two of them, Matt would continue his reading to Tommy, and Tommy—who knew himself to be no judge of books—still couldn't help but feel a chill creep up his limbs as Matt's dark vision unfolded in language that Tommy could only listen to in spellbound admiration.

After the book was accepted and published, Matt began to keep a secret scrapbook of reviews. To everybody else, Matt displayed a calm, cool indifference to the critical accolades that *The Shadowstealer* gradually began to garner. But with Simmy and Tommy, it was different. To Simmy he would always read the latest entry aloud. "Why, ain't that grand," she would declare. "To think folks all the way up there in Chicago's reading your book." And Tommy thought it was pretty grand, too. "Why," Simmy remarked to Peter, "I believe

Mr. Tommy's prouder of that book than your daddy is."

And even now, eight months after Matt had given Tommy his copy, Tommy found himself opening it a couple of times a week, in order to reread the words he had committed to heart the first time he had seen them: "To Tommy, who shared with me the dark secrets."

Yeah, Tommy thought, he was being silly. Besides, as was well known, Matt and Cathy had met at a McDonald's. So at least she had to be human.

5

It was true, they had met at a McDonald's.

Later, Cathy enjoyed telling her mother that. "Is his name Ronald, dear?" Mom had replied coolly. Of course, Cathy should have known better. After all, it was one of her mom's many mottoes: Cavanaughs did not evince discomposure. For Cathy's mother, God, in addition to being the Creator of the Universe, was also a role model. As she had often instructed her daughter: "You must rise above everything." The tragedy was, Mrs. Cavanaugh did. "Did you and your friend have Large Macs?"

"Big Macs," Cathy corrected her mother. They were talking by phone. "They were delicious. I had no idea."

"I'm sure you didn't, dear."

"He's published a book. It's brilliant. It's called *The Shadowstealer*."

"What kind of book is it?" Mom asked, ready to pounce.

Cathy hesitated. "It's a ghost story," she said, for lack of a better description.

"Oh?" Mom's voice dropped a chilly, withering octave. "One of those little horror things?"

"Henry James wrote a ghost story, too, Mother."

"Henry James also frequented male bordellos," Mom retorted. Cathy gritted her teeth. It was hopeless. She should have realized that long ago. As a child, she had set her mind to a single purpose: One day she would be smarter than her mother. (Mom was a professor of Classics at Smith and had published distinguished translations of Sophocles and

Euripides.) It was possible, surely. Cathy's SATs had been resplendent (Verbal 800, Math 789); she had graduated from Williams College Summa Cum Laude, had obtained an M.A. in German Literature from Yale. She had sent her mother a copy of her master's thesis: "Demonic Pathology in Heinrich Kleist." Her mother had sent it back to her, corrected. A note was attached, "My dear, you are on the path that leads downward to Dostoyevsky! Beware."

"Well, dear, do you intend to make this Ronald James person—"

"Matthew Hardison, Mother."

"Do you intend to make him—what is it they call it nowadays?—your Significant Other?"

And much to her surprise, Cathy said, "Yes, I do."

Actually, McDonald's had not been Cathy's idea. She had originally wanted to meet Matt at The Blue Nile, an Ethiopian restaurant in the midtown section of Atlanta. But he had demurred. He didn't eat at places where they serve things that—as he put it—could get up in his lap.

Her first impression on seeing him was, My Lord, that can't be him.

He was sitting, with his back to her, out on the patio, in the shade of a grinning and garish lifesize statue of Ronald McDonald. He was reading a book, his elbows on the concrete picnic table—it was littered with empty Bic Mac foam boxes and ketchup-smeared napkins. He was dressed in an ill-fitting pair of tan polyester slacks—they had, Cathy suspected, been pulled off the rack at K Mart's at some time in the past. No belt. His shirt was a dingy white, with a collar that was as rumpled and wilted as a two-week-old head of lettuce. His shirttail stuck out inelegantly in the back. His severely battered tennis shoes—he wore no socks—had Georgia red clay caked around the soles, even though it hadn't rained in the last two weeks. His hair looked as if it had gone uncombed during the same time period. She glanced down at the photograph on the back of the book. No doubt about it, it was him, though somebody— his mother, his editor?—had taken pains to spruce him up for the snapshot. If he had a wife, she was obviously either very sweet or very blind. There was no way of knowing. No one she had talked to at the magazine had ever heard his name.

As she tried to size him up, she was unable to see the man in front of her as an author, let alone the author of a book like *The Shadowstealer*. As the editor of the trendy, upbeat Atlanta magazine *Southview*, she had been handed the novel by her book reviewer. "You have to read this. We've got to write an article on this guy." Cathy was unexcited. After all, she knew it was supposed to be one of those "little horror things," as her mother had put it—and had expected a tedious, shabbily written tale of a little girl who could hurl refrigerators around the room by means of her telepathic powers. But *The Shadowstealer* had defied her expectations. It was wonderful, and it was terrifying. The characters had a life of their own: She felt that if she saw one of them walking toward her down the street, she would be able to recognize him at once. Then, too, it had a strange power not only to grip her as she read it, but to linger in her mind after she had put it down. Already she had awakened twice in the middle of the night, scared to death, convinced in the depths of her soul that the horror had somehow slipped from the pages of the book that lay on her nightstand, only to coil beneath her bed. And as she had stared up into the darkness she had caught herself wondering: Is it possible for someone to be too gifted?

At that moment he turned and looked at her. He smiled. Not the kind of polite little smiles she was used to, but a big, openhearted smile—warm, whimsical, and just a tad shy. She also noticed that concealed beneath the nerd look, there was a nice face, a face incapable of malice or cabal. He quickly closed his book and turned it over on its back. Was he trying to keep her from seeing what it was, or was he deliberately arousing her curiosity? He got up and walked over to her—Cathy noticed only the slightest hint of a limp in his right foot, the only remaining outward sign of his childhood handicap: the fifth and final operation had proved a remarkable success. Matt offered his hand. "I bet you're Cathy Cavanaugh."

"And I bet you're Matthew Hardison." She laughed.

"I'm not sure about this," he confided in her immediately. His voice had a pleasant country drawl.

"About what?"

"Being interviewed. I always thought it was other people who got interviewed."

"Why? You're a fabulous writer. People are going to want to know all about you."

"That's what I'm afraid of," Matthew said. "You probably want to know what I think about things."

"Yes, that's true."

"Can we eat first?"

Cathy stayed outside on the patio. When he was safely out of sight—they had decided on two Big Macs—Cathy walked over to the picnic table where he had so carefully placed his book facedown. She leaned over and peeked at its spine. It read *Freddy the Detective*. (Later, Cathy discovered that Matt was a member of an organization called Admirers of Freddy.)

When Matthew returned with the food, the conversation went from Freddy the Pig to Stephen King, from the Gothic tradition to Henry James. Matt's reading, she learned, was eccentric, even willful, his opinions strong and a little arbitrary. Yet it was evident to Cathy that Matt, in everything, made up his own mind, paying no attention whatever to the prevailing conventional wisdom. Finally, she turned to the obvious personal questions. What made him want to be a writer? When had he first realized his sense of vocation? How did he develop his ideas? Who had influenced him the most?

To the last question he answered, without hesitation, "My Aunt Hester."

Puzzled, Cathy looked up from her Big Mac, not sure whether Matthew was teasing or not. Then he launched into the story of how the idea of his book had first come to him, when at the age of twelve, he and his friend Tommy had sneaked into Aunt Hester's room, and how, the very next day, he had commenced writing it all down. "Of course, it grew over the years a bit. Though I'm not sure it got any better." Matt took a robust chomp out of his Big Mac, then grinned. "The funny thing is, Tommy and me, we used to sit up nights, trying to come up with a plausible explanation of how all those things could have happened. You know, like what *really* made her brother, Wiley, scoop his eyeballs out." Matt noticed Cathy as she frowned at the remnants of her meal. "Oops, sorry. But there was one very obvious explanation we never thought of."

"What was that?"

"Well," Matt said, "it never occurred to us that Aunt Hester was crazy as a loon. Which Aunt Hester was. But, later on, I realized something. That it didn't really matter. So she wasn't quite 'right.' Who cares? What counted was the intensity of her vision, the fact that in telling her story, she got us to believe, in our heart of hearts, that it was all true. Lord, you don't know how many times I've been walking at night and I've really felt it, this tingling on the back of my neck. And I've had to stop and turn around, to see if *it's* there, lurking inside my shadow, ready to reach up with its claw and grab me."

Cathy, who after reading the book had had her share of such spells, smiled and said, "I know what you mean." She finished her last bit of Big Mac. "I kept wondering, as I read the book, if you hadn't been inspired by some folktale. It certainly sounded like it should have been a folktale."

"Maybe it is. Somewhere," Matt added with a laugh.

"And I kept thinking about C. G. Jung, too." The name, surprisingly, did not ring a bell with Matt. So Cathy explained. Jung, the Swiss psychologist, in developing his theory of human personality had postulated a concept he called The Shadow—*Das Schatten*, in German, she offered. For Jung, The Shadow is the darkest, most terrifying recess of the soul, a place teaming with all of our most hidden and horrific impulses and urges. The Shadow is that which cannot be brought to the light of consciousness without risking doom and self-destruction. It is that which we must always run from, but which, in the end, always catches us.

"Hmmmm," Matt commented. "Didn't know I was so profound." He hesitated, then said, "Actually, all I was trying to do was to scare the shit out of people."

"Well, you did."

"Yeah, I did, didn't I?"

Cathy laughed, then looked at him with her spookiest eyes. "Did it ever occur to you—way back in the deep dark part of your mind—that maybe by telling this story, you'd let the thing loose? The way it happened in the book?"

Matt shrugged. "Who knows what goes on in the deep dark part of my mind? Maybe I did. Hell, maybe that's what I really wanted, deep down." Matt arched his eyebrows demonically—or as much as he could get them. "But like I say: Nobody has to read it if they don't want to."

They chatted for a while more, then Matt said, "I've got an idea. Why don't we go out to Stone Mountain. It's only a little ways down Memorial. You ever been there?"

Cathy shook her head no.

"How about it then?"

It was one of those decisive moments that you look back on and wonder about. She could have delicately told him that her afternoon was tied up, that she had work she needed to do—which was even true. She could have insisted that she was there to learn about him, not for him to learn about her. But she didn't say any of those things. At the time, she wasn't sure why, though later she would put it this way: Even within the brief time frame of that first encounter, Matt had already begun to cast the same spell upon her that he had cast so long ago on his childhood friends; he had wrenched her out of her prosaic world and dragged her into one of his own devising. What he did with his stories, he did in life, too. He created a world with its own laws, its own gravity (or lack of it), its own light, its own darkness. And she was held spellbound by it, even at those moments when a voice within her whispered: "Let me go. Let me return to my world."

Yet only once did Cathy try to break the spell. That was two weeks later, by which time Cathy was aware of the depths of Matt's feelings for her, although never once had Matt risked putting it into words. They saw each other nearly every day, and yet it was all under the guise of an extended interview. Acting a bit like Scheherazade, Matt managed to string Cathy along—talking about her, about everything except Matthew Hardison, mentioning himself only as he was about to leave, at which point Matt would let out some darkly tantalizing bit of autobiography. "Course, it's too late to go into tonight. But how about tomorrow night?" And each time, Cathy fell for it.

But something told her it was time to stop.

They had been to see a movie and afterward they had stopped by Zesto's for a milk shake. "I really have enjoyed this so much," she told him. But it was time she got back to her "normal life." Aside from actually writing the article on him, there was, she said, mountains of backlogged material that required editing.

Matt was silent, but Cathy knew he was hurt.

On the way back, something happened that summed up, for Cathy, everything that she loved in Matt. They were coming up

Morningside Drive. The headlights of the car caught a gleam in the middle of the road. Matt swerved. Cathy asked, "What was that?"

Matt told her it was a cat. "I think it's still alive." He pulled over to the curb and got out. He walked to where the animal was lying. Cathy followed. He knelt down and stared at its sides: It was still breathing. But there was no visible blood, no wound or gash. "It must've just been grazed." Cathy asked what he was going to do. He hesitated a few seconds, then said, "There's an animal hospital over in Tucker. It's open twenty-four hours. We'll take it there." Gently he lifted the cat up and carried it to the car. "Can you drive?" he asked.

He held the cat cradled in his lap. It gave out low, pained meows, its eyes fixing on Matt restlessly, then disappearing as the animal buried its head under Matt's arm.

At the clinic, Matt carried the cat into one of the cubicles. The animal was spread out on the table and for ten minutes, the attendant worked to save its life. "It's not going to make it," the man said.

"Just keep trying," Matt told him. The cat looked up one more time, its dazed, but still lustrous green eyes staring directly into Matt's face, then laid its head back down and died.

"That'll be twenty-five dollars," the attendant said.

Outside, Matt was silent. "It must have been more seriously injured than it looked," Cathy commented.

"The way it was staring up at me when it died. Almost like it knew. I thought only we knew," Matt whispered, his eyes on the used car lot next to the clinic. Cathy looked over at it, and saw a Porsche, and recalled how, on her last date with someone, she had sat and listened to an insufferable monologue on the resale value of the Porsche versus the BMW—her date was a stockbroker and drove a Porsche, of course. Matt, on the other hand, wouldn't have recognized a Porsche if it ran over him. "I always thought that's what it means to be human: to be haunted by what isn't. I thought animals were luckier."

"What do you mean, haunted by what isn't?"

"That's all imagination boils down to, I think. For the rest of creation, there is only what is. They don't look beyond that. But we do. We can see all the shadows that creation casts—shadows of what could have been, or should have been. Shadows of regret and hope, of longing and remorse.

It's like, our highest faculty is both a blessing and a curse. To see what isn't there, but could be." Matt frowned. "When I was a boy, I went to this revival." And Matt told Cathy of the fire that had swept through the tent outside Mt. Jephtha many years earlier, the catastrophic outcome of Tommy's granny's efforts to heal Matt's "afflicted" condition. "Afterward, I was eaten up by doubt. Why did it happen? Why would God let it happen? People said that it was God's will. But I couldn't accept that for a minute. Later on, I realized why. Because, like every other human being, I could imagine what it would have been like if the fire hadn't happened. I was haunted by what wasn't, by what hadn't been." Matt frowned. "And then, too, in a crazy way I felt guilty for it."

"Guilty?"

Matt nodded, then told Cathy how Tommy's granny had, much against Matt's own will, pushed him up onto the platform, in order to be healed, and how, when Odum looked down at his foot, a change swept over his face. "It was as if he were scared to death. By my goddam foot. I know it wasn't the prettiest thing to look at. Still isn't. But, Lord, talk about overreacting." Matt went on to tell how Odum had started whispering to himself crazily, saying all matter of weird and untoward things. "How he had buried me, and such. Assuming I wasn't hearing things." Matt glanced away. "No telling why he said it, or what he was thinking. But whatever it was, I couldn't shake off the feeling that if I hadn't been up there, if he hadn't looked at me, the fire would never have happened. And all those people would have been alive."

"It wasn't your fault," Cathy told him.

"No. And yet, it happened because I was there. You see what I mean?"

And Cathy nodded. She was familiar with the idea from her knowledge of Greek literature. A man can be culpable simply by being who he is. Sometimes he must pay dearly even for the unintended consequences of his most innocent actions. In other words, a man may be required to atone even for his fate.

Matt stared out the car window and sighed. "Anyway, that fire showed me something. It showed me the dark underside of the world. Though sometimes I wish like hell I could forget I ever saw it."

"*Lacrymae rerum*." When Matt looked at her, puzzled, Cathy translated and explained. "It's a phrase from Virgil's *Aeneid*. It means, literally, 'the tears of things.' All the melancholy, all the little sadnesses, and the big ones, too, that make up existence. To feel them makes us human," Cathy said. "But you're right. Sometimes we do have to forget about it, don't we? If we didn't, life would be awfully unbearable."

"Yeah." Matt sat pensively, then said, "Did I ever tell you, I have a cat that can talk?"

"Pardon?"

And Matt proceeded to tell Cathy about Tigger the Talking Cat. He even offered what he referred to as his own poor imitation of Tigger's voice. When they got back to her apartment, he said, "I wish Tigger were here now."

"Why?"

" 'Cause sometimes he can say things I can't. It's almost like he can read my mind. I don't know how he does it, but he can."

"Well, once a cat can talk, there's no telling what else he can do."

Matt nodded solemnly. "It's like he can get things off my chest for me, things I'm too shy, or too proud, or too stubborn to say for myself. You know?" He bit the corner of his lip nervously and shot Cathy a timidly appealing glance.

"What would Tigger say if he were here right now?"

"Oh, I don't know, Miss Cathy," Matt said, falling into his best Tigger impersonation. "I reckon I'd tell you how much you mean to my daddy. How he's worried you're not going to want to see him anymore."

"Oh."

"To tell you the truth, I think Daddy's in love with you. Only he's afraid you're too good for him. I mean, Daddy has his points—I ain't saying he don't—but he ain't had all the advantages you've had. I mean, just think if you'd met poor Daddy back when he used to work in that gas station, cleaning out them toilet bowls. I bet you wouldn't have gone out to a fancy place like McDonald's with him then, would you?"

Cathy stared out the window, a lump embarrassingly in her throat. "Tigger," she said after a moment, "your daddy is very kind and very good. And he means very much to me, too. But—"

"Oh, no, here it comes, Daddy. I told you."

"But right now, I just don't know what I want."

"Yeah," Matt said in his own voice.

That night, by herself, Cathy searched her soul. If she had been a character in a book, how would she have judged herself? After all, the first thought that went through her head was, What would people say? Mom? My friends? Here was a man who bought his clothes at K Mart, who had worked the night shift at the 7-Eleven, who genuinely enjoyed eating Big Macs, and who seldom stepped foot inside a restaurant without a drive-thru. He had the savoir faire of a lumberjack and the social graces of a construction worker. His education consisted of night courses at a junior college. He drank Budweiser and smoked Marlboros, and what he knew about art and music could be put inside a can of Copenhagen—which, to Cathy's horror, he confessed to once "dipping." One night he had taken her by where he used to work. They had gone in and he had introduced her to Hakim, the Pakistani cashier. Afterward, he had joked with her: "Can you see yourself coming in there back when I used to work the night shift? I can imagine me starting up a conversation with you, what you would have done." Cathy could imagine it only too well. "You'd've given me a look that would have turned my blood to ice water." He was right: he wasn't her kind of guy. And yet, he was a genius. The only genius she had ever come up close to. And he was also the kindest human being she had ever met.

You're a goddam snob, Cathy suddenly told herself in an epiphany of horror. All your life you've been rebelling against your mother's elitism, and here you are, its leading disciple. And yet, at that moment, she knew that her mother had possessed her too thoroughly, too completely, for her to say anything other than "I guess you're right."

The next day she called him up. "Let's go to dinner." When he came by, he was wearing a suit. He was so proud of it that Cathy thought he was going to come busting out of his vest. He had ordered it rush, a week earlier. "I actually let this guy stick his hand up my leg," he told her. They went to the Blue Nile that night, and although he was perhaps a little overly inquisitive about the ingredients used in the main course—"You sure that's just lamb?"—he carried it off with aplomb.

"I guess Daddy's being kinda obvious, ain't he, Miss Cathy," Tigger remarked.

"Yeah, a little." They were in front of Cathy's apartment. She hesitated, then said, "I was a fool, Tigger. I mean, about the things I told your daddy last night. I guess it was just a little scary for me."

"Oh, I know. It's scary for me, too, Miss Cathy. Us cats, we ain't had no mommy in a long time." And Matt gave Cathy one of his little-boy looks. They both smiled.

"Well, you two want to come in for a Bud?" she asked.

They ate at the Waffle House the next morning.

6

They were there.

Matt glanced over uneasily at Cathy. "Is it so bad?"

Her eyes wide, she shook her head, then broke into a giggle. "Oh, I love it. It's gorgeous. I mean, it's a little strange, but it has such—"

"Character?"

They were talking about the Lumpkin house. As Matt had turned into the long gravel driveway, Cathy had been able to get only a few tantalizing glimpses through the azaleas and magnolias. She held her breath. She wanted to love it, just as she knew Matt loved it. He had warned her that it was old, that it needed repairs, that it epitomized the most extreme excrescences of the Gothic revival. All of which was true. And yet, as Cathy got her first proper look at the house, she felt her heart flutter in a way that is traditionally indicative of the state called "Love at First Sight."

"I told you Great-grandpa Lumpkin saw it in a dream."

"I can believe it."

His architectural motto, Cathy reflected, had clearly been "More is more."

"Some people thought he was crazy," Matt commented. Then on further reflection, he said, "Actually, *everybody* thought he was crazy. Especially Great-grandma Lumpkin. But he wasn't the kind of man you argued with."

"I can see."

"I think he wanted to make a statement: Lumpkins are different."

"Living in a place like that, I don't see how they had any choice." Cathy laughed. "God, no wonder you have such an imagination."

Of course, Matt went on, it does need work. "But I'll go along with anything you say."

That was part of the plan. Now that Matt had money, he wanted to fix the old house up right. Only, he confessed to Cathy, he didn't have any idea how to go about doing it. He would rely on her judgment completely. After all, she knew about such things, just as she seemed to know about everything else. "My God," he once asked her, "how can you have learned so much in so little time?" To her, it was touching. Here was Matt—certainly the most brilliantly gifted human being she had ever known—and he was constantly asking her to tell him what books to read, what music to listen to ("Is this guy Schubert good?"), what this or that philosophical idea was all about ("What's utilitarianism?"). He even had a reading list—it was by now four pages long—of all the books she had mentioned to him in the course of their talks—a list that promiscuously paired off *Das Kapital* with *De Profoundis*, *The Memoirs of Hadrian* with *Emma*. At times Cathy expressed doubts about his project—"My God, you've managed to do pretty well without knowing all this stuff," she once told him—but he was determined. "I just don't want you to get bored with me," he told her.

The same solicitude was apparent when he had first timidly suggested: "You know, maybe we could live in Mt. Jephtha." He knew, after all, what he was asking of her. But it was obvious he had thought it all out. "You could be a free-lance editor. All you need for that is a mailbox, right? Besides, remember, you said you always wanted to try to write a novel. You could write your novel, I could write mine."

Cathy had given him a sly look and said, "Yeah, but what if I just want to settle down and have kids?"

Matt had grinned and said that would be fine, too. "Course, we'll have to get Peter's approval first."

7

"Hon, your daddy's here," Simmy said.

Peter was standing in the hallway by the window. He was dressed in his best suit, with a polka-dot bow tie. His face was scrubbed pink and his hair slicked down. He frowned glumly and stared out the window at his dad and the woman with him. Two weeks before the wedding, Matt had driven up from Atlanta, taken his nine-year-old son out on the porch, and sat him down in a rocking chair. Matt had never been so nervous in his life. Earlier, he had asked Cathy what he should say. "Just tell the truth. He's going to have to find out sooner or later." So Matt did just that.

"I'm getting married."

Peter had stared up and said, "Why?"

"Because it's hard for me to be alone."

"You're not alone. I'm here, and Simmy's here."

Yes, Matt had conceded. "But, you see, I love her."

"More than you love me?"

Oh, Lord, Matt had thought. "No, I love you both. More than anything in this world."

"But you just met her. How can you love her as much as me?"

And Matt had started into a rambling discourse on how there were different kinds of love, but he saw that Peter wasn't listening to him. At that moment, the only kind of love that interested Peter was the love he was afraid of losing. Matt had stopped, lifted his son up, and set him in his lap. "Just give us a chance, her and me. That's all I'm asking. Can you do that?"

Peter had hesitated, then had reluctantly nodded, "I guess."

Simmy, on the other hand, was easy. For years she had told Matt how he needed to find himself a good woman. "None of these here low-lifes, but a woman who 'preciates you, way you ought to be 'preciated." Delirious upon learning of the impending marriage, Simmy had immediately set to work on making Peter come around, although in her own peculiar way. "What you and your daddy goin' to do when Simmy's been took up to Jesus, hon? You need you a momma, both a you. Somebody to cook and clean and wash your dirty ol' drawers."

But Peter was unconvinced: The idea that Simmy was in imminent danger of being took to Jesus seemed to him—considering the woman's frenetic level of energy—as remote a threat to his world as the melting of the polar ice caps. "What if she doesn't like me?" Peter had asked, the day before the wedding.

"Course, she's going to like you."

"What if she's mean to me?"

Simmy had laughed and said, "If she's mean to you, Simmy's going to take that big old mop she's got, and she's going to chase her on back down to 'Lanta with it, you hear me talking, hon?"

"You promise?" And Simmy gave the boy her solemn word on it.

Still, as Peter stood behind the curtain and watched the strange woman—he had seen her only once, and that was at the wedding—he felt the butterflies whirling around in his stomach.

"Why just look at her. Ain't she fine!" Simmy exclaimed grandly: She was right behind Peter, with her hands on his shoulder. "Your daddy, he's done hisself proud this time. Now you go out there and you do your daddy proud, too," Simmy said.

Peter looked back at her. "You remember your promise, don't you?"

Simmy smiled. She leaned down and whispered, "I got my mop all ready, if I needs it. Now you go on out there and you show her how good Simmy's done brought you up. You hear?"

Matt and Simmy were sitting in the kitchen. Peter had taken Cathy off upstairs, to give her a grand tour of the house.

"We all going to be happy now," Simmy announced. "Gonna be a real family."

Matt nodded. "It's almost scary sometimes."

"Scary? How come you say such a thing?" Simmy demanded.

"I expected a lot of things out of life. But I never expected to be happy."

"You crazy."

"Maybe."

"Daddy!" Peter tumbled into the kitchen, Cathy in tow. "We got a surprise for you. Up in the attic!"

Peter was already attempting to shove him out of his chair. Matt grimaced and protested.

"Go on, Mr. Matt," Simmy chimed in. "You going to be real pleased."

"Tell me what it is first."

"Then it wouldn't be a surprise."

Peter was pushing his daddy from behind. Cathy took hold of his hand and said, "Be brave now." Matt looked at her and frowned. If she wasn't going to tell him, nobody was. He sighed and acquiesced. A few minutes later he was standing at the door at the end of the narrow flight of steps. The door opened into the huge, dank, cavernous attic.

"Close your eyes."

"You gotta be kidding," Matthew said. "You know what lives in attics?"

"We chased the monsters out, Daddy."

Matthew heaved a sigh. He closed one eye, leaving the other a trembling slit. Peter reached up and opened the door.

"You can look now."

Matthew was already looking. His mouth dropped.

"Me and Tommy and Simmy did it."

"Tommy did it mostly, Mr. Matt."

Matthew went up the last step and stared at the room in front of him, still dumbfounded. "It's got walls, and a floor. I've never seen them before."

"Tommy come by and he worked every day, hard as a mule. Toting all them things out to his truck. Except, a course, Mr. Leon's books." By which Simmy meant Matthew's uncle's two thousand odd blue notebooks. "We put them in the other part of the attic. Tommy put up them walls, too, and then him and us we done painted them up good."

"Come over here, Daddy." And Peter led his father to a wall that had never been there before. He opened the door and Matt gazed into the neat room. There, in front of the attic's solitary window, sat his word processor. Overhead there was a neat row of fluorescent lights. On either side of the room there were bookshelves and filing cabinets.

"Tommy did all this?" Matthew asked. He walked into the room and Peter rolled the swivel chair—it, too, was brand-new. Peter pushed him down into it.

"We knew you'd never do it," Peter said. "So we did it for you."

"Tommy'd've been here hisself, but he had one last load to tote. But he's coming back, quick as he can."

Simmy put her hands on Peter's shoulders and said, "Come on downstairs, hon. I need you to taste the icing for me." And Peter followed Simmy back down the narrow steps, the old woman reaching back from time to time and saying, "Now you take Simmy's hand. Don't want old Simmy breaking her hip now."

Cathy went over and kissed Matt. "You sure got them fooled. Me, too," she said as she plopped down into his lap.

"Yeah. I just hope I can keep you fooled."

Cathy glanced at the doorway. A huge, long-haired tabby cat stared up at her with grim, imploring eyes. She grinned. "That's—"

But before she could get the name out, Tigger said, "Would you please mind getting out of my daddy's lap, you strange person."

"You can get up here, too, Tigger."

Tigger glanced away uncertainly. Then he looked back up at Cathy and in a single bound jumped into her lap. She nuzzled him behind his ears. His green eyes closed in blissful distraction. "Oh, Daddy, I like her already. I think you made a good choice."

Matt kissed Cathy on the neck. "Me, too, Tigger."

8

After taking a shower, Tommy got back in the truck and drove to the field behind the trailer park. On the far side was a stand of pine trees, and beyond that the old water tower.

Tommy's son, Jimmy, was there with three of the other kids from the park. They were playing horseshoes, which, along with hide-and-seek and football, was the favorite activity of the Happy Home kids. Two of the kids, Opal and Leroy Cates, were brother and sister. She was twelve, Leroy was eleven. They could have swapped faces without anybody noticing the difference. They both had grim, stern casts to their watery blue eyes, and could stare at you long and hard with no more self-consciousness than if they had been standing on the invisible side of a one-way mirror. They lived in a run-to-seed trailer at the far end of Joy Lane. Their momma, Venita, worked the day shift at the Waffle House. Her hair was blond, up to a certain point—which changed over the course of the month— and was normally piled up on top of her head, as if she were trying to see how much she could get up there without keeling over.

The other boy was Curtis Poke. At fifteen, he was the oldest of the group. A good-humored country boy, he lived with his dad and stepmom in one of the nicer trailers. All the little kids in the park looked up to him: He was never known to back down in a fight, and he never picked on you, unless you started it first.

As Tommy got out of his pickup, he overheard a dispute between Opal and his boy, Jimmy. "That ain't near to no ringer," Opal maintained. "Tell him, Curtis. It ain't even close."

Jimmy protested and looked over at Curtis. "Whatchew think?"

Curtis knelt down and examined the horseshoe's position on the ringer. "Opal's right."

Jimmy reddened. "That ain't no fair. You always take up for Opal."

"No, he don't. He give you the last one. Remember?"

But Jimmy, who was not always the best of sports, was not willing to drop his protest. "These horseshoes got something in 'em. Magnets, like."

"You just getting your ass whupped, s'all," Leroy said. And it was true.

Just as Leroy was about to take his turn, Opal noticed Tommy. She waved and smiled. She didn't often smile, but then Opal, like the other kids in the park, liked Tommy. He was always willing to take up for them, as he had done a week before, when ornery old Mr. Proopes took his BB gun out and shot at Opal and Leroy's dog, Sparkle, claiming it had been heading in the general direction of his prized rosebushes.

"Your daddy's here. Hey, Tommy."

"Hey," Tommy said back amiably. "Who's winning?"

"I am, a course," Leroy declared in no uncertain terms. The only terms that the boy ever made use of. Tommy grinned. At the tender age of eleven, Leroy was what anyone would recognize as a real character. He was blunt, outspoken, self-assertive beyond his years. What he thought, he spoke. And if you didn't like hearing it, well, that was your problem. Yet the boy had brains. Not the kind of brains that led you to write poetry or to speculate on the mysteries of the universe. In fact, Leroy's grades in school were seldom more than kindly bestowed C's. But the brains were there, and Tommy had seen them in action. What inspired Leroy was the concrete and the mechanical. Once Tommy had taken Leroy and Jimmy with him to wash Mt. Jephtha's old fire truck—Tommy was one of the town's volunteer firemen. Jimmy grumbled the whole time, displaying no more interest in the fire engine than he would have shown in an exhibit of Sumerian funereal artifacts. But not Leroy. He wanted to know everything. What this switch did, how the pumps worked, where the water went in. The truck, to Leroy, was like a big three-dimensional jigsaw puzzle, and he wanted to find out where all the pieces fit, a trait that probably explained the boy's startling flair for fixing things. Broken radios and ruptured air hoses, malfunctioning circular saws and fractured bicycle wheels—none of them posed the slightest obstacle for Leroy. He merely examined the ailing item with his harsh, critical gaze, then silently set to work. And woe to him who foolishly asked Leroy if he knew what he was doing! The scowl he directed at such doubters was enough to freeze blood. "Course I do."

Once, when talking to Matt about the peculiar boy, Tommy had suggested that Leroy was the perfect mirror image of Matt. One was all soaring imagination, the other all gritty reality. "Think what you two could do if you ever got together," Tommy had joked.

Jimmy came over to his daddy. He was holding out his horseshoe. "Something's wrong with mine." He sulked.

"That a fact?" Tommy said, unimpressed. Always a good sport himself, Tommy did not much care for Jimmy's constant efforts to put the blame on somebody or something else. It was one of those truths of life that a man can learn only by being a parent. Before, Tommy always thought that a kid, any kid, could be gently guided to see the errors of his ways. If something was wrong, it could be set straight, provided you were prepared to be patient and sympathetic. And so, time and again, after one of his outbursts, Tommy had taken his boy aside and tried to reason with him. He took Jimmy over each step in the argument, and the boy accepted each premise with a sullen nod. But each time Tommy went to draw the logically required conclusion from the premises, Jimmy would flare up, "Naw, that ain't right." And Tommy would sigh and try to start all over again.

"Maybe it ain't the horseshoe, son."

"You try it. You'll see."

Tommy took the offered horseshoe out of his son's hands, aimed, and tossed. It was a dead ringer. "Seems like it works fine to me."

Jimmy ran over and fetched it back. "Naw, it don't do it with you," Jimmy murmured. "It just does it with me."

Tommy stared at his son. He was about to ask Jimmy if horseshoes could tell the difference between the hands that threw them, but Opal cut in, "You gonna play with us?"

"Nope. Gotta get going. Come on, Jimmy."

As they were leaving, Curtis ran over to Tommy and said, "I almost finished that book."

A couple of weeks before, Tommy had loaned Curtis one of his two spare copies of *The Shadowstealer*. A year earlier Tommy had discovered, quite by accident, that Curtis loved to read. Of course, it wasn't the kind of thing that a boy like Curtis wanted to let get around. After all, he had his reputation to consider.

"What you think?"

"I think it's pretty scary. Where'd he come up with all them ideas?"

Tommy smiled at the boy. "You got me."

"I keep thinking something's sneaking up behind me, when I read it. I keep having to turn around. To make sure nothing's there."

"Me, too," Tommy said. "Anyway, y'all be good." And the three kids said they would be.

As the Bronco pulled off, Leroy cast a cold eye on Curtis. "Whatchew want to be reading some book for? There ain't even school."

"Nothing's wrong with reading, Leroy," Curtis said. "Lot of people read."

"I don't care about no goofy ol' story," Leroy said. " 'Bout shadows coming to get you. That's crazy."

"You gonna play or ain't you?" Opal yelled at her brother.

"Gonna play," Leroy answered. But he was still shaking his head. "Shadows with claws and eyeballs." Leroy, too, had seen the cover. "Whoever heard of such a thing?"

9

"Would you like another beer?"

Tommy Buford nodded. "Yesum. If you don't mind."

Cathy glanced from Tommy to Matt. "Yesum?" She repeated with a quizzical smile, then went back into the kitchen, leaving Tommy and Matt out on the back porch of the Lumpkin house. Outside, near the edge of the woods, they could hear their two boys, Peter and Jimmy, whooping and hollering.

"She sure is something," Tommy said.

For the last half hour, Matt and Cathy had been telling Tommy about their honeymoon vacation: They had spent a month in Italy, where Cathy had taken Matt to enough museums to last him the rest of his life. Right before going to get more beer, Cathy had been talking about Donatello.

"Don't see how she pronounces them names," Tommy declared. "And here I always thought you was smart."

"That shows how much you know."

At that moment Tigger the Cat sat down on his haunches smack dab in the kitchen doorway. He stared up at Tommy, then Matt. Tommy called to him, but the cat went right over to Matt and jumped up in his lap.

"See if I save you from Simmy anymore," Tommy scolded the animal.

"I got my daddy back now."

"Sheeet."

Cathy returned with the beer and sat down. "So Tigger talks to you, too?"

Tommy stiffened in his chair and nodded. "Yesum." But this time he caught himself. "I mean, yes." He glanced over at Matt, then fixed his eyes on to the top of his beer can. He lifted it to his mouth, then noticed that he hadn't snapped off the top. He blushed and corrected his error.

There was an awkward silence. Tommy looked up and braced himself. "It sure is . . . is halcyon tonight."

Cathy and Matt glanced at each other, in puzzlement. Tommy, while he had memorized a list of fifty very impressive words, had overlooked the question of pronunciation. The word that he had screwed up all of his courage to utter had come out sounding like hal-*key*-on, the stress falling resoundingly, in Tommy's version, on the second syllable. Proceeding on the sincere assumption that this was some kind of quaint Southern turn of phrase, Cathy asked Tommy what he meant.

Shifting uneasily in his chair, Tommy said, "You know, 'quiet,' 'peaceful.' That's right, ain't it?" He appealed to Matt.

"Oh, you mean halcyon," Cathy said without thinking.

Made aware of his error, Tommy blushed. Followed quickly by Cathy, who suddenly understood what had happened.

"Sheeet," Matt said, lifting his beer to his lips, "I don't know what the hell you two are talking about. Us ignorant country boys, we don't go in for all them fancy words. Not like you two city slickers."

While Matt was able to dispel some of the tension, for the next fifteen minutes Tommy didn't say a word. Finally, glancing down at his wristwatch, he stood up and said he reckoned he best be going.

"What for?" Matt said. "Whatchew got better to do?"

"Just thought I'd leave you two together. Anyway, I sure am glad you're back."

After Tommy had left, Cathy shook her head. "I'm really sorry I embarrassed him. I honestly didn't mean to." And then, as Cathy tried to explain, Matt walked over and kissed her.

"It's not your fault."

"But I feel terrible."

"Don't worry. You got to give Tommy a little time, that's all."

"I wish he didn't keep saying 'yesum' to me."

"It's just a reflex."

"I try to be as nice to him as I know how. But it's like I intimidate him."

"You do," Matt said with a laugh. "Shit, you intimidate me."

"I don't mean to."

"I wish you could've heard yourself, the way Tommy heard you. Borronmini and Gucciardini and Titsy-ritzy-ardini. My Lord, he's just not used to that."

"I'll try to be nicer."

"It isn't that, Cathy. It's what you are. See, people like you, they're not supposed to be nice with people like Tommy."

Cathy looked up at Matt and for the first time he saw anger flash from her eyes. "What on earth do you mean, people like me?" she asked him. "Goddammit, at what point are you going to start seeing me for what I am myself? So, my parents had money. So, I went to a goddam good college, and yes, I dress well and I've read a lot. What is that supposed to prove? If I was one of those goddam 'people like me' I'd be married to a goddam stockbroker living in Connecticut, remember."

And Matt quietly said, "I know that."

Embarrassed by her outburst, Cathy squeezed Matt's hand. "Of course, I'd be going nuts. But I just wish everybody would treat me like I was normal. Because I am." Matt patted her hand and said, "Don't worry about Tommy, he'll come around."

10

An hour earlier Curtis Poke had been in his room. He was on the last few pages of *The Shadowstealer*. Suddenly the door had burst open and in had come Jesse Dillard, Curtis's best friend. "Shit, didn't you hear me knocking?" Startled half to death, Curtis looked up, his mouth open. "I figured you was in here playing with yourself," Jesse said, then, catching sight of the book, he went over and took it from Curtis's hands.

"And shit, here you was, jus' reading a book." Jesse shook his head in consternation. "I swear, Curtis Poke, sometimes I don't know about you." Jesse sat down on the bed and stared at the cover. "What the fuck's that?" Curtis explained. "Shit, maybe I'll read it." But then, on second thought, Jesse flung the book down on the bed. "Hell, it'd take me a year to read that fucker. You coming to the rink or not?"

The skating rink—Jasper's was what everybody called it— was located two miles north of Mt. Jephtha. It was one of the two hangouts where the kids of Claudell County went on the weekends. Either there or the Dairy Queen, on the other side of town, with the balance of the evening spent cruising between the two hangouts. Set back in the woods, about three hundred yards off the main road, it would have been easy for an out-of-towner to have missed the old weather-beaten wooden sign that stood—or rather leaned—at a ninety-degree angle at the entrance to the narrow gravel road, and which dimly displayed the rink's hours, also advising that Wednesday night was Ladies Night, while on Fridays the rink was open until dawn, for what was called the Teen Skate-athon.

At ten o'clock Curtis and Jesse were in the parking lot, drinking Budweisers out of a brown bag and leaning up against Jesse's black Cougar, with the radio on. Jesse Dillard was something of a legend among the kids of Claudell County, famed for his wild and unpredictable nature. A good fighter, Jesse was known never to have backed down from anyone or anything. He was also handsome, in a rough country way, with eyes, deep blue and glistening, that said more to you in a second than most people could in a lifetime of running their mouths. He seldom wore a shirt, even when it got to be wintertime, and his body—at once as smooth as a child, and as muscular as a man's—seemed like the incarnation of some elemental force, each movement conveying the impression of wild and restless energy, as unpredictable as rain, as irresistible as a cyclone. Jesse was always getting into fights, either up at the rink or over at the Dairy Queen, though, in fairness to him, they were seldom his fault. There was just something about the boy that provoked it. The weekend before, Jesse had merely walked inside the rink, but that had been enough.

"What you looking at him for?" Bobby Lee Pinkham had snapped at his girlfriend, June Lively, as her well-mascaraed eyes oozed up and down Jesse's legs and torso.

"I ain't looking at nobody. 'Sides, none of your business who I look at."

"Oh, yeah?" Bobby said. "You just watch me." And Bobby Lee, itching for a fight, strode over and grabbed Jesse by his arm. "Why you looking at my June that way?"

"I wasn't looking at nobody no way," Jesse replied in all honesty. But it was too late. The code of honor had been violated and Jesse was obliged to beat the shit out of Bobby Lee. Ten minutes later the dust cleared in the parking lot of the rink. Jesse stood over Bobby Lee's limp and bleeding body. Jesse, who didn't even have a cut on his cheek, shook his head in dismay and even a bit of remorse: "What you go and start running your mouth for, Bobby Lee? You knew I was going to have to whup you. Say!"

To which Bobby Lee only whimpered, "I won't do it no more, I promise."

An hour later, Jesse, always quick to forgive, was sharing a joint with Bobby Lee.

"Reach in there and get me another Bud, Curtis." Jesse snapped open the top of the can, then tossed the metal tab back over his shoulder. He took a sip. "Who's that coming?"

Curtis glanced up and saw the headlights up over the ridge of the hill that separated the rink from the highway. "Looks like ol' Wally's patrol car," Jesse said. Like a lot of kids in the country he could tell nearly any make of car from just a glance at its headlights.

All the kids in Mt. Jephtha knew Sheriff Clark simply as "ol' Wally." It wasn't that Wally couldn't be tough: Everybody knew, if you deserved it, Wally made sure you got it. But his toughness was always tempered by a face-to-face knowledge of the people he was dealing with. He knew the names of all the kids who came up to the rink. He knew what their mommas and daddies did. He knew who was rowdy, who started fights, who drank too much.

As Wally Clark pulled his car up in front of the two boys, he stuck his head out the window and gave them his best Official Police Business scowl. "What you got in that paper bag, son?"

"This one here?" Jesse held up the sack in which his beer was concealed.

"You ain't got a Bud in there, do you?"

"No, sir, Wally. It's a Nehi Grape."

"A Nehi Grape?" Wally repeated. "You got you another one of them Nehi Grapes in a Sack?"

"Sure do. You want one?" Jesse asked. He jumped down from the hood of his car and carried one of the brown-bagged Budweisers over to Wally. Wally took it, popped open the top, and drank.

"Don't make them Nehi Grapes like they used to."

Wally shone his flashlight down at Jesse's pants. "Woo-whee, where d'you get them things? Frederick's of San Francisco?" It was the same question that Wally had asked Jesse ever since the boy had saved up the sixty dollars—about a year back—to buy the flashy red parachute pants. Wally shook his head in dismay. "When I was your age, if me and my buddies seen a boy come 'round Mt. Jephtha dressed in them tight red pants you got on, why, we wouldn't have known whether to fuck him or shoot him."

"Sure hope you would have shot me, Wally," Jesse quipped, then, nudging Curtis, he added, "Why don't you get you some?" And the boys laughed at the image of portly Wally snug inside a pair of silky pants.

"You got any idea what my Matilda'd say if I come home one night wearing them red pants? I wouldn't get me any for the next four years. Not that I get me that much as it is."

"Hell, it might turn her on."

Wally shook his head. "Turn her *on*? Hell, I got enough work on my hands just turning her *over*." Wally took a sip from the Bud and sniffed the air. "What kind of perfume you call that, boy?" he asked, wrinkling his nose up as if at the scent of something nasty.

"It's Brut," Jesse said. "Smells good, don't it? And it ain't cheap neither."

"Yeah, but it makes you smell like a French whore, son. Not that I done smelled many myself."

To which Jesse made his routine answer. "Least I don't smell like no chicken shit." Since he was six years old, Jesse had helped his grandmother run her chicken barn, and in the last few years, on account of her arthritis, Jesse had taken over the entire burden of egg gathering. He boasted that he could gather eggs faster than anybody in Claudell County and that was probably true. Still, the barn had disadvantages. When he was younger, some of the kids in school had made fun of him for smelling like chicken shit—an unavoidable hazard of life in the barns. So, when he was twelve, Jesse had hit on the expedient of dousing himself liberally with cologne.

Wally shook his head and laughed. "Well, I'll tell you what, Jesse Dillard. You drink you about four, five of them Nehis, and then you head on back home. And you let Curtis there drive, hear? Sometimes them Nehis in a Sack kinda go to your head."

Just as Wally was about to pull back out, Leroy came up to the car. The boy, along with his sister, Opal, had gotten a ride up to the rink with Jesse and Curtis. "Howdy," Leroy said, not even a flicker of a smile on his face.

"How you been, Leroy?"

"Can't complain," Leroy told him. Then Wally said he had been meaning to talk to Leroy. He pulled a walkie-talkie out from the glove compartment and handed it to the boy. "Don't know what's wrong with it. Just upped and quit on me. You think you can fix it?"

Leroy examined the walkie-talkie, then nodded. "I expect."

"You fix it, I'll give you ten bucks. That a deal?"

Leroy thought a moment. "Make it twelve."

"Fair enough."

"I'll have it for you next week."

With difficulty, Wally tried to return Leroy's grim, solemn expression. "I know you will, Leroy."

11

Back home, Melinda was getting ready for bed.

"Whatchew wanta wear tomorrow, hon?" her momma asked her. She was standing in front of the girl's closet: It was crammed full of frilly, lacy dresses. Because of her size, Matilda saw no sense in spending much money on clothes for herself, but the longing was still there. When she went shopping for Melinda's dresses, she made the girl try on everything two or three times, and then would look at her daughter as if staring into a reflection of herself in a magic mirror. "I just can't make up my mind. They all look so pretty."

Melinda had been invited to a birthday party at one of her girlfriends, tomorrow afternoon. Matilda, who liked to decide the night before what her daughter would be wearing to school the next day, was in a particular mood tonight, loathe to let her pride-and-joy be outdone by anybody else's little girl.

"I wanna wear my gardenia dress," Melinda said. This was Melinda's favorite, so-called because of the gardenia motif that was printed on the polyester fabric in profuse bloom. But Matilda had never much cared for it. For one thing, it was cheap-looking, probably because it was: Wally's Pentecostal sister who lived down in Decatur had bought it at Sayre's, and hadn't even bothered to take the marked-down price tag off. For another thing, it wasn't pink. "Oh, hon, won't you wear the one we got when we was down at Rich's?" It was both expensive and pink.

"I won't." And Melinda reaffirmed her preference.

Matilda was holding out the nice pink expensive one. "But this one's so pretty on you." Still, Matilda knew that when her daughter made up her mind, that was it: a trait she had always suspected came from her daddy's side of the family. "Alright, hon," Matilda said as she gazed sadly at the pink dress. "You do what you want."

Matilda replaced both dresses in the closet and then shut the door, jiggling the door when, as always, it got stuck.

Her girl was lying in bed now, with her stuffed Garfield cuddled next to her. "When's Daddy coming home?"

"Around twelve, I reckon."

They kissed each other and hugged, then Matilda turned off the lights.

In the kitchen, Matilda fixed herself a bowl of peach ice cream, then carried it back into the den. She sat down to watch TV until Wally came back. She was just about to take her first bite when, glancing over to the armrest of the sofa, she saw the library copy of *The Shadowstealer*, with Wally's place in it marked by a piece of pink toilet paper: Wally had been reading it that afternoon on the john. She stared hard at the cover of it, at the gleaming eyeball that peeked out from underneath the black oozing shadow.

She twisted around. From outside, through the open window, she heard a scratching noise. She frowned, trying to place what it was. Probably, it was Trix, the neighbor's cat, prowling around the screen door to the back porch.

Still . . .

She got up and looked out the window.

The backyard was teaming with shadows. And beyond that stood the woods. The woods stretched from that point all the way up to the Tennessee border, sixty or seventy miles of it. And all the shadows seemed to be coming from back there, as if deep in the woods was a spot where they spawned and bred, creeping their way out when they were big and black and long enough.

Matilda shivered at the image. Lord knows where she got it, metaphor never having been her strong suit.

She listened, but the noises had stopped. The cat must have gone on. Sometimes, she would see Trix, jet-black and slinky as an eel, roaming around at night and Matilda would marvel at its capacity not to be afraid, no matter how dark it was, or how deeply it wandered back into the thicket behind the row of old houses. Animals, they know only one kind of fear, she found herself thinking, the kind of fear that made sense, where you were afraid of something that was standing right there in front of your nose, ready to cause you some kind of easily recognized pain. Only human beings are afraid of what isn't there. Like shadows with claws and eyeballs peeking out at you.

Before sitting back down, Matilda glanced again at the cover of the book.

She turned it facedown and began to eat her ice cream.

12

Jesse was drunk as a dog.

Curtis, who had stopped drinking after his second Bud, was driving the black Cougar.

"What you want me to do?" Curtis asked after they had left the rink.

Jesse muttered, "Can't go back to Granny's. She'd kill me dead."

They stopped twice before getting to the trailer park, to let
Jesse throw up on the shoulder of the road. By the time they
got to Curtis's trailer, Jesse was passed out cold. "You going
to sleep out here?"

Jesse's mouth hung open. A thin line of spittle ran down
onto his bare chest.

Curtis shook his head. "Reckon I'll see you in the morning."

In his bedroom, Curtis groped in the dark for the light
switch. He clicked on the light, then stopped dead. His mouth
open, he stared at the sheet that was hanging halfway out the
open window.

"Goddammit," he whispered to himself. He went over to
it and quickly pulled the sheet inside. He stared down at the
urine stain in the center of it. That morning, he had taken it
off the bed and had hidden it in the back of the closet. He
was going to wait until both his daddy and his stepmomma
were gone, and then he was going to try to wash the stain
out. But, between the last few pages of *The Shadowstealer*
and Jesse's sudden entrance, he had forgotten. His stepmomma
must have gone snooping through his closets and found
it there.

His heart racing, Curtis walked over to the window and
looked outside. No telling who might have seen it there.
"Goddammit," he whispered, and sat down on the edge of
the bed. He felt his eyes fill with tears.

He got up and crumbled the sheet into a ball and set it in a
closet. He went quietly into the bathroom, where he idly stood
over the toilet and tried to pee. Sometimes he'd stand there
for ten minutes before going to bed, in the hope that anything
inside would come out then, and not later. He figured it must
work, because sometimes he could go a whole week without
it happening.

Nobody else knew. The last time his stepmomma had hung
a sheet out the window was back when they had lived down
in Stockbridge. Nobody in Mt. Jephtha knew a thing about it,
and Curtis wanted to keep it that way. If anybody ever found
out, he would die of shame. He knew it.

Of course, it wasn't easy. Like the times Jesse insisted that
Curtis spend the night at Jesse's granny's. They always slept in

the same bed. If an accident happened, Curtis knew that there would be no way of covering it up. He had no choice: each time he would stay awake the whole night long, hoping that he wouldn't drift off to sleep, even for a split second. Twice he did, and he woke up, terrified, jumping out of the bed to inspect the sheets. Both times, he was lucky.

But one day his luck would run out and then what?

Curtis zipped up his fly—no luck—and went over to the mirror above the bathroom sink. He stared at himself. What was it inside of him that did it? His stepmomma said he was too lazy to get out of bed.

Yeah, like he liked waking up in his own piss.

Though that wasn't what bothered him the most. It was something else, hard to put a finger on. This feeling he always got, as if something had crept inside of him without his knowing about it, something that he didn't want to be part of him, and yet was.

At least, Jesse had passed out in the car. That was good. Curtis would be able to get some sleep.

13

"Momma? That you?"

Melinda, her Garfield clutched to her, sat up in her bed and pushed her hair out of her eyes. She looked from the door to her room, which was closed, over to the window. Her momma wasn't anywhere.

Yet Melinda knew she had heard the door of the closet rattling, just the way Matilda always rattled it whenever it got stuck and wouldn't open.

She lifted her legs over the edge of the bed and rubbed her eyes.

A diagonal slash of moonlight cut across the door of her closet. The top was dark, the bottom bathed in light.

She was about to get up when she noticed a black streak near the crack under the closet door. Not a streak, exactly, either, but a wavy line, nearly zigzag. And yet not just a line, but wider than that, wide as a man's arm. It suddenly wiggled—

Melinda quickly scooted her feet back into the bed—then disappeared into the crack.

Her first thought was, Snake. Black snake. But it was both too wide and too thin. Too wide across, too thin up and down.

"Momma?" she called, then held her breath, waiting to hear Matilda calling back to her, and the sound of her firm footsteps in the hall. But, instead, what she heard was the doorknob rattling again, louder, even violent, like somebody was on the other side of it trying to burst the door from its hinges.

"Momma!" she yelled out, and clutched Garfield's neck so hard that she could almost hear him gasp.

The door was opening.

Melinda pushed herself back against the headboard and stacked her pillows up in front of her, to fend off whatever was coming out of the closet.

It was all the way open.

She blinked, confused, and saw her gardenia dress hovering right there in the middle of the closet. Like there was somebody back there, holding it up on its hanger, about two feet from the floor.

The gardenia dress floated out across the threshold of the door. The big flower pattern glowed in the diagonal slash of moonlight. But set in the darkness, right above the collar, Melinda saw something. It stood out against the dark background because it was blacker.

"Who's doing that?"

It came closer.

"Don't you recognize me?"

Melinda shook her head.

"Why, you see me every day."

Melinda stared at the black thing above the collar. It was like a face—big enough for a child's face—and it had something falling down on either side of it, like hair, only neither the face nor the hair had a single feature. It was like a silhouette.

Melinda's.

"I know what you are. You're my . . ." But she couldn't say it. It came closer and Melinda saw that there were arms and legs.

Something twinkled in the face. Twinkled at exactly the spot where an eye would be, if shadows had eyes.

Then the hands reached out.

Only they weren't hands.

14

Jesse opened the door of the Cougar and scowled out into the night. "Curtis, where the fuck you go to?"

He pushed himself out of the car and shut the door after three tries.

He looked around and recognized Curtis's trailer. He clutched at his crotch and then staggered off to the side of the trailer.

"Goddammit," he muttered as he tried to undo the zipper of his parachute pants. They were always getting stuck, though only when he had to pee like "a fucking English racehorse," as he always put it, not that he had ever come across such a thing, peeing or otherwise. He tugged and twisted and felt his bladder throbbing for relief. "Come on, you fucker."

At last the zipper came loose. Jesse was peeing before he got it out good. He eased into the bushes. His whole body shivered as he closed his eyes and enjoyed the pure and unmixed pleasure of relief. As he was finishing up, he glanced around and said, "Don't nobody be stealing my shadow back there, hear?"

He chuckled. On the way up to the rink earlier, he had made Curtis tell him about the book he had been reading. Of course, Jesse knew he would never get around to reading it himself—it was hard enough getting through the diddy little stories they made him read in ninth grade—he had been held back two years, on account of nonattendance. But Jesse liked a good story, and he insisted that Curtis tell him every little detail of it. "Don't leave nothing out, hear?" And Curtis didn't. At first, Jesse could tell, the other boy had been reluctant to talk about the book, probably figuring that Jesse was such a redneck that he would think Curtis was some kind of fag for liking to read. But while Jesse would be the first to admit he was a redneck, he also insisted that he "wasn't no *stupid* redneck." And if anybody knew there was a difference, it was Jesse.

Once he had been watching a Kung Fu movie on TV with his Uncle James, who was in his twenties. James had remarked, "Look at them Mexicans fight."

Jesse had looked hard for the Mexicans, then realized what James was saying. "Them ain't Mexicans. Them's chinks."

"Mexicans, chinks—they's all the same to me." And that was true, Jesse had noticed, everything was much the same to James.

But to Jesse, it wasn't like that. People sometimes asked him why he hung around Curtis—he was two years younger, after all, and wasn't much of a hellraiser. Jesse always told them, "Fuck, that boy, he's smart as hell. Sometimes I jus' like listening to him talk." And it was true. Jesse could pester Curtis by the hour, wanting the boy to tell him things. Once he had asked Curtis what was north of America, what was south, what was west of it, and what was east. When Curtis had easily answered all the questions, Jesse could only shake his head in amazement, "How you know all them things?"

Jesse got his fly back up, careful not to damage himself in the process.

He felt another shiver, this time right on the back of his neck. He stiffened. "Ain't nothing back behind me, is there?" He said, recalling what Curtis had said about that book he was reading, how you could always tell when the shadow thing was sneaking up on you, because the little hairs on the back of your neck stood up. And Jesse also remembered the other part, how, when it was there, you could not, never, under no circumstances, turn around to look at it. *'Cause if you did, you was fucked.*

He eased his way out of the bushes. He looked in front of him, but his shadow wasn't there. But then, Jesse noticed with relief, neither were the shadows of anything else around.

He took a deep breath, then twirled around, nearly losing his balance. "You there, motherfucker?"

It was there, right at his feet. His own shadow. Jesse kicked at it. "You ain't got nothing hiding inside you, now. You let me know if you do," he said, joking with his shadow in much the same spirit that he joked with the chickens in his granny's barn.

He walked back to the door of the trailer. It was open, except for the screen. He pushed it and walked inside.

"Curtis," Jesse whispered as he stumbled against the closet of the other boy's room. But Curtis, his face full of moonlight except for his open mouth, was long gone. Jesse sat down on the bed and tried to take his pants off, but gave up. "Fuck them," he said. He leaned back onto Curtis's bed, shoved the sleeping boy over a little bit, then lay down.

Jesse put his arm around Curtis and said, "Don't be getting no ideas now."

15

Wally stepped through the door and Matilda was on him.

"Slow down, woman," he told her.

He went to the refrigerator, but she slammed the door shut as he opened it.

"Ain't you listening to me?"

"I got a choice?"

And starting somewhere in the middle, Matilda told her husband what had happened. How she had been watching TV an hour earlier, and had been startled nearly out of her wits by the screaming. "I thought something had got holta her," Matilda said. "When I got to her room, she was crying her eyes out. She had had her a nightmare."

"A nightmare?" Wally was about to head for the hallway, to check on Melinda, but Matilda took his arm and stopped him. "She's done already gone back to sleep now. No use in stirring her up again."

"I wasn't gonna stir her up. I was gonna see if she was okay."

"That's mighty fine of you. Seeing how it was all your fault, anyhow."

Wally frowned. "All my fault? What the hell you mean by that?"

"She says her shadow done come out of her closet, wearing that gardenia dress. Now where you think she got her an idea like that?" Matilda asked, her ample arms majestically folded across her even more ample bosom.

"I dunno," Wally said weakly. He had a feeling he knew what was coming, though.

"She got it from that book! Why, just looking at that cover's enough to scare the daylights out of near anybody."

"Well, I won't keep it around where Melinda can see it, that's all."

Matilda glanced away. Her tone quickly changed from righteous anger to shame-faced embarrassment. "I reckon you won't have to be worrying about that."

"Whatchew mean?"

"I done something with it."

"You done what with it?"

"I stuck it down in the garbage disposal."

Wally walked over to the kitchen sink. He lifted up a damp page. "Hon, that was a library book. What are we gonna tell ol' Miss Avery?"

"The truth, I reckon," Matilda said with dignity. "I'll tell her. I say it ain't fit to be lending out a book like that anyhow. Scaring the daylights out of folks."

"You ain't even read it, Matilda."

"I don't need to. All I gotta do is think about it and I get goose bumps."

Wally shook his head. "That book, it costs seventeen dollars and ninety-five cents."

"I'll pay for it. That ain't the problem."

"But I hadn't finished reading it. You know how long I had to wait to get aholta it?"

"I reckon you'll have to wait a little longer."

Wally sighed. "Hon, I think you're kinda taking this the wrong way. Kids, they've been having nightmares for as long as the world's been around. And they's gonna go on having 'em."

"Not like this one here. You shoulda seen her. Why, I had to take everything out of that closet of hers, just to show her wasn't nothing in it. Why, you know what she made me do?"

Wally had sidled his way to the refrigerator. He opened it and discreetly pulled out a Bud. "What, hon?"

"I had to take that gardenia dress and go out and put it in the trash. She didn't even want it in her room no more."

"Well, hon, that ain't nothing for you to get all riled about." Wally knew how Matilda had always felt about the dress. "You been dying to do the same thing, and don't say you ain't."

"That ain't the point," Matilda said testily.

Wally pulled open the tab of his beer can. "She'll get over it. Don't you worry about it no more, alright?"

In bed, Matilda pouted for a while, but, after about ten minutes, she cuddled up next to Wally. "Way I see it, there's some things ain't fit to be wrote about. Even if they ain't real."

"Maybe so, hon."

16

"Goddam," Curtis gasped.

In the harsh morning light that came through the one window in his room, Curtis stared down at his undershorts. They were soaked. He looked at the sheets he had just jumped out of, then at Jesse. "Oh, shit," he whispered. He kept repeating the word, then sat down at the end of the bed, careful to avoid the huge yellow stain that covered half the sheet. He stared at Jesse, who was still asleep. Curtis looked at the parachute pants, Jesse's pride and joy.

Jesse must have been nearly on top of him. His pants were as badly soaked as Curtis's own shorts.

Curtis felt limp, numb, dazed.

It had happened, and there was no way out. Even if he could roll Jesse off the sheets, then pull the sheets out without waking him up, there were still the parachute pants. Jesse was a sound sleeper, but the pants were on so tight that they could only be removed with Jesse's active cooperation.

He was trapped.

He sat there, too stricken to cry. "Shit," he kept whispering.

Curtis jumped up again. Jesse had rolled over onto his side. He groaned and reached down to the crotch of his pants. He felt them. Was he awake? Or was he just fidgeting in his sleep?

Please, Lord, Curtis prayed, let this just be a dream. Let this—

Jesse sat straight up in the bed. He scowled as he looked down at his pants. He got out of the bed, looked at himself, at the sheets, at Curtis. "Shit, Curtis, you done peed on me," Jesse said in a flash of enlightenment. "You know how much these pants costs. I should fucking kill you, you little faggot."

"I'll buy you new ones," Curtis said, his face ashen. "Just don't say anything to anybody."

Jesse looked up at the other boy. A vexed frown crossed Jesse's brow. "You fucking did it in your sleep, didn't you?"

"I do it sometimes," Curtis stammered, unable to let his eyes meet Jesse's. "I don't know why. My bladder's too small, or something."

"Shit, that's why you never liked sleeping the night at the farm. Ain't it?"

Curtis nodded, his eyes on the floor.

"Man. I thought you did it on purpose," Jesse said with a laugh. "Shit, man, I didn't know you couldn't help it. Fuck, I'm sorry." He looked back at the sheets. "What's your stepmom say when you do it?"

"She gets mad."

"Guess so." Jesse chuckled. "Pissing in the fucking bed when you're fifteen. Ain't that something?"

"I'll buy you some new pants."

"Shit, these was getting kinda old, anyhow. You get you an extra pair of jeans or something?"

Curtis nodded, then hurried over to his dresser. He opened a drawer and handed Jesse some clean blue jeans. Jesse pulled off the tight, soaked parachute pants and tossed them in the corner. "How 'bout a towel?" Curtis got one of those, too, and gave it to Jesse. He dried himself off. He pulled on Curtis's jeans, sucking in his muscular stomach in order to zip them up. Jesse then turned back to the bed. "I bet your stepmom's going to raise some hell," Jesse said, shaking his head. "Oh, well, ain't but one thing to do." He went to the bed and began to pull the wet sheets off, careful not to touch the stain. He balled up the top sheet, then turned to Curtis. "Ain't you even going to help?"

"Help what?" Curtis said, confused.

"Whatchew think? We got to get this shit up to the laundromat, 'fore your momma finds out. Wash my pants, and them drawers of yours, too. Come on. Put some clothes on and grab that other sheet there."

Stunned by the other boy's reaction, Curtis didn't move a muscle.

"What's your problem?" Jesse said as he looked at Curtis's face. "You look like you seen a ghost."

"I thought you was going to be pissed."

"Sheeet, I had a cousin used to fucking shit in the bed. Ooowheeee, you can't believe what them sheets smelled like. Had to wash them fuckers three, four times. It was worse than sticking your nose down in the floor of Granny's barn." He looked around and got the blanket off the foot of the bed—it was untouched. "Here, wrap all that shit up in this. That way won't nobody notice nothing when we go to wash them things."

Curtis got dressed and did as Jesse told him. When everything was bundled up, Jesse said, "You 'bout ready?"

"Yeah."

Jesse stopped at the door. "You really think I was going to tell folks, Curtis Poke? What kind of friend you think I was?"

"I figured," Curtis began, but didn't finish.

Jesse shook his head in dismay. "Shit, man, every fucking body's got something they don't want nobody else to know 'bout. So do you, looks like. And this here ain't the worst, neither."

PART THREE

....

1

In the week following Matt's return to Mt. Jephtha, Tommy dropped by the Lumpkin house only a handful of times, and on no visit did he stay more than fifteen minutes. Or, as Cathy couldn't help noticing, as soon as she stepped into the same room with him. Even a glimpse of her was enough to make the usually ebullient Tommy tongue-tied. "What am I doing wrong?" Cathy asked Matt, after the second incident. "I don't want to come between the two of you." But again Matt only counseled her to give Tommy time.

But time obviously wasn't the answer. Something had to be done. And bright one morning—the second week back—Cathy bounced onto the porch where Matt was reading. "Remember, you said I could fix up the house?"

Matt nodded, a little wary.

"We're going to start tomorrow."

"We?" Matt exclaimed in horror. "You don't mean 'we' as in 'you and me'?"

"No, of course not." After all, Cathy had by this time learned that, as Matt first put it to her, "Reality is not my forte." He had taken after his Uncle Leon in not being much of a handyman. "I mean, Tommy and I."

"Tommy?"

"Isn't that a great idea? We could work together. That way, he'd come to see I was human."

Matt expressed his reservations. After all, no matter how hard Matt might try to avoid actually doing something—and he could try very hard—the restoration of the Lumpkin house was bound to disrupt him. Cathy tried to reassure him. "You won't have to do a thing."

"But what if I have to step over something?"

Cathy sighed. "We'll carry you."

That night, Matt talked to Tommy. He had been laid off
for the past week, due to the lack of work, and he readily
agreed to the offer. Though, at Cathy's insistence, Matt had
to pretend like the idea had been his.

Monday morning Tommy was there at six. He was to begin
on the dining room. The wallpaper was stripped by two that
afternoon and Tommy had just set up his ladder and was about
to commence with the painting when Cathy walked in, dressed
in overalls and a T-shirt. Tommy stared at her, a little abashed.
"Can I help you?" he asked.

"No," Cathy said, "I'm going to help you."

"Help me what?"

"Help you paint, of course." She took the roller, dipped it
directly into the can of paint, carried it dripping to the bare
wall, took a deep breath, and began to smear crazy zigzag
swathes of peach paint across, up and down, and sideways.
Tommy, who was patiently and carefully pouring the paint
into the pan, looked up at her work, his mouth slightly open.
"You ever painted before?"

"Oh, yes. I took a summer course at the Boston Institute of
Fine Arts," Cathy said airily.

"They have a class in house painting?"

"No. Abstract expressionism." Cathy went on, making spirals and loops of color on the wall. She stepped back a little,
as if to admire her work, then shook the paintbrush at the wall,
dabbing it with specks. "I'm almost sure this is how Jackson
Pollock did it." She turned around and, with the appearance
of absolute innocence, asked, "I *am* doing everything right, I
assume."

"That kinda depends on what you mean by 'right.' "

When Matt came downstairs an hour later, Tommy was
patiently demonstrating to Cathy the fine points of painting
a wall. "Like this, you mean?" Cathy said, holding the roller
the way Tommy held his, and carefully pressing it against the
wall. "My, that does look nice, doesn't it?"

Matt stared at Cathy's wall—it had still not been painted
over. "You do that?"

"Well," she said, blushing a bit, "it was my first effort."

Later, when Tommy and Cathy took a break, Matt went out

to the porch. Tommy had gone to pick up Jimmy.

"You think you're really clever, don't you?"

Cathy looked up. She had dabs of peach-colored paint on her golden hair, peach freckles across the bridge of her nose. (The peach had been Cathy's idea.) Again, the innocent look. "What are you talking about?"

"I think you know," Matt said, sitting down on the porch steps next to her. She sipped her beer. "I haven't the slightest idea what you're talking about."

"You told me you painted the walls of your apartment, back in Atlanta. Remember? You said they were purple, and that you had to repaint them yourself. They looked pretty good to me."

"Did I tell you that?" Cathy said.

"Yes, you did."

"Hmmmm."

"You were just trying to make Tommy feel smarter than you."

"Well, he is. In a lot of ways. Look at all the things he can do."

"I know that."

"But I don't think he does," Cathy said. She frowned—the most adorable frown in the world, Matt always thought—the frown of a precocious little boy who has just been troubled by his first glimmer of metaphysical doubt. "You think I was wrong to do it?"

Matt kissed her on the neck. "It worked, didn't it?"

By the following Saturday, Cathy and Tommy were like old buddies. The day before, Tommy had begun on what had been designated as the library. Around two in the afternoon, Cathy brought Tommy and herself a beer—Matt was upstairs reading. " 'Preciate it," Tommy said with a smile. He set down his circular saw and snapped the beer tab. He took a sip, then leaned back against the open window, the frame of which he was in the midst of replacing. They chatted for a few minutes about how the library was coming along, and Tommy explained to her, with his customary thoroughness, the exact steps involved in the proper replacement of a window frame, making digressions to tell her the various pitfalls that waited a less skillful carpenter.

And Cathy sat there with him, totally engrossed. It was a kind of revelation to her, listening to Tommy.

For most of her life, the workaday world had been invisible to her. If something broke, it was fixed. The concept was always expressed in the passive mood: "it was fixed," not "somebody had to fix it." But, since knowing Tommy, she began to see what was really involved in the day-to-day upkeep of the world. *Somebody* had to do these things. The material world that, to her, had always operated smoothly and as if by magic suddenly revealed a stubborn tendency to fall apart, requiring, each day, a massive injection of skilled human energy just to keep it at the same level of order that had been taken for granted the day before. The Second Law of Thermodynamics acquired a brutal, new significance for her. It was a daily struggle against the forces of chaos—a struggle that, like others, had its heroes. Perhaps unsung ones, but heroes nonetheless. Like Tommy. Of course, Tommy got paid, but there was a passion in what he did, a true love and joy. Cathy saw it in the way he caressed a certain piece of wood that he had patiently sanded and resanded, in the smile he had as he showed her, step by step, how a piece of dull, ragged sheetrock is transformed into a smooth and glistening wall. Cathy shook her head in genuine admiration: "I really don't know where we would be without you."

"It means a lot, having somebody to appreciate what you do," Tommy said, glancing at her for a moment, then looking off quickly. Then he went on, "My ex-wife, there was only one thing in this world she ever appreciated, and that was money. It didn't make any difference how you made it, either, long as it got made. Maybe it was the way I was raised, but I always felt what counted was doing what needed to be done and doing it best you can." Tommy had been looking down at the floor when he added, "Matt's real lucky to have somebody like you. Somebody who knows how to make a man feel like he's worth something. Aside from his bank account. I wish I had found me somebody who could've done that for me. You know?"

"There's so much I never understood," Cathy told Matt that night. "So much that Tommy's teaching me." And over the next few weeks, as Cathy continued to listen to Tommy's stories about his life, she began to see that there was another side to human existence, one which she had been dimly aware of, and even then only through books. In the world she had come up in, she had known of people who suffered, people who put bullets through their heads or who spent half their lives in and out of treatment centers. But, looking back, such suffering as she had come across struck her as a rarefied luxury, a masochistic self-indulgence, even a kind of demented joke. A friend of hers, a brilliant freshman at Cornell, had jumped into one of the gorges of Ithaca after making a B+ in a calculus course. It was his first (and last) B+. He left a note to his parents saying he could never face them again. And he genuinely couldn't have. Another boy she knew had been given a Porsche on his fifteenth birthday, had been accepted to Harvard at sixteen, had graduated Summa Cum Laude. He hanged himself two weeks after the graduation ceremony. His note, alluding to the penultimate aphorism of Wittgenstein's *Tractatus Logico-Philosophicus* (he had been a philosophy major), said: "The solution of the problem of the meaning of life lies in the disappearance of the problem. The problem (for me) has just disappeared."

But through Tommy, Cathy came to understand that for most of humanity the problem is not the meaning of life, the problem *is* life.

When Tommy had first come by the house, Cathy had noticed there was a bumper sticker on the front of his truck. It read: SHIT HAPPENS. She had seen them before, down in Atlanta, although always (she observed) on battered old pickups and derelict Chevies. There was a reason for this, she surmised condescendingly: Such people have simply accommodated a vaguely Lucretian metaphysics in order to justify the haphazardness of their own undertakings. Why think anything through? Why plan ahead? Why take responsibility? SHIT HAPPENS, so what's there to be responsible about? Eat, drink, and be merry, for tomorrow we die. Or, smoke dope, snort cocaine, down twelve-packs of Bud, burn Marlboros into your lungs, go home and beat the wife and kids, lose your job, because, after all, there's nothing you can do to make life better: Shit happens.

But as she came to know Tommy, she began to look upon the motto differently. It still disturbed her, deep down, and yet it made sense to her now. For people like Tommy, there was precious little that happened in their lives over which they had any control whatsoever. Just listening to him talk about his work showed Cathy how true this was. Work for him depended on a hundred imponderables: whether it was raining, how cold it was, whether the boss liked him, whether the contractor actually paid what he had promised he would pay, and, of course, on whether you fell off a ladder, or ran a circular saw over your fingers, or got hit in the head by a dislodged roof beam. And love wasn't much different from work. Tommy had told her how his wife, Arlene, had come to him when they were both seventeen. She was pregnant. "I reckon we got to get married." That was how it happened. And there was no one to tell Tommy any different. You just did these things, and didn't ask questions. Some years into the marriage, when Arlene started being unfaithful to him, Tommy knew nothing else to do, except to put up with it. He drank a lot, got into brawls with Arlene, ran around on her himself—but still, they stayed married. Even after Jimmy was born, Tommy went on with it. But one night, during one of their fights, Arlene said something that brought the whole unhappy thing to a sudden end. She had come back to the trailer at three o'clock in the morning, and was drunk. He knew where she had been. With Bruce Cochran, her boyfriend. The fight started, and Arlene began yelling about how much money Bruce made (he was a car salesman) and how much more of a man he was than Tommy. Jimmy, who was only four at the time, woke up and staggered into the kitchen where the fight was going on. Tommy told the boy to go back to bed. Arlene grabbed Jimmy up and started slobbering and crying over him, saying, "Oh, my poor baby."

Tommy pulled the boy away from her and carried him back to bed. When he returned he said, "I want a divorce. And I want to keep Jimmy."

She looked at him and hissed, "You don't really think he's yours, do you? You ain't that dumb." She proceeded to narrate the exact night when she claimed to feel this funny tingling inside of her, right after she and Bruce had made love in the backseat of one of the demos he got to drive around in.

After Tommy had slapped her silly, he said, "I reckon maybe I shouldn't have, but I did."

And later he told Cathy, "I can't say I don't wonder some-times about it. Only I can't let myself think thataway. I mean,

I'm the one who raised him and loved him and all. So the way I see it, no matter what Arlene might have done, I'm his real daddy."

Later that night, when they were in bed, Cathy mentioned this conversation to Matt, who matter-of-factly said, "Yeah, I know about it."

"You think it's true?"

"People say Jimmy has Bruce's mouth, whatever the hell that means."

"What a horrible thing to tell somebody, whether it's true or not."

Matt grunted, then said, "Shit happens."

And as Cathy stared out the window, she nodded sadly. The phrase she had once found so repugnant now struck her as if it were charged with a Virgilian pathos, a *lacrymae rerum* of the working class. "It does, doesn't it?" Then she reached over and put her arms around Matt.

"But not to us."

When Matt said nothing, she squeezed him. "Right?"

"Yeah," he murmured sleepily, "of course."

2

It was after one in the morning.

At Wally Clark's house, there was not a single light on, except for the tiny Garfield night-light in Melinda's bedroom. Before Wally had gone to sleep, he had read his daughter a story and then, as he had done for the previous two weeks, he had checked her closet for her. "See, nothing's there. You just go on to sleep now."

Outside, behind the old two-story house, the wind shook the leaves of the pecan and pine trees, making their shadows waver and undulate over the fenced-in backyard. The sky was full of swiftly moving clouds and Wally, as he had stood out on the back porch earlier, had figured that there would be rain by the morning.

Overhead there was a wedge of moon. It vanished, then reemerged in the endless procession of pearl-gray clouds. During the period when it was gone, the shadows in the yard all tended to merge into each other, to ebb away in the surrounding sea of darkness. But with each reappearance, the shadows resumed their identities. What identities they had.

Farther, on the other side of the fence, lay the woods, and the deeper shadows within.

There, in the midst of all the other shadows, one moved alone. It moved even during those moments when the wind stopped and the trees were still.

It moved toward the very faint glow of light that came from one of the bedrooms in the back of Wally Clark's house.

Sitting up in the bed, Melinda's eyes went straight for the closet. She looked at the knob, then at the crack under the door. She stared at it, to make sure nothing was seeping out or seeping in.

She waited, her Garfield clutched to her side.

She knew her daddy had gone through the closet earlier, to make sure nothing was lurking inside. She knew he did it to make her feel better. She had even pretended like it helped.

She got up, opened one of her drawers, and pulled a towel out. She carried it within a foot of the closet, crouched down, folded the towel, and pressed it against the crack.

She stood up and looked around the room.

Everything was okay. She could go and get a drink of water now.

In the kitchen, she set the glass back on the counter, her Garfield still carefully lodged between her arm and her side. Through the window, over the sink, she could see the woods behind the house. And all the shadows.

They told her she had been dreaming. That it was just a nightmare. Shadows didn't go into little girls' closets and put on their dresses. Shadows just didn't do anything like that at all.

Certainly they didn't talk to you.

What were they, anyway? she wondered. Nobody needed them. They were like nothing. And yet they weren't quite nothing, either.

They were in-between.

But where was that, this in-between place?

Melinda turned around and began to walk back to her bed-room. She stopped.

There was a tingling feeling on the back of her neck. A mosquito, maybe. She rubbed the back of her head against her hunched shoulders.

It went away.

She was back in her bedroom.

She stared down at her little night-light. Small as it was, even it cast shadows.

She turned and looked at the wall on the other side of the light. The table leg was there, huge, going all the way up to the ceiling. Her pink frilly wastepaper basket, into which nothing had ever been thrown, was also there, but no longer pink, and now as large as her momma and daddy's king-size bed. Even her stuffed raccoon was there on the wall.

Melinda frowned. Right there, midway up the wall, was a shadowy blob. It didn't seem to come from anywhere.

She crunched her Garfield tighter.

She stepped closer and the blob got bigger. Something like an ear stuck out. She turned and the ear stretched longer across the wall, up toward the table leg.

She looked down at Garfield. She uncrunched him from between her arm and her side and held him up.

Garfield's shadow floated on the wall, growing larger as she held him closer to it, and smaller as she pulled him back.

Only nothing was holding him.

Not her arm. Not her.

She tucked him back in his place, her eyes still fixed on the wall.

She wasn't there. Of all the other things that cast a shadow against the wall, only she was missing.

It was then she felt Garfield slipping out from where she had tucked him, as if somebody or something was slowly pulling him from behind.

That was when she turned around.

3

An hour later that night, over in Happy Home Trailer Park, Curtis Poke had just gotten undressed. He was standing, stark naked, in front of the mirror on the back of his door, looking at himself from every angle. He knew it was crazy, but he was prompted by the whispering he kept hearing in his head, the voice that went on insisting, against his better judgment, that what had occurred an hour earlier out in the hay barn had left a trace on him, some change in his very physical appearance, a funny way of walking, or some kind of brand etched into his skin.

But there was nothing.

Nothing he could see.

But the voice went on, taunting, hissing, saying the dreaded words.

Curtis put his underwear back on and got into bed. He stared up at the ceiling.

Maybe it hadn't happened.

But he knew it had.

And he knew why it had.

It had started up at the rink earlier.

He and Jesse had been drinking Buds in the parking lot.

At a little after eleven, June Lively, Bobby Lee Pinkham's girlfriend, had wandered out to Jesse's Cougar. "I ain't s'posed to tell you this," she began coyly. "Bobby Lee'd kill me if he found I done told you."

"Tell me what?"

"They's planning to git you for what you did to Bobby Lee."

"I didn't do nothing to Bobby," Jesse protested. "He's the one started it. All I did was give him a whupping when he ast for one."

"They's saying they's gonna make you eat a bag of chicken shit. They's gonna steal it out of your granny's barn."

"Fuck, I ain't afraid of Bobby Lee and his fag-ass friends."

"He jus' gets so jealous. 'Specially of me and you. Wonder

why that is? You think maybe Bobby Lee can feel some kind of electricity between you and me?" And June brushed up close against Jesse's chest. "Course, all the girls like you. I can't blame 'em none, neither. I'd go out with you."

"You got you a boyfriend already," Jesse said. He wasn't even looking at June.

"So. Look at all them girls you go out with?"

And that part was true. Jesse had a new girlfriend nearly every week. This week it was Tammi Jenkins. June looked around her. "I don't see Tammi."

"We done took her home, Curtis and me."

June looked over at Curtis with a frown, as if she had just noticed him. She turned back to Jesse and brushed up against him again. "Why don't we take me for a ride in your big ol' Cougar."

"Me and Curtis, we supposed to be going someplace."

This was news to Curtis.

"Whatchew want to be with him for, anyway?" she said, then added in a whisper, "I think he's a gayfer."

"Curtis ain't nothing like that," Jesse said. "Now you go on back inside and don't make no trouble, you hear?"

Disappointed, June pushed herself away from Jesse. She gave Curtis a dour look and said, in a mocking, sissified voice, "Bye-bye, Curtis."

Jesse watched June as she sashayed up the steps to the rink. "Bitch." He downed a few more sips of his beer, then said, "You know what I wisht sometimes, Curtis? Sometimes I wisht there wasn't no girls. No girls hanging all over you, calling you up night and day. Sometimes I wisht there wasn't nothing but you and me, and maybe Granny. I reckon we could keep her around."

Curtis glanced at Jesse. Curtis had had a girlfriend for a while, the way everybody was supposed to. But a few weeks back, she had started going out with somebody else. Her name was Melody and Curtis had asked her up to the rink one night, along with Jesse and his girlfriend, Tammi. Actually, it had been more Tammi's idea for them to go out—Melody was her best friend. Curtis liked Melody okay, except when she would call him up and tell him about the soap operas she watched in the afternoon. Curtis would sit there, his mind a million miles away, and say, "Yeah . . . yeah . . . yeah . . ." Sometimes he'd lie and tell her he had to go and do some chores, just to make her stop talking.

Jesse suddenly looked over at Curtis. "Shit, you feel like hanging around here?"

"Whatchew mean?"

"I feel like getting fucked up." Earlier Jesse had bought a couple of joints from Jason Howell, who was thirteen. "I'm about ready to fire one up."

They drove back to Jesse's granny's chicken farm. Jesse still had a six-pack left and they had gone out to the barn where the hay was kept. They both had a few more Buds, then rolled and fired up a joint. They talked some more, then Jesse got on top of one enormous mound of hay and declared himself King of the Mountain. Before Curtis knew it, they were tussling crazily in the hay. Curtis would sink in about two feet deep and Jesse would have to pull him out. Or Jesse would leap on top of him and together they would roll over and over down the slope of hay.

That was when it happened.

They had rolled over and over, and Jesse had ended up on top of Curtis. The barn was dark, except for the moonlight that crept in. It fell across Curtis's face. Jesse wasn't wearing a shirt and his body was pressing down on Curtis. Curtis struggled to get up, as if Jesse were trying to pin him. But then he realized, they weren't wrestling anymore. Jesse wasn't trying to beat him or make him say Uncle. Jesse was on top of him for another reason.

"This here's more like it, ain't it?" Jesse whispered.

"Whatchew mean?"

Jesse's blue eyes were looking straight into Curtis's. Neither of the boys moved. Neither breathed.

Then Jesse said, "Fuck all them bitches." And suddenly Curtis felt Jesse's hand reaching down inside his blue jeans. "Feels good, don't it?"

And before Curtis knew what he was doing, he nodded.

Jesse slowly unzipped his blue jeans, lifted the younger boy's butt up, and pulled off his pants. Jesse laughed. "Looks like ol' Curtis got him a hard-on, don't it? Reckon I know what you're thinking about," he said as he reached his hand inside Curtis's underwear. Curtis said nothing. He felt Jesse's hand tighten and squeeze. "You're thinking 'bout some of that pussy you been getting off Melody. Ain't you?"

And Curtis nodded, grinning with relief. "Yeah."

Jesse glanced down at the crotch of his silk parachute pants. "Reckon I must be thinking 'bout ol' Tammi."

And Curtis chuckled nervously. "Yeah."

"Reckon I oughtta let it out to get a little air," Jesse said. He stood up, unzipped his pants, and pulled them off. He wasn't wearing underwear. He never did. Jesse crouched down and matter-of-factly put his dick right up against Curtis's. "Daddy Bear and Baby Bear," he said, rubbing them together. "Shit, I'm horny as fuck. Sure wish Tammi and Melody was here, don't you? You could take ol' Melody over on that side of the hay, me and Tammi could do it right here. I'd be fucking the shit out of her right now, if I could," Jesse said. "How 'bout, you close your eyes and you think real hard 'bout ol' Melody. I'll think real hard 'bout Tammi."

Actually, at that moment, Curtis's mind was a whirl of dizzying sensations and images, none of which had the slightest relationship to Melody. But he closed his eyes tight, and dutifully tried to think of the time he and Melody had halfheartedly had sex: five minutes into the ordeal, he had pretended he was coming, and had gasped and panted appropriately. She had thrown up, complaining that he didn't know how to do it, then confessed—the next night—that it had been her first time. His, too, though he didn't tell her that. The whole thing reminded him of the handful of football games he had played down in Stockbridge back in seventh grade— he was on the second string. Like everybody else, he was supposed to be excited, supposed to want to get out there and whup ass. And yet, minutes before the game, he would have to go to the bathroom and throw up. Other guys, he noticed, did the same thing, but, like Curtis, pretended they didn't, or, if they were caught, said it was something else— the flu or the chili dog they'd eaten earlier. And that's how it was with Melody. Later, he said all the things he knew he was supposed to say, how she had been a great piece of pussy, and how he couldn't wait to get inside it again. He and Jesse even joked about it. But not a word of it was true.

But what he felt in the barn wasn't like that. Not once did he ask Jesse to stop, or push his hand away, or murmur. And yet his body was trembling the whole time, the way it did when he had a fever, and afterward, his teeth were chattering, even though the night was warm. Jesse kept saying things to make it seem like what had happened was really something else. And, of course, at no point did either of them mention the dreaded words: "Fag, queer, gayfer, homo." Maybe Jesse didn't even think them. But Curtis did.

As Curtis lay in his bed, back in the trailer, his eyes shut, he kept hearing the words Jesse had whispered to him in the barn. "Feels good, don't it?"

It did, but it couldn't. There was no way.

When Curtis was seven, he had come across his first real queer. Curtis was up at the garage where his daddy was a mechanic. This guy had come in driving a brand-new Corvette. When Curtis had wanted to look inside, his daddy had come over and pulled him away. "You stay over here, where I can keep an eye on you." And Curtis saw the way his daddy looked hard at the man. He even noticed that the man moved funny, more like a woman. Later, when the guy left, his daddy took him aside and said, "You know what that was, don't you, son?" Curtis said no, and his daddy said to him, "That was one of them *thangs*." Curtis asked what he meant, and his daddy said darkly, "Fellers like that, they do to each other what the Lord never meant to be done."

"One of them thangs." That, even more than the other words for it, was what haunted Curtis as he stared up at the ceiling. It was as if what they had done wasn't just wrong, but something that wasn't even human—like having sex with a dog or with a dead person—something that made you into a kind of deformed and twisted thing, like the baby with two heads he had seen in his momma's copy of *World Weekly News*.

But worst of all, for Curtis, was the sense that there was something that had crept inside him uninvited, a shadowy presence that was at once part of him and yet which couldn't be part of him.

He looked over at the book he had been reading. He still hadn't finished it, though he only had a couple of pages left. *The Shadowstealer*. In it, one of the characters talks about how, deep inside everybody, there is something alien, thinglike, something we don't want there, but which always follows us, wherever we go. Follows us like our own shadow.

We may run from it with all our might, but whenever we glance behind us, it's still there.

And that's how Curtis felt now.

He rolled back over onto the pillow.

What had Jesse said up at the rink? How sometimes he wished that there was no one in the whole world, except him and Curtis?

Curtis remembered the way Jesse had looked at him when he had said this. Saw his eyes—they were looking at him just the way they had been later in the barn.

And Curtis again felt all strange and funny inside. Because he knew there was only one way it could be like that. It could be like that only if the world just upped and went away, if everybody else in it—Tammi, and Melody, and all the kids at the rink—just disappeared in a puff of smoke, only if everything that ever was suddenly wasn't.

4

"Hon. Wake up!"

Wally rolled over. Matilda was sitting up in bed. "You hear that?"

"Hear what? What time—"

"I must be losing my mind. I thought I heard the garbage disposal going."

"What in hell would the garbage disposal be running at three o'clock in the morning for?"

Matilda shook her head, to indicate that she certainly didn't know either. "I must have been having some crazy dream." She leaned back onto her pillow, puzzled. "I could've swore I—"

This time both Wally and Matilda jumped up. They looked at each other, to make sure that they were both hearing what they thought they heard. "What the hell?" Wally got out of bed, snatched his pants off the back of the chair, and was already out in the hall before he got them over his knees. Matilda came right behind him. He was fiddling with his fly when they got to the kitchen door. Again the sound of the disposal unit stopped.

"Melinda?"

Wally walked toward the kitchen. "Hon, you okay?"

The girl was standing over the sink. She had her face right in it, as if she were looking for something that had fallen. Her long auburn hair was hanging down on one side of her head. Her left hand was clasped to her left ear. Wally walked over behind her.

Again the disposal unit came on—she was clicking the switch with her free hand.

"My Lord, God, her hair!" Matilda shrieked. The tips of the girl's hair had been sucked down the drain. They had caught on the blades of the disposal unit. Matilda went to pull Melinda back from the sink.

"Don't," Wally said and reached over and flicked the switch to OFF.

Matilda gasped, "What are you doing?"

"Turn it back on!" Melinda demanded.

"What's wrong? What is it?" Matilda asked, her voice hysterical. She looked at Wally. "What's she saying?"

The girl sobbed. Her hand went up and struggled to pull Wally's off the disposal switch. "I don't want to hear them no more. I don't want to hear nothing no more."

"Hear what?" Wally said.

Matilda was trying to ease the girl's hair out of the drain, but it was too tangled up in the blades. "I gotta get my scissors," she said, then hurried into her bedroom.

"Can't you hear them?"

"I can't hear nothing. Hon. Who you talking about?"

" Them kids screaming. 'Don't cut no more. Don't cut me no more.' "

Aghast by his daughter's words and behavior, Wally stared at her face. There were tears in her eyes. Unable to turn the disposal back on, she had stuck the index finger of her right hand into her ear. She kept shaking her head. "I can't get 'em to stop. Make 'em stop."

Matilda was back with the scissors. She reached down into the sink and began to snip Melinda's hair free of the drain. "What'd she say?" Matilda asked her husband. She absently let the scissors slip from her hand into the sink.

" 'Bout kids screaming," he said.

Matilda looked at him. "What kids?"

Wally's face was pale. Beads of sweat raced down his temples. "I don't know. I don't know what the hell she's talking about. It's like she's gone—"

"Crazy," Matilda said, staring bug-eyed at her daughter. "Look at her hair, how it's all chopped up. She was so proud of her hair, too. Why'd she go and do something to it?"

Wally was trying to pull the girl away from the sink. "Come on, hon, you was having a nightmare," Wally offered. "That's all."

"I can't hear nothing but them," the girl wept. She looked around at her daddy.

"I told you, you was just—"

"I can't hear you. I can't hear nothing. Nothing but that screaming." The words came out in between convulsive sobs.

"My Lord, Wally, we got to get her some help."

Wally nodded. "You go call Dr. Lowery. Tell him to get over here fast." Matilda hurried back into the hallway.

Melinda tore loose from Wally's hands. She turned back to the sink and grabbed up the pair of scissors. She opened them all the way, then grasped one end in a fist. The other she lifted up to her ear. "Whatchew doing?" Wally got out, but all at once he understood. She lifted the tip of the scissor blade and jabbed it into her ear. He grabbed her hand and twisted it back, but she kept trying to gouge it back in. Wally saw the blood: It was coming from inside her ear. "Oh, my Lord," Wally whimpered, feeling his knees go weak beneath him. He wrestled the scissors from her and flung them inside the china cabinet, breaking three of Matilda's little ceramic whatnots.

Her hand went back to the disposal switch. She clicked it on and again put her head down into the sink, trying to get as close as possible to the terrible grinding noise. Her finger pushed its way into her left ear and Wally watched helplessly as the blood dripped down her slender wrist into the sink below. He lifted her hair back out of the way.

"Make it stop, Daddy. I can't hear nothing but them. I can't hear nothing."

Wally nodded his head and whispered, "I'll make it stop. I'll make it—"

That was when Matilda stepped back into the kitchen and screamed.

PART
FOUR

···

1

It was ten o'clock in the morning. Peter had just finished eating his breakfast. Simmy was doing the dishes. "Is Daddy through working yet?"

"You'll know when your daddy's through."

Four days earlier, Matt had retreated to his attic study, in order to start working on his new novel. In part, this was owing to deadlines—the "Unnamed Hardison Thriller," as it was called in the contract, was due in eight months. But it was also, as Matt told Cathy, a way of escaping from the unwonted hustle and bustle that had taken over the Lumpkin house in the past few weeks, the lower rooms being filled with ladders and paint buckets and drop cloths and circular saws and lumber.

Peter frowned. "Yesterday when I went up there, he wasn't doing anything. He was just sitting there."

"Your daddy works even when he ain't doing nothing," Simmy said.

Peter wrinkled up his nose. "How can he be working if he's not doing anything?"

" 'Cause he's special, that's why."

"You think he's getting those writer's blocks again?"

"Oh, Lordy, I hope not," Simmy said in a hushed and fearful voice, as if even the mere utterance of the thought was something to be avoided at all costs.

Over the years, Peter and Simmy had learned to tell almost exactly how many pages Matt had written on any one day. If he came out of his room beaming, joking with them, poking at Peter, teasing Simmy, then they knew he had probably written ten pages. Smiles and normal good humor meant around five. But no pages at all—they could tell that one even before he came into the room. They would hear him coming down the hallway, muttering to himself under his breath. Then they would grab on to anything and hold on for dear life. On such days, everything was wrong. Peter was too noisy. Simmy's eggs tasted like warmed-over superglue. Mt. Jephtha was the armpit of the universe. The sky was too blue, the sun too yellow. And if the slack period went on a week or more, then both Simmy and Peter resorted to tiptoeing around the house, an ear cocked for approaching footsteps, at the first sign of which they both ran for their lives.

"What are they? Writer's blocks?"

"They sure is bad, whatever they is," Simmy said. "I reckon, they's kinda like the piles, only worser."

Peter stuck a piece of bacon into his mouth and frowned. "Daddy doesn't seem special to me. He just seems like Daddy."

"That's 'cause you don't know no better. If you had any sense, you'd see it, way everybody else does." Simmy paused, then said grandly, "Your daddy, he done wrote a book."

"Yeah, I know," Peter said wearily.

"And one day when you're older, you'll read it and you'll see just how special your daddy is."

"You've never read it."

"I don't need to," Simmy said. "I keep it right under my pillow every night. That's better than reading." After *The Shadowstealer* had been published, Matt had presented Simmy with her copy. On the front page he had written: "To the only woman in my life." Aglow, she had promptly wrapped it in Saran Wrap and set it on top of her knickknack shelf in her bedroom, as if it were an heirloom too precious to be touched by human hands. (Though more than once, in the middle of the night, Simmy would wake up and turn the book around, so that its cover didn't show.) " 'Sides, Mr. Matt done read most of it to me hisself," Simmy went on loftily.

"Is it really scary?" Peter asked skeptically.

Simmy turned around and looked at him. "Is it scary?" she asked him. "You don't want to know how scary it is, I tell you that."

"How can some old book be scary? All it is, is words. It's not like a movie."

Simmy looked around at Peter. She shook her head. "Not them words your daddy writes. They's alive," she whispered, in nearly the same tone of voice she used to tell how, as a girl, she had seen her dead grandmother wandering across a field of chick peas. "Your daddy, he can make you see what ain't there, just like it was there."

"How can he do that?"

Simmy shook her head uncertainly. "I reckon, it's like a gift. Way some folks can see ghosts. Suppose it got to come from someplace, hon. Only I ain't so sure I want to be knowing whereabouts that place be."

"He says it's Storyworld. He says that's where all the monsters come from."

A year before, when Matt had tried to explain to Peter what he did, he had come up with the idea of Storyworld. There were two worlds, he told his son. The real world, the one everybody thinks they know about, the world of chairs and buses and schoolrooms. But in addition, hovering somewhere beyond the world of ordinary fact, there was another: Storyworld. "You see," he explained to his son, "Daddy isn't smart enough to make up stories. He has to wait for the stories to come to him." Peter was puzzled by the difference, so Matt reminded him of an incident that had happened when the boy was seven.

Matt had bought Peter a G.I. Joe action figure for his birthday. One day Simmy found it in his room, mysteriously burned. Simmy, with her horror of fire, had a fit. "He's going to burn hisself right up," she told Matt.

When he asked his son what had happened, Peter had explained to his father that a monster had come into his room and done it. Matt had taken out a notepad and a pencil, then asked Peter for an exact description of the creature. Any claws? Fangs? How long? Dripping blood? Bloodshot eyes? Protruding? How far? When Matt had compiled his dossier, he told Peter to wait a minute, he was going to check his copy of *The Observer's Guide to North Georgia Monsters*. He returned and said, "We have a problem, Peter. The suspect you described is (dramatic pause) Tibetan."

"Oh?" Peter said feebly, his head hanging.

"It lives only in the high Himalayas. The book says it has never been seen at an altitude below forty thousand feet, or at a temperature greater than ten degrees Celsius." Matt waited for this revelation to sink in. "You have anything to say to this?" Peter shook his head. Matt went to the bed and put his arm around Peter's shoulder, then said sotto voce, "Just between you and me, that crypto-fascist pig had it coming anyway."

Whereupon Peter nodded and said, "That stuff about the monster, I just made it up."

Matt smiled at his son and said, "I know. You know how? Because your monster didn't come up behind me and grab me by my throat. It didn't make me believe in him. And that's what a monster's got to do—make you believe in him, no matter how hard you try not to."

"I don't know about no Storyworld, hon," Simmy said. "But wherever he gets them things, I sure hope nothing ever gets loose that shouldn't be."

"Which d'you mean?"

Simmy, who had been scrubbing dishes, looked up and shook her head uncertainly. "I recollect, when he was reading to me and Mr. Tommy about them shadows, right out yonder on the back porch, I was looking off into them woods, wondering and wondering."

"Wondering what?"

"Maybe there's some things shouldn't be messed with. Some things you shouldn't even give a name to, maybe, much less be telling no stories about."

"Why you say that?"

Simmy's thin back hunched and shivered. "My great-grandmomma, she used to call 'em whatalls. That's 'cause you couldn't rightly say what they was. She believed that there's a whole mess of them whatalls out there, circling around us like them ol' buzzards do, just waiting to swoop down. Sometimes, late at night, I'd see her sitting out on her ol' porch, looking straight ahead of her, not looking this way or that, and not saying a word, neither. And she'd be trembling, from head to toe. And I'd ast what was wrong with her, and she'd tell me, 'One of them things is circling around.' And I'd go to look, to see where it was, but she'd grab holt of me with her hand and say, 'Don't you be eyeing it. That's all it's a-waiting for. For somebody fool enough to think he can go looking at it straight in the eye. Can't pay no attention to it. Can't talk about it. Sure can't call it to you, neither.' And sometimes her and me, we'd sit out there near all night long, so still not hardly breathing, not looking one way or the other, till old Great-granny'd whisper, 'It's gone now, hon. It's done went somewheres else.' "

Peter frowned skeptically. "How'd she know it was there, if she didn't see it?"

Simmy sucked in a cheek pensively. "Sometimes it's best not to know something, hon. 'Cause there's things out there, once you seen 'em with your own two eyes, there ain't no way of ever unseeing 'em again." She stared down at the dishes, then said, "What you doing, getting ol' Simmy to be thinking 'bout them things for, anyhow? She won't sleep at all tonight, nohow."

2

Five minutes later Peter was standing on the last step before the sacred doorway. Across it was the forbidding sign that read in big black letters:

THOU SHALT NOT DISTURB
THE LORD THY DADDY!

The boy took a deep breath, pushed the door open, and called out, "Got any monsters yet?"

Matt jumped halfway out of his chair. His glasses, which moments before he had been idly twirling in his hand, were catapulted into a far corner of the attic.

"Goddammit, Peter!" Matt hissed at his son. "You're going to kill Daddy one day."

Peter giggled. Like most children, making an adult jump out of his skin always gave Peter a gratifying—and no doubt compensating—sense of his own power. "I scare you?" He smiled.

"What do you think, you little shit?"

"You little shit," Peter mocked. He had never been able to take his father's mean daddy routine very seriously. After all, this was the same man who, instead of waking Peter up for breakfast, used to lift him out of the bed and carry him to the kitchen table. True, Daddy might hint darkly at excoriation or disembowelment—he had even explained to Peter, in too vivid detail, what those things meant. But long before, Peter had decided, the threat of gradual dismemberment was preferable to the actuality of the mildest spanking.

"Find my glasses," Matt said.

"Say, 'Please.' "

"I'm going to bury you up to your neck in the middle of the woods, and I'm going to pour honey all over your face."

Peter shook his head. "Not if you can't see me."

"I'm going to put a cage over your head and fill it with starving rats, and they're going to eat your eyeballs out."

"Say, 'Please.' "

"Okay. Please."

Peter walked over and picked up the glasses. He held them up to the light that came in through the solitary window, then shook his head. "They're dirty," the boy scolded, and he was right. Peter breathed a heavy fog onto the lens and then carefully cleaned them off on his T-shirt. Peter sighed and handed the glasses to Matt.

"You still want me to bury me up to my neck?"

"Not right now, Peter. I'm busy. Ask Simmy if she can."

"You don't look busy to me," Peter observed. He was now nuzzling against his daddy.

"Yeah, I noticed," Matt said. He tousled his son's hair. "You think maybe the monsters don't like me anymore?"

"The monsters will come back, Daddy," Peter assured him. "They're just up in Storyworld, remember?"

"Let's hope so." Matt put his arms around his son's waist and lifted him into his lap.

Firmly planted now in his father's lap, Peter put his fingers on the keyboard.

"Want me. to help?"

Matt shrugged. "Give it a shot."

"Okay." Peter closed his eyes tightly, obviously under the impression that this was the surest method of obtaining inspiration. Then, after hitting CAP LOCK, Peter began. Peck by peck, the letters magically appeared upon the screen:

THER E WAS ONCEE A MONSTERHE LIVED UP IN STORY WORLD AND HE WANTED TO COME DOWN AND EAT PEOPLE BUT HE COULDN'T

WHY NOT? Matt typed.

BECAUSE NOBODY HADEVER TOLD A STORY ABOUT HIM

Peter twisted around and grinned at his father. This was their typing game, where the two of them would talk back and forth, without ever using spoken words. Matt smiled and said, "I think I heard this one before," then brushing his son's hands away, he typed:

AND EVERY NIGHT HE WOULD LISTEN OUT, TO HEAR IF SOMEBODY DOWN IN THE REAL WORLD WAS TELLING A STORY, AND HE WOULD HOLD HIS BREATH, HOPING TO HEAR A STORY THAT WAS ABOUT HIM. HE WOULD HEAR STORIES ABOUT ALL THE OTHER MONSTERS, BUT NEVER NEVER DID HE HEAR A STORY ABOUT HIM.

THEN ONE NIGHT

Matt relinquished the keys. "Go on," he said to Peter. "Finish it, smartass."

The boy frowned.

DADDY TOLD THE MONSTERS STORY AND LET IT LOOSE AND IT CAME DOWN AND ATE EVERYBODY UP

Peter laughed. "You like that, Daddy?"

"Great ending," Matt said.

3

Matt and Cathy sat out on the back porch. In the library, Tommy was putting in bookshelves, while Cathy had spent the whole morning and most of the afternoon painting the downstairs bathroom. Peter and Jimmy had gone back into the woods somewhere. Every now and then you could hear a whoop or a holler from them.

Cathy—in between fixing up the house—had been editing the manuscript of a friend of hers. She and Matt had been discussing the young man's novel, his first. Earlier in the week, Cathy had gotten herself in hot water with Simmy over the book. On Monday, when Simmy had taken Cathy her morning coffee, the old woman had been puzzled by the sight of the disheveled manuscript spread out from one end of the bed to the other, with pages spilling onto the floor. Each page had typing on it, and then, piled on top of this, every sort of curlicue and scribble that Simmy could imagine. "I'm editing a novel for a friend," she explained.

Simmy had stared at her with a faintly scandalized expression. "A man friend?" Simmy asked.

"Yes, he's a very gifted young writer."

At which Simmy seemed even more disturbed than before. "I don't know about that," the old woman muttered to herself, more than a trace of cool indignation in her voice.

Later, Cathy had brought up the incident to Matt. She was puzzled, but Matt only laughed. "Imagine this. Simmy walks in and finds you rolling around in bed with another man. Then you look up at her and you say, 'Oh, but he's so gifted.' That's how she saw it."

"Because I was editing another man's book?"

Matt nodded. "You see, for Simmy, there's only two books in the world worth paying a mind to, the Bible and the one on top of her knickknack shelf."

Cathy had promptly set everything straight. She took Simmy aside and inducted her into the intricacy of editing. She even showed her a list of proofreading notations, then went over a page she had been working on. It was covered with red ink. "That fellow done all them things wrong?" Simmy asked.

Cathy hesitated, then compromised: "Let's say, he didn't do them right."

Simmy reflected, "So's you kinda like one of them schoolteachers. Picking at what folks done wrong."

Cathy smiled. "A little."

"Course, Mr. Matt, he don't need that editing, I reckon," Simmy commented and glanced significantly at Cathy. It was her chance to be readmitted to a state of grace.

Cathy gave her best serious look and said, "Matt? Oh, no, of course not."

"So you's just helping out some of them that ain't near as smart as Mr. Matt. That it?" And Cathy, relieved to have won back the old woman's respect, nodded and said that was right.

Matt set the book he was reading in his lap and stared into the woods. As part of his program at getting "a real education," as he called it, he had decided to read the Greek tragedies—earlier in their relationship, when Cathy had made an allusion to *Oedipus Tyrannous*, Matt had asked if it was a kind of dinosaur. He had only been half joking, as Cathy later discovered.

Matt had started with Sophocles and was now reading Aeschylus, *The Orestia.* He had just gotten to the second play in the trilogy, where the hero, Orestes, is being pursued to the point of madness by the Eumenides.

"What are these Eumenides do-hickies?" Matt asked, mauling the pronunciation. Cathy took her reading glasses off, set the manuscript on the table next to her, and pronounced the word correctly. Matt eased back in his chair: He always loved it when she explained things to him. It made him feel like he was back in first grade, he once told her.

"They're better known as the Furies."

"What are they supposed to do?"

"Well, according to Greek mythology, they lived under the earth. Came from it. I guess you could say they symbolized that part of us that we can't escape from—what binds us down to the past, to our animal origins. When blood is spilled, they come forth to demand revenge."

"But what does the word mean exactly?" And again Matt tried to pronounce it.

"Eumenides?" Cathy smiled. "Literally, it means the Good Ones. The Well-meaning Ones. Though nobody ever really thought of them as good at all. It's just the way the Greek mind worked. If something was truly terrible, you weren't permitted to say so. I guess, the basic idea is that there are some things so plain awful that you aren't supposed to look at them or speak of them. Because any time you do, you're risking destruction. And who knows, maybe they were right."

"What d'you mean?"

Matt slid down another notch in his chair: He could tell that Cathy was really cooking now. Looking into her eyes, he could almost see the sparks of thought flashing out of them. She hesitated, then said. "There's a fatal flaw in all knowledge."

"Oh?" Matt loved a paradox.

"Knowledge is irreversible. Once you know something, you can't unknow it. Like in Oedipus. Once he had discovered the terrible truth of who he was, of what he had done, he couldn't go back again. And in the play that's what everyone tells him, the closer he comes to unraveling the mystery, 'Stop, don't go any further.' But he had to. He was driven to acquire the knowledge that would destroy him. In a way, it's like the story of Adam and Eve, and the Fall of Man. The same thing. Human beings are compelled to discover the truth—in this case, the Knowledge of Good and Evil—but in doing this, they destroy their own innocence and happiness."

"Ignorance is bliss?"

"Not really. Because that makes it sound like we have a choice. We don't. And that's just the point."

Matt frowned, his lip stuck out the same way it used to be when as a boy he would think deep thoughts. From inside, they could hear the sound of Tommy's circular saw. "I guess, it's like Tommy."

"Tommy? How d'you mean?"

"What his wife told him about Jimmy—how he wasn't really Tommy's son. I guess, if he had a choice, Tommy would prefer not to know—or even think—something like that. But he doesn't have that choice now, does he? I mean, he'll always know, and there's nothing that can ever make him forget."

Cathy nodded. "It's like what we talked about, the night we found that cat in the road. How do you forget? If something really terrible has happened, is it ever right to forget about it? But if you don't, then how do you go on? I heard Simon Wiesenthal talk one time. He's the one who's devoted his whole life to tracking down Nazi war criminals. And I thought, Yes, he's right. There are atrocities that should never be forgotten. And yet, what does that do to the man who has to devote himself to pursuing and punishing the criminals? What would it do to any man's soul if not an hour passed without thinking of what was done at Auschwitz? I just can't imagine that."

"Yeah," Matt whispered.

"I guess that's why I asked you, back at McDonald's, if the Shadowstealer came from folklore. Because of the prohibition against looking back at it. Also because it can only 'get' someone who knows about it, who thinks to himself that it is following him. It's like the Shadowstealer is that part of us—of humanity, maybe—that we can't admit to, we can't allow ourselves even to glimpse. Because once we've seen it, once we've turned to look at it, face-to-face, we can't go on the way we did before."

The sound of the circular saw was no longer in the air. Matt looked up. Tommy tapped tactfully on the screen door, then stuck his head through. "You guys want a beer, or you wanna go on being profound a little longer?"

"I think we'll take the beer," Matt said.

4

"My Lord, that's a tyrannosaurus rex," Cathy said. "I didn't know they were orange."

Matt grinned. "I told you I'd show you things you'd never seen before."

It was seven-thirty. Cathy and Matt, along with Tommy and the kids, had decided to go to Sir Gooney Land, a miniature golf course where each of the eighteen holes was presided over by a garishly colored dinosaur. In some cases, its role was purely decorative, though in a few, the dinosaur's anatomy was incorporated into the game. For example, when you came to the blue stegosaurus (Hole No. 7), you had to hit the ball into the creature's mouth and hope it would emerge, moments later, from its heavily armored tail. Predictably, Tommy was a hard-driven competitor and a superb putter: He patiently studied the layout of each course, then made dazzlingly accurate angle shots, despite the fact that between him and Matt a good bit of beer had been consumed so far that evening. Matt's approach was—of course—inspired and a bit haphazard, though he did manage a dazzling hole in one at the orange tyrannosaurus. It was obvious that Tommy loved the game because it was a game, while Matt loved it because of the dinosaurs. When they finished the first course—Tommy won, Cathy came in last—they let the two boys play the second course by themselves, while the adults sat out on one of the picnic tables and sipped their Buds out of Coke cups—Tommy had smuggled in a six-pack under the fence, and had hidden it between the hind legs of the triceratops.

Matt and Tommy were reminiscing about Matt's childhood passion for dinosaurs: "I guess I identified with them because they were extinct," he commented wryly.

"He used to make me play dinosaurs with him," Tommy said. "Shit, he used to make everybody play dinosaurs with him."

"How did you *play* dinosaurs?"

"Same way we played anything else. Just the way Matt told us to."

"I was always the triceratops," Matt explained. "A very lovable and witty triceratops."

Tommy grinned. "I was the tyrannosaurus. I reckon I wasn't so lovable."

"What would you guys do?"

"Mainly, I would try to talk Tommy out of eating me," Matt said.

"He'd usually talk me into eating Bobby Jaspers—he was the brontosaurus."

"So you guys just roamed around Mt. Jephtha, pretending you were dinosaurs?" Cathy asked.

"Isn't that how everyone spends their childhood?"

Tommy laughed. "You know, I used to think that. I figured everybody had a Matt when they was little, to tell them what to play. I reckon we didn't know back then how lucky we was," Tommy said. He had obviously intended his remark to be tongue-in-cheek ribbing, but as he looked at Matt, his eyes betrayed something else, Cathy noticed. It was a deep and genuine love.

"You never complained."

"Sheeet, I used to complain all the time. I always wanted to play baseball."

"I played baseball with you sometimes."

"Yeah, but only if we pretended we was dinosaurs while we were doing it. And you kept wanting to change the rules," Tommy complained. "Like that rule you come up with, about how triceratops couldn't have nothing thrown at 'em, on account of how they was too slow and delicate."

"Well, they were slow," Matt said.

Tommy grinned and shook his head in mock dismay. "I never saw nothing wrong with somebody wanting to live in his own little world," Tommy said. "Problem with Matt's always been that he wants everybody else to live there, too."

Cathy and Matt sat out the next round and watched as Tommy patiently demonstrated his putting technique to the two boys. A frown crossed Cathy's face. "Just look at the way they are together," Cathy said, her eyes on Tommy and Jimmy. "I would never have thought it was possible for a man to be like that. I mean, to have such doubts in his mind and yet never to let them show, not even for a split second."

"Yeah, but sometimes I can't help wondering what really goes on in Tommy's mind," Matt said.

"Why do you say that?"

"Like earlier, when Jimmy kept missing the pterodactyl's mouth." Cathy recalled the scene. The boy, after having exceeded the five-putt limit, threw a minor tantrum. He had hurled his putter into the bushes, narrowly missing Peter's head, then stormed off to sit out the next two holes on a bench, his face screwed up in flushed indignation. Tommy, a supremely good sport, had been visibly embarrassed by his son's behavior. Too embarrassed even to call the boy down. "Didn't you see it in Tommy's eyes?" Matt asked Cathy. "Maybe it was just my overactive imagination. But it was like I could almost feel what was going on inside Tommy at that moment. Feel this—" Matt hesitated. He stared down at his cup of smuggled-in beer. "It's the kind of thing that hurts inside, even to think about. But it was like in that glimpse, I knew exactly what he was thinking. He was thinking, My own son wouldn't act that way. My son would've been a good sport, like me."

Cathy turned away in silence. Matt was right on both counts. She saw it, too. But she also felt that it was one of those little things it was wiser to pretend you didn't see.

A little awkwardly, Cathy tried to change the subject. "At least, I think Tommy likes me now."

"Yeah, I noticed. He's starting to look at you the same way he used to look at Dolleen Tilman, back in seventh grade," Matt remarked. "I sure hope he doesn't remember about our deal."

"What deal?"

"See, Tommy and I, we both had crushes on Dolleen. In fact, we almost got in a fight over her, but Tommy at the last moment didn't have the heart to beat me up. Which, of course, he could have done with one hand tied behind his back. So he said, 'You can have Dolleen. But I get the next one.' And I gave him my word of honor."

"The next what?"

"The next girl we both fall in love with."

"Was there a next one?"

"Nope. Not until now."

Cathy stared at Matt. "Come on, you can't be serious."

"I know ol' Tommy pretty well. I know that look he gets in his eyes."

"But why?" Cathy said.

"Aside from being beautiful and sweet and brilliant and charming, aside from listening to him with sympathy and compassion, I have no idea."

"Daddy?" Peter ran over to them breathlessly. "Can I spend the night with Jimmy. Tommy says it's okay."

Matt looked over at Cathy. "It's up to you."

"My God, my first maternal decision," Cathy reflected.

"Pleasepleasepleaseplease!"

"Sure. Why not?"

As Peter ran breathlessly back to the lavender pterodactyl—"They said I can, they said I can"—Matt examined Cathy: "That wasn't so hard, now was it?"

She leaned back against him. "Like falling off a log."

5

At the Happy Homes Trailer Park, the two boys took off the moment Tommy pulled his pickup into his gravel driveway. "Y'all be back by eleven," Tommy told them, and Jimmy yelled okay. "And don't get in no trouble, hear?"

"Where're we going?" Peter asked.

"Over to Leroy's."

"What for?"

"To see if he wants to do something."

"Like what?" Peter asked sarcastically.

"I dunno. Something."

Fat chance, Peter thought glumly. Since he had first met Leroy, it had always been a mystery to Peter why Jimmy liked hanging around him. All Leroy ever wanted to do was to play horseshoes and talk about cars and football. When Peter and Jimmy were alone, they never ran out of things to be doing, or mostly things to pretend like they were doing. But to Leroy, the whole fabulous realm of the pretend simply did not exist. He was as literal-minded and as devoid of imagination as a slab of concrete and, in Peter's judgment, about as much fun to be around. Nor was Leroy the kind of boy who, lacking imagination himself, can still be seduced by the imagination of others. His mind and heart were set against anything that he wasn't already familiar with. "That sounds goofy to me," was Leroy's standard retort whenever Peter made a suggestion. Once, they had invited Leroy to come play with them at the Lumpkin house. Upon stepping foot inside, Leroy had looked around and said, "I don't like this place. It's goofy. It ain't like no trailer." Which Peter couldn't argue with. And there was no way of persuading Leroy that the Lumpkin house, while admittedly lacking the advantages of a trailer, might still possess other virtues, such as novelty and individual character. But then, to Leroy—as Peter slowly discovered—anything unique, anything different, was, for that very reason, highly suspect. Peter could see it in the other boy's eyes, that grim, hard, unyielding look that he offered to anything out of the ordinary.

And the worst part of it, to Peter's mind, was the fact that Leroy's attitude always seemed to rub off on Jimmy, at least whenever his friend was around the other boy. When Jimmy was with Leroy, the talk was cars and engines and four-on-the-floors, or the Georgia Bulldogs, or horseshoes.

When Jimmy and Peter got to the other trailer, Leroy was sitting out front. His sister, Opal, was inside, with one of the neighbor kids she babysat for. They were watching *Magnum, P.I.* A yellow light flickered off and on overhead.

Leroy glanced up without a smile. It was another thing Peter had noticed about him. He never smiled, and nearly never laughed, either. Peter had seen the same behavior in some of the adult men of the county, the ones who wore caps that said Budweiser or Jack Daniels or Bocephus on the front. It was like they weren't going to smile unless somebody paid them.

"When's your Momma supposed to get back?"

"No telling."

"Where'd she go to?"

Leroy glanced down, glum. "I reckon where she always goes to."

Both Jimmy and Peter knew what that meant. Everybody in the trailer park did. Leroy's momma, Venita, spent nearly every night at the bar over in Homersville, The Drop On Inn. It was the closest bar to Mt. Jephtha—Claudell County was dry, like many counties in North Georgia. Sometimes she came home, sometimes she didn't. Sometimes she would bring a man with her, a trucker passing through, maybe, or a local. Leroy would wake up in the morning and he would find the unshaven man sitting at the breakfast table, his eyes dark and heavy with hangover. "This here's your Uncle Mike," Venita would tell Leroy, and the man would grunt and halfheartedly wave at the boy with a piece of toast. When he was lucky, the man would leave before nine or ten in the morning and Leroy would never set eyes on him again. But from time to time, they would stay. Nobody had stayed now for about four months. The last one, Uncle Bob, had stolen Opal's baby-sitting money and beaten Venita up before he left. Sometimes kids would come by and say, seeing a semi out front of the trailer, "Who's your new uncle today?" But Opal had knocked one up the side of the head, and after that, nobody said anything. Opal could be as mean as any boy.

"I hope she don't bring nobody back," Leroy said. "I wisht she'd just stay at home."

"You feel like doing something," Jimmy asked.

"Dunno. It's too late to play horseshoes."

Jimmy shrugged and glanced over at Peter for suggestions. "Whatchew think?"

"We could play hide-and-seek." It was one of the standard pastimes at the park. Three square areas of trailers allowed plenty of hiding space.

"There ain't enough people."

"There's three. That's enough."

Leroy frowned. "Naw."

"We could go to the old water tower."

Jimmy didn't seem too excited about this idea, either. "What we going to do there?"

Peter hesitated, then offered, "We could climb it and pretend we were on a spaceship."

"That sounds goofy to me," Leroy said. "It's just an old water tower. Ain't nothing there worth doing. I wisht I coulda gone up to the rink."

"Yeah."

Peter sighed and gazed off into the woods on the other side of the cemetery. Above the tops of the trees, he could see the water tower. He and Jimmy had climbed it before—without Leroy—and they'd had a pretty good time, though now Jimmy was acting as if going up there was the most boring thing in the world.

"I'm leaving," Peter suddenly announced.

Jimmy—who was now sitting next to Leroy—looked up. "Where to?"

"I dunno. Some place. I don't want to sit around here doing nothing."

Jimmy checked Leroy. "You wanna come, too?"

"Naw, man." But then—in typical Leroy's fashion—after the other two boys had gotten up and were heading off, Leroy changed his mind. He yelled, "Wait up," ran after them, then said, "Don't know why I'm even coming with you anyhow. There ain't nothing to do."

6

It was a little after ten. Cathy and Matt were on their second bottle of champagne.

They were in the backyard. Matt had brought a blanket outside and had spread it under one of the huge pecan trees near the edge of the woods. The salient windows of the house were both dark—Peter's and Simmy's. "You know," Matt said, "we could do just about anything we want to, and nobody'd be the wiser."

Cathy giggled.

"Don't you ever listen to Dr. Ruth? 'You should try doing it in your own backyard,' " Matt mimicked in his appallingly bad imitation Dr. Ruth. Besides, as Cathy had noticed, all of Matt's vocal impressions had a tendency to sound like Tigger the Talking Cat.

Cathy, who was already stretched out on her back, with her head in his lap, smiled up upside down at him. "You're talking serious edification, aren't you?"

Matt nodded.

"Edification" was Mattspeak for what Cathy's mom referred to as "coitus vulgaris." Oddly, Matt—who normally called things what they were—didn't like any of the existing words for the act of sexual intercourse. "Fuck" was out. "But you use it all the time," Cathy pointed out.

"Yes," Matt conceded, "but only in the correct context, such as 'Hey, pal, what's your *fucking* problem?' " "Copulation" was even worse: "I think of dogs piling on top of each other, like an accident on the interstate." And "Screw" was totally inadmissible: "I just can't think of you as a wobbly table leg."

"But we have to call it something," Cathy had said, whereupon Matt had suggested "edification." It was funny, Cathy thought later, how Matt's thinking resembled the savage mind (she had read her Lévi-Strauss, along with nearly everything else). To him words were not symbols that stood for things. They *were* things. Magical things, capable of making a separate world. As Matt indicated when, at the end of their first hour of edification months before, he had said—and with absolute sincerity—"Now tell me the truth, wasn't that a lot better than fucking?"

And she had to admit it was.

"I want you to edify my brains out," Cathy whispered, looking up at his face, circled by a halo of stars and pecan limbs overhead. He put his hand inside her loosened blouse and caressed gooseflesh out of her shoulders. A few moments later, she had slipped out of her clothes. Her long moonlit hair fell to cover half her face. "I feel so naked." She laughed. Then, as she looked up into his eyes, she felt a strange mixture of sorrow and exultation: She had noticed it before, the way Matt looked at her. His eyes, as they gazed on her body, glistened with tears. She reached up and touched her index finger to the corner of his right eye. She felt the drop of moisture on her fingertip and then brought it down to her mouth. She stuck her tongue to it and tasted the salt. "Why do you cry sometimes, when you look at me?"

"Because I love you so much that it scares me."

"Why?"

"Because I never had anything I was so afraid of losing."

"How are you ever going to lose me?" Cathy said.

Matt said nothing. He continued to caress softly the length of her stomach, up to her breasts, making gentle circles around her nipples. Once, earlier in the marriage, he had told her that he could easily dispense with sex, as long as she just let him touch her like that. "You know," Cathy said, "I will always be here for you. Always. I've never loved anyone else." Then she sat up. "I want you to believe that, with all your heart! Do you?"

Matt looked away. "I want to."

"Who else could I possibly love?"

"Maybe someone who doesn't exist. Who never really existed," Matt said. He was looking off into the depths of the woods. "I just don't want to let you down. Maybe you thought you were marrying someone else—someone who had gifts I don't have."

Cathy looked at him. There were times when he could have the saddest face she had ever seen. Times when her heart wanted to break for him, simply recalling what he had been through, the sorrow and the long years of humiliating struggle. She looked at him and thought of the him stooped over the filthy toilet bowl at the all-night service station where he used to work. He had once told her how he had volunteered to clean it up, simply because no one else who worked there would do it, and because—as he told her—it needed it so badly. (Though, as Matt explained, there was another reason: "*I* could always think of something else. They couldn't.")

"It doesn't matter anymore," she said softly. "I admit, maybe that did have something to do with it at first. Maybe I first fell in love with you, because of that wonderful, magical world you could create out of nothing. But now it's different. I love you for being what you are. For making another world wherever you go, even when you're not writing. Everything you touch, you make magical. Like Tigger. It's so funny; everybody— me, Tommy, Simmy, Peter—you make us all believe, in our heart of hearts, that Tigger really can talk. And you do that with everything. You create your own world just by breathing."

Matt said nothing. Cathy scooted closer to him and reached

her hands out to his face. She turned his eyes back to her. Now it was her turn for the tears. "You've made bearable all the tears of things," she whispered. "It would kill me if I thought you didn't believe me—believe how much I love you. I love the Matt Hardison who makes holes in one at the orange tyrannosaurus at Sir Gooney Land. I love the Matt Hardison I read to at night. I love the Matt who talks like Tigger. I love the Matt who is so good and kind to Simmy. And to Peter. And to Tommy. And to me. Do you understand that?"

He looked at her and smiled. She leaned forward and kissed him, then eased down onto the blanket. "Stay, O moment, thou art so fair," she whispered. She was gazing over the tops of the trees at the water tower. She sat up suddenly. "Awwwww."

"Awwwww what?"

"Look, it's got writing on it. I can't read it, but I bet it says, 'Somebody loves somebody.' "

"Good guess."

"You know what?"

"What?"

"Nobody ever wrote my name on a water tower."

"Ahh, bwess her whittle heart."

"I think it'd be sweet. I can just see it, Matt Loves Cathy. We could lie out here when we were old and gray and we could look up at it and remember."

"It'd have to be in pretty big letters."

"So. I'll buy the spray paint," Cathy said. "Come on, be a sport. Just think. We could take a picture of it and send it to my mom. She'd love that."

Matt's eyes were fixed on the water tower. "You know something. I went swimming up there once. Me and Tommy. At night, too. Jesus, it was like swimming inside a black hole. It's amazing the things you do when you're little."

"How did you hold on?"

"The best we could."

Cathy grinned mischievously. "You know, that would be kind of fun."

"What would be?"

"You and me, inside the water tower. In the dark." She looked at him, wide-eyed. "I'm serious."

"Guess I'd better tell you what I told Peter."

"What's that?"

"If I ever catch him up on that water tower, I'm going to tan his hide."

"But that's not fair. You did it!"

"A parent is not obliged to be consistent."

"I think it'd be thrilling."

"Frankly, I can think of something even more thrilling for us to do."

"Shucks." Cathy grinned.

7

"I don't see what we come up here for, anyhow."

It was Leroy talking. The boys had just negotiated the forty-foot metal ladder up to the platform of the water tower. It stood at the summit of a small hill, in the center of a clearing, and allowed the boys a view of the cemetery and the trailer park, on one side, and of the ravine and the town of Mt. Jephtha on the other. Peter could even see the roof of the old Lumpkin house, separated from the tower by a mile-deep stretch of woods.

The moon was low above the trees, but full. Its light flooded the empty field around the tower, casting long shadows in the direction of the trailer park. A light breeze brushed against Peter's face. He sat down on the platform and let his legs dangle over the edge, his arms resting on one lower railing. "I like it up here," he whispered. "You can see everything."

"You can't see everything," Leroy snorted. "You can't see Atlanta. Or Nashville."

"My daddy come up here a long time ago and went swimming," Jimmy said. He, too, had heard the story.

"Mine, too," Peter said.

"Why'd anybody want to go swimming up in some ol' water tower?"

Jimmy walked around to where the metal door was. It was half the height of a regular door, but the same size across. He stared down at it, glanced back at Peter with a mischievous grin, and pulled the door open.

"Whatchew doing that for?" Leroy asked.

"Whatchew think?" Then Jimmy turned to Peter. "You want to?"

"Want to what?"

But Peter didn't need to ask. He could tell from the way Jimmy's eyes were gleaming, the same gleam he had seen in them all the other times he had talked Peter into doing something risky and foolish.

"I don't know." Peter looked into the tank. Enough moonlight fell inside for him to see just how dark and uninviting the water was. He reached over and stuck his hand into it. "It's kinda cold."

"Naw, it ain't," Jimmy said, doing the same thing. "You chicken or something?"

Peter—of course—shook his head no. "I don't have my swimsuit," he said lamely.

"Whatchew need that for?" And Jimmy, as if to demonstrate, was taking his shirt off. Peter watched, then turned back to the tank.

"What if there's something inside there?"

"Like what?"

"Snakes, or something?"

"*Snakes?*" Jimmy put his shirt over the railing and was pulling his blue jeans off. "How's a snake gonna get inside a water tower? Climb the ladder?"

It was, Peter had to admit, unlikely. "Could be something else, though."

"Naw. Ain't nothing in there, 'cept water."

Stripped down to his underwear, Jimmy leaned over and called out, in a spooky voice, "Anybody in there?"

A faint echo came from the tank, though in a voice deeper and more genuinely spooky. Peter looked at Leroy.

"You're a goofy fuck if you do it," Leroy declared.

"Come on. Ain't nothing gonna get you."

"What if the door got stuck or something?"

"How's it gonna get stuck, 'less somebody closes it? Say?" Jimmy asked. " 'Sides, Leroy ain't coming in. I know that. He's too big a pussy. Ain't you, Leroy?"

His face hard, Leroy did not deign to respond to Jimmy's remark.

"Come on. It'll be fun. Just think, we can tell folks what we done."

Yeah, *you* can, Peter thought. It was one of Jimmy's most annoying traits, bragging and exaggerating his accomplishments, what there were of them.

Jimmy put one leg over the rim of the door and looked back at Peter. "Well, whatchew gonna do?"

"I'm coming, I guess."

Jimmy grinned and sneered at Leroy. "Pussy," he called, then turned and dropped into the water. Peter heard him splashing around, hooping and hollering his redneck yells. He stuck his head up, his elbows on the door, his hair wet and dripping halfway down over his eyes. "Come on. It's warm once you git in."

And reluctantly Peter took his blue jeans off. He placed them on the railing, then went back to the door. Leroy was shaking his head.

Peter glanced at the boy. He was about to say, "You ain't leaving, are you?" but he realized that this might suggest a lack of courage on his own part.

"Shit," Jimmy called out from inside, "you coming or ain'tchew?"

"I'm coming."

"How much longer you two gonna be in there?" Leroy called out, peering into the tank. He could hear the two boys splashing and yelling; they had been inside for no more than five minutes, but, out on the platform, alone, it had seemed much longer to Leroy.

Much longer.

Leroy glanced back down at the moonlit field. Twice already he had told them that he was leaving to go on back to the trailer park. But so far, though he had walked over to the ladder a few times, he had changed his mind each time about leaving.

After all, to get back to the park, he knew he would have to walk through the woods. It wasn't a great distance, less than a fourth of a mile, but at night, and alone, it was more than Leroy cared to undertake right then.

Not that it would have given any problems a few weeks before.

That was what disturbed Leroy. Though he wasn't much of a daredevil, Leroy had never exhibited any signs of being a scaredy-cat, either. In both cases, it would have required an exercise of imagination, and that was something Leroy saw little point in.

But in the last week, something had been happening. Before, Leroy had always had sensible dreams. He dreamed he was driving a big semi, like the kind he wanted to drive when he grew up. Or he dreamed he was playing horseshoes or football. Once he had been chased by a big dog, but he had easily jumped over a fence and had gotten away from it. And that, up until last week, had been Leroy's idea of a nightmare.

It wasn't anymore.

Leroy stared down at the shadow of the water tower. It stretched downward to the woods, going about half the way there.

To Leroy, up until last week, trees were trees, woods were woods, and shadows were shadows. Which was precisely how Leroy liked things.

But then he had been over at Curtis's trailer, in the other boy's room, and he had come across that goofy book he had been reading. Leroy had picked it up and examined the cover. "What's this supposed to be?" he asked with a scowl, and Curtis had told him. Told him, too, of the thing that lay concealed in the shadow of the running boy. Of course, Leroy, at the time, and later, had scoffed and mocked at the very idea of such a thing.

Until he had his dream.

It had been sitting on him. Right on top of his chest. He woke up and saw it. It was black, except for one eyeball in the face. "Who the fuck are you?" Leroy asked, decidedly pissed off.

"I been following you, Leroy. Ain't you never felt that tingling right there on the back of your neck?"

"Bullshit, you ain't real. You's just something somebody made up, s'all."

But as the thing spoke to him, he had felt that tingling. "Ain't you never wanted to look back? Look back and make sure it ain't me?"

"Naw, why should I?"

" 'Cause," it whispered, " 'cause one night, real soon, Leroy, you'll gonna be walking back through them woods, and you feel it, this here tingling, only this time, you gonna have to look, Leroy, no matter how hard you try not to."

Leroy went to say "Bullshit" again, but he couldn't get the word out.

"And then, Leroy, you're gonna see what's hiding inside. See something you never even imagined was in this here world."

When Leroy woke up, he was shivering all over. He had even crawled in bed with his sister, Opal. He nudged her until she was awake and then asked her to tell him how it was going to be when she became a rich and famous country-and-western singer, and about the saddest song. And then he had gone back to sleep.

But since that night, it had come again. And again. And every night he had been out walking anywhere by himself, he had felt it, the tingling. Only he had made damn sure that he didn't stop, and even surer that he didn't look back.

And that's why Leroy didn't move from the water tower.

He knew, even if he ran home as fast as he could, he couldn't make it through the woods without feeling it on the back of his neck again, without stopping, without at least peeking around behind him.

Inside the tank, Jimmy was treading the patch of water that was in the moonlight. Peter had one hand up, holding with it on to the door ledge, resting.

"Wonder how far down it goes?" Jimmy said.

"Dunno."

"I'm going down and look."

And before Peter could say anything, Jimmy took a deep breath, grabbed hold of his nose, and disappeared. Peter pushed himself away from the door and swam around to the other side of the moonlight.

At first, it was spooky being inside. Looking up, you could see nothing, only the black dome of the tower. Despite its age, it had not rusted through anywhere. But Jimmy had kept splashing and saying how there was nothing to be scared of, and Peter had gotten used to it. He swam over and felt in the dark for one of the ribs of the tank—even wet, they were easy to hold on to, whenever you wanted to take a rest.

He waited for Jimmy to come back up for air.

He looked at the door.

It was crazy, but the idea occurred to him again: What if the door suddenly slammed shut? What if it locked? He looked back at the patch of light. What if Jimmy didn't come back up again? And the image flashed through his mind of Peter alone, locked inside the tank, with Jimmy down there somewhere at the bottom.

"Leroy?" he called out, his own voice echoing in the darkness.

He listened, then called again. But Leroy didn't appear in the doorway.

Just then Jimmy bobbed up to the surface. He gasped for air. "Sumthin's down there."

"Whatchew mean?" Peter asked, startled.

"Dunno. Sumthin'. I'm going back down to see." And again Jimmy sucked in a huge breath, and plunged under.

"Jimmy! Wait a second!"

But it was too late.

Again Peter called out for Leroy, louder this time. He waited to see the boy's grim disapproving face peering into the darkness. There were times when even Leroy was a welcomed sight. Maybe especially Leroy.

Peter swam to the door and pulled himself up far enough to stick his head out.

Leroy was standing at the railing. His face was turned away, like he was staring at something down in the empty field.

"Leroy? What is it?"

"Somebody's down yonder," Leroy said. Only his voice didn't sound right. Didn't sound like you expected it to sound, flat and grim. It sounded agitated.

"Where?"

"In them woods. Like they was watching us."

"How you know?"

"I see where its shadow goes."

"Its shadow?"

"Sticking out."

Peter turned back around. He thought he had heard a splash, like Jimmy would make coming to the surface. Shit, he thought, how long had he been down there? He called out the boy's name, confident to get an answer. But no answer came.

Peter stared at the moonlit patch of water. The water was churning, bubbling.

"Jimmy?"

Peter squinted and scanned the far side of the tank. Probably Jimmy had already come up and was holding on to one of the metal ribs, trying hard to keep from bursting out laughing at Peter.

"You over there? You ain't scaring me. I heard you come up."

Sumthing's down there.

Peter's eyes were still on the spot where the bubbles kept churning up to the surface.

Sumthing's down there, and now it's got hold of Jimmy. And in the darkness, Peter could see the scene being enacted beneath him. The dark oozy thing that was entwining itself around Jimmy's body, its tentacles thin as a garter snake, only longer, much longer, whizzing through the dark water, and wrapping and coiling, and Jimmy's mouth wrenched back into a desperate shriek, only out of his lungs came not the cries of terror, but only a mocking row of bubbles, sliding up to the surface of the tank, where Peter watched them break, and where it was almost like within each one there was a faint replica of the suffocated scream beneath him.

Help me, Peter.

Then, from behind him came Leroy's voice.

"It's coming."

Peter turned and lifted himself up again.

"It's heading this way."

"What?"

"Something ain't right," Leroy was saying.

Peter turned back around. Before, Peter had managed to sound calm, but there was now a real urgency in his voice. "Jimmy? Stop fooling around. Something's outside. Leroy's seen something. So stop fooling, okay?"

At that moment Peter heard it, the sound chilling his whole body as if the water had, in a heartbeat, been brought within a quarter of a degree of freezing. Somebody was gurgling right beneath him.

Gurgling, *Help me, Peter! Help me!*

Peter twisted himself around and reached up to the door. He flung his arm over and was about to pull himself free when the thing jumped up from the water, grabbed his legs, and tugged him back into it.

Terrified, Peter twisted around and saw the dead face. Through each of the empty eye sockets, something squirmed and wriggled, like the heads of two snakes, poking out toward him. Peter's head went under, taking in a mouthful of water as he did—he was in midscream. He struggled and knocked his head against the metal of the tank, and again he felt the thing on him, entangling him. It was pushing him now.

His eyes were open but there was nothing except the blackness of the water.

It was pulling him by the arm, but Peter, in his panic and confusion, didn't know which way it was dragging him, up into the air or down to the bottom of the tank.

He broke the surface, gagging.

"Peter, you okay?" And again he was being pulled up. "It was just me."

Jimmy was next to him, trying to pull him up to the door ledge. "What was that?" Peter managed to get out between his chokes and gasps for air.

"A dead cat, s'all. Must have got stuck inside and drowned. I just put my fingers through its eyes, s'all. I dropped it when you got scared, or I'd show you."

With Jimmy's help, Peter clambered over the ledge. He collapsed, still trying to catch his breath.

Jimmy patted him on the back and kept saying he only meant to scare him. But then Jimmy stopped. He was looking over at Leroy. Something had caught his attention there.

"See it?" It was Leroy speaking. Peter struggled up to his feet and followed Jimmy.

"See what?"

Shivering, Peter leaned against the railing and stared down where the other two boys were looking.

Directly below them lay the shadow of the water tower, still stretching halfway down the field, as when Peter had first seen it from the platform. Then it had been the only shadow on the moonlit field. But now there was another.

Jimmy stared at it. "Look. What's it doing?" he whispered. "It's like it's—" But Jimmy didn't finish his thought. He didn't need to. Peter and even Leroy knew what he was going to say. The tip of the shadow that had emerged from the woods had at first been a single blur of darkness, like the shadow cast by somebody walking with his arms down by his side. But now two shadow arms were extending out from the main body of the shadow. The shadow arms slithered slowly toward the tower over the moonlit field, undulating back and forth the way a black snake moves through grass. Peter had seen his own shadow do that, when it moved over uneven ground, the up and down of the surface causing the shadow to look like it was wriggling back and forth.

"Why don't he come out of the woods, whoever it is."

"Maybe it's somebody trying to scare us. Opal, maybe."

"Naw, it's too big for Opal."

It kept moving. Peter, as he watched it, remembered how in school, whenever the teacher set up the ancient movie projector, the window blinds drawn down tightly, some of the boys would jump out of their seats and would hold their hands up into the dust-filled shaft of the brilliant light, manipulating their fingers and palms into a bizarre assortment of shadow creatures: birds with fluttering wings, elephants with dangling trunks, and Indian chiefs with enormous warbonnets. Maybe, that was it, Peter reflected, somebody back in the woods was deliberately wriggling his arms over his head like that, so that they'd cast funny shadows like they were doing.

"You think we should yell at him?" Jimmy asked.

"Uh-uh," Leroy whispered. On his face was a scowl. "It ain't right. Don't you see?"

Peter watched as the long shadow hands slinked and stretched closer and closer to the long shadow cast by the water tower, the distance between them growing smaller and smaller. But still, nothing, no one, had stepped out of the woods. Peter tried to imagine in his mind's eyes the required posture of whoever it was doing it. Maybe he started out squatting down at the edge of the woods, then slowly stood up, then little by little raised his arms up over his head, then spread out his fingers, just the way the fingers of the shadow were beginning to open up as they drew nearer the shadow of the tower, each of them growing at the tips as if—

"Whatchew mean, it ain't right?" Jimmy asked.

"It's going the wrong way," Leroy whispered.

Peter looked over at the other boy and blinked.

"Look how the shadow of the tower is. Then look at that other one. It's going wrong."

With all his attempts to imagine how the shadow was being made, that hadn't occurred to him. He glanced back at literal-minded Leroy, who alone had noticed the obvious: The shadow could not have been cast by the moon.

"That ain't possible," Leroy said, his tone of voice firm and determined, as if, with that statement, the errant shadow could be expected simply to coil back up into itself, like a caterpillar before a flame. But the shadow didn't cooperate.

It touched the shadow of the water tower. It spread through that other shadow, blackening it.

"Look," Jimmy said. He was pointing at the woods. At the spot where the shadow had first emerged. It was no longer dark there. Instead there was moonlight. The shadow was farther up the slope. And nothing and no one had stepped out of the woods.

"It wasn't nobody," Jimmy whispered. "Nobody atall."

Leroy grimaced, as if bitterly offended by what he was watching. "This here, it ain't right. It's goofy," he declared. "I'm going."

"Wait," Peter told them, even though as he said this he didn't know what he was asking them to wait for. But the two boys weren't interested in finding out. They had already made a dash to the point where the metal ladder met the platform. Leroy went first. He had gotten down four steps of the ladder when Peter saw it.

"It's coming up," he said. "It's coming up the ladder."

Leroy saw it, too. But all Peter could hear him say was, "Naw, naw."

"You see what it is?"

Jimmy, who had been set to follow Leroy down, backed off quickly. "Shit, it's coming up."

"Get off the ladder, Leroy," Peter yelled, leaning over the railing. Step after step disappeared below Leroy, not the way something grows dim as a shadow passed over it, but as if whatever it was, was engulfing the steps in an rising tide of liquid tar.

"Leroy, get off!"

But Leroy didn't budge.

Jimmy grabbed Peter and they hurried to the other side of the tower. They crouched down, holding their breaths.

"What is it?"

"I don't know."

"Leroy?" Jimmy called out. "You see it yet?"

But there was no answer from the other boy. Just complete silence. Then Jimmy poked Peter in the side.

"Look."

There, about eight or nine feet from where they were crouched down, the side of the water tower fell into momentary darkness, then that part of the platform directly below. Within seconds, the moonlight had returned. Jimmy stood up and went to the railing.

"It's going."

Peter was next to him. He watched as the shadow thing oozed from the base of the tower back into the woods. It was heading for the path that led down to the old swinging bridge.

"It's gone," Jimmy whispered.

The two boys went around to the other side of the tower. They saw Leroy. He had gotten back up the ladder and was standing on the platform, his eyes staring in the direction that the shadow thing had disappeared. Even when they spoke to him, he didn't turn his head or even acknowledge their presence.

"You see it?" Jimmy asked.

And Leroy nodded, a dazed, distracted nod. "I seen it."

"What was it?"

"Just this here shadow," he said softly.

Peter glanced at Jimmy, then asked, "You okay, Leroy?"

In Leroy's face there was an expression that neither of the other two boys could ever have imagined being there. It was a look of confusion and bewilderment. For the first time in Leroy's existence he had stumbled across something that didn't fit in anywhere. Something that wasn't normal, but something that he could no longer dismiss as merely goofy, either.

Leroy's tongue slid across his upper lip. A frown furrowed his brow. "Something was hiding under it, like," he whispered.

"Whatchew mean?"

But the other boy only shook his head. "I don't rightly know."

Peter shivered, then said to Jimmy, "Let's get back, okay."

• • •

It took the boys only five minutes, running hard, to get back to the park. Leroy did not say another word to them about what he had seen. He just went to his trailer—his momma wasn't home yet—without even telling them good night. Peter and Jimmy held a conference before going inside.

"You think we should tell your daddy?" Peter asked.

"What can we say? That we seen a shadow?"

Peter frowned. Jimmy was right, that didn't seem to capture the enormity of what they had witnessed. But what could they say?

" 'Sides, you know what they'd do if we was to tell 'em we'd been up there," Jimmy said. " 'Specially, swimming."

"Yeah." Peter's daddy had told him enough times what would happen. Boiling in oil was one option. Jimmy was already on his way in.

"But what if it *was* something?" Peter asked.

Jimmy glanced uneasily around him at the thousand shadows that haunted the trailer park at night, and the thought struck him, A shadow was a terrible thing to be afraid of. "Let's just go to sleep, okay?"

8

It was after twelve. Cathy and Matt were lying cuddled up. Stars gleamed through the sparse outer limbs of a pecan tree overhead. "I wish we had that one on videotape," Cathy murmured.

"Cathy!"

"No, not for that reason. Something else."

"What?"

"I don't know. I just got this eerie feeling." She gave him what would be a significant glance in anybody's book. "I think Something Special happened."

"Just how special?" Matt asked, sitting up and looking over at Cathy.

"Pretty special," Cathy whispered. "I mean, wouldn't it be nice to come into the world tonight? And to know that you were created in an act of genuine, passionate love—not just some accident."

"That's why you wanted the video camera? For *baby* pictures? 'Yes, and here we have junior caught in the act of being conceived. Isn't he adorable?' "

"I guess it does sound crazy. And I suppose it wouldn't do to show them to the child until he was reasonably mature, of course. But still, don't you think it would make him feel awfully good about himself? Or am I just being wacko, as usual?"

"I wonder how many of us would want to see the same moment in our own lives. I think it could be pretty sobering."

They were silent for about a minute, then Cathy—struck by the somberness of Matt's last words—stared at him and, emboldened by the champagne, asked a question she had long contemplated, "Do you have a secret? Something you've never told me?"

Matt looked up. "Why did you say that? Just now?"

"I don't know. Because sometimes it seems that way," Cathy hazarded.

"You know what my oldest memory is?" Matt asked. He was sitting up now. A shiver crossed from one shoulder blade to the other. "It's so old, I don't even know if it was a dream or if it actually happened. I was standing in the hallway on the third floor of the Lumpkin house. Outside Aunt Hester's old room. Leon was in there and they were talking. But all I could see were two shadows, but I knew it was Leon and Hester—this was back when she could still get around. Hester was saying, 'You know he's going to ask one day. You know he's gonna want to know.' She was talking about me. And then she said—" Matt stopped and glanced at Cathy, to underscore the significance of what was coming. "She said, 'When he asks you about his momma and daddy, you gotta make up something about 'em. You gotta make up something so terrible that he won't never ask you again.' "

There was not a sound in the backyard. Cathy squirmed and put her hand on Matt's bare back. She hesitated. "Maybe it was just a dream."

"I don't know." Matt was staring over the top of the woods. At the water tower.

"What did Leon tell you?"

"He said that my parents died before I was born." He looked

over at Cathy and raised his eyebrows. "I guess not many people can say that, huh?"

"How?"

"My mother was carrying me. Close to term. She and my father were traveling back to Mt. Jephtha—they were living in Chicago at the time. She wanted to have her baby here. Anyway, they had a flat tire. The car was pulled over to the side of the road. She was in the car. A drunk in a car came over the hill and hit them. They got them to the hospital. But it was too late. That's when they realized I was still alive. See, my mother was dead when I was born." He shook his head. "Sounds like some kind of legend, doesn't it? I think that was where Uncle Leon got the idea I was destined for something. Saved for God knows what."

"Maybe you were," Cathy said.

Matt frowned and shook his head. "But you see, I've never really believed it—what Leon told me." And Matt again repeated Hester's words. " 'Tell him something so terrible that he'll never ask again.' And I never did."

"Lord, it's hard to imagine anything much worse."

"Not for me it's not." He leaned back, his eyes still drawn to the water tower. "Remember what I told you, the night we took that poor cat to the clinic? About the fire at the revival? And what Odum said to me?"

"Yes."

"It sounds crazy, but you don't know how many times I've thought of those words. 'I buried you. You can't be.' It was like he knew who I was. And I'll have dreams. About him, and the fire. About being in this tiny box, buried underground. Crying. Afraid. And when I wake up from them, my foot's always going nuts. Like . . ."

"Go on."

"Almost like something is clutching on to it. Holding with all its might. Trying to pull me back somewhere. Or pull itself out." And again Matt shivered.

"You're cold. I think we'd better go back inside. Okay?"

For a moment, Matt didn't answer. She put her hand on his chin and forcibly turned his eyes away from the water tower in the distance. "It's time to come back to earth," she whispered softly.

9

Jimmy and Peter lay in bed.

They hadn't spoken for ten minutes, though their minds had been on the same thing.

Then, without a word of explanation, Jimmy got up and left the room.

Peter saw him, less than a minute later, come back. Only he was carrying something.

He sat down and turned on the light next to his bed. He was holding a copy of Peter's father's book. He was staring down hard at the cover, at the thing that trailed behind the terrified boy.

Peter looked at Jimmy. "You thinking what I'm thinking?"

Of course, Peter didn't need Jimmy to put it into words. He knew already the answer. He took the book from Jimmy and stared at the eyeball hidden underneath the shadow.

"Remember what Leroy said, how it was like something was hiding under it, what we seen."

"Only he didn't say what."

"Maybe 'cause he was too scared to."

That was possible, Peter reflected, judging from the way Leroy's face had looked.

"But it's just something my daddy wrote this book about. That's all."

Jimmy's eyes were wide. "But what if it ain't?"

Peter was looking at the claws of the shadow as it reached out for the boy's feet. "He always says there's this place where he gets his stories from. I used to think it was a real place. Storyworld, 'cause Daddy, he talked about it like it was. Not exactly real, but kind of." Peter glanced up at Jimmy. It was a crazy thought, and he didn't know how to put it very well, but he stammered it out anyway. "My daddy, he used to read me *Peter Pan*. I know it's kinda dumb, but remember when Tinker Bell dies? Peter Pan asks everybody if they believe in fairies. He says if enough of them believe hard enough, they can make Tinker Bell come alive. And she does."

"Yeah," Jimmy said skeptically, not convinced that Tinker Bell was a proper topic of discussion for boys their age.

"What if this is like that? If enough people believe in the Shadowstealer, maybe it comes alive. You think?"

And again the two boys stared at the cover.

"So it's kinda like, writing about it, your daddy done let it loose?"

And Peter nodded.

There was a long pause. "If he did, you think there's a way he can put it back up?"

10

As Cathy was getting dressed, she noticed something out of the corner of her eye. She turned and stared at it. There, at the edge of the woods, was a streak of darkness. She squinted at it—it must have been her imagination, but when she had first caught a glimpse of it, it seemed to be undulating slowly across the grass. But now it wasn't moving.

"Matt," she whispered. "I think somebody's watching us."

Matt stood up. "Where?" Then he saw what Cathy was pointing at. Matt walked a little closer to it. "Anybody there?" he said. He turned back around and shrugged. "I don't think it's anybody. Besides, why should you worry about it? *You* wanted to put it all on videotape."

Together they walked inside. Cathy stopped on the last step up and glanced back around into the yard. "It's gone now."

"What's gone?"

"Whatever it was."

"So?"

"But it shouldn't be. I mean, it should still be there, shouldn't it? If it was just a tree or something."

Matt frowned and stared out into the dark, shadow-filled yard. "Hell, I can't even tell where it was."

"Yeah. I must have just gotten disoriented."

11

Leroy was in bed. Leroy had not said a word to his sister about what he and the other two boys had seen up on the water tower. Instead, he stared somberly at the shadows on the wall in front of him and repeated to himself, like a mental exercise, "It was jus' some goofy ol' shadow, s'all. It was jus' some goofy ol' shadow."

Outside, he heard a car pull up, and then the familiar laughter of his momma. The man was laughing, too. Opal came into the room and closed the door behind her.

"Looks like she done found her another one," Opal said cynically from the other twin bed.

"I sure hope they ain't too noisy."

"Me, too."

"They sound drunk?"

"Yeah," Opal said. She stared up at the ceiling, her mouth fixed into a hard unforgiving pout. They did not speak for the next fifteen minutes, though each of them knew that the other was awake. Leroy listened to the drunken talk that came from the other part of the trailer. He had heard it all before. Finally, at a little after twelve, the trailer grew quiet.

"They're starting to do it, ain't they?"

Leroy looked over at his sister's bed. "Ain't they?" he repeated.

"Hush up, Leroy. They'll hear."

His face dark and attentive, Leroy listened a moment, then lay back on the pillow. Through the paper-thin walls, he could hear the monotonous click-click of the little .45 record player in their momma's room, the noise it always made when the needle came to the end of the groove. The record player was supposed to be theirs, a gift from one of the series of uncles. But Venita had taken it into her room two months before.

They were playing Elvis now, his momma and the new man with her. "Love Me Tender, Love Me True." When Elvis died, Leroy's momma had gotten drunk and cried all night and the next day. After, she went out and bought anything that had Elvis's picture or name on it. The worst spanking that Leroy ever got was when he knocked over and broke her whiskey decanter with Elvis on top, his guitar in his hands. His Uncle Carl had gotten it for Venita when he took his semi through Memphis.

Through the wall he heard a laugh. "You play that fucking thing one more time, I'm going to break it." He wasn't teasing, it didn't sound like.

"Hush, I don't want my babies to hear," Venita said, then gave a drunk laugh. "I don't want 'em hearing us make looooove." There was a thud, a giggle, then the needle skipped and screeched across the well-etched surface of the old .45. "Shit," his momma said, "I near always do that. You hear what I done?"

"You put that on again, I'm going to bust it."

And again he meant it. But Venita wasn't paying him any mind. "I heard you," she said, her tone bold and fearless the way it always was when she got drunk. She could stand in a big man's face and spit right in his eye, and yell, "Hit me again. Hit me again." And the big man usually did what she asked. Once again Leroy heard the needle hit the middle of the record, then slid all the way off the turntable. The sound made a shiver go down his spine.

"Sheeet. Come on you little fucker." She was talking to the record player.

"I done fucking told you!"

But Elvis was somehow singing through all the scratches. Leroy had heard it before. Nobody had ever troubled to tell Leroy that there was any beauty in the world, or what he should expect it to be like whenever he came across it. But he had found it in the way Elvis sang, and he knew at once what it was. Listening to him, Leroy's eyes filled with tears.

There was a crash: Elvis gasped, squalled, shrieked, metal on metal. "Look what you done now! You son of a bitch! That there belonged to my babies."

"I told you I was going to bust it."

Don't let him start hitting on her, Leroy whispered to himself.

But Venita was still raising hell.

Don't hit her, please.

Leroy held his breath, listened. "Why, you old horndogger." His momma's voice had that sexy sound she liked to give it.

Through the walls he could now hear the dull, monotonous clump-clump, clump-clump, clump-clump of the bedsprings. The man was panting, and his momma was making the noises she made, high-pitched, drunk. They got louder and louder, then, in the middle of it, she said, giggling, "Hush, you gonna wake up my babies." But the man kept on groaning. And so did she.

"He busted the record player," Opal said.

"I can fix it," Leroy told her. It wouldn't be the first time he had to fix something one of his momma's boyfriends had broken.

Ten minutes later, the whole trailer was quiet. But Leroy was still awake. He was staring at the closet across from his bed. At the shadows cast by the moon. And again he saw it loom up, the way it had loomed up over him on the platform of the tower, and the things he had seen underneath it, dangling down. Once Jimmy had caught a garter snake and had chased a girl around the trailer park with it. Leroy had watched the crazy twisting, flailing of the snake's tail. He didn't like it, the way it wiggled and squirmed.

On the tower he had almost told them: That was what it was like, only as if there were thousands and thousands of the tiny wiggling squirming tails, lashing and thrashing in the dark, and dripping something down, an ooze like the stuff that frogs made in ponds, where tadpoles come from. He had almost said that was what it was like, but he couldn't.

He had almost told them about the eyeball, too.

But he didn't.

He stared at the wall, and again repeated, "Jus' some goofy ol' shadow, s'all. Jus' some goofy ol' shadow."

12

Back inside, Matt, a little tipsy, fell asleep within a minute or two. But Cathy lay awake. After twenty minutes, she got up and went to the window. She searched the backyard for the spot where she had seen the shadow. There was nothing along the edge of the woods that matched it. It was gone. She was about to get back in bed when she frowned. She was staring down into the yard, at the shadow of the Lumpkin house. It fell toward the woods. Lord, I must be going crazy, she thought. Whatever it was, it couldn't have been a shadow in the first place, because there was nothing that could have cast it. Anyone standing at that spot at the edge of the woods would not have thrown his shadow forward in the first place. So, once again, she had just let her imagination run away with her.

There was nobody watching them.

Nobody at all.

Cathy got back in bed and promptly fell asleep.

PART FIVE

....

1

Jimmy and Peter were walking around the base of the old water tower, searching for any trace that the shadow thing had left from the night before. That had been Jimmy's idea. He had gone on the analogy of it being some kind of giant slug and figured it might have left some oozy residue. At least it might have left a trail of flattened grass and leaves. But the two boys found nothing.

In fact, as they climbed up the ladder and looked down on the field full of brilliant morning sunlight, it was hard to conjure up, even in their imagination, the thing that had so frightened them the night before. Jimmy frowned. "Maybe we was just seeing things. You think?"

Peter shrugged. "Maybe."

On the way back to the trailer, Peter got quiet and thoughtful. He had heard people use that expression before, saying that so-and-so was "just seeing things." But he still wasn't clear what that was supposed to mean. Once, when he was about five, Peter, in an effort to imagine something, had patiently sat for half an hour at the bottom of the staircase at the Lumpkin house and stared up at the top step, in a laborious but futile effort to make someone materialize on it. And then there had been Johnny Morrison, in first grade. You couldn't ever sit next to him in the lunchroom, because of Moose. Moose was a football player who weighed three hundred pounds and could easily beat up even the strongest sixth-grader. Moose's only drawback was that he was invisible. At least to everybody else.

Peter's first taste of ontological speculation came one afternoon when Cindy Halpern accused Johnny of flat-out lying: "He don't really see no football player. He's just saying that."

Their teacher, Miss Jackson, demurred and defended Johnny. "What about when you dream?" she had asked Cindy. "Don't you see things that aren't there?"

"Well, yes," Cindy conceded. "But that ain't the same thing. 'Cause I know they ain't there."

"While you are dreaming?" Miss Jackson asked.

And Cindy said, "Well, no. But when I wake up, I know."

"But how do you know? How do you know you're not dreaming right now?"

Cindy was stumped, but tried to rally: " 'Cause I can pinch myself."

"But you can pinch yourself in a dream, can't you? Have you ever thought that maybe Moose is just as real to Johnny as your dreams are to you? Maybe Moose is just a dream that got loose," she added, à la Dr. Seuss, and asked them all to make up stories about how somebody or something in their dreams had gotten loose, and whether this would be a good or a bad thing.

It was, to Peter, heady stuff.

But maybe that explained what they had seen. Maybe it had crept out of someone's dreams. His daddy's, maybe. Only, unlike Moose, it could became visible not just to one person, but to a whole bunch. And Peter recalled Simmy's remarks of a week earlier, when she had told him that his daddy could make you see what ain't there, just like it was there.

And Peter recalled another experiment he had undertaken when he was younger. In social studies period, Miss Jackson had told them about tribes in Africa and places, where there were people, witch doctors and such, who believe that by using just words they can do things, like heal and make rain to come and even kill their enemies. Only they had to get the words just right. Like in a spell. One little slip-up, and no go. And Miss Jackson had asked them, "Do you ever use words that way?" Everyone shook their head no, but Miss Jackson smiled patiently and said, "Sure you do. Haven't you ever wanted something to come true, where you kept saying, over and over, 'Please, please, make Momma and Daddy buy me a new bicycle?' Or a doll, maybe? Now haven't you all done that?" Nods and smiles. "Now think about it. When you say something like that over and over, aren't you really hoping, way down deep, that if you say it enough times, it will come true?"

And that afternoon Peter had gone home, sat in his bedroom, and repeated to himself, as if it were a magic formula, "Please, let Daddy get me a G.I. Joe." He did, too, though, admittedly, it was a couple of months later, and only after Peter had begged for it.

On the way back to the trailer park, the two boys stopped by the field and found Leroy playing horseshoes with his sister and some other kids. Leroy glanced at Jimmy and Peter, giving them his stoniest face, then looked away and tossed a ringer. He was the same when they got him off to the side. When they again tried to get him to say what he had seen the night before, Leroy scowled, "Ain't nothing to talk 'bout, anyhow. Wasn't nothing but some ol' shadow."

But, Peter pointed out, how could it be a regular shadow? A shadow had to be the shadow of something. And this one wasn't. Not to mention, it was going the wrong way, as Leroy himself had observed. "So?" Leroy responded. "Could be all kinds of things. I ain't gonna worry 'bout it none."

And Leroy went back to his horseshoes.

"So what you think we should do?" Peter asked as they walked to Tommy's trailer.

"Nothing, I reckon. 'Cept wait."

Yeah, for what? Peter wondered.

2

"Whatchew doing in bed, Curtis Poke? Here it is, near twelve o'clock. Come on. Get your lazy ass up. You was supposed to help me with the run." By which Jesse meant the afternoon egg run in his granny's chicken house. Jesse was sitting on the edge of Curtis's bed. He had lifted the covers back and was checking out Curtis's underwear.

"Don't that thing ever go down?" Jesse laughed.

Curtis preemptorily jerked the covers back over him. He gave Jesse a harsh scowl. "It's jus' the way it gets in the morning, s'all."

Jesse went to pull the cover back down, but Curtis had it tightly gripped in his hand. "Hey, cut that out, okay, man?"

Only mildly affronted, Jesse said, "It ain't like I never seen it before, Curtis."

"So? What's that supposed to mean?" Curtis asked, more than a hint of resentment in his voice.

"Nothing. It don't mean nothing," Jesse said amiably.

His hand still on the cover, Curtis eased up onto the pillow. "You got a cigarette?"

Jesse stood up and pulled his box of Marlboros out of the pocket of his jeans. He tossed them to Curtis. Then he noticed something sticking partway out under the bed. He leaned over and picked it up. It was a battered copy of *Playboy*.

"I know what ol' Curtis has been doing." Jesse opened right to the foldout and let it drop to its full length. He held it up admiringly. Curtis glanced up at the playmate's body, the preternaturally tanned flesh as glossy as the surface of the artificial fruit that his momma decorated the dining-room table with. "I wouldn't mind jumping on that right now. I'll tell you. Whatchew you think?" Jesse asked, displaying the centerfold for Curtis's benefit.

"Yeah," he mumbled.

The night before, Curtis had taken his prize copy of *Playboy* out from its hiding place under his mattress. He studied it for fifteen minutes, then began to jerk off, intent on visualizing the unlikely scene with as much clarity and detail as he could. He pressed his eyes closed and tried to see himself spreading her legs apart. She was licking her lips with her tongue, her finger fiddling with her smooth-shaven pussy. "You want to fuck me, don't you? Don't you?" He tried to imagine what her voice would sound like, but somehow, looking at the picture, it was hard to conjure up any sound that could come from between those lips, except sighs and pants and groans. But Curtis kept doggedly at it.

They started in his bed, then slipped off into Jesse's granny's hay barn. But now she had crawled on top of him. She was twisting the nipples of her titties, grinning down at him. He reached up and caressed her smooth taut stomach. He closed his eyes again, and the stomach began to ripple. Ripple with muscle. Then a hand touched him there, going unerringly to where it felt best, and her lips were there, too, and her tongue. "Feels good, don't it?" And he smelled the fragrance on her.

Only it was Jesse's cologne.

"Feels good, don't it?" he whispered. And Curtis, jacking off hard now, wished him away, made every effort to see her and not him. But Jesse's muscular arms were pressing down on him, his hands were moving from his stomach downward.

His body arched, his head pressed into the pillow, he had let go, and he and Jesse did again in Curtis's mind what they had done that night out in the hay barn. When it was over, Curtis sat up, threw the magazine down on the floor, his teeth chattering as they had been the first time.

"Man, I could jerk off right now, just looking at that piece of pussy." Jesse grinned. "Whatchew think?"

Curtis glanced up at the other boy. " 'Bout what?"

"Shit, ain't nobody here." Jesse sat back down on the bed. He poked at Curtis through the sheets. "Looks like you're as horny as me. Fuck, man. Ain't no point letting it go to waste."

Curtis scooted back quickly.

"What the fuck's your problem?" Jesse asked. "You and me, I thought we had us a pretty good ol' time out in the barn."

Curtis was looking at the wall. "It ain't right."

"What ain't?"

"What we done. It ain't natural."

"Whatchew mean, it ain't natural? I thought it felt pretty fucking good. So'd you, looked like."

"So?"

"Shit, man, way you're acting, you'd think we was fucking gayfers or something. You know we ain't."

Curtis looked over at Jesse, taken aback by the other boy's breezy dismissal of that possibility.

"I mean, how could you and me be something like that?"

"What the fuck's the difference?" Curtis asked, point-blank.

Jesse's eyes got a strange, puzzled look. "What the hell's wrong with you? You think we act like gayfers or something? Say, Curtis!"

"No."

"So what's the big fucking deal?"

"I just don't want to do it no more. Okay?"

Jesse got up from the bed. "You saying I'm some kind of faggot?" His face had a look, both stricken and angry at the same time.

"Naw."

"You'd better not be. You know I'd have to whup your ass,

and you know I don't wanna do nothing like that."

Curtis was silent. He was staring at the wall again.

"I know I ain't smart, the way you are, Curtis. I don't read books and shit like that. But, fuck, I know when something feels good. And you know it don't mean nothing when we do it. It's just 'cause they ain't no girls around to do it with, that's all."

"Then why don't you go over and do it with Tammi?" Curtis said, his eyes on the wall.

"Fuck, man, maybe I will." Jesse threw the *Playboy* down and went toward the door. He stopped and looked back. "You're a real dumbass, Curtis. You'd better hope nobody finds out 'bout you peeing in the bed at night. Sure would be embarrassing as fuck, people knowing I hang around with somebody does shit like that."

As Jesse slammed the door behind, Curtis's eyes were burning with tears. He tried to hold them back. Inside, it was a mess. He jumped up and went to his window. He looked out and saw Jesse, mad as hell, walking toward his Cougar. Call him back, something said inside him. But it was drowned out by all the other voices, the ones that had hissed and whispered and mocked him all night long. He turned from the window and collapsed, his head facedown, into his pillow.

One of them thangs.

One of them thangs.

One of them thangs.

One of them thangs . . .

3

Earlier that morning Cathy and Tommy had been painting the main hallway. At a little after twelve, Tommy had left, to go pick up the boys from the trailer park. Cathy, her hands and face still speckled with paint, decided to go up and see if Matt was working.

The attic door was open. No Matt.

She called for him, but there was no answer. She went to their bedroom. The door was closed. She tapped on it with her knuckles. Inside she heard a stricken groan.

"Matt?"

Another groan. Actually, it was more like a moan this time.

She tried to turn the knob without getting any paint on it. But it was impossible. "Shit," she said, gave up and just grabbed it.

Matt was lying on the bed, his face buried melodramatically under the pillow.

"Honey, are you okay?" Cathy tiptoed over to the bed.

"I'm going to call Alison." Alison was Matt's angelically patient editor.

"Why?"

"I'm going to tell her I can't do it. I'm no good. A fake. I'll never write another word in my life."

"Oh, sweetheart, you're just having a rough time. It happens to everybody." She went to stroke his back, but stopped, remembering that she still had paint on her.

"I'm washed up."

"You're being silly."

"No, I'm not."

"Hold on," Cathy said and went into the bathroom to clean her hands. When she came back, she pulled the pillow off Matt's head and sat down next to him. Tigger was lying on the bed, curled up at Matt's feet. "Even Tigger thinks you're being silly." Then in her imitation of Matt's imitation of Tigger's voice, she said, "Oh, Daddy, you just having writer's block, that's all. They's just like the piles, only worser." (Simmy had mentioned her theory to Cathy earlier.)

"Stop trying to cheer me up."

"Oh, Daddy, you going to write such a wonderful novel," Tigger said.

"That's easy for you to say, Tigger."

Cathy laughed. And even Matt cracked a smile. "Oh, Daddy's really feeling sorry for himself, isn't he, Mommy?"

"Yes, he is, Tigger."

Matt sat up and looked at Cathy. "You two think this is just hilarious, don't you?"

"No. We're just trying to make you feel better."

Matt sighed. "Don't you understand? I don't know how to write anymore. I'm going to have to start working at 7-Elevens again. And won't Mommy like that, Tigger? What do you think

Mommy's going to say when Daddy starts working the night shift at the Pac-n-Sack?"

"She's going to say, 'Fuck off, Daddy.' "

"Yes, that's exactly what she's going to say, Tigger."

"She's going to say, 'You don't expect no classy broad like me to be married to no loser, do you?' "

"I think Daddy's getting a little hysterical, Tigger."

"No, he's not, Mommy. You know it's true. You only married him 'cause he wrote some goofy ol' book. But he can't write no more goofy books and you won't love him no more."

Cathy looked from Tigger's somber cat face back to Matt's. It wasn't funny anymore. Looking into his—Matt's eyes—she saw that beneath the veil of humor there was a dead seriousness. Matt really meant what he—or rather Tigger—said.

"You can't really think that?" she asked him.

"Why not? You don't know how I feel up there, staring at that goddam blank screen for six hours a day," Matt said. "I keep feeling like I've let you down. Or worse, like I deceived you."

"Daddy's just scared of losing you, Mommy, that's all."

Cathy shook her head. "He's not going to lose me. Tell him that, okay?"

Matt frowned. "I don't goddam understand it. When I was writing *Shadowstealer*, that last revision, the words poured out. It was like I was hearing the damn story being whispered into my ear. It was almost frightening, as if I had tuned into something I shouldn't have tuned into."

"Why do you think they call it inspiration?"

"I know. But why can't I turn it off and on when I want to, like a spigot? Be nice, wouldn't it?"

Cathy smiled. "It will come back."

From downstairs, they heard three rings of the telephone. They waited a few moments, then heard Simmy—whose voice could carry when she wanted it to—yelling upstairs at the top of her lungs. "Mr. Matt, it's that agent of yours on the phone."

"Frank," Matt said. Some years before, Frank had given Matt his break. While an assistant editor, he had mercifully rescued an earlier manuscript of *The Shadowstealer* out of the slush pile at his publishing house. Later, when he became an agent, he told Matt that the book still needed work, and helped him at every step. "He's probably calling to tell me to fuck off."

"I'm sure he's not."

When Matt left, Cathy and Tigger sat on the bed together. "Your daddy sure can get awful gloomy sometimes, can't he?"

"You said a mouthful, Mommy."

Five minutes later, Cathy looked up. Matt was standing in the doorway. His face was pale. He lifted his hand to the door and Cathy saw that it was trembling.

"What's wrong?"

Matt stumbled into the room, like a drunken sleepwalker. He said nothing. He simply sat down on the edge of the bed, and put his hands between his knees, and stared down at them.

"What is it?"

"Spielberg."

"Steven Spielberg?"

"Told Frank."

"Yes?"

"Wants to make a movie."

"Oh?" Cathy asked, puzzled.

"*Shadowstealer.*"

It was like playing charades, almost. Cathy's heart skipped several beats as it dawned on her. "You're not kidding, are you?"

And Matt shook his head no, his mouth hanging open.

Tigger, who during all this had gotten up and stretched, nudged Matt's arm aside and crawled into his lap. He looked up into Matt's face, then turned his head upside down. "Tigger, you're gonna be one rich fucking cat."

And for once, even Tigger was speechless.

"What is it? What's wrong?" Simmy asked when Cathy and Matt came downstairs. "Why was Mr. Matt looking that way?"

Cathy told her.

Her eyes widened, and she stepped back: Cathy was almost prepared to catch her fall. Simmy's hand went over her heart. "My Lord, my Lord," she whispered. "Mr. Matt, you done it now."

"Yeah, I have, haven't I?"

4

Back at his trailer, Tommy made himself a sandwich. He was just about to leave, to try to round up the two boys, when he heard the crunch of gravel out in his driveway. He went to the door and saw Wally Clark's car.

Puzzled, but pleased, Tommy called out, "What brings you around?" When Tommy was younger, back when Wally and Matilda were hopelessly without child, Wally—the kind of guy who was born to be somebody's dad—had vented his longing for paternity on the Mt. Jephtha Methodist Softball Team, of which Tommy was the star pitcher. Wally was probably closer to Tommy than he was to any of the other kids: To Tommy, this was because his own dad had died when Tommy was just eleven. To Wally, it was because Tommy was, in his own words, the kind of son a man wanted to have.

But today, as Wally pulled his hefty frame from behind the steering wheel, Tommy noticed that his smile wasn't on him right. Usually, Wally's smile was as big as Wally himself, and as open and genuine. But there was something lacking in it now: Wally was *trying* to smile, and not doing a very good job at it.

They chatted for a while on the porch steps. Wally had heard that Tommy was fixing up the Lumpkin house, and asked how it was coming. Finally, Wally said, "You think we can go inside and talk. I got this problem."

"Sure."

Tommy got Wally a Bud out of the refrigerator and carried it to him. Wally was sitting on the sofa, and Tommy saw that Wally's eyes were fixed on the coffee table, on the copy of *The Shadowstealer* in the center of it. He reached out and pulled the book closer to him, staring down at the black shadow that trailed the boy on the cover.

Tommy, who had been holding out the Bud without getting Wally's attention, said, "Here you go."

Wally jumped a little, as if startled out of his reverie, and took it. " 'Preciate it." He snapped the top and took a deep, long drink. "Whew," he said.

"Something wrong, Wally?"

Wally stared up at the other man. Wally wasn't much for confiding in anybody, Tommy knew. What problems he had, he had always kept to himself. But right then, as Wally studied his face, Tommy knew he was about to say the kind of thing that a man like Wally normally wouldn't say to another human being. Tommy sat down.

"Yeah, there is, I reckon. I just don't know what."

"Can I help?"

"I ain't sure anybody can help." His eyes went to the book again. "I don't know if I'm goin' crazy, or if it's just—" He stopped. "It's Melinda," he said. "Something's been happening to her."

For the next ten minutes, Wally recounted what he knew. How they had found Melinda standing over the garbage disposal two weeks earlier. How she had been crying. How she said she kept hearing these voices—the voices of children being tortured, and maimed, and mutilated. How she had grabbed hold of her momma's scissors and had tried to poke her eardrum out. Luckily, Dr. Lowery said later, she didn't, though she had come close, cutting the lining of her ear canal. "He put her on sedation. They wouldn't take at first, so he kept giving her stronger and stronger doses. Finally, she quieted down." Wally paused, again his eyes wandering to the book. "He tried to bring her off of them, but it'd start up again. It's like she can't hear nothing. Not a word you say to her. Nothing except that screaming she calls it."

Tommy watched as Wally kept touching the edge of the book, moving it first to the right and then to the left, and then centering it again. "Doc Lowery, he says it could be this thing he calls—shit, I never can get it right—tintin . . . tinatinnatus. Something like that. When it ain't so bad, it's like a ringing in the ears that don't go away. But sometimes it gets a whole lot worse. And then you hear these loud-ass noises in your head, day and night, all the time, and there ain't no way to get rid of them." Wally bit his lip and glanced up awkwardly at Tommy. "Only Doc Lowery, he says he never read of a case so bad. He's called around and asked. But nobody's done heard of anything like this. 'Specially 'cause of what she thinks she's hearing. Ain't nobody knows of a case where it's little kids screaming and crying."

Wally let go of the book and stood up. He looked away from
Tommy. "Don't even know why I come by here. It was Matilda
wanted me to. She's got this crazy ass idea in her head. Shit,
she wanted me to go by and talk to Matt instead. But I told
her I was gonna talk to you about it first. 'Fore I start making
a fool of myself."

"What she want you to talk to Matt about?"

" 'Cause she thinks it's that book he wrote. She thinks that's
what done it."

Tommy's mouth hung open for a few seconds. He lifted
up his Bud, but he didn't take a drink. "Why would she be
thinking something like that for?"

And Wally told about Melinda's nightmare. "She had seen
me reading the book. I never did finish it, 'cause Matilda tore
it up and put it down the disposal. Course, Melinda didn't read
a word of it. But she seen that picture on the front. And she'd
heard about it, a course. I reckon everybody 'round here has
by now."

"Sorry, Wally, but I still don't see how a book could do
something like that. I mean, it's just a book, s'all."

"Don't you think I done told her that? But the way Melinda
talks. Even when she's on that sedation Doc Lowery gives her,
you go in there, and she'll be whispering. 'Bout something
come up behind her, and done stole her shadow from her."
Wally stopped. "And how she had to give it something to get
loose."

"Give it what?"

Wally glanced at Tommy for a second, then away. "Give it
her ears."

Tommy looked at the top of his can of Bud and took a sip.
It suddenly tasted stale.

"Shit, I don't know why I'm even telling you this. It's all so
fucking crazy," Wally said. "Anyhow, you know how Matilda
is. Once she gets an idea into that head of hers, ain't no way
to get it back out again. And she keeps on me to find out
where Matt got them ideas from. Whether, maybe, it come
from somewheres, or whether he just made it up out of his
head. I mean, she's got hold of this idea that there's something
out there, like the thing in that book," Wally said, pointing to
the cover of *The Shadowstealer*.

"I was going over there in a little bit. To Matt's. I'll talk to him about it, if you want me to."

"I don't reckon it can hurt none. 'Cept he's gonna think ol' Wally done flipped his lid. But shit, who knows, maybe I have."

Tommy stood on the tiny porch of his trailer and watched as Wally's car pulled again.

Pounding in his head were the words he and Matt had heard so long ago, up in Hester's room, on the third floor of the Lumpkin house.

I give it my eyes.
I give it my eyes.

5

The two boys, who had been riding in the back of Tommy's pickup, jumped out and ran up the porch steps.

Peter stopped cold.

There, standing in front of him, was a sight unlike any he had ever seen, or had ever expected to see. It was Simmy and she was drinking out of a champagne glass. Drinking *champagne* out of a champagne glass! Peter could tell by the bubbles.

"Whatchew doing, Simmy?"

And out it came. "The Lord's decided to make a movie outta your daddy's book, hon!"

"A movie?"

Peter stood there, dumbfounded. There had been talk about it, of course. But his daddy had always pooh-poohed it.

"For real?" Peter turned to Jimmy. "You hear that?" Then he raced into the house. Simmy was waving at Tommy as he walked up the steps.

"You drunk, Simmy?"

"Lord a-Mercy, *yes*!" she declared. Then she repeated what she had told the boys.

Tommy stared at her, his mouth hanging open. "No shit," he whispered.

"They's out on the back porch celebratin'. You go on out there and be with them. 'Cause you deserve to be, Mr. Tommy. You sure do. You been so good to him all these long years.

Just the way ol' Simmy's been." Simmy leaned over and kissed Tommy on the cheek. "You know something, Mr. Tommy. I ain't never kissed a white man before."

"Reckon that makes two of us, Simmy."

Out on the back porch, Tommy shook his head and grinned. Tigger was sitting in front of a champagne glass, a forepaw lifted over it. He stuck it in, pulled it out, then daintily licked the champagne from his fur. Cathy was in Matt's lap.

"Get a glass."

"I'll just take a Bud, if that's okay."

"Today, everything's okay."

6

Tommy and Matt were sitting out in the backyard. Inside, Cathy and Simmy were busy making dinner. It was getting to be evening, and Matt had been soberer in his life. He was reminiscing about the past, about all the hard times, about the nights he had worked in 7-Elevens, about how Tommy had always been there, encouraging him.

Matt had his arm around the other man. "But we did it, didn't we?"

And Tommy nodded. "Remember that night, the night we snuck up to Aunt Hester's room. The night you talked about putting on that skit? I was gonna be Wiley, Arlene was gonna be Hester, and you was gonna be Mr. Eprin?"

"Course."

"You said everybody in town'd want to see it, and folks would hear about it down in Atlanta, and then one day somebody out in Hollywood, he'd drive through and he'd see it. And then they'd make a movie about it.

"I remember thinking to myself, 'Matt sure is full of it tonight.' Reckon I was wrong, huh?"

"Actually, I was full of it. You were right." Matt laughed and brushed his hair back. "Christ, it's almost scary, the way it worked. Like something's been going on behind my back. You know? This person happened to know that person who happened to know this person who happened to know. You know? And, somehow, my goddam book ends up on Steven Spielberg's nightstand. Bedtime reading. Frank said he was up all night reading the fucker, called him first thing in the morning. Six o'clock. You believe that shit?"

"I believe it. I believed it when you didn't, remember?"

Matt stretched out and propped his head up in his hands. "Shit, all my life I've never been sure what's real and what isn't. I hope to fuck this is real."

"It is."

But Tommy remembered something else from that night. How he had reminded Matt of the core of the story. How the Shadowstealer could only get somebody who, somewhere or other, had heard the story of it. Matt had grinned way back then and said, "Yeah, that's the best part."

Tommy hesitated. Probably it wasn't the time or the place to bring it up, but Tommy couldn't get it off his mind. "Wally come by today."

"Ol' Wally?"

"Yeah. His girl, Melinda, she's been—" Tommy hesitated, not sure what word to use. He decided on "sick."

"What's the matter with her?"

"They ain't sure. She started having these nightmares. Wally thinks it might be on account of . . ." Tommy looked down at Matt. He had turned over and was looking up at him, genuinely concerned.

Fuck, here it is the greatest day in your best friend's life, Tommy thought to himself, and you want to say something like that.

"On account of—" Tommy shifted his glance over to the woods. "Something she ate."

"Oh?" Matt said, registering a sense of anticlimax. "Well, I hope she feels better."

"Yeah," Tommy said softly, "me, too."

7

Tigger sat impassively on the front porch and watched the commotion. Tommy was carrying out the luggage, while Matt kept saying, "Shit, I forgot something else," and would have to hurry back inside. Cathy yelled at him and asked if he had his toothbrush. Simmy ran out and handed a can of shaving cream to Cathy, who then had Tommy open a suitcase, where she put it inside.

Matt stood by the door of the car and kept saying, "I know I forgot something. I know I forgot something."

Simmy went over and hugged Matt and Cathy. She was crying. She said, "Don't you be forgetting about ol' Simmy now."

Tommy checked the things in the back of the car, then closed the trunk.

Then the car went off and Tommy and Simmy and Peter and Jimmy all waved at it until it was gone.

For the last two days, everybody had been talking about it. Mommy and Daddy were going to Hollywood.

The ones who were left kept talking about it a little longer, then Jimmy and Tommy got into the truck and they drove off.

Simmy came over to Tigger and said, "Don't you worry now, he's coming back. Real soon, too. Mr. Matt ain't gonna forget about us, nohow." Peter knelt down and scratched Tigger under his ruff, then he followed Simmy inside.

Time passed. Tigger stood up. He looked around, licked himself, then ambled down to where Jezebel was curled up, on the bottommost step. Jezebel was an orange calico who had wandered up to the house six years ago. Tommy, at the time, had wondered if there was telepathic hotline for stray cats. FLASH BULLETIN: THERE'S A REAL SUCKER WHO LIVES UP IN MT. JEPHTHA. CHECK HIM OUT. Jezebel had been named by Matt, five months after the cat's arrival—Matt always claimed that a cat's name was never, properly, a matter of arbitary convention, but had to be divined, and then after long familiarity, and, in most cases, a few six-packs of beer. The one exception to this rule had been Tigger, who had been named by Matt's ex-wife, Arlene, back before they got married. From time to time Matt vainly tried to rechristen Tigger, giving him a name more consonant with the cat's stature in the ecology of the feline household. For a whole week Matt had gone around calling him Judas Maccabees, but somehow it never caught on.

Tigger offered the top of his head to Jezebel's tongue. The calico licked it, then stopped. Tigger then buffeted Jezebel's ear with his head, and Jezebel resumed his preening of the older cat. It was standard Tigger procedure, often remarked upon by Simmy, who'd snort and say, "Look at that worthless ol' cat. He's too lazy to clean hisself. Always getting somebody else to do it." With a look at Matt she added, "Reminds me of somebody I know." Still, even with the help of a half-dozen other cats, Tigger never managed to look quite presentable. His ruff, in particular, tended to get matted up in knots, which Matt would patiently try to disentangle. In severe cases, however, there was no choice but to resort to the expedient of Alexander the Great when confronted with the Gordian knot. The result was both pathetic and ludicrous. Shorn of his magnificent mane, Tigger slouched around for weeks in despondency, his neck bare except for a narrow strip of fur along the top of his head, which gave the normally staid and sober Tigger the appearance of a feline punk rocker, complete with multicolored mohawk.

Preening time over with, Tigger set his head on Jezebel's back, where together they napped until evening. Then he got up and went into the pantry to check on the food supply. Nemesis was eating. She was the smallest cat in the house. Solid black, short-haired, lean, and mean. She glanced hostilely over her shoulder and gave Tigger a hiss of staggering ferocity. A tyrannosaurus hovering over a freshly killed prey could not have been more convincing. Tigger got the message, and ambled back out into the kitchen. It wasn't that Tigger lacked courage. He simply wasn't "confrontational." Though, more than once, Tigger had been observed by independent witnesses (i.e., anyone other than Matt) as he repulsed the territorial intrusions of mindlessly jovial neighborhood dogs, intrepidly stalking them back to the property line of the Lumpkin house.

"Whatchew doing in here?" Simmy snarled. She was cooking dinner for herself and Peter. Tigger gazed up at her attentively. She shook her spoon at him. "Mr. Matt ain't here to save you now. So you better watch out."

Tigger lifted his front paw straight up in the air, then scratched himself under his arm.

"Go on. Git."

Tigger never needed to be told twice.

He went out onto the back porch. It was dark now. He sat a moment, then went down the steps.

The moon was right above the horizon. The yard was full of its familiar shadows.

Tigger sat down on his butt and cupped his huge tail in his forepaw. He closed his eyes and blissfully licked himself where the sun seldom shone. "Don't you wish you could do that?" Matt once asked Tommy.

Tigger stopped and looked up. He was staring into the woods. He sniffed, blinked, then sniffed again, his tail still in his paw. He was about to resume his licking when he uncurled and stood upright.

Tigger—usually not the most alert-looking cat in the world— was looking alert. He went down the remaining steps and walked out into the yard. He crouched, the way he did when he was pretending to chase birds. His tail wagged rapidly back and forth.

Then he made his sprint.

He stopped, crouched again, after traveling about ten feet closer to the edge of the woods.

He watched it.

In his thirteen years of prowling the backyard, Tigger had seen many things. But what he watched now was not among them.

It wasn't a bird.

It wasn't a squirrel.

It wasn't a rabbit.

Matt and Tommy had once watched Tigger confront a garter snake. It was what Matt referred to as a classic instance of Approach/Avoidance. Over and over Tigger had stretched out his paw, consumed with the desire to touch it *just once*. But each time the snake spun around, its tail whizzing through the grass, Tigger immediately sat right back down, to stare up at

Matt for further instruction. But Matt wasn't here now. And what Tigger was watching wasn't a garter snake.

It only moved like one.

In the moonlight Tigger's eyes glinted yellow. His huge haunches, raised up in the crouch, trembled with the urge to spring.

It slithered closer, each undulation of the coils of blackness immediately registered by a darting head movement of the cat.

Tigger sprang.

It arched up, inches in front of him. Tigger let out a hiss. His ears went back, the fur stood up stiff all along his spine.

His green eyes mirrored the darkness.

8

There was a full moon.

That was probably what was doing it, Curtis Poke thought. He had seen a TV show once, where they went to an emergency room of a big city hospital and talked to the nurses, and they all agreed, they were always busier when there was a full moon. There was something about it that made people go crazy.

Maybe, Curtis reflected, that explained what was happening at the rink.

It was only a little after ten, but Jesse was already as drunk as Curtis had ever seen him. In fact, Jesse was already drunk two hours earlier, when he and his girlfriend, Tammi, had picked Curtis up at the trailer park. Curtis got into the backseat of the Cougar. Little Opal was already there. Jesse often gave her and Leroy a ride up to the rink on Fridays and Saturdays.

"Where's Leroy?" Curtis asked.

"He ain't coming," Opal told him. "He ain't left the trailer hardly the last week. Don't know what's got into him. He just sits around and watches TV now."

Jesse asked Curtis if he wanted a beer, and before Curtis could say a word, Jesse had tossed him a Bud. Tammi glared, then started in on Jesse about his drinking—she was always on him about how he shouldn't drink or smoke dope as much

as he did. Usually Jesse just shrugged it off, but not tonight. He
slammed down the brakes of the Cougar, the tires squealing.
Curtis tumbled forward and Tammi slid off the front seat.
"Listen, bitch, ain't nobody telling me what to do. You hear?"
Then he gave Tammi one of his famous scowls. Normally,
Jesse's face was as open and sunny as a summer meadow.
But when he got pissed, his nose retracted into his eyebrows,
his mouth twisted, his nostrils flared. It was a face to make
anyone think twice.

Tammi didn't say another word. She knew better. When
Jesse got like that, you just shut up and took it, if you had
any sense. Especially when he was driving. Always wild and
reckless behind the steering wheel, Jesse, when pissed off, was
terrifying: Every curve was taken at seventy, stop signs were
ignored, red lights run through. On the little gravel road leading
back up to the rink, the Cougar literally flew off the ground as
he throttled it up the last rise before spinning out in the parking
lot, narrowly missing T. J. Cummin's '76 Chevelle.

Once at the rink, Jesse got out and chugged three Buds in
a space of five minutes, staring hard at Tammi as he snapped
open each can, as if daring her to say a word about it. Tammi
tried to ignore him, pouting—which was probably the worst
thing she could have done. As he finished the third, Jesse told
Tammi to hand him another one.

"Git it yourself," she said, glancing at him angrily.

"Whatchew say?" he asked her, his eyes flashing.

"You heard me."

"I done told you, bitch, git me a fucking beer."

That's when Tammi started screaming at him, calling him
a son of a bitch.

"Don't you never call me that!" Jesse grabbed her, twisting her wrist hard. Tammi burst into tears and ran inside
the rink.

"Jesse, man," Curtis asked, "what's wrong with you?"

Jesse gave Curtis the same look he had given Tammi earlier.
He pointed his finger right up in Curtis's face and said, "Don't
you be starting, too."

And Curtis shut up.

It didn't take June Lively more than three minutes to seize
the opportunity. She had been inside when Tammi came in,
crying and carrying on. June's boyfriend, Bobby Lee Pinkham,

had gone off a little before, with two of his football player friends. They had told June they were running down to the Pac-n-Sack to buy beer, but June had heard them whispering to each other conspiratorially and had caught enough key words to know what was going on. Among them "barn" and "chicken shit." Right before they left, Bobby Lee had said, "Looks like fuckhead's here." That was just when Jesse's Cougar pulled into the parking lot. Then Bobby Lee and his two buddies piled into Bobby Lee's TransAm and drove off. It wasn't hard, even for June, to put two and two together.

Outside, June went up to Jesse. "I got something to tell you. Bobby Lee and them friends of his, they's goin' to try to git you."

"Whatchew mean, git me?"

She told him. They were going to wait until Jesse was drunk as a dog. Then Joe and Andy, Bobby Lee's pals, were going to hold Jesse down—they were both bigger than he was, by about fifty pounds apiece. Bobby Lee would proceed to perch on top of Jesse's chest, a bagful of fresh chicken shit in his hand—they were planning to get it from Jesse's granny's barn, as a way of adding insult to injury. Dribble by dribble, Bobby Lee was going to empty the contents of the bag, while Joe and Andy pried open Jesse's mouth. Bobby Lee had said he'd only stop when Jesse begged him to, and then he'd have to yell out, at the top of his lungs, right there in front of everybody, "I'm a faggot. I'm a cocksucking faggot." This last twist, June told Jesse in a stage whisper, was because of how Jesse was always going off with Curtis Poke, a well-known homo, allegedly to do all kinds of gayfering things. "Course I know it ain't true about you," June added, with an emphasis on the last word. "But everybody knows 'bout Curtis."

Jesse snorted contemptuously. "I ain't worried 'bout 'em. They can all go fuck theirselves." And then he chugged another beer.

"I just don't want nobody hurting you, Jesse. You always been real sweet to me," June said. "Why don't you and me go off somewheres, 'fore all them goobers get back? You and me, we could have us a real good time. Whatchew think?" June was rubbing up against him.

Jesse got a funny look in his eyes. He was staring into the woods behind the parking lot. June wasn't even sure that Jesse had been listening to her. "I was goin' do something tonight," he said, his voice strangely solemn.

"Do what?"

"I always wanted to do something ain't nobody ever done before. Something people'd be talking about for years."

"Like what?"

"Something," Jesse whispered, then staggered over to the driver's side of the Cougar. "Get in."

"Where we going to?"

"You'll see."

"Jesse, man, you know you shouldn't be driving," Curtis said. "What if Wally catches you? Way you been drinking tonight?"

"Fuck ol' Wally." Jesse collapsed behind the steering wheel. June went around to the passenger side. Curtis hadn't moved. "You coming or ain't you?" Jesse said to Curtis.

Curtis hesitated, then said, "I reckon." He went around to where June was standing, opened the door, lifted up the front seat, and crawled into the back.

"Whatchew want him coming along for?" June asked. But before she could repeat her question, Opal came running after them.

"Where you all goin' to? I wanna come."

"You stay here," Curtis said.

"Naw, man, she can come if she wants," Jesse said. "Get on in."

Opal got in, much to June's dismay, and Jesse gunned the Cougar and did a donut in the middle of the parking lot, coming within inches of hitting Tod Oakley's new Toyota pickup. June slid across the front seat like her butt was fastened to a pair of roller skates.

"I thought you was going with Bobby Lee," Opal said as she stuck her head between the two front seats, addressing June.

"Just 'cause I come up to the rink with him, it don't mean he owns me or nothing."

"You think Bobby Lee's going to be pissed?" Jesse asked, looking into the rearview mirror at Curtis. "Say!"

"He's got him some big friends, Jesse," Opal said. "They's football players."

"Sheeet, I ain't scared of no fucking football players. They's all fags anyways, if you ask me. Ain't that right, Curtis?"

Curtis didn't answer him.

"Say, Curtis! Ain't they all fags?" Jesse looked in the rearview mirror at Curtis. Curtis was staring out the window. "I done asked you a question, Curtis. You gonna answer it?"

This time, when Curtis still didn't answer, Jesse glared at him. "What you showing your ass for, Curtis, anyhow?"

"I ain't the one showing my ass."

"What the fuck you mean by that?"

"Nothing. I don't mean nothing."

Jesse put his arm around June, who quickly cuddled up next to him. "I know me a secret," Jesse said, his eyes, via the rearview mirror, fixed intently, gloweringly, on Curtis's.

"What's it 'bout?" June asked. "I just looove secrets."

"It's about ol' Curtis back there. Something he does, ain't nobody supposed to know. Something I caught him doing once."

Staggered by Jesse's words, Curtis looked at the mirror. His stomach felt as if a can of Drāno had just been emptied into it. His throat went dry. Tears of pain welled up in his eyes. He turned away and tried to stare out the window, to keep from looking at the reflection of Jesse's face. Don't let him do it, he prayed. Let the car fucking wreck first. Anything.

"Oooooo," June squealed. She cast Curtis a malicious, mascaraed glance over her shoulder. "I bet I know what it is." She snuggled closer to Jesse. "You tell me if I'm right." June leaned and whispered something in Jesse's ear.

"What's she saying?" Opal asked.

But Curtis couldn't say a word. The Drāno was going crazy in the pit of his stomach. He rolled the window down, ready to throw up.

"Naw," Jesse said, "that ain't it. Guess again."

Once more, June tittered and eyed Curtis, then put her lips to Jesse's ear. He laughed. "Naw. Naw. You ain't even close."

"Jesse, man!" Curtis said. "Stop the car."

"What's your fucking problem?" Jesse snarled.

"I think I'm gonna be sick."

"You ain't had enough to drink to be sick."

"Come on, tell me what it is," June pestered. "I done guessed twice."

"Fucking let me out, Jesse."

At that moment the car slammed to a screeching halt. Smoke from the burnt rubber poured from behind the car. Curtis was knocked forward into the back of Jesse's seat. Opal collapsed against her elbows. June fell onto the floorboard.

"What'd you say, Curtis?" Jesse was already turned around and leaning at Curtis over the back of the seat. He grabbed the boy by the collar and shook him. "What'd you say?"

Curtis looked up at him. There were tears in his eyes. "Just let me out, s'all."

Jesse's crazy face stayed on a few seconds longer. He looked at Curtis's eyes. "Tell 'em, what I caught you doing, Curtis."

"I don't know what you're fucking talking about, man."

"Tell 'em."

"No."

"Come on, Jesse, tell me. I wanta know." June was squealing. "I'm gonna tell everybody."

"Whatchew doing this to me for?" Curtis said, fighting back tears.

"You know." Jesse said. And all at once, his crazy face disappeared. His eyes were looking into Curtis's the same way they had looked that night out in the hay barn.

"You tell me right now," June was saying, a pout starting up around her mouth. "You don't tell me right now. I'm getting out and goin' back to the rink."

Jesse's eyes hadn't moved. "I caught ol' Curtis here in his room," Jesse said. "And you know what he was doing?"

"What? Tell me. Hurry up." June was jumping up and down in her seat.

"He was reading a book."

June's face wrinkled up in disappointment. "Is that all?" she exclaimed. "Why, everybody knows Curtis reads books. How you think they know he's a gayfer?"

"He ain't no gayfer," Jesse said. He turned to June, his face full of threatening signs, none of which June seemed to pick up on.

"Why, just ask anybody 'round. Everybody knows he is, Jesse."

"I done told you, he ain't. So stop running your mouth about it."

"You ain't telling me to stop running my mouth. I don't know why you hang 'round him in the first place. Everybody knows—"

"I done warned you once."

"Whatchew want to be with him for, anyhow?"

" 'Cause he ain't no fucking redneck, way I am. 'Cause he's got brains in his head. Which is more than you got."

"I got enough brains to know gayfers when I see 'em," June said, in full pout. "You jus' go on and take me on back to the rink. I ain't driving 'round with no fucking gayfers."

There was a passage of time—not a very long one—during which June was unaware that she had said the wrong thing. "You fucking slut puppy," Jesse hissed.

"What you—"

But before June could get her words out, Jesse had flung open the car door, jumped from the Cougar, went around to the passenger side, pulled the door open, and reached inside.

"What's he doing now?" Opal said.

Jesse grabbed hold of June's arm. She let loose a shriek. "Let go a me!"

"Get the fuck out."

"I ain't."

"Oh, yes you are." He tugged her harder and June fell from the car seat onto her ass. She bounced to her feet, yelling, and slapped Jesse on the face. He looked at her, then hauled away and knocked June onto the shoulder of the road. Dazed, she groped back onto all fours, then began to scream. "You sombitch! You sombitch!"

"All you fucking bitches are the same," Jesse said.

"Bobby Lee, he's going to kill you. I'm going to tell what you done, and him and them friends of his, they's going to kill you," she howled as the blood began to ooze from her nose.

Jesse walked back to the other side of the car and got in. "Get up here in front with me, Curtis." Curtis didn't move for a moment. Jesse looked at him through the rearview mirror. "You shoulda knowed I wasn't goin' say nothing."

Curtis had never heard Jesse's voice sound as it did at that moment. There was a sadness in it that nobody, not even Curtis, could have imagined being there. "I done lied to you, Curtis. I wasn't thinking of Tammi that time we was in the hay barn. I wasn't thinking of her atall. I was thinking about you, Curtis," he said softly. "Maybe them things ain't right, like you say. But that don't give you leave to treat me like no dog. You hear?"

"I hear," Curtis whispered. And again, but for a different reason, Curtis could not keep looking into Jesse's eyes. At that moment, they had to be the saddest eyes in the whole world.

"Least we can be friends," Jesse said. "Now get up front."

And Curtis did.

Opal leaned over, baffled by the boys' train of conversation. "Whatchew two talking about?"

Neither of the two boys answered. On the shoulder of the road, June was still hollering. "Wait till I tell Bobby Lee what you done to me! He's goin' to *keeeeell* you. Both you two. You ain't nothing but a pair of faggots, s'all."

"She sure does yell a lot, don't she?" Opal said, unperturbed by the whole incident. She had seen worse back at the trailer. "Where we goin' to now, Jesse?"

Ten minutes later, Jesse pulled his car up in front of what used to be the JCPenney's, but which was now a Wal-Mart.

"What we stopping here for?" Opal said.

Jesse opened the car door and staggered out. Curtis stared at him, then jumped from the Cougar and ran as fast as he could to where Jesse was. Opal followed. "What's he doing, Curtis?"

"I ain't sure," Curtis said, though, in the pit of his stomach, he knew otherwise.

The three of them walked through the alley between the Wal-Mart and the hardware store until they came to the end of the overgrown sidewalk that had once led to the swinging bridge. Ten years earlier, a storm had demolished the bridge itself, leaving only the cable wires. Gleaming in the moonlight, they made a graceful downward curve to the middle of the ravine, then rose up to the far side. Curtis's eyes followed them from one side to the other. It had never seemed so far away as it did at that moment.

"I always wanted to do what nobody else's ever done," Jesse whispered. "Always wanted to do something special."

"Jesse, you ain't going to make it. You're too fucking drunk."

"If I don't make it, you get the Cougar."

"I'll call Wally. I mean it."

Jesse easily pushed Curtis off him. "What's ol' Wally going to do, come out there and bring me back?" He began toward the point at which the cable could be reached by hand, down toward the ravine about ten feet from the sidewalk. Jesse stood on tiptoe, but couldn't quite get to it.

"He's crazy," Opal said. "You think he can do it?"

Curtis shook his head. "Ain't no way."

"He'll kill hisself."

"Fuck!" Jesse squatted down and jumped up at the cable. He grasped it for a second, then lost his hold. He fell and tumbled about six feet down toward the edge of the ravine. Opal screamed, but Jesse stopped before rolling over the edge. "Shit, that was close."

"Come on back, Jesse. Please. We gotta talk."

"Ain't nothing to talk about, Curtis," Jesse yelled as he climbed back up to the point at which he had made momentary contact with the cable. Again he jumped up. One hand fastened on to the cable, he lifted himself up from the ground. Both hands were on it now. Jesse swung himself back and forth and made crazy "Wheeeee!" sounds.

"Catch y'all later!"

Curtis and Opal stood there, their mouths open, and watched as Jesse began, inch by inch, hand over hand, to crawl slowly out from the edge of the ravine. He stopped after going fifteen feet and looked down. At that point there was nothing to stop his fall. Nothing except the riverbed, fifty or more feet below him.

"He's crazy," Opal said. "He ain't even doing it for no money. He's just plum crazy, ain't he?"

"Yeah," Curtis said, his eyes fixed on the figure of the dangling boy.

9

Jesse was hovering smack dab over the middle of the ravine.

Opal said, "Looks like he's going to make it. Whatchew think?"

"I don't know," Curtis whispered.

Jesse was hooping and hollering. "Shit, I'm near halfway there," he shouted back to Curtis and Opal. Confident of his triumph, Jesse began to swing back and forth. He gave out a few Tarzan yells.

"What's that?" Opal turned around. "You hear it?" Curtis had. It was the screech of tires, coming from where Jesse had left the Cougar. Curtis listened to the engine—it was the sound of what Curtis would have admiringly called a "bad engine" if he hadn't recognized whose it was.

"Who is it, Curtis? You know?"

He nodded. It was Bobby Lee Pinkham's '72 Trans Am. "Shit."

"What's he want?" Opal asked.

There wasn't much doubt about that part. Curtis stared up at the path that led from around the side of the Wal-Mart. He could hear the voices. Bobby Lee had clearly not come alone.

"I'm going to kill that fucker."

"I done told him what you was doing to do." This was June talking: She was doing her best to keep up her hysterics. "But he kept saying how he wasn't afraid of you. He says you's a faggot, Bobby Lee. He call all y'all faggots."

"He's the fucking faggot," Andy Long said. He weighed two hundred forty pounds. He had broken the knee of a fifteen-year-old kid playing football the year before, and had gone around bragging about it. With him was Joe Dodd, even bigger and at least as mean. Joe and Andy were carrying cans of Bud and, like Bobby Lee, were drunk. Crazy drunk.

But that wasn't all they were carrying. Bobby Lee was holding it, a brown paper sack, its bottom soaked through.

"I don't see him. All I see is them two down yonder," Andy said. "That little faggot friend he's got."

Curtis glanced back apprehensively at Jesse. Go, go, he whispered to himself. He knew that there was no way out for himself: Bobby Lee would be on him in a heartbeat if he tried to make a run for it back up the side of the Wal-Mart.

There was only one way of escaping from them and from their chicken shit. And that was to follow Jesse.

"Where the fuck he go to?"

That was when Bobby Lee saw Jesse. "Shut up, y'all. Look."

"Shit, man, that's one crazy fucker," Joe Dodd said, grinning, a grudging trace of admiration in his voice.

Jesse had not yet noticed the arrival of Bobby Lee and his pals. He was still whooping it up. "This here's fun," he exclaimed. "You ought to try it, Curtis. Don't be a pussy now. Come on."

Curtis had stepped as close to the edge of the ravine as was possible without falling in. He glanced back at Jesse, all the while waiting for Bobby Lee and his pals to make their move.

"Well, looky there. If it ain't ol' Curtis," Andy Long said, coming down to him and grabbing hold of his shoulder.

Curtis tried to pull away, but the football player's grip was too strong. "Let go of me, fuckhead," Curtis said.

But Andy grinned. "What you think we should do with this one?" he asked Bobby Lee. "You think we got enough of that chicken shit for 'em both?"

Andy peered inside the bag and wrinkled up his nose into a scowl of disgust. "Don't that smell good?"

Billy Lee snatched the bag. "We got enough."

"You gonna make Curtis eat some, too?" June asked. She was smiling now.

"What're we gonna do about fuckhead out there?" Andy said, meaning Jesse.

"Watch me," Bobby Lee said. He went over and he found a rock about the size of a golf ball. He held it in his hand a moment, staring out at Jesse. He hissed, "Fuck with my June, see what happens," then he threw the rock out into the ravine. Curtis watched as it whizzed past Jesse, missing him by not more than a few feet.

"What the fuck was that?" Jesse called back. That was when he noticed the others. "Curtis, who's that with you?"

"Move your ass, Jesse!" Curtis screamed.

Andy twisted the younger boy's arm, then shouted, "We got your little fuck buddy. And you ain't believing what we're going to do to him."

Curtis jerked his arm loose from Andy's grip, turned, and delivered a swift, surprisingly effective punch to the football player's rock-hard beer gut. "You son of a bitch," Andy hissed. Curtis scrambled down to the point where earlier Jesse had jumped up and taken hold of the cable.

"Come on, Curtis!" Jesse yelled.

Curtis stood there, staring up at the gleaming cable, then looking down at the ravine.

Behind him, higher up on the embankment, Bobby Lee and the others waited to see what Curtis was going to do. "That little fucker ain't got the guts."

"Jump up and grab holta it!" Jesse shouted. "You can do it, Curtis."

His eyes on the hidden depths of the ravine, Curtis stood as if paralyzed. "I can't."

"Yes, you can, Curtis. You and me, we can cross over yonder. We can leave all them goofy ass motherfuckers behind."

Curtis shook his head. "I ain't got the guts to."

"Yes, you do. I know you do. Come on, Curtis," Jesse implored him. "What we got to lose, you and me? You want to eat chicken shit all your fucking life? Or you want to come with me?"

Hearing Jesse's word, Curtis suddenly understood: It was no longer a matter of getting away from Bobby Lee and Andy Long and Joe Dodd and June Lively. The wire cable, gleaming in the moonlight, was all at once transformed into something else. And what was required to cross over was not simply physical courage and agility.

"Fuck, Curtis! All them over yonder, they ain't nothing! Them words in your head, they ain't nothing, neither! Just words, Curtis. All that matters is you and me. S'long as it's just you and me, it don't make no difference what all them assholes think."

"You hear what they's saying?" June tittered. "I done told you they was a pair of fags."

Curtis raised his right hand toward the gleaming cable wire.

"You gotta jump to catch it," Jesse yelled.

And Curtis said, "I want to." There were tears in his eyes now.

"Then fucking do it!"

Curtis's arm dropped. "I can't, Jesse."

"*Motherfucker!*" Jesse hollered. "What do I got to say, Curtis? I don't care no more. I don't care about nothing no more. 'Cept you and me. Don't care what no assholes call me. If I got to, I'll say it. Say it right out loud."

A chill went up Curtis's spine. "Don't."

"What's he goin' to say?" June tittered.

His voice desperate and exhausted, his throat hoarse from yelling, Jesse called out through the darkness. "There ain't nothing in this world I ever done loved, 'cept you. There ain't no point in living, ain't no point in doing nothing, 'less I can say it out loud."

The words echoed down the ravine. Openmouthed, scandalized, June turned to Bobby Lee. "You hear what he said?"

Bobby Lee snickered. "Sounds like ol' Jesse's a homo, don't it?"

And Joe and Andy snickered, too.

Jesse's words curled in Curtis's guts. He shook his head in horrified disbelief and stepped back away from the point closest to the cable wire, stepped back up the embankment toward where the others were waiting for him. "He's just drunk, s'all," Curtis said. "S'all it is. He don't know what he's saying." He turned to the others, and repeated his feeble words of explanation.

"So you two are fuck buddies." Andy Long grinned.

Curtis shook his head no. But before he could get another word out, he was pinned to the ground. Joe was sitting on one arm, Andy was crouched on the other. He pressed his knee down hard and Curtis let out a scream.

Bobby Lee was sitting on top of him.

That was when Jesse started back.

Curtis twisted his head and watched the boy as he came scrambling back toward them. He was screaming bloody murder. "You touch him, I'll kill you."

"That's right, open your mouth like a good little faggot." He grinned up at Andy. "Do it again."

The brown paper sack, laden with chicken shit, was right over his face. Curtis could smell it. Andy ground his knee into Curtis's arm. Curtis gritted his teeth, trying not to open his mouth.

"Come on, open wide."

"Maybe if you was to stick your dick in it, he'd open it," June said.

"I'll get his mouth open," Joe Dodd said. Without getting up from Curtis's arm, he reached down and put one hand on his nose and the other on his lower jaw. He began to wrench them apart.

"Say 'Ahhhhh.' " Bobby Lee chuckled, and tilting the paper sack, the first few gluey strands of chicken shit began to drip from the bag. It dribbled around Curtis's chin and lips, then, as Bobby Lee moved it upward, into his forcibly opened mouth. At the first taste of it, Curtis began to gag.

"I think ol' Curtis likes it."

Curtis tried to spit it out, but Bobby Lee put the sack right against his mouth and was letting it ooze in.

Jesse was yelling. "You better fucking let him up! I mean it. You fucking hurt him, I'm goin' kill you."

"Don't use it all up," Andy cautioned. "We gotta save some for Jesse."

Bobby Lee looked inside the bag. "Awww, looks like we didn't bring enough to go around. Ain't that right?" He got up off of Curtis and said to the other two boys. "Might as well let him be. I think he's done had his fill already."

Curtis rolled over onto his face, gagged, then threw up. He lifted his face from the dirt, his mouth smeared with vomit and chicken shit. Through his tears he saw Jesse scooting closer and closer.

"Go on back!" Curtis managed to yell out at him, but Jesse had that wildass look on his face—Curtis could see it in the moonlight—as he came back toward them, slipping one hand quickly over the other hand, writhing from side to side. Bobby Lee grabbed up another rock and threw it at him. June found another one and gave it to him.

Curtis struggled to get up on all fours as he watched one of the rocks—it was the size of a baseball—hit Jesse in the chest. Jesse's left arm lost its grip and the boy was flung sideways.

"Jesus," Curtis gasped, but Jesse still held on.

June was yelling out to Jesse, with sickening self-satisfaction. "I done told you, you homo. I told you Bobby Lee was going to git you. I done told you."

"Let the faggot come on back," Joe Dodd said. Curtis, who was trying to get to his feet, looked up at Joe and saw genuine fear in his face. Curtis thought it was a good sign.

It wasn't.

"What you stopping for, Bobby Lee? You know what he done to me."

"You fucking slut," Curtis yelled at her.

"They's going to get you, too, you little queer," June hissed. She found Bobby Lee two more rocks. She handed them to him. "Hit him again," June said, her eyes flashing. "Go on. You know he can't hold on much longer, Bobby Lee. Go on and do it."

But Bobby Lee just stood there, looking at the helpless boy. He shook his head. "Let him come back."

Jesse repeatedly tried to grasp on to the cable with the hand that had come loose. He was hissing and screaming, his threats and insults now aimed at June.

"You hearing what he's calling me?"

"He's calling you a slut," Opal said. It was the first word out of her.

"Who you calling a slut?" June said. "Your momma's the biggest slut in North Georgia."

"Don't you call my momma a slut," Opal said.

But June ignored the younger girl. Her eyes fixed on Bobby Lee, she said, "What you waiting for?"

"I done told you. I'm going to let him come on back. If he can."

"What for?" June said. "You done heard what he's saying about me. You gonna let him call me them things?"

"She went off with Jesse tonight. I seen her," Opal said. "Curtis did, too. We seen how she was all over Jesse's ass. Kissing and hugging on him. Doing whatall up in that front seat. Putting her hands right there on his pecker."

"She's lying," June exclaimed. "He done made me go off with him. He said he was going to hurt you if I didn't. Hurt you real bad. I swear. I swear to God. I just didn't want him a-hurting you, Bobby Lee."

"Don't believe her. She's lying," Opal said. "Ain't that right, Curtis?"

"Shut up, you little bitch!"

Bobby Lee was staring right into June's heavily made-up eyes.

June said, "You ain't gonna believe her against me?"

When Bobby Lee said nothing, June exploded. "You all a bunch of faggots, you know that." She took one of the rocks and threw it as hard as she could at Jesse—he was just at the point of getting a grip on the cable with his flailing hand. It hit him in the stomach. His hand missed the cable. He twisted around, nearly halfway. In his face Curtis saw the struggle, the pain of trying to keep the one remaining hand clutched to the cable.

"Cut it out," Joe Dodd yelled at June. "You hear?"

"You ain't telling me what to do." She was clutching the other rock.

Jesse's face was wrenched with exhaustion and strain. Curtis watched as again he reached up, his loose hand struggling to clasp the cable. He groaned and hissed, then, somehow, he caught hold of the cable. He steadied himself. His head was down.

"He ain't moving."

"He's trying to catch his breath."

Curtis could see Jesse's face. Something peculiar was going on. Jesse was no longer yelling or screaming—though that was probably due to exhaustion. But there was a look in his face that Curtis had never seen in it.

Jesse looked scared.

But even that wasn't what Curtis noticed most. Somehow, he knew that the scaredness had nothing to do with what was happening on the side of the ravine. The scaredness was coming from something down beneath him. Something he was staring at.

"What the fuck is that?" Jesse gasped. "You see that down yonder."

"What's he talking about?" Opal asked.

Jesse's face was fixed on something that must have been hovering below him down in the darkness of the ravine.

"Shit," the boy gasped. And then, as the others watched, Jesse began to climb hand over hand, not toward them, but toward the opposite side of the ravine.

"Whatchew doing?"

"He's getting away," June said. "Look, you're letting him get away."

Jesse stopped and began to thrash his legs wildly, as if kicking something away from his feet, while at the same time, he was frantically trying to climb up on top of the cable. "Get the fuck off me!" he was screaming.

Then all at once Jesse's legs stopped moving. They dropped straight, as if a boulder had suddenly been attached to each of his feet. Even the cable wire sagged.

"Jesse!" Curtis shrieked.

At that moment June hurled her last rock out into the ravine. It disappeared in the darkness. No one, standing on the edge of the ravine, was sure whether it had hit Jesse or not. But something happened. Jesse let out a howl.

There was not another sound as he slipped from the cable and dropped into the darkness below him.

Both Andy and Joe let loose of Curtis at the same moment. "Goddam," Joe whispered.

Curtis stood there a moment. They waited to hear the thud of the body against the rocks below, but there was nothing. Not a sound. Not the echo of a sound.

"You fucking killed him, you stupid bitch," Andy Long said.

"He ain't dead," Curtis whispered. "I know he ain't. He can't be." He walked to the edge of the ravine and looked down into the darkness. But there was no sign of the boy's body.

"I'm getting out of here," Joe Dodd said. "Come on, Bobby Lee. We got to get out of here." Joe took hold of Bobby Lee's arm.

June looked at Bobby Lee. "You heard them things he was saying about me, didn't you? Didn't you? I had to. You heard them things."

"You fucking cunt," Joe Dodd hissed.

"You heard him, Bobby Lee. You heard what he's saying to me."

"I heard him," Bobby Lee said. He was swaying, both drunk and stunned.

"Come on. Let's git."

Joe Dodd took hold of Bobby Lee's arm and pulled him up the path.

"What 'bout me?" June said.

"Leave her, Bobby Lee."

And Bobby Lee nodded. He and his two friends walked back up the path toward the Trans Am.

"What you doing?" June screamed.

"We're leaving your ass," Joe Dodd told her.

"You can't," she screamed. "Bobby Lee, he started throwing at him first. I ain't taking the blame for it. I ain't taking the blame."

But the three boys were already gone.

June looked around at Opal and Curtis. "You seen him. He started throwing first. Bobby Lee did." June glanced back at the ravine, then ran up toward the sound of the Trans Am's engines revving up. She was yelling at Bobby Lee not to leave her.

Opal had come up to the edge of the ravine. She was standing next to Curtis. "I seen it," she whispered. "I seen it grab holta him."

Curtis looked at the girl. "Whatchew mean?"

"You couldn't hardly see it, it was so black. It come at him. From down there."

"What're you talking 'bout?"

Opal shook her head uncertainly. "I ain't never seen nothing like it. It was blacker, blacker than anything I ever did see in my whole life. And there was something else I seen." She looked up at Curtis. "This twinkling. Kinda like an eyeball peeking out. Peeking out of nothing."

10

Peter was in bed.

There had been a good bit of protestation—after all, Matt and Cathy let the boy stay up till ten—but Simmy had prevailed. "Simmy's done raised more little insignificant white boys than both them two put together," she said, clasping her hands over her ears to indicate that she was deaf to any further pleas. She was about to close the door to the boy's room when he jumped back out of bed.

"Where you going to?" Simmy demanded.

"I'm gonna get Tigger."

"Tigger? Whatchew want him for?"

"To sleep with me."

"Whatchew want to be sleeping with that worthless ol' cat for?"

Peter didn't bother to respond to this. After all, he had only been sleeping with Tigger for the last four years, during which period Simmy had been asking the same question. Sometimes—when Matt wasn't there—Simmy actually tried to put the cat out for the night, along with the rest of the menagerie, using subtle devices like setting a saucer of cream on the back porch. Simmy adhered to the school of thought that credited cats with the power to suck the breath out of babies—and, in her eyes, every night Peter slept with Tigger, he was running the risk of feline suffocation. Peter tried to argue with her—not about the basic premise, which he realized was hopeless—but about the minor one: "I'm not a baby anymore. Don't you think I'm big enough to push him off me if he was trying to suck my breath out?" But Simmy was undeterred: Her belief in Peter's fragility was one of the underlying motives of her behavior.

The safety matches, which she had to use four or five times a day to light the oven, were kept hidden at the top shelf of the pantry. To retrieve them, Simmy had to mount a stepladder, at considerable risk to health and hip. Anytime Tommy or Matt left a book of regular matches around the house, they had hell to pay. "What if Peter was to get holta them?" she scolded, briskly confiscating the alleged items of danger. In her mind, Peter was as fully flammable as the Hindenburg, ready to blow up at the slightest spark.

"I done told Mr. Matt," Simmy went on, "one morning I'm going to come in here and find you with that big ol' worthless cat a-sitting on your face, the breath clean sucked out of your lungs."

"He sleeps between my legs, Simmy."

"I don't know 'bout that. Wouldn't want nothing sleeping between my legs."

"Can I just go down and get him? Please?"

"I reckon, but you be fast."

And Peter hurried down the steps.

On the back porch, Peter stood and stared at the dark corners of the yard. He had been calling for Tigger, but so far Tigger hadn't appeared. Which wasn't like him. Usually, when it was Peter's bedtime, Tigger would come racing up the back steps at the first call, sometimes getting to the top of the stairs before Peter did, so that by the time the boy got to his room, Tigger would be waiting for him at the foot of the bed.

Simmy came to the screen door that led from the kitchen.

"He ain't come yet?" she asked.

"Uh-uh."

"Wonder why that is?"

"Dunno."

"I expect he's out in them woods, prowling."

"It's not like him. He likes to sleep with me."

"What's that over yonder?"

"I thought that was him, too. But it's not moving."

"Looks like something," Simmy said, craning her neck to get a better glimpse of the dark patch in the far corner of the yard.

"It'd've come if it was Tigger."

"I reckon." She put her hands on Peter's back. "Why don't you get you one of them other cats to sleep withchew?"

"They're not as good as Tigger."

"Maybe so," Simmy conceded. "Well, you go on to bed now and I'll keep calling for him."

"But I can't sleep without him."

"I ain't never heard such a thing. Can't sleep without some ol' cat."

"He ain't some ol' cat. He's Tigger," Peter said. "What if something's happened to him?"

"What's gonna happen to that cat now? He gonna live to be old as Simmy."

"Yeah," Peter mumbled. Her hands on his back, Simmy turned him around. "You gonna keep calling for him?"

"I done told you I would."

"Okay," Peter said reluctantly. He was about to go out to the kitchen when he stopped. "Leave the screen door open for him."

"I will. Now you go on up to bed."

11

It was after eleven. Tommy Buford had been watching TV in the living room of his trailer. He had just finished the last sip of his Budweiser and was about to go to bed when he heard his son's voice calling out to him from the boy's bedroom.

Tommy stuck his head in the door. "What you doing awake?"

"I can't sleep."

Tommy frowned, then took a sip from his can of Budweiser. "Something the matter?"

"Uh-uh."

"You sure?"

Jimmy hesitated, then said, "Maybe if you did Toodles."

"You're too old for that."

"No, I'm not."

Tommy looked into the boy's eyes. Inside, there was one of those rapid shifts of emotion he felt so frequently with Jimmy. At first, a voice, shockingly harsh and callous, that whispered, "If he was really yours, he wouldn't be afraid of the dark." But the moments the words came to him, Tommy felt like his guts were being wrenched out of him, felt a pity and a guilt that swept away everything else. He walked over and sat down on the bed next to him. "Okay," he said softly. "I'll do Toodles."

Tommy pulled his son's pajama tops up to his shoulders. "Toodles" was by now a family tradition. Tommy's daddy had played it on his back until Tommy was nine, and no telling how much longer it might have gone on if Tommy's daddy hadn't been killed—he had been crushed to death when a semi jackknifed and rolled over on top of his Chevy pickup. To any outsider Tommy's daddy seemed the epitome of tough redneck macho. He certainly had all the credentials: a construction worker, an ex-Marine, he drank hard, displayed an immense potbelly, went deer hunting every weekend, sported enormous suntanned arms with tattoos from his shoulder down to his wrists. But, tempered in with this, Tommy's daddy had that peculiarly backwoods tenderness for his male offspring, calling both Tommy and his brother variously "sweetheart," "honey," and sometimes even "darling," right in front of other people, and all without a trace of self-consciousness. He would set them down in his lap, especially when he was drinking, and ask for "sugar," then proceed to hug and kiss their necks until, giggling uncontrollably, they would break away. Toodles was part of this cult of paternal affection.

It began one night when Tommy had gone into his parents' bedroom and tugged on his snoring daddy's undershirt. "I had me a bad dream," he told him.

His daddy tucked him in next to him—Tommy's mother slept through the whole incident—and said to his son, "You

ever hear the story 'bout Toodles?" Tommy said no, and
his daddy rolled him over. Toodles, he told his son, was
the name of a wayward young train. All the other young
trains managed to stay on the tracks. But not Toodles. While
the other trains run up and down the main line—represented
by Tommy's spine—Toodles, try as hard as he might, just
couldn't keep himself to the straight and narrow. One morning
he went out and he saw a beautiful field full of buttercups—
Tommy's daddy described how the sunlight shone off of them,
how they glistened with the morning dew. Toodles tried to
control himself, but he just couldn't. He looked around, to
make sure no other trains were looking, then darted off the
tracks down to where the buttercups were—the buttercups that
always grew about four inches below Tommy's shoulder blade.
There Toodles whiled away the whole morning long, sniffing
and admiring the buttercups. Of course, a grown-up train came
along and upbraided him. The first rule of being a train, he
sternly pointed out, is *never ever go off the tracks.* And so the
story went on, with truant Toodles roaming through field and
meadow, brook and pond, always determined to do right, but
always ending up going wrong. Though, as Tommy listened to
his daddy's soothing words, and felt his strong hand caressing
his back, it was difficult for him not to believe that Toodles
had a point. Sometimes the buttercups were worth it.

Jimmy made it only a little ways beyond the buttercups,
then drifted into sleep. But Tommy still didn't get up. He
lay there and continued to weave the errant path of Toodles
for a few minutes more, listening to the deep, reassuring
sleep sounds his son made. He looked down at his son's
quiet face and frowned. Had Jimmy been awakened by a
bad dream? Probably. It was strange, Tommy thought, how
sometimes he would know that his son had had a nightmare,
and yet never once had he asked him what the nightmare was about. Just as his own daddy hadn't asked him about
his nightmares. Were all fathers like that? Better to soothe
the nightmare away, to pretend it wasn't there, than to face
up to it.

Tommy smoothed Jimmy's hair. Did something similar lurk
behind his own son's peaceful brow? What did we really know
of anyone else, Tommy caught himself thinking, until we know
their nightmares.

• • •

He got up and closed the door to his son's room behind him.

Back in the living room, he picked up his copy of Matt's book. Earlier in the day, before Matt left, Tommy kept trying to work up the courage to tell him about the conversation he had had with Wally the day before. He kept putting it off, until, at last, Matt and Cathy had driven out of the driveway, on their way to Hartfield Airport in Atlanta. And from there, out to California.

Tommy sighed.

Of course, it was crazy thinking that way. Whatever was wrong with Melinda, it had nothing to do with Matt's book. How could it?

Besides, even if he had told Matt about the girl, what difference would it make? There was going to be a movie of *The Shadowstealer*, just as Matt had prophesized so many years before. And not some little low-budget thing, like the *The Attack of the Giant Crabs*. No, it was going to be a major studio release, opening across the country, to be seen by millions

and millions

and millions . . .

In time, everybody would know the story that Aunt Hester whispered into the windowpane, convinced that when she died, the story would die with her.

It hadn't.

And the chances were now, it never would.

12

For the fifth time in the last half hour—it was already after twelve—Simmy stood on the uppermost step leading down from the back porch. Muttering imprecations on Tigger's head, she surveyed the dark corners of the yard.

She had already reached the stage of bargaining. First came the offers of food, favorite food like fried chicken. Then came conciliatory gestures, like telling Tigger she would never again threaten to fry him in her frying pan. And this last time Simmy had totally capitulated: "You come back right now, when you finish eating that chicken I done fried up, you and me, we gonna sit down and have us a long talk."

But it was in vain.

There was still no Tigger.

In the kitchen, Simmy resumed her work. Knowing full well that she couldn't sleep until Tigger was back safe, she had decided to begin making a heap of her famous preserves. An enormous stewing pot simmered and steamed on top of the oven, filling the house with its pungent scent of peaches. She removed the lid and stirred with her big spoon. As she stared down at the seething chunks of fruit, she recollected, with a tinge of conscience, how often she had threatened to make talking cat preserves.

She replaced the lid and went to the pantry, to check on her supply of mason jars. "Hmmm," she murmured, counting only three.

The rest were down in the basement, on a high shelf that Simmy had to use a box to reach up to. They were all ancient, coming directly from old Leon's mason jar factory, and Simmy was immensely proud of the fact that in the course of sixty years, she had broken only one of them.

Simmy turned and stared at the basement door. It was cracked, about four inches. That was peculiar. Normally she saw to it that the basement door was shut. This was to keep the cats out: "I ain't having my basement full of no cat poop," she'd declare. She pulled it open and stared into the dark.

Simmy didn't like going down the stairs. Not that she was afraid something would get her—that would have been foolish, and Simmy had no tolerance for foolishness, even her own. No, it was because of her hip. Least, that was what she told herself and what she told Matt and Peter, too. Usually she could persuade one or the other of them to run down there and fetch anything she needed. If she had to do it herself, she always took Peter with her, to watch and make sure she didn't fall and break her hip. Her hip was what worried her, mainly.

Not the dark.

"Ain't nothing in the dark ain't in the light," she used to tell Matt, when as a boy he was afraid. And it was true. Least, that was what Simmy had always told herself.

No, the jars could wait. No preserves were worth risking her hip.

Simmy was about to close the door when she heard it.

The crash and shattering of glass on the concrete floor of the basement.

Something had toppled over one of Simmy's mason jars.

She stuck her head back inside. "Who's that?" she called out.

She waited, then heard it again.

A second mason jar plummeted to the floor, and broke to pieces.

"Who's doing that?" she said angrily. In a flash, two plus two equaled four. That's where Tigger had gone to. He had snuck off down the basement steps, to avenge himself on Simmy by wreaking havoc on her precious jars. That's what it was. "You worthless ol' cat, you done it now!" she exclaimed. After all, Tigger's lack of feline agility was legendary. His massive tail alone, during a quick spin, had been known to knock over beer cans and iced tea glasses. And now he was down there, prowling in and out of her row of mason jars.

The only question in her mind was how Tigger, given his lack of leaping prowess—fat body, short legs—had gotten up on the shelf in the first place.

As Simmy was turning this riddle over in her mind, the third jar bit the dust.

"You done gone and made Simmy angry now." She reached around and turned on the light switch. There was only a single exposed bulb down there, and by turning it on, as much darkness seemed to be created as had been dispelled. Before, there had been nothing. It might as well have been a sheet of black paper stretched across the opening. But now the darkness had been broken up, as if the shadows were all pieces of something that had once been one, and which now lay broken and scattered, much like the shreds of Simmy's prized mason jars.

Simmy gripped the railing in her hands and began down the steps, all thoughts of truce with Tigger renounced in a new batch of threats.

Midway down the stairs, a fourth jar exploded.

"You wait till Simmy gets you. You wait—"

She stopped on the bottom step and squinted into the shadow-fretted basement. The shelf of her jars stood on the other side of the wooden partition. Leaning against it was Simmy's old cat-chasing broom. She grabbed it up and carried it with her as she went around to the other part of the basement. "I gotchew now."

There was a space of about five inches between the partition wall and the ceiling. It let in enough light for Simmy to see the row of jars. She saw the places where the jars had been. She looked down and saw the shattered remains of the four jars that had already fallen. She looked back up again, squinting. One jar sat perched right on the edge of the shelf. A breath could have knocked it over.

But nowhere was there a sign of a cat.

"Where'd you go to?"

Simmy advanced cautiously deeper into the sectioned off room. She looked in the corners, checked the shelving on the far side. But still no cat. She muttered a few more curses, saying how he had gotten away this time, but she was going to find him. With the broom, she began to sweep the fragments of glass up into a pile. This done, she pulled an old crate underneath the shelves. Supporting herself with the broom, she reached up to the endangered mason jar, in an effort to slide it back to safety.

She had just touched the glass when she heard it, the noise from behind her. A glimpse followed, caught out of the corner of her eye.

Huge and black, the thing jumped up at her, quick as a flash of lightning, only the streaks were not of blinding brilliance, but of a blackness that Simmy had never known in her life, blacker than pitch, blacker than the bottom of a cistern on a moonless, starless night.

Simmy whirled around, nearly losing her already precarious balance on the old crate, and saw it, looming up toward her.

She gasped, "Lord Jesus" as the jar slipped from her fingers. The broom fell to the floor. Her eyes followed the hurtling downward of them and her body registered the sensation as if it had been her own.

But she hadn't fallen. She had only collapsed back against the partition. A mason jar fell and crashed, and that was when she looked up at it again.

Her mouth opened.

She stared across the floor at the shadow on the opposite wall. The shadow cast by the light that came down through the open space between the ceiling and the partition wall. She clutched at her heart and knew she was still alive, and she looked back at the moment of terror as she might have looked down into a deep chasm that she had somehow managed, her eyes shut, to leap across, only to see that the chasm was not deep, but bottomless.

Her own shadow was on the wall.

"My Lord, Jesus Christ, Simmy, you done nearly scared yourself to death," she let out. She looked at her feet, at the box that she had come within a heartbeat of slipping off of, down to the dreaded peril of broken hip, broken neck, or worse. Simmy recollected the old childhood taunt, teasing a fraidy-cat by saying so-and-so was scared to death of his own shadow. As she stared down at the floor, she could see herself lying there, her eyes staring up lifeless, her neck half twisted off, dead. And why? 'Cause of her own shadow. 'Cause she would have been scared to death—literally—by her own shadow.

"You crazy," she hissed to herself, then swallowed the after-taste of fear. Supporting herself with one hand, she eased down from the crate to the floor. She shook her head in vexation and picked up her broom. She pointed and shook it harshly at the wall, scolding her shadow as if it had been a wayward child. "Don't you be scaring Simmy like that, you hear? You liked to have her break her poor ol' neck. 'Sides, whatchew going to do without me? You ain't nothing but an insignificant ol' shadow anyhow. Can't go nowhere without me." She glanced at the floor, and counted the casualties. Six shattered jars in all. "And look here whatchew made me do."

She swept the additional shards into the previous pile, then set her broom back against the wall.

She snapped her shadow a stern look and said, "I done had 'bout enough out of you tonight." She turned and went back into the main part of the basement and began up the steps.

Halfway up the steps, she stopped. She went to turn around, to glance back into the basement, just to make sure. But she recalled how, in Matt's book, that was when the thing got you, when you turned around to see if it was there.

Pooh, she thought to herself, you going crazy. Don't matter if I turn 'round or not. Who'd be wanting to steal ol' Simmy's shadow, anyhow?

But still Simmy kept her eyes in front of her.

She was only three steps from the door to the pantry.

That was when she felt it.

It was a tingling. As if somebody, standing right behind her, had reached out and just barely touched with his fingertips the down on the back of her neck. She went to look back around, but stopped herself. "Ol' Simmy, she knows what it is a-following her up them steps. She knows what it is alright."

She went up the next step.

Again it came, the tingling. And inside her a voice whispered, "Look back around. One little peep can't hurt none." But Simmy scolded the voice back into silence, telling it how she had done learned her lesson once. "You just go on now, shadow. You done made a fool outta Simmy once tonight. You ain't gonna do it no more."

She lifted her foot slowly, her hand clutched tight to the banister, and then she felt the coldness shoot all the way up her spine as something soft wrapped around her ankle. She froze.

"Look," the voice inside of her head screamed crazily. "Turn around, Simmy!"

She pulled her foot up. Her ankle slid out of it.

"Them cobwebs down there playing tricks on ol' Simmy. But she ain't gonna look back. She ain't no fool."

She was on the last step. She reached up to the door and the voice said this time, reasonable and calm, "You safe now. Might as well go on and have you a peek. Just turn around and look. Can't hurt none."

And Simmy nodded and thought, Just one little peek. She went to turn away when suddenly she heard the door in front of her creak open.

"Lord Jesus Christ!" she exclaimed. She clutched on to the railing, to keep from falling backward. There, standing by the door, was Peter.

He, too, nearly jumped out of his skin.

"I thought I heard Tigger," Peter said as soon as they both realized they weren't dead.

"You nearly scared ol' Simmy to death this time. Now you help me up this last step."

13

Jimmy Buford opened one eye. He murmured, still half asleep.
"That you, Daddy?" His one eye closed again. He thought he
had fallen asleep long before, while his daddy was playing
Toodles on his back. The last thing he remembered were the
buttercups. But he must have been wrong. Because Toodles
hadn't gotten to them yet. He was still inside the station.
Maybe he just snoozed for a second, and dreamed about the
field of buttercups. The hand made tingling circles on his
shoulder blade—that was how he knew that Toodles hadn't
left the station yet, because that was where his daddy's hand
always started from.

Only Daddy wasn't telling the story anymore.

Slowly the hand moved down along the curve of the boy's
spine, and Jimmy felt the tingling that spread out over his
whole back, up his shoulder blade, and out to his arms. As
the hand went lower, toward the small of his back—where
the buttercups were—the tingling shot out down his thighs
and legs, going all the way to the tip of his toes. One eye
opened a slit, then closed again, and the boy saw the meadow
full of buttercups and the little train in the middle of them, its
iron cowcatcher intertwined with flowers—that was how the
big trains could tell where it had been. Toodles sniffed the
buttercups and the hand made its small caressing circle in
the small of Jimmy's back, at the place where the buttercups
always were.

Then Toodles began to move. Only he wasn't going back to
the tracks, the way he always did before in the story, whenever
he got his fill of sniffing buttercups. He was going someplace
else, someplace he had never been to before. It was down
beyond the field of buttercups. And there was something else
wrong. The hand, it didn't feel like his daddy's. The fingernails
were too sharp.

Much too sharp.

"Daddy?"

"Toodles wants to go into the water tower," a voice whispered. "Something's waiting for him at the water tower."

"What?" Jimmy asked.

"Same thing's waiting for you."

Jimmy did not move. "You ain't Daddy, are you?" he asked, his voice trembling.

There was not a sound. And Jimmy felt them as they began to sink into his skin.

It wasn't a hand anymore.

It was a claw.

It was dripping with something, cold and slimy. Jimmy could feel the ooze of it as it trickled onto his spine.

Everything inside of him shouted, "Roll over, look at it!" Jimmy clutched his pillow, struggling against the urge to flip over onto his back, to stare up into the thing that was hovering above him in the darkness. His face down, so that only his right eye was peeking out, he saw something cross the outermost periphery of his vision—something that twisted and squirmed, like the tail of a small snake, then disappeared.

"Whatchew want?" the boy gasped.

The claw sunk in deeper, then Jimmy heard a sharp, mocking hiss, right in his ear. "Your hands."

"No!" Jimmy screamed. He clutched to the nightstand and pulled himself up.

Don't look at it. That's what it wants you to do.

Jimmy dashed to the door of his bedroom, knocking it open. He pounded on his daddy's door, and screamed. But there was not a sound from the other side of the door. "Daddy! Wake up, wake up!" He felt the claw as it crawled up toward his neck, the tingling prickly and sharp: Jimmy shuddered violently, and tried to knock it away with his hand. Against his knuckles he felt it—it was like touching something mucky at the bottom of a lake, soft and oozing and cold. *"Go away!"* he yelled, but again it whispered, only this time something slimy and long was wiggling its way into his ear. "One little ol' peep can't hurt."

Jimmy shrieked, ran into the living room, burst out the door of the trailer, and hurled himself into the yard. He tumbled down. He went to look back, as a reflex of getting up, but caught himself in time. He closed his eyes as tight as he could. He heaved himself upright, opened his eyes, and began to race through the dark streets of the trailer park. All around him lay the shadows of things. Of trees and telephone poles, of cars and trailers. All of these shadows obeyed the law that shadows were meant to obey. The moonlight behind them, they fell forward. But as Jimmy ran breathless with terror, he looked down at the ground directly in front of him, where his own shadow should have been.

There wasn't even a trace of a shadow. It was behind him—cloaking the thing whose mocking whisper he kept hearing as he ran and ran. He couldn't outrun it. It would always be there, behind him, no matter how far he went, or how fast. He could run all night long, until he died from pure exhaustion, but still it would hang on to him, never lagging back, never stopping to catch its breath. It would follow him wherever the moon cast a shadow. It would follow him, until gasping for air, Jimmy would collapse, look back into it, and be yanked forever into the shadow world.

He saw the water tower. He had been running toward it all along, as if something has already told him that this was where he had to go.

Pain shooting down his side, Jimmy cut behind old Mr. Proopes's trailer, trampling under his prize bed of roses, then headed to the path in the woods. His legs ached, but always he felt it clutching at it, dragging it along behind him. *"Can't look back. Can't look back!"* On and on he ran, stumbling, righting himself, stumbling again. He knocked into a poplar, but kept on.

He was in the open field in front of the tower. He could see the writing on the side of it, the painted-on avowals of love that had once meant something to somebody, and he remembered hearing how long ago his daddy had painted words like that on the water tower for his momma, back when they had loved each other.

He ran and ran, and he remembered, too, how the boy had been running in the picture on the book, with the thing trailing behind him, inescapable, reaching up with its claws, peering at him through the darkness with the single eyeball gleaming.

He was the boy now.

Jimmy collapsed. He looked up. The ladder was less than twenty feet away. He panted and heard it whisper behind him. "Your hands." He shook his head furiously, but was unable to get even the word "No" out of his exhausted lungs. But he picked himself up and went on running, falling into the ladder, grabbing hold of it, and staring up at its daunting height.

He couldn't make it. He was too weak. Too afraid.

He began up the ladder. He couldn't look down or behind him. He knew that. He couldn't see how high he was up, or how closely it was following him.

He had climbed ten rungs and then held on to the next one, his arms looped around the cold metal. And starting at the back of his neck, he felt the tingling of the thing as it spread. He gasped for breath and began to clamber up the ladder again. He was only a few rungs from the top when one of his hands slipped.

He twisted around, flailing, but the other hand somehow held. For a split-second, he was facing it. But he shut his eyes in time. Desperately, frantically, he kept repeating, *"Can't look back. Can't ever look back."*

Jimmy gasped, clutched the rung tighter, and again somehow managed to go on, up the remaining steps. He pushed himself over the last one, and was now on the platform. He groped his way onto his feet.

He staggered along the railing, stopped, doubled up with pain and exhaustion, and stared, and stared out down into the moonlit field, the place where he had first glimpsed the shadow thing.

All at once Jimmy knew why he had come there. Once he had had a nightmare. He had been up on the water tower then, too. A monster had been chasing around it. Desperate to escape, he had mounted the railing, and had pushed himself off, plunging downward in the empty dark. Only, way before hitting the ground, he had awakened. It was something his daddy had told him before: If you fall from someplace high in a dream, you always wake up before you hit the ground.

And that was why he had climbed the tower.

It's a nightmare. That's all.

Besides, it couldn't keep hold of me, Jimmy thought, not if I was falling through the air. Your shadow can only touch you if you're on the ground. But not in the air. It would have to let go, and when I woke up, I would be back in my bed, and my daddy would be there with me, and everything would be okay.

He stepped up onto the first rail, his heart beating crazily.

"It's just a nightmare. I won't feel nothing. I'll be awake before I hit the ground. Way before.

He glanced down and he saw the claw dripping the black slime on his shoulder. It squeezed.

"No!" the boy screamed. And screaming, he lifted himself up and hurled himself from the tower.

Hurtling head first down into the moonlit field, he saw it, only a patch of darkness at first, then, with staggering, unimaginable swiftness, growing larger and larger and larger, the shadow that had been waiting for him all along.

PART SIX

....

1

Wally Clark sighed.

"You want to tell me what happened one more time, son?"

Curtis, his head hanging—he was both sleepy and exhausted—began once more to tell Wally what he had seen that night.

They were sitting at the bottom of the footpath, about half a mile down from where the swinging bridge used to be, and which led, through a couple of zigzags, down to the riverbed. They had both been searching the ravine for the last three hours.

When Curtis had called Wally earlier, the boy was in a state of panic and hysteria. His words came out garbled and confused, but Wally was able to piece enough of his report together to understand the thrust of it.

When he and Curtis got down to the riverbed, Wally went right to the spot beneath the wire cables of the old bridge. It would have been a straight drop from there, Wally figured.

Curtis kept calling out Jesse's name, though Wally didn't have the heart to tell him that this was probably a waste of breath.

Flashlight in hand, Wally searched a swath of ten feet on either side of the invisible line that ran parallel to the cable wire, fifty some feet overhead. He reckoned that even if Jesse had dived from the top of the cable, he couldn't have gotten much farther than that.

But, for some reason, Wally couldn't find a body.

As he stood, puzzled, in the shallow riverbed, Wally stared up at the cable above. It was possible that Jesse might have survived the fall. Maybe, Wally speculated, the boy, while seriously injured, had been able to crawl off somewhere into the undergrowth of the ravine, to pass out or die. If he had gone very far, they would have to wait until it got light.

That was when they had walked back to the bottom of the footpath, where Wally had sat down and asked Curtis to repeat the story.

It still wasn't clear, even in Curtis's mind, exactly why Jesse had fallen. Had he slipped? Or was it because of the last rock that June Lively had hurled at him? The legal implications were mind-boggling. A boy was dead, but, Christ, he had been out there swinging on the goddam cable wire. Bobby Lee, his two friends, and June—they had been acting like assholes, but had they actually broken the law? And could Wally do anything, aside from scaring the shit out of them?

And then there was the other thing. Along with everything else, Curtis added little Opal's account, how it wasn't that Jesse lost his grip. It was that something had come up out of the ravine, something black and shadowy, which had seized hold of Jesse's feet, and then yanked him down. She said she had seen it. Of course, he could ask her about it, in the morning—she had walked home, according to Curtis, right after the accident.

And, puzzlingly enough, Curtis even lent some degree of confirmation to Opal's report. He said that before Jesse fell, his legs went straight down, like something was hanging on them. And, in his second version, Curtis added that even the cable wire had sagged, sharply and suddenly, at the moment Jesse's legs stopped flailing.

As if . . .

As if what, Wally asked himself. A month before, Wally would have dismissed this part of the story. He would have attributed it to hysteria, or to a child's overactive imagination. But he could no longer do that so easily. The last weeks had taught him otherwise. There were some things he could no longer take for granted.

Like a child's nightmare.

Or the crazy words a little girl whispers in her sleep.

Or a shadow.

Something black and shadowy, he thought. Much like whatever it was that had stepped out of his daughter's closet, wearing her favorite dress. The thing he had told her was just a dream.

When Curtis finished his account, the two of them walked silently up the path.

At the top, they heard something.

It was the sound of a car engine being revved up.

"What's that?"

Curtis had stopped. His mouth open, he went to shake his head, to show he didn't know. But all at once there was a flash of recognition in the boy's face. "Shit," he whispered and took off, running as hard as he could along the edge of the ravine.

"Hold up," Wally shouted.

Ten minutes later, Wally cut through the alley between the Wal-Mart and the hardware store.

Curtis was standing on the sidewalk. He was staring into the square.

Jesse's black Cougar was missing.

"You see who took it?"

Curtis nodded, but said nothing.

"Who was it?"

That was when Curtis finally turned and looked at Wally. "It was Jesse," he whispered.

2

Tommy was up at seven.

He took a shower and was getting ready to fix breakfast when he went to Jimmy's room. He opened the door, then called to him, "Come on, sleepy head, up and at 'em." Without even glancing at the bed, he clicked on the light. Then, as always, he repeated, a little louder this time, his exhortation: After all, the process of getting Jimmy out of bed usually occupied half the morning. Sometimes Jimmy would sit up on the side of the bed, his head nodding on his chest, and say, "I'm up," only to collapse right back on his pillow the moment Tommy left the room.

"Come on, time to—"

Tommy stopped. Taken aback, he saw his son sitting up in the bed. His eyes were open. And it was obvious they had been open for a long time.

"Lord, you're awake," Tommy commented. "What brought this on?"

"Make 'em stop," the boy whispered. His voice sounded unlike anything he had ever heard out of his son.

"Make what stop?"

Jimmy was staring down at the sheet: It covered him up to his chest. Tommy walked over to the bed. "They keep doing it," Jimmy said.

"What are you talking about?"

Jimmy was moving his hands under the sheet. Tommy could see the outline of them. That was what his son was staring at, the two little lumps in the sheet that were moving back and forth. "My hands."

"What about your hands?"

"I want 'em to stop."

"Stop what?"

"Stop moving."

"Well, just make 'em stop then," Tommy said, stumped.

"I can't."

Tommy sat down on the bed and watched the two lumps made by Jimmy's hands as they made tiny circles. "Let me take a look, okay?" He pulled back the sheet and all at once the hands stopped. They lay still next to Jimmy's body. "Looks to me like they done stopped."

Jimmy stared first at his right, then at his left hand. "Yeah."

Puzzled by his son's behavior, Tommy examined the boy's eyes. "You ain't still asleep, are you?"

"Maybe," Jimmy said.

That would explain it, Tommy thought. "Well, wake up, okay. I'm taking you with me over to the Lumpkin house this morning."

"I did what you told me to."

Tommy had just gotten up from the bed and was heading to the door. He stopped and looked around. "Did what?"

"You said, if you was having a nightmare and you jumped off something high, you'd wake up."

Tommy nodded, he remembered saying something like that.

"It don't work," Jimmy said.

"Oh?" Tommy waited for his son to go on, but he seemed to be finished. "Oh, well, sorry about that. You go on and get dressed now, you hear?"

3

On the way to the Lumpkin house, Jimmy sat slouched up against the door of the truck. Tommy tried to get a few words out of him, but the boy only nodded or mumbled. But, at eight o'clock in the morning, that wasn't unusual for him.

"You sure you ain't sick or something?"

"Maybe," the boy said. For the third time since they had left the house, Jimmy looked at his hands. Each time he stared hard at them, the palms first, then turning them over to look at the back. One finger would wiggle, then another.

"They hurt or something?" Tommy asked.

Jimmy shook his head no. "It's like . . . they ain't there no more."

"Maybe they went to sleep. Way your leg does sometimes. You know?" Tommy offered, while from the corner of his eye, he watched as his son scraped the back of his hand against his knees, once, then twice.

"They ain't got no feeling in 'em."

An uncharitable thought occurred to Tommy. The night before, he had told Jimmy that he needed some help at the Lumpkin house the next morning—just a little painting, was all. Is that why Jimmy's hands had started acting funny, so he wouldn't have to do any work? And it was true, Jimmy could be awful lazy. "You telling me you won't be able to help me out this morning?"

The boy was staring at his palms again.

"Course, I suppose that means you won't be able to play, either."

But Jimmy didn't answer him directly. All he said was, "I can't feel nothing no more," and went on looking at his hands.

At the house, Tommy got out and said, "Grab that paint bucket."

Jimmy reached into the back of the truck and put his hand, palm down, under the handle of the paint bucket. He stood there, looking like he didn't know how to turn his hand right way up. Tommy, whose uncharitable interpretation of his son's ailment was growing stronger by the moment, yelled, "If it ain't too much trouble, that is."

Jimmy frowned, as if he didn't know what to do next. "They won't go right," he said. But before he had finished his sentence, his hand turned over, and Jimmy was able to grip the handle.

"Looks like maybe you're gonna live, after all. Tote it on in."

Jimmy lifted the paint bucket and headed toward the front steps. Tommy got out the rest of the things from the truck. As he started up the walkway, there was a crash. Tommy looked and saw the paint bucket rolling down the steps. The intensity of the second thud popped the lid off halfway down the steps. Paint flung everywhere.

"What the hell d'you do that for?"

"I didn't do it," Jimmy said. He was staring down at his hand. His fingers were wiggling around, as if performing some kind of bizarre piano exercise.

"What you mean, you didn't do it?" Tommy exclaimed. "Look at this goddam mess. What in hell's wrong with you?"

"It let go," Jimmy repeated. He hadn't taken his eyes off his hands.

Yeah, same way your horseshoes cheat on you, Tommy thought bitterly. "Can't you even say you're sorry, for Christ's sake? Why you always have to have some sorry ass excuse? Some goddam sorry ass excuse for everything you do."

Simmy pushed open the screen door. "Lord a-Mercy, what happened?"

"Jimmy dropped the damn bucket of paint everywhere," Tommy said. "I don't know how in hell we're gonna get this shit cleaned up."

"I'll go get my mop," Simmy said, then turned to Jimmy. "You go on in the kitchen. I was just fixing up my eggs and bacon. Peter's sitting at the table already."

His eyes still on his hands, Jimmy wandered in the house.

Tommy had taken some rags out of the back of the truck and was trying to wipe the paint from the steps. Simmy came out with a mop and a bucket of water. "Ain't nothing to fret about. We can git it all up. Won't even know nothing happened."

"I don't know what gets into him sometimes. I swear," Tommy fumed.

"Boys, they was done created to mess things up. Remember all that King Konging and Giant Crabbing you and Mr. Matt used to be into. So don't you go telling Simmy something she don't know already."

"Least me and Matt, we always knew when we'd messed up. Just once, I'd like to hear that boy take the blame when he's done something wrong. Is that asking too much?"

"Mr. Tommy, sometimes I think asking anybody to change anything about theirselves is asking too much."

Simmy dropped her mop. There was a scream from inside the house. It was Peter. He was yelling at the top of his lungs, "Simmy! Uncle Tommy! Come here! Quick!"

"What the hell—"

"Lord a-Mercy," Simmy cried. She raced through the screen door. Tommy followed after her.

He stopped at the door into the kitchen.

Peter, his face pale, was still yelling. "I didn't even know what he was doing. I thought he was going to get some bacon out."

"Oh, my God." Simmy put her hand up to her mouth.

Tommy stepped into the room. His mouth open, he saw his son's hand in the skillet of bacon. The flesh was sizzling. But, somehow, instead of yelling or grabbing at him, Tommy said, "What are you doing, son?" After all, his hand couldn't be in the skillet. If it had been, the boy would have been screaming. He would already have taken it out. But instead Jimmy just stood there, his face not even registering a hint of pain, only a kind of numb bewilderment. It had to be a trick he had seen on TV, Tommy thought, the kind where they say, "Don't try this at home, kids."

Only how did he get the grease to hiss and splatter like that?

"I can't feel nothing," The boy said, staring down at the hand. He lifted it out: The scalding grease dripped from his fingers. They were fiery red, and already more severely blistered than anything Tommy had come across in his ten years of being a volunteer fireman. The boy stared at it, just as Tommy had seen him do earlier, the way you look at an unfamiliar object whose use eludes you.

"It wasn't no nightmare," he whispered.

4

Simmy had emptied all the ice trays out of the refrigerator. Peter fetched a towel and handed it to her. She set the towel on the kitchen table, filled it with ice cubes, then wrapped it around Jimmy's hand. Tommy had called Dr. Lowery, who said that the boy should be taken at once down to the emergency room at the hospital in Cleveland. Tommy asked Simmy if there was anything in the house to kill pain. But Jimmy said, "There ain't no pain."

"You'd better get him on to the hospital."

Tommy nodded. He went to lift his son into his arms, but the boy pulled away. "It don't matter none."

"What d'you mean?"

"It don't matter where you take me to. It ain't mine no more."

"What are you talking about? You gotta get to the hospital. Your hand's been burnt, burnt bad."

"But it ain't mine no more, Daddy."

Simmy frowned, "Whose hand is it, if it ain't yours?"

Jimmy looked up at his father. "I did what you told me to. But when I jumped from the water tower, he was waiting for me down at the bottom. You told me I'd wake up, but I didn't. And he was waiting. He caught me. That's why I had to give him my hands. They're his now."

Tommy swallowed hard, then glanced up at Simmy and at Peter. They were both wide-eyed. "We're getting you to the hospital, fast." He leaned over, picked his son up, and carried him out to the truck.

"What was he talking 'bout, Simmy?" Peter asked out on the front porch.

"I dunno, hon." Her face had a troubled look.

"He said he give somebody his hands. Who'd he mean?"

"Folks, when they's had accidents like that, they get to talking crazy. It was some of that delirious talking, s'all."

"Is he gonna be okay?"

"Sure he is. Them doctors, they's gonna fix him up like he was new. You'll see."

5

It was nearly five o'clock in the afternoon.

Wally Clark sat in his office.

He had just come back from Jesse's granny's farmhouse. It was the third time he had driven by. He had hoped to find Jesse there, alive and kicking. Hoped that somehow it would all turn out to be a hoax. "Let's scare the shit out of good ol' Wally." But Jesse's granny hadn't seen him since the night before.

He had talked to the other kids involved. Yeah, they said, they saw Jesse fall. They had been there, according to their account, to try to talk the boy out of trying to do such a dumb-ass thing in the first place. Obviously, they had gotten their stories straight—they all agreed, nobody had thrown a single rock. Sure. "Then why didn't one of you boys call me about it?"

Andy said he guess it just slipped his mind.

Wally took out a pad of paper and wrote down: FACTS. Underneath, he scribbled:

Jesse fell. Everybody saw that.

Jesse's car got drove off. Fast.

Curtis says it was Jesse inside. But maybe he was wrong. Could be somebody else stole it. Bobby Lee or one of his friends.

If Curtis had been wrong, Wally reflected, then maybe Jesse's body was still down somewhere in the ravine. Also, there was a second possibility: That somehow Jesse, in a state of semiconsciousness, had managed to get out of the ravine, unaided, had gotten into his car and driven away, lost and confused. In which case, he was bound to turn up at some point. It was just a matter of waiting.

Which left just one alternative.

6

At the trailer park, Wally found Venita's trailer. She was working, but Opal was there.

Up until the final moments, Opal's story was the same as Curtis's.

"Curtis says you think you saw something else. You remember about that?"

Opal nodded. "I seen this thing." Big and black and long, she told him, and it had been reaching up. "You couldn't hardly see it, it was so black. But I knew it was there, on account of how you couldn't see nothing through it."

"You got any idea what it could have been?"

Opal shook her head. "They found his body yet?" Opal asked.

"Nope."

"Too bad. He was always real nice to me."

As Wally was heading toward his car, Leroy came up behind him. "I done fixed your walkie-talkie for you," he said and handed it to him. "I figured you must've forgot."

"Reckon I did. I've had a lot on my mind," Wally told the boy. He was about to get into the patrol car when Leroy took him by the arm. "How much I owe you now?"

"Don't worry 'bout it," Leroy said.

"Oh?" Wally raised his eyebrows in surprise. It wasn't like Leroy to provide his services for free. But as he looked into the boy's face, he saw that Leroy had something on his mind.

"Sheriff Wally?" The boy was staring up at him hard, but there was a trace of hesitancy around his mouth. He glanced over his shoulder.

"Yeah?"

"I seen it, too."

"I didn't think you was there, son."

Leroy shook his head, to show he didn't mean that. "I seen it before. We was up on the water tower. Peter and Jimmy, they was in there swimming. And I seen it coming across the field. So'd they. Only they didn't want to get into no trouble. About being up on the tower."

"What did it look like?"

Leroy glanced away. "This here big ol' shadow," he said. "Only it was going the wrong way. And there wasn't nothing to cast it, neither. Nothing at all. And . . ."

"Go on, son."

"And it had an eyeball. Underneath. I seen it," Leroy said.

"An eyeball," Wally repeated. Like everybody who knew Leroy, Wally was aware of the boy's attitude toward make-believe. Shadows with eyeballs were not what you would normally expect out of Leroy.

"I reckon you know I ain't making this up," Leroy said firmly.

"I know you ain't," Wally said, surprised at the conviction he put into his assurance.

"It was the thing in that book Peter's daddy done wrote. That Shadowstealer. I know it was."

Wally said nothing. He glanced up at the tower over the woods. " 'Preciate you telling me that, son."

"Jesse must've look back down at it," Leroy said, as Wally wedged himself behind the steering wheel. "That's how come it got him, I figured. You can't never look back at it. No matter what," Leroy spoke like an authority on the subject.

"I'll try to remember that," Wally said uneasily. "Be seeing you, Leroy."

7

Wally drove up across the park, to where Tommy's trailer was, but as he glanced at the empty driveway, he realized that Tommy was probably still working at the Lumpkin house.

The day before, Wally had heard about the famous phone call. The girl at the Piggly Wiggly had told Matilda about it. Only in her version, the call had come directly from Steven Spielberg. "You know, the one who directed *E.T.*," she reminded Matilda. On coming back to the house, Matilda—who hadn't let up on blaming the book for their daughter's condition—said, "Like enough people ain't heard about that thing already." And with grim humor, Wally found himself imagining T-shirts that said, "Shadowstealer, call home." Wherever, whatever the fuck home was for it. And maybe little black cuddly Shadowstealer dolls, a single eyeball fixed to its featureless face. Motorized, maybe, so that they could sneak up behind you at night.

Wally pulled up the driveway of the Lumpkin house and went to the front porch. He tapped on the screen, and Peter came to the door.

"Tommy here?"

Peter shook his head. "Who's that, hon?" Simmy asked coming from the kitchen.

"Mr. Tommy done took his boy to that hospital down in Cleveland."

"What for?"

Peter glanced at Simmy, then said. "He got burnt." And then, together, Peter and Simmy told the story of what they had witnessed out in the kitchen that morning. Wally listened, his face expressionless, and nodded. He walked to the railing on the porch and stared out into the yard. "I hear Matt's gone out there to Hollywood."

"That's right."

"Gonna sign a big juicy contract to turn that book of his into a movie." Talk at the Piggly Wiggly was of million plus for the film rights. He turned back to Peter. "You want to show me 'round the house, son. I kinda wanted to see how Tommy's been coming along, fixing it up."

Simmy went back to the kitchen. Peter took Wally into the library. Wally ran his hand along the shelving and said it looked like Tommy was doing a fine job. Then he turned to Peter. "There's something I want to ask you about."

Peter waited, wide-eyed, for the question.

"I want to hear about what you and Jimmy and Leroy seen that night you boys climbed up the water tower."

Abashed, Peter glanced to the floor.

"Oh, I ain't worried about you-all climbing there. I'd do it myself, if I was your age, and could. I was only interested in what you boys thought you saw up there."

And Peter told him. The shadow thing had come from the woods. It had wiggled its way to the tower, heading in the opposite direction from all the other shadows around it. And everything it fell across went black, not just dark. So black you couldn't see through it.

"You sure you wasn't just imagining it?"

"Pretty sure," Peter said. He hesitated, then added, "Anyway, even if I was, Leroy sure wasn't."

Back out on the front porch, Wally stood and thought. The phrase "mass hysteria" crossed his mind. He knew such things happened. People go along with their normal lives, and then suddenly, out of the blue, a crazy idea of some sort infects one member, and then another, and then another, until everybody believes the same crazy thing. A girl whispers, "Witch," and soon the whole town is out hunting and burning innocent old ladies—and, strangely enough, even the innocent old ladies, by this time, are convinced that they are witches. Wally wasn't much of a philosopher, but he knew that what a man thinks is really out there depends less on what he sees with his own eyes than on what other people tell him is supposed to be there.

But Peter's final words kept going through his head. "Even if I was imagining it, Leroy wasn't."

Wally turned back and called to Simmy.

"You don't happen to have the phone number of where Matt and his wife are staying out there, do you?"

"Course, I do."

"You think you could give it to me?" Wally asked with a smile.

Simmy hesitated, then said, "I reckon so. Hold on." And she went to fetch it.

"Here it is." Simmy handed Wally a piece of paper with the phone number scribbled on it. Wally thanked her and went out to the car.

He looked down at the number.

Shadowstealer, call home, he thought to himself.

"Jesus," he whispered, and his imagination running ahead of him, he could picture it, calling up Matt and saying, "This here's ol' Wally. Wally Clark. Got a favor to ask you, Matt. Forget about that million plus. Tell that Spielberg fellow to go and take a flying fuck. Tell him to make *Bambi, Part II*, instead. Tell him anything you want to, only get back here fast."

And Matt, of course, would say, "Sure, Wally. No problem."

Yeah.

8

Tommy was sitting in the waiting room at the Cleveland General Hospital. He had read every article in the *Field and Stream* three times, and had been reduced to taking a quiz in the *Cosmopolitan* called, "How Sophisticated Are You?" and had rated "Not Very." He got up and wandered down the bleak off-white corridor to the room where his son was being taken care of.

The door was open an inch.

Tommy pushed it a little farther and saw Jimmy, with his bare back to the door. A middle-aged nurse was tending to him. (The same nurse who, earlier, when Tommy had tried to explain what had happened, kept staring at him as if to say, "You expect me to believe that?" Of course, he knew what she was thinking. Not that Tommy could blame her. After all, he had been there himself, but even he had trouble believing his own story.) And now she was in there, asking Jimmy leading questions. Like, what does your daddy do when you've done something naughty? But Jimmy wasn't paying her any attention. He was talking a mile a minute.

"It comes up behind you. You can't look back at it. It follows and follows you. If you run, it starts to run," the boy was going on, not unlike a kid might typically be expected to do after seeing a scary movie or TV show.

"You have to give it something you got," Jimmy said. He glanced down and said, "I give it my hands."

Tommy closed the door.

When the nurse came out a few minutes later, she went up and told Tommy icily, "Your son certainly has a vivid imagination." But in her eyes, Tommy could almost see her thinking, You don't think you're going to get away with this, do you?

After the nurse left, Tommy sat back down and looked over the quiz page of the *Cosmopolitan*, idly wondering which questions had done him in. "I like to eat at ethnic restaurants. True or false." "I would prefer a pickup truck to a sedan. True or false."

Anything to block it out, the words that kept going on in his head, crazy and threatening to drown out every other thought.

I give it my hands.

I give it my hands.

9

Peter was despondent.

He was slumped on the back steps. Simmy came out and asked him if he wanted some lemonade. He shook his head. "I wish Daddy'd come home."

"He'll be coming back soon, hon."

Peter turned and looked up at Simmy. "You think Jimmy's going to be okay?"

"Oh, I'm sure he will be."

Peter sighed. "I wish Tigger'd come back. I miss him."

With a worried frown, Simmy gazed out into the backyard. It was nearly eight, and the shadows were beginning to stretch across the grass, darkening, deepening. "He'll be a-coming back. I know he will." But even Simmy couldn't manage to make her voice sound hopeful.

"I don't think he will," Peter said sadly.

Simmy sat down and put her arms around the boy. "If he don't, he done lived a good life. You know that. He cheered folks up and made them happy. Not too many human folks can say the same."

"Yeah."

Simmy glanced down at the bottom step. There was a plate, with two pieces of chicken in it. She had set it out there earlier, in the hope of luring Tigger back home. But the food was untouched. Strangely, even the other cats in the house—who normally had to be shooed away from the kitchen whenever Simmy made her fried chicken—hadn't even come close to the plate. It was like they knew something.

She patted the boy's shoulder. "Ain't too much longer 'fore Jesus is gonna be taking ol' Simmy up to him, anyhow. If something done happened to Tigger, first thing she's gonna do when she gets there is ask Jesus where he keeps all them good cats, and she's gonna go and fix him up all the food he likes in that big ol' kitchen they got up yonder. And then, him and me, we'll sit around in rocking chairs on this great big porch and we'll look down at you and when you cry, Simmy and Tigger, they'll be a-crying, too, and when you laugh, we'll be laughing. You hear me talking?"

"I hear," Peter bit his lip. It was trembling. She hugged him to her. "If you wanna cry, ain't no shame to it, hon. Ain't no shame in tears at all."

By the time Peter finished, it was dark.

10

Back at his house, Wally had barely gotten out of the car when Matilda was at the side door. From her face, Wally knew something was wrong. Bad wrong.

"I been trying to get holta you," she yelled. "I been calling and calling."

"What's wrong?" Wally asked, his heart thumping, knowing already: It was starting again, Melinda was starting again.

"I don't know where she found 'em. I done hid 'em, hid 'em good."

"Hid what?"

"Them scissors," Matilda gasped.

"What she done?"

"Nothing. She just sitting there. I talk to her, but she don't say nothing back."

Wally hurried into the house.

Overhead, on the porch, there was a yellow light bulb. Moths knocked into it, then flew away. Ten feet from the bulb, hanging from the hook in the ceiling, was the porch swing. Melinda was sitting in the middle of it, rocking slowly back and forth. In her hand was a pair of scissors. Next to her lay a stack of old newspapers—Matilda had been saving them for the upcoming paper drive at her daughter's elementary school. Melinda was carefully cutting out strips of newspaper. Loops of twisted paper covered the floor right beneath her feet. The girl frowned in deep concentration, as if each snip of the scissors had to be exact. Wally walked over to her and asked what she was doing.

"Making cutouts."

"Oh? Some special reason?"

She shook her head no.

"Well, they sure are pretty," Wally said, glancing down at the crazy pile of cuttings. "But I think you done enough." Wally took a step closer. "Why don't you hand me them scissors. Don't want you hurting yourself with 'em."

She shook her head, without looking up at her daddy. "Mr. Shadow said I had to keep them."

"Mr. Shadow," Wally repeated. He came closer. Close enough to reach out and grab the scissors out of her hands. Wally stared at the scissors. Her fingers were tight in the metal loops. There was no way he could snatch them from her hands. "He say why?"

"To help him with."

"How're a pair of scissors goin' to help him, hon?" Wally said, trying to humor her, all the while easing within range.

"They can help make you believe in him." The sharp tips of the scissors gleamed in the light of the overhead bulb. "He wants you to believe in him."

"Why's that?"

"Because each time somebody believes in him, he gets stronger." Melinda frowned. "That's why he wants you and Mommy to believe in him." She bent over the scissors and snipped slowly, carefully: an S-shaped loop appeared. "I believe in him, Daddy."

"Give me those scissors, hon."

"I can't," the girl said softly, her eyes on her snipping.

"A course, you can. Now hand 'em to me, Melinda."

Again she shook her head. Wally bit the corner of his lip. It was crazy: She was acting just the way she usually did when she had gotten her feelings hurt or when she was pouting. Except for the scissors and her reference to Mr. Shadow, the scene could have come right out of their life before, one of the many occasions on which Melinda, sullen and spoiled, tried to coax her daddy into letting her have her way about something.

Wally was right next to her, squatting down by the swing. "Tell you what, I'll say I believe in Mr. Shadow if you just give me them scissors? That fair enough?" Wally asked.

Again no.

"Why not, hon?"

" 'Cause."

" 'Cause what?"

"Mr. Shadow will know when you believe in him." Melinda had snipped her next letter. It was an "h."

Wally sighed. There was no point in talking to her anymore, he realized. It was now a matter of doing something, anything, to bring all the craziness to a screeching halt. "Okay," he said cagily, then pretended to be getting back up to his feet. At the last second, he turned and went to snatch the scissors from his daughter's hand.

"Jesus!" Wally gasped as he flinched back. He grabbed his right hand with his left, and looked down at the cut that the blade of the scissors had made across his palm. A thin trickle of blood seeped out. "Shit, hon, look what you done. I was just trying to—"

Wally glanced back up at his daughter.

The girl was twisting the tip of one of the blades into the palm of her hand. His mouth fell open. The girl's expression was not one of pain, but of heavy concentration: He had seen the same grave frown on his daughter's face when, a few years back, she used to make crayon drawings on the kitchen table, holding the crayon tight in her hand, and bearing down hard on the waxy tip, her mind totally absorbed in her work. And as Tommy had done earlier, when his boy had put his hand in the skillet of hot grease, the absence of any external sign of pain had the effect of paralyzing Wally's normal reaction, as if he were half expecting his daughter to start laughing at him for being silly enough to think she was really doing what it looked like she was doing.

That was when he saw the gleaming tip as it poked through the back of the girl's delicate hand.

He reached to grab the scissors, but Melinda had already pulled them out. She spread them open, so that the two blades were separated by about three inches. She held them right up to her eyes, and stared at her daddy.

Wally stopped in midmotion.

The girl's lips were trembling. A tear rolled down her cheek. Her gaze slowly turned from her father's face down to the tips of the scissors—they were only a quick jab away from the girl's eyes. Wally's heart seemed to be no longer beating as he looked into the once sparkling irises. They were baby blue. People were always so quick to wonder where the girl had gotten her eyes from, his and Matilda's both being garden-variety brown. The eyes that, in Wally's mind, always suggested a miraculous and benign disruption of the course of nature, indisputable proof that their child was less the outcome of ironclad genetic laws than a gift of mercy that had been inexplicably bestowed upon them.

"I think I got real pretty eyes, Daddy," she whispered. "Don't you?"

Unable to speak, Wally nodded.

"He says I can keep 'em, if you and Momma do what he wants." Melinda went on, her voice conveying a desperate hope against hope.

"Okay," Wally managed to get out. "We will."

"You promise?" she said, wistfully gazing back into his face.

"I promise."

Her eyes returned on the tips of the scissors. "I didn't want to believe in him, either, Daddy. But he can make you believe.

"You.

"And Mommy.

"And everybody."

11

"Lord, I'm still in a state of shock."

Matt and Cathy were sitting out on the terrace of the hotel. Earlier that day—it was just getting to be evening in LA—they had a three-hour lunch with Steven Spielberg, along with two of his associates. Also present were an expert in special effects, Matt's Hollywood agent, and, of course, Matt's long-time New York agent and friend, Frank. Frank was supposed to be meeting them in the next half hour. "I think Spielberg liked the book."

Cathy smiled at Matt's coy understatement. "Yes, I think he did, too."

Matt took another drink of champagne and leaned back in

his chair. He smiled, basking in the glow of the recollected litany of praise. "What was it he said now?"

It was hard for Cathy to keep a straight face. Since lunch earlier, Matt had kept pestering her to recall various superlatives that had been heaped, Hollywood style, upon Matt's book. "Bigger than *E.T.*, was it?"

"That was one of them, yes."

"Goin' to knock *Jaws* right out of the water?"

"That was another."

"The greatest thing since *The Old Testament*?"

"No, Matt, no one said that."

"Oh."

Matt finished his glass of champagne and Cathy poured him another. "I'm getting kind of fond of this stuff."

"So I've noticed."

"You know what I've been thinking about all day long?"

"Yes!" Cathy laughed. "I never thought the day would come when I'd see a smug Matthew Hardison."

"Well, aside from that." Matt grinned. "I guess it's from reading all this Greek tragedy stuff, but I've been thinking a lot about Fate. The idea that some things—both good and bad—are destined, and that there's no way of getting around them. And I keep feeling that this was one of those things. It would have been so easy for me never to have heard that story. Or to have heard it and forgotten it. But it was like, we were meant for each other. Like two people who are passionately in love always think they are, where it becomes impossible for one of them to imagine what life would be like without the other. And that's almost how I feel. Bizarre, isn't it?"

"No. I think you were fated to tell that story."

Matt chuckled. "Did you hear what Sidney said?" Sidney was Matt's Hollywood agent. "He introduced me as the Nightmare Man. I'm not sure how I feel about that one."

"Somebody asked me how I could sleep in bed with you at night."

"I've wondered the same thing myself." Matt grinned. He stuck his nose into his glass of champagne, to feel the bubbles. "I really liked that Bert fellow."

Bert was the special effects whiz kid that Spielberg had brought along. At the tender age of twenty-three, he was reputably the hottest and most original talent in the business, a man who could bring anything to life on the screen. He had just finished the book the night before and was all fired up about it. He had tried to explain to Matt some of his initial flashes of inspiration, but, unfortunately, like so many whiz kids, the guy was so deeply absorbed in his own world of technical brilliance that he was unable to communicate anything to people on a lesser plane. He kept talking in jargon that eluded Matt, although the basic idea came dazzlingly across. The challenge, the whiz kid said, would be to find a compromise between something and nothing, between substance and shadow—to use the words of *The Twilight Zone*. Bert said he wanted to capture the hallucinatory intensity of what he called "The Glance Behind." Everyone has experienced it: The momentary conviction that there is Something Terrible hovering just over our shoulder, right at "the outermost edge of the fringe of the penumbra of the periphery of our vision," as Bert put it. A tad too much, and the lurking latency becomes crass and dismissible. A tad too little, and you get zip. "I want the back of every neck in every theater across the country to feel the tingling when the Shadowstealer is creeping up on someone."

And speaking of tingling, Matt recalled one of Spielberg's anecdotes. It was about a B-grade horror movie he had seen as a boy. A Vincent Price extravaganza called *The Tingler*. The eponymic creature in the film could enter the human body only when its victim was in a state of extreme terror. Parasitelike, it crawled and lodged within the victim's spine. Paralysis and death ensued. The neat thing about it, Spielberg pointed out, was the quality of self-reference. It was fear of the tingler that allowed the tingler to enter into you. To fear it was to create it. "It sounds kind of hokey, I know, but toward the end of the movie, the screen is suddenly plunged into darkness. Even the exit lights go off. You can't see a damn thing around you. And then you hear Vincent Price's voice. And he says, 'Ladies and gentlemen, the tingler has gotten loose in the theater.' Every damn knee in the whole place was jerked up to the chin. People were screaming, yelling." Spielberg smiled at the recollection. "It was *wonderful*."

And that, he went on to say, was the quality that appealed to him in *The Shadowstealer*. The basic concept: a Nothing that, through the agency of the mind, could transform itself into Something. "Only in your story, the last hokey element is removed. After all, in the movie you kinda knew that the tingler couldn't really have torn its way through the movie screen. But the Shadowstealer isn't like that. Here the thing that gets you, ultimately, isn't some creepy-crawly whatchmajigger. It's the story itself. Just hearing it once is enough to make you fair game for it. It's as if the mind, the imaginative faculty, has turned against itself, has created something out of its depths, then projected it out there, into the realm of the not quite visible, cast it behind us. Like a shadow. And the neatest part is that each time the story is repeated, each new mind it takes hold of, the stronger, more terrible it becomes. Just think about it. In the course of the movie, the audience will become aware that by merely watching the screen, they are unwillingly helping to create the thing they are afraid of."

"Perceptive guy, that Spielberg," Matt commented.

They chatted for another fifteen minutes, until Frank arrived, buoyant and upbeat as always. Everything was arranged, he told them. Tomorrow, at lunch, the contract would be signed. The final terms came out at a little over a million and a half dollars, as had been confidently predicted by those in the know down at the Piggly Wiggly. "Not bad at all," Frank said with forgivable smugness. "You got a great agent, pal."

They talked about the tedious negotiations for a half hour. Cathy listened and Matt pretended to. Then, out of the blue, Frank said, "I tell you about the kid of my friend back in New York? He's a writer—not the kid, but his dad. And I gave him a copy of your book. He loved it, of course. But the funny thing is, his son's only eight. A smart kid, but not much of a reader. His daddy told him the story and the boy started reading it. A third way into the book his dad had to make him stop. He told me, 'I never thought I'd have to make my son stop reading a book.' The boy started having these wild nightmares, you know. Shadows stepping out of his closet. Crawling under his bed. It really kind of spooked him. The dad, I mean, not just the son. The dad said something that was kinda funny, in a way. He said, 'Shit, I hope this Hardison guy doesn't get any better. I don't think the world's ready for it.' " Frank chuckled. "I wonder if anybody's ever been held liable for causing nightmares? I can just see the possible headlines in *The National Enquirer*, 'Author Sued for Mental Suffering

Caused by Novel.' 'The People of the United States Versus Matt Hardison.' 'Can a Story Drive You Insane?' "

Frank took a sip of his champagne, and got a straight face. "Course, who knows, maybe I shouldn't be laughing."

12

Leroy and Opal were watching TV. It was ten o'clock.

"This here's boring," Opal said. "I wisht we was up at the rink." It was, after all, Saturday night. Their momma had come home from the Waffle House, and had stayed long enough to get dressed, go through Opal's drawers looking for her hidden cache of baby-sitting money (she hadn't found it: it was under Opal's mattress this time), and leave. Later Opal had baby-sat four-year-old Kevin Oakley until nine-thirty, when his parents came and took him home. Since then she had been idly switching channels on the TV, usually just when Leroy was getting interested in a show.

Opal got up and went to the open door of the trailer. She looked out. "Wisht there was something to do." Opal glanced back at her brother. "I reckon we could walk on up to the rink."

Leroy shook his head a firm and determined no. "I ain't gonna go out there."

"Ain't nothing gonna get you, Leroy."

"I didn't say nothing was. I just ain't going out there."

Opal went out onto the stoop.

"Where you going?" Leroy asked in alarm.

"Nowheres. I declare, I don't know what's got into you."

"Nothing's got into me." And ain't nothing going to, neither, Leroy added in silent reflection. Since the night up on the water tower, Leroy had not stepped foot outside the trailer, not after dark, not even for a second. Even Opal, who sometimes failed to notice things, recognized a change in her younger brother. "You don't want to go nowheres no more," she had said the night before, when leaving to go up to Jasper's skating rink. And, to Opal, there was something else peculiar. Almost every night for the past two weeks, she would wake up about four o'clock in the morning and find Leroy snuggled in bed with

her. As close to her body as he could get it. This, the same
Leroy who wouldn't let anybody squeeze or hug on him, not
since he was old enough to do anything about it. The first time
he got in bed with her, Opal had raised hell. "What you think
you're doing?" She figured it was some kind of prank. But
Leroy, his eyes wavering uncertainly, told her he'd had him
a bad dream. "S'that all?" Opal asked.

And then Leroy, in a bizarre about-face, said, "Tell me
that story. About when you become that famous country-and-
western singer, and about that saddest song." Before, whenever
Opal broached this topic—it was her most deeply held fan-
tasy—Leroy scoffed and scorned. "You ain't gonna be no
famous singer. You can't sing worth shit." But she insisted
that one day it would happen, and she'd tell about what she
called "The Saddest Song That Ever Was." It was going to be
a song of heartbreak such as the world had never heard before.
She couldn't tell you what it was about, not right yet, but one
day she would wake up and there would be tears in her eyes,
and she'd go and write it down, and she'd become rich and
famous, and drive a different Cadillac every day, maybe even
some of the ones that Elvis had owned. And Elvis, he would
be so moved by the song that he would come out of hiding
up where he was, in Wyoming or Michigan, so that he and
Opal could do a duet of it, The Saddest Song, and it would
be so sad that all up and down the highway, whenever it was
played, people, even truck drivers, would have to pull off to the
shoulder of the road, because of the tears that would be blinding them, the way people did in a real bad thunderstorm.

But now, when Leroy got in bed with her, instead of scoffing
at her story, he'd beg her to tell it to him, and when she
finished, he'd keep on asking her to describe the big house
they'd have, and everything in it.

"Wonder if Cyndi's still up?" Opal asked.

"What for?"

" 'Cause, I was thinking 'bout going over there, to see
what's she doing, Leroy. Something wrong with that?"

"That's clear across the trailer park!"

"So. I done walked clear across the park before," Opal
rejoined. "I swear, Leroy, I don't know what's wrong with
you. Ain't nothing gonna get me 'tween here and there."

"Whatchew going do if it comes up behind you?"

"Reckon I just run back home. I sure ain't looking back behind, I tell you." Opal had been thoroughly coached by Leroy about what to do in case she was ever out by herself and felt a tingling on her neck or noticed that her shadow wasn't where it should be.

"What if it tricks you into looking 'round?"

"It ain't gonna trick me."

"I ain't gonna let you go out there." Leroy was up from the sofa. He was standing by the door.

"Whatchew gonna do to stop me?" Opal didn't ask this as a threat: It was more like curiosity. Opal could handle any boy her own age, much less her brother.

"Dunno," he conceded.

"I ain't gonna be gone that long, Leroy. Ain't nothing gonna happen. I promise."

"Opal!" Leroy called after his sister. She turned around and was going to say, "Lord, Leroy, stop acting like a baby," but she didn't say it. Looking into her brother's eyes, she saw something she hadn't seen in them since their momma's boyfriend, Dexter, had accidentally slammed the door of his rig on Leroy's finger.

Leroy had tears in his eyes. "I'll listen to your story."

Opal hesitated, spooked by Leroy's peculiar behavior. She looked back out into the shadow-filled trailer park. "I won't be ten minutes."

He called out for her one more time. But Opal had already taken off. Just to be on the safe side, she was running, careful to stay as much as she could in the patches of moonlight that filled the park.

13

It was ten-thirty when Tommy got back to the trailer. He carried Jimmy inside and put him into Tommy's own bed. He set the boy's heavily bandaged hand on top of a pillow. As he did, Jimmy stirred. His mouth sagged up and words dribbled out.

"Coming."

Tommy held his breath and listened.

"Tonight," the boy moaned. "Coming for hand."

Then the boy turned his mouth into the pillow and the words stopped.

In the living room, Tommy went to the phone. He stared at it. He reached in his pocket and pulled out Matt's number. He repeated it silently.

And if he did call him, what would he say? What could he say?

He picked up the receiver, but the number he dialed was Wally's.

The phone rang. Tommy waited. It had already been ringing for a while when he started to count. At ten he put the receiver back down.

He looked at his watch.

Somebody had to be there. He dialed again, on the off chance that he had made an error the first time. But again, it was the same thing.

No answer. Nothing.

Tommy stood up and went to the door of the trailer. The park was quiet for Saturday night.

Outside, the moon was still full.

Tommy picked out one shadow, darker than the others, and stared at it, watching to see if it moved, if something hidden underneath it gleamed in the moonlight.

And Tommy caught himself thinking. This is how people go crazy.

He turned away and went back into his room. He lay down next to his boy, but his eyes were wide open. He knew he wouldn't be sleeping anytime soon.

14

Melinda was still in the swing.

Through the window Wally and his wife could glimpse the profile of the girl as she bent over her cuttings. "D," "O," "W," "S," "T" were now curled on the floor. She was working on "E."

He pulled out the phone number he had gotten from Simmy.

"I'm going to call Matt. I got to do something. I just can't sit here with my thumb up my ass."

Wally went to the telephone and picked up the receiver. He began to dial the number. Matilda kept glancing back to the door that led out to the porch. "Don't talk too loud, okay?"

The last number dialed, Wally waited for an answer. It rang three times. Then a woman's voice politely announced the name of the hotel where Matt and Cathy were staying. "May I help you?"

Wally glanced down at the slip of paper. He said, "Room 423."

The hotel switchboard operator pleasantly asked him to hold one moment.

And again the phone began to ring.

"What's going on, hon?"

His heart racing, Wally said, "They're ringing his room."

"Any answer?"

Wally shook his head.

He counted them. Ten rings. Then a voice.

"Matt?"

"Sorry, sir, I'm afraid there's no answer."

"You know when they'll be back?"

"I'm sorry, but I don't have that information. If you would like to place—"

But Wally didn't hear the rest of the woman's polite little routine. The receiver tumbled from his hand.

"Oh, my Lord!" Matilda gasped.

Wally jumped up. Melinda was standing in the doorway. A trail of looping, connected letters fell from the blade of the scissors. "He wasn't there, was he, Daddy?" the girl said.

"No."

"Mr. Shadow knew he wasn't. That's why he let you call."

Matilda walked over to where the girl was standing. "Oh, Lord," she whispered. She slapped her hand to her mouth and began to step away. "Oh, my Lord God. Look!" The yellow light bulb was directly behind the girl's back.

"Look how her shadow goes. Wally, look how—" But Matilda couldn't finish her sentence. She shook her head and ran from the room.

Wally stared at the figure of his daughter, silhouetted in the harsh yellow light. There was no shadow in front of her.

Instead, something black stretched behind her. It reached to the edge of the porch and then went off into the darkness. Although Melinda stood absolutely motionless, the blackness behind her undulated back and forth, up and down, sliding this way and that like the coils of a huge snake.

"You believe in him now, don't you, Daddy?"

Wally, his mouth open, nodded. "I believe, hon. I believe in him now."

15

It was after twelve-thirty when Opal left her friend Cyndi.

For the last hour, Opal and Cyndi had been on the phone with a boy, taking turns talking to him, and by the time she left, she had totally forgotten her earlier fears. Her life, heretofore, had been a rapid succession of quick, violent shocks, scenes and events occurring so fast that nothing much had time to register for her: At most, she merely witnessed things, then passed on to something else. In fact, as she cut through Mr. Proopes's backyard, the last thing in the world she was worried about was whether her shadow had something hidden in it. She walked at her normal pace and had gotten halfway across the park when she stopped and casually glanced back behind her.

A dog was rummaging in a somebody's overturned garbage can.

Opal started walking again. Only then did she remember Leroy's admonition, how on no account, and for no reason, was Opal to look behind her on the way back.

Oh, well, nothing had got her.

And her mind turned again to the burning issue of the moment, whether Jason Winder liked her or Cyndi better, judging from the way he had talked to one or the other on the phone.

She could see the trailer at the end of the road.

That was when Opal felt something on the back of her ankles. It wasn't much, just a wisp of something crossing her flesh.

It was followed by a sharp tingling on the back of her neck, like somebody's finger was softly caressing the down there.

She took another step forward, and the tingling came again, sharper.

She froze. All up and down her spine the tingling spread. She slapped at the back of her neck, wondering if it was maybe a mosquito doing it.

Then she remembered Leroy's warning. That was how you knew, the first hint that it had hold of you, that the dark ooze of it had filled your shadow and was creeping up behind you.

Recalling her brother's advice, Opal looked over at the telephone pole that rose up only a few feet to her right. Its shadow stretched toward her own trailer. Then, as if one shadow might not be enough, she glanced at everything else to her right. A tricycle in the Hendersons' front yard, their battered Chevy pickup, the birdbath, a beach ball that lay next to them. In each case, the shadows concurred. Every one of them stretched away toward her own trailer.

The moon was behind her, overhead.

She glanced down, puzzled at the expanse of moonlight that spread out before her eyes, reaching all the way to the shadow of the Henderson trailer.

Nowhere in the puddle of moonlight did she see even a trace of her own shadow.

It was gone.

Every bit of spit in her mouth evaporated in an instant. *Don't look back at it.* She recollected. *Whatever you do, don't look to see if it's there.*

She took a step forward and stopped.

Her head motionless, she strained impossibly to see around her shoulder, strained until the muscles in her eyeballs ached with fatigue.

Slowly, one careful step at a time, Opal walked back toward her momma's trailer, keeping her spine straight and her head rigidly forward, much as if she had been practicing her posture at a finishing school for girls. Fifty feet short of home, her and Leroy's dog, Sparkle, sat up and looked at her, his tail wagging anxiously. He started to go to her, then stopped. He tilted his head in puzzlement at what he saw coming toward him.

"Sparkle, stay."

The dog obeyed, but only for a few moments, then began trotting toward Opal. When he came within ten feet of her, he stopped and changed his course, deciding to go wide of her.

As she looked into the dog's face, Opal saw that Sparkle's eyes were intent not on her, but on the invisible space right behind her. He stopped and began to bark.

"Go away," she called, her throat so dry with fear that the words came out a hoarse rattle. "Go—"

Just then Sparkle lunged behind her, the same way Opal had scolded him for lunging at the mailman when he came by the trailer. The dog yipped and growled as he scooted somewhere behind Opal's back. Instinctively, Opal went to turn around, to call to the dog, but she stopped herself. She teetered, nearly losing her balance. But she held steady. "Sparkle?"

The dog made one last bark.

Or almost one.

It was as if Sparkle had been a dog on TV and some-one had clicked the set off in mid-yelp. The only noise that now came from behind her was a strange sucking, slurping sound. It reminded her of the noise that the drain in the bathtub made when too much hair got in it and stopped it up.

Sparkle.

She wanted it to be a sound. But it wasn't. It was lost some-where between her heaving lungs and the sandpaper lining of her throat.

It was going to do the same thing to her. Just a glimpse over her shoulder was all it needed. Just a peep.

That was when she felt it.

The tongue licking her ankle. Licking it the way Sparkle did. Always before, the dog drove her crazy doing it, and she would kick him away. But now, feeling the tongue, she wanted to burst out laughing. Sparkle was okay. He was back there. Which meant nothing else was back there. Which meant it wasn't going to get her.

"Sparkle, you okay, boy?"

On the last word, Opal turned around.

The tongue was still licking her. Only it was no longer Sparkle's. It belonged to something else now. Out of the pitch-black puddle at her feet, the red tongue glistened as it stretched out higher and higher toward her face, still lick-ing.

"Uh-uh," she whimpered.

16

Leroy sat up and looked around. He was in the living room of the trailer, where he had fallen asleep waiting for his sister to come back. The TV was still on, only it was after two o'clock in the morning. "Goddam you, Opal," Leroy said. He went to the door of the trailer and looked outside.

No sign of Opal.

Maybe she had decided to spend the night at Cyndi's, he fumed. Sometimes she did that, just going off and forgetting about him. Usually the nights when his momma didn't come back home, not even with some man.

He turned back and went into the bathroom and peed. Then he stepped to the door of his bedroom. He frowned. In the moonlight, he could make out the back of Opal's head, asleep on her pillow.

That was funny. She had come back, only she hadn't woke him up, the way she usually did when he fell asleep on the sofa, saying, "Come on, Leroy, it's time for bed." Or maybe she had tried, but failed to stir him.

Anyhow, she was there.

He'd be safe.

He got undressed and into his bed.

He stared for a few moments at the shadow on the closet door in front of him, then rolled over and went back to sleep.

17

In the hotel room, Matt collapsed on the bed.

"Damn."

"What's wrong?"

He had sat up and was furiously rubbing his right foot as he muttered and grumbled to himself. "It hasn't happened in years. My foot. I told you how it goes nuts sometimes."

Cathy nodded and sat down next to his leg. "You want me to rub it?"

"If you don't mind."

"Does that feel better?"

"A little. Keep on."

Matt lay back on the pillow. He put his arm over his eyes and said, "When I was a boy, Uncle Leon used to say to me how I was touched by the hand of Fate. I always wondered if that's where it touched me. My goddam foot."

Cathy smiled. "Like Oedipus. The name in Greek means 'swollen foot.' " And she reminded him how when Oedipus is born, his parents, in a desperate effort to avert the decree of Fate, abandon the newborn child on a hillside. To make extra sure, they even chained the boy's ankle. Hence his nickname when, a few days later, the child was rescued.

Matt smiled. He remembered the various profundities Cathy had pointed out in his book. Profundities that Matt assured her he had never intended to put there.

"There's always a hidden meaning for you, isn't there?"

She smiled. "Maybe that's because there always is."

18

"Leroy! Wake up."

Leroy opened his eyes. Across from him, in the other twin bed, Opal was sitting up on her knees, her face cut in half by a slash of moonlight. "You're having one of them bad dreams, Leroy."

The boy rubbed his eyes. If there was one thing Leroy knew, it was when he'd had a bad dream. He'd wake up, drenched with sweat, his eyes wide in terror, the echo of his own screams all around him. But Leroy couldn't even remember dreaming. "I wasn't having no bad dream."

"Quick! Leroy, wake up!"

Opal's tone of voice was the same as it had been when Leroy first heard it. He sat up higher in the bed. "You deaf, I said I wasn't—"

"Leroy, wake up!" she went on, her voice still frantic, cutting him off in midsentence.

"What's got into you, Opal? You're acting—"

"Leroy, you gotta wake up. Hurry, Leroy, 'fore it comes out

that what wasn't there usually wasn't there for a damn good reason.

Like black ooze with tentacles that came slithering out from beneath your closet.

Leroy suddenly felt Opal's hand go around his waist. It was funny. Sometimes he did that to her, if he was certain she was dead asleep. But never, all the times they had slept together, had she done it to him. But right then, Leroy certainly wasn't going to complain. It felt too good and comforting.

"Opal?" he whispered. "Tell that story. About The Saddest Song."

And, strangely, Leroy felt her body as it snuggled closer to him.

And Opal began, her mouth so close to his ear that the voice might as well have been coming from inside his head. At her first word, he closed his eyes. And the chill he felt began to warm as he listened to her tell about the boy who was like Leroy, who had a sister who was like her, and how they lived in this trailer in a big trailer park. And at night the sister would tell her dream of how one day they would live together in the biggest house in Nashville, with a swimming pool the size of a football field. And how they would have all the money they ever dreamed of wanting, and how they would be able to go skating anytime they wanted to, because they would have a skating rink down in their basement, and their friends would all come over and skate with them. And Leroy began to smile dreamily as he listened to Opal talk about all the nice things they would have, a bowling alley, and a big stereo that nobody could ever break, and all the records and tapes of Elvis that had ever been made, and they would drive around on Sundays in one of the famous pink Cadillacs that Elvis used to own.

And it would all have come true, too, Opal whispered, except for something that happened to them one night.

See, the boy had a bad dream. It was real bad. So bad that the boy didn't know he was dreaming. Didn't know he still dreaming even when he thought he was woke up.

Even after he had crawled into bed with his sister.

Even after she had put her arms around his waist.

Leroy opened his eyes. "Opal? What you saying that for?"

Because the thing that he had seen oozing out from under the closet, it wasn't under the closet at all. No, it was right there in bed with him. Only he didn't know it. He didn't know

*it was snuggling next to him in the darkness. He didn't know
that it was curled up right there—*

"Stop it, Opal," Leroy said, "I don't like that story. Go back
to the other one."

*And then when the boy tried to jump out of the bed, he
couldn't. Because of the arms that were around his waist, the
arms he thought were his sister's, but weren't, because that
thing had already gotten hold of her out in the moonlight.*

"I done said, I don't wanna hear no—" At that moment,
Leroy went to jerk Opal's arm away from his waist, but he
couldn't.

That was when he felt the sharpness of the things at the end
of what he thought were his sister's fingers.

"Opal?" he gasped.

He felt his body being squeezed tighter. He looked and saw
her hair falling down over part of his face, only each strand of
the hair was moving, wiggling, the way a box full of worms
at a bait and tackle store wiggled and squirmed and coiled.

And he felt it, the cold slimy ooze of the thing that had its
arms around him. He tried to yank his body out of its grip, but
he couldn't. And the flesh he felt was no longer like flesh, but
was like putting your hand into the box of worms.

It wasn't her anymore.

It was—

"What you done with Opal, you motherfucker!" Leroy
shouted. He twisted, got his one free hand down to the
floor, groped frantically by the side of the bed. He clasped
his sister's lucky horseshoe. He took a deep breath, hauled it
back, and with all his might, he slammed it into the thing, then
again, and again, and again.

It let go.

Leroy leapt from the bed. For a split second he was going to
look at it, to see if he had hurt it. But the words came rushing
back, and he snapped his eyes shut. *Can't look at it.* He turned
and bolted from the room. Only at the end of the little dirt road
did he stop and dare to look back.

Panting, terrified, confused, the boy wiped his forehead, then
stared down and saw he was still holding Opal's lucky horseshoe. He held it up in the moonlight and saw the black ooze
dripping off of it, a trickle just starting to drop toward his waist.

He threw the horseshoe into Mr. Proopes's rosebed, then
ran some more.

19

Peter stood at the window of his room.

Outside, there was a plaintive, muffled meowing. Peter knew at once it was Tigger's. His meow, when troubled or lost, was as recognizable to Peter as Simmy's voice or his own.

Which meant: *Tigger was alive!*

Peter dashed out into the hallway and yelled up to Simmy's bedroom on the third floor, "It's Tigger!" He didn't wait for Simmy to wake up, but hurled himself headlong down the stairway and was out on to the back porch only seconds later.

"Tigger?"

He went down the back steps and looked around the yard. The meowing was closer now, but it still sounded muffled, like Tigger was trapped or stuck somewhere. Which would explain why he hadn't shown for the last two nights.

The only question was, Where would he be stuck?

Peter called out for the cat, and the meowing got more plaintive. "I'll get you out, Tigger, but I got to find where you are first."

He turned around and stared at the back porch. There was a space underneath it, enclosed by a latticework, except for a small opening. Sometimes he and Jimmy used to crawl under it and wait until Simmy came out to sit on the porch, at which they would start to make growling monster sounds, or maybe they'd start to bump the underside of the boards, in the hopes of getting Simmy to think that one of her great-grandmomma's "whatalls" had sneaked under there, waiting to get her. Not that Simmy was ever much deceived. "Sounds like two insignificant little white boys done snuck under the porch, trying to scare ol' Simmy."

The only thing was, Peter had checked the spot three times that morning, and there had been no sign of Tigger. Maybe he had been out in the woods then, and had gotten hurt, too hurt to climb up the porch steps, and had curled up in the safest place he knew.

Peter went to the tiny opening—usually he and Jimmy had to crawl through it on their stomachs. He peered into the dark and called out.

The meow came back instantly.

"I'm coming in to get you. Just hold on, Tigger."

Peter got down on all fours and began to wiggle his way through the hole in the latticework. Inside, he looked around: the moonlight took up the lattice pattern, only the squares were more elongated, due to the angle at which the light fell.

"Tigger?"

He couldn't be very far, the whole area being not much larger than a normal carport. Peter crawled on all fours closer to the side of the house.

He groped his hand out and touched fur. A meow followed, inexplicably sadder than all the other meows before.

"Come here, Tigger."

Peter found Tigger's collar and began to drag the cat closer. He stopped. Tigger's face had emerged into one of the moonlit patches. Only there was something wrong. It was featureless and white, as if something had erased Tigger's eyes and nose and mouth. Peter let go and jumped back. "Tigger?" he gasped. But the meowing kept on. The boy's heart at full stop, he stared at the face, then lifted his finger to it and touched the soft mesh. He pulled on it and two green eyes gleamed at him.

"You stupid cat," Peter whispered, breathing again. "You got caught in some cobwebs." He continued to pull the webbing off the cat's snout and whiskers. He rubbed the loosened cobwebs against the dirt, to get them off. Then he reached back to take hold of Tigger's collar. That was when he heard it.

The boy stopped, thinking that his imagination was just playing a trick on him.

He stared into Tigger's face. His eyes were fixed on him, hard and with an intensity that he had never seen in them before. The mouth was in shadow.

Since as long as he could remember, there had always been a Tigger voice. His daddy had used it a thousand times, and in a hundred different contexts: to cheer Peter up, to tell him stories with—The Further Adventures of Tigger the Talking Cat, Part CXXVI—to sass Simmy, to make fun of, or, alternatively, to wax lyrical about, himself—"Oh, Daddy's so wonderful, Peter. You have no idea how lucky you are." Peter had heard Tommy do the same thing, and more recently, Cathy, too. And, of course, there were times when Peter would try it himself, although his Tigger voice was never quite up to the standards of Daddy, or even Tommy.

But now, in the darkness of the space beneath the porch, he had heard a voice that hadn't come from Daddy, or from Uncle Tommy, or from Cathy.

It had come from something else.

From what he had grasped hold of, there in the dark.

From Tigger himself.

And what Tigger had said was, "Don't look behind you."

Or, at least, in a momentary onrush of fear, that was what it had sounded like, the voice menacing, even with a trace of mockery in it.

But, of course, as everybody knew, cats couldn't talk. Not really.

Not even Tigger.

The green eyes gleamed, as Peter looked into them. But they were not gleaming at him, but on something that, estimating from the angle of Tigger's line of vision, had to be hovering just over the boy's right shoulder, maybe even only inches from the back of his neck. It was a trick cats like to play, Matt had more than once observed to Peter, this intense and sudden focusing in on nothing whatsoever, their eyes huge and full of rapt attention, as if to intimate, "If you could only see what I see."

"What is it?"

"What Daddy let loose," the voice went on.

The hairs on the back of Peter's neck stood up. At that same moment, Tigger began to let out another sound, not a voice anymore, but the horrible anguished wail that Tigger made anytime they boxed him up to take him down to the local vet, piercing and awful.

Peter felt the thing on his shoulder. He looked down at it.

It was a claw.

And as he turned to see what the facelessness that it was connected to, he heard the blood pounding against his temple, pounding out the plea that welled up from inside of him, *Don't look at it. Don't look at it.*

• • •

Tigger watched, then quickly darted from beneath the porch out into the moonlit yard.

The fur standing up on his back, he turned around and stared at the gaping hole.

There was a shriek, and then silence.

And slowly it coiled out, the hideous blackness of the thing, oozing around the base of the porch and twisting so that it was now turned toward the steps to the back porch. Tigger watched as, coil upon coil, it made its way up.

Just then a voice came from inside.

It was Simmy's. She was calling for Peter.

Tigger crouched and waited.

"Who is that?" she called in alarm. "Peter? Was that you?"

As the last coil disappeared over the last step, Tigger heard the familiar squeak of the hinges of the screen door that led from the kitchen onto the back porch. "Hon?"

Tigger opened his mouth wide and let loose an enormous hiss, as if to warn her, to tell her what he had seen slinking up to the place she was standing.

In the moonlight Tigger watched as Simmy went to the door and looked down the steps into the yard.

"What's that?"

His green eyes saw as the old woman quickly turned around, her face fixed on something that moments before had been behind her.

As quickly as a bird darts up out of a clumsy old cat's paw, the darkness rose up and covered her.

Tigger turned and dashed as fast as he could toward the woods.

20

"Is she asleep?"

Matilda shook her head uncertainly, then whispered to her husband, "I don't know. I can't tell no more."

Out on the back porch, Melinda was curled up in the swing. Matilda had just tiptoed out, to see if the girl's eyes were closed. They were. But then she had also noticed that the scissors were still tightly wrapped around Melinda's fingers.

"We got to get them scissors from her," Matilda said.

"I ain't trying that again," Wally said firmly. "She could gouge both of them eyes of hers out 'fore I even knew what was happening."

Matilda nodded: He was right. She clutched at her shoulders and shivered. "Least, that thing's gone. What's it want from us, anyhow? What's it doing here?" she asked.

"Dunno."

"It's the same thing as was in that book, ain't it?"

"I reckon."

Suddenly Matilda's eyes brightened with hope. "They must've gotten rid of it somehow, in that book. How they do it? Whatever they done in the book, we could do, too."

Wally cast his wife a sharp, bitter glance. "I never got to that part. Remember? You done tore it up 'fore I could get to it."

"But somebody's got to know."

"That's one of the reasons I wanted to call Matt about."

"But, Tommy, he oughtta know. There's whole bunches of folks 'round here who done read it. We just gotta ask one and find out."

"You figure she's goin' to let us?" Wally asked, nodding out toward the porch.

"Even if she jus' playing possum right now, she's gotta sleep sometime, don't she?"

"I don't know no more," Wally whispered.

Matilda jumped. "You hear that?"

"Yeah." Outside, there was a voice. A boy's voice. It was calling, "Sheriff Wally." And it was frantic. Before Wally had gotten to the door, whoever was there had commenced pounding on the other side. Wally pulled it open—it was the door at the side of the house—and saw Leroy standing there, his face pale, beaded with sweat. "It got my sister," he told Wally. "That motherfucker, it done got Opal."

They were outside, by Wally's car.

Matilda was standing at the door. Wally had told her to stay there as a lookout. Every few minutes, she had to hurry into the dining room, where she was able to see if Melinda was still on the swing or not.

Wally listened to Leroy's account of what had happened at the trailer. Leroy had not expected Wally to believe a word he said, and kept swearing by his momma's grave that it was all true. But Wally only said, "I believe you."

"Whatchew gonna do?" Leroy asked.

"Listen, and listen good. There ain't nothing I can do right now. But you can."

"What am I supposed to do?" Leroy's face was full of blank amazement.

"Here." Wally glanced over his shoulder and shoved a piece of paper in his hand.

"I know you can drive. I done pulled you out from behind enough steering wheels. So you take that station wagon yonder"—it was Matilda's—"and you drive over to Tommy Buford's. You tell him to call this here number and say . . . say that Matt's gotta come back here. Quick. But tell Tommy he can't be calling here, no matter what. You understand that? I'm taking a big enough chance already." And again Wally glanced over his shoulder at the door to the kitchen. Matilda wasn't there. She had gone again to check on Melinda. "And if Tommy don't—or can't—do the calling, you gotta do it yourself. I got your word on that?" Leroy nodded. "You tell Matt something crazy done got loose."

Wally handed Leroy the car keys, then watched as the boy raced to the station wagon and started it up.

It was then he heard Matilda's scream.

"Wally!" she was yelling. "Comeer, hon! Quick!"

Wally ran back inside the house. He stopped dead. His daughter was on the threshold between the back porch and the living room.

"I told you, Daddy," Melinda said sadly. "I told you what I'd have to do. Didn't I?" The scissors were splayed. She was holding them two inches from her face. "I thought you believed in him. You said you did."

"Hon, don't do nothing, please. Don't—"

"He just wants us to believe in him, that's all."

"I do. I saw him. Hon, I believe in him. Your momma and I both do. Ain't that right?"

"We do," Matilda gasped.

"Mr. Shadow doesn't think so," the girl whispered. She raised the tip of one of the blades closer to her eye.

"No!" Wally screamed. He lunged toward his daughter, in a desperate effort to grab the scissors away. But it was too late.

Only two feet from his daughter, Wally closed his eyes and collapsed to his knees. "No, no," he whimpered, his face staring down at the floor, unable to look up.

He had not seen the blade go in.

He hadn't needed to.

He knew when it had happened from the terrible, inhuman gurgling that his wife made as she had tried to scream out, "Not your eyes, hon. Not your eyes."

21

Only half awake, Tommy Buford stumbled to the door of the trailer. Leroy, who had made it to the park in five minutes flat, going ninety miles an hour the whole way, tried to blurt everything out all at once. Tommy collapsed back onto the sofa and said, "Slow down, son."

Leroy did, but not by much.

"Sheriff Wally, he seen it. That shadow thing. Seen it a-coiling up behind that girl of his. It done already got her," Leroy said between gasps. "You gotta call this here number Wally give me."

Tommy glanced at the piece of paper: It was Matt's number in LA.

"Tell him he's gotta get back here and do something."

"I gotta call Wally first." Tommy reached for the phone, but Leroy jumped up and grabbed it from him.

"He done said you can't call him. She'll know. His girl will."

"What am I supposed to tell Matt? He'll think I lost my goddam mind," Tommy whispered.

"Anything. Just get him back here."

Tommy scanned Leroy's face. He knew the boy too well to doubt what he was telling him. Maybe it wasn't exactly like he portrayed. But it had to be damn close.

Tommy set the phone in his lap. He dialed the number and handed the slip of paper back to Leroy. Tommy got the switchboard operator at the hotel and asked for Matt's room.

"He answering yet?"

Tommy was about to shake his head no, when he heard Cathy's voice on the other end. "This is Tommy. I hate to call so late. But I got to talk to Matt. Yeah . . . I figured he'd be asleep. But . . . I gotta talk to him, anyways. No. Yeah. Something is wrong. No, it ain't Peter or Simmy. Please, Cathy, just let me talk to him."

"Who's that?" Leroy jumped up and went to the screen door. "It's Wally's patrol car," he whispered to himself, then turned back to Tommy and repeated what he had just said, loud enough to get Tommy's attention. Leroy watched as Wally got out of the patrol car and he instantly knew that something wasn't right. Wasn't right at all.

Wally had his gun out.

But that wasn't the only thing.

It was the way Wally's face looked. Devastated, hollow. Leroy had seen the same face on prizefighters on TV, but only after they had been knocked senseless three or four times, and are somehow still struggling to get to their feet.

"Put it down, Tommy."

Tommy looked up, his mouth open. Wally's gun was aimed right at Tommy's face.

"I'll shoot if I have to," Wally said. "I don't have no choice. You hear?"

Leroy looked from Wally back to Tommy. The phone was now in Tommy's lap. Just then Leroy heard the faintest sound of a man's voice coming through the earpiece of the telephone. "Tommy? Tommy, it's Matt. Tommy? What's wrong?"

"Hang the fucking phone up. *Now!*"

And Tommy did.

"You got to come with me."

"Where? What for?"

"Do what I say, and don't ask no questions." But Wally wasn't able to keep his eyes on Tommy's face for more than a moment. "Melinda . . . she . . ." Wally, as he tried to stammer the words out, covered his face with his hand. "Them scissors she got holt of, she—"

"She poked her right eye out with 'em."

Leroy nearly jumped out of his skin. There, in the hallway that led into the living room, stood Jimmy Buford. He was

235

the one who had just spoken. As he spoke, he was slowly unwrapping the bandage from his hand. "She done it 'cause her daddy made Mr. Shadow unhappy. He doesn't like it when you make him unhappy." Jimmy was looking into Tommy's face. "And now you've gone and made him unhappy, too, Daddy."

The bandage trailed to the floor as Jimmy walked into the kitchen. He opened a drawer and with his unburnt hand, he lifted out a meat cleaver. The blade glistened in the overhead light; Tommy had always been a stickler about keeping his knives sharp.

Just then the phone began to ring. "Don't answer it," Wally said to Tommy. "It's Matt, calling back." Tommy went to get up from the sofa, but Wally barred his way. Tommy looked from Wally back to his son. "Son, what the hell are you doing?"

"I ain't your son. I never was. Mr. Shadow told me so," Jimmy said. "He's my daddy now."

Tommy took hold of Wally's arm, to try to push it away, but Wally knocked him back down on the sofa. In disbelief, Tommy stared at the older man, the man who had been his friend since he had been a boy. "What d'you do that for?"

" 'Cause I ain't got no choice."

"Look what he's doing, for Christ's sake. Look."

"I can't," Wally said. "You'd best not, either. There ain't nothing you can do."

"That's crazy." Tommy was staring into the barrel of Wally's gun. "You couldn't kill me. You know goddam well you couldn't."

"I don't know what I can do no more."

"Look," Leroy said. Jimmy had set his hand palm down on the counter, right by the sink.

"Shit, what's he goin' to—" But Leroy didn't have time to get the question out. Jimmy had already lifted up the meat cleaver. It hovered there a moment. "This is how Mr. Shadow makes people believe in him. Watch." A smile flickered on Jimmy's lips. Tommy let out a scream, jumped up, and knocked Wally's arm away.

"Jesus Christ," Tommy shrieked as he watched his son bring the cleaver down with a sickening thud. The burnt hand was severed clean.

Leroy was on his feet. "I ain't believing this. I ain't believing this."

For a moment the hand lay still on the counter. Then a finger twitched, and another.

The phone was still ringing, but nobody made a move to unplug it. It went on and on like a stammered scream of horror.

"Looky," Leroy said, "it's moving."

Slowly the fingers rose up. They were dragging the severed hand across the back of the sink, over the faucet handles. The fingers reached up to the ledge of the window and pulled the rest of the hand onto it. It crawled to the latch and unfastened it. The screen came loose at one end, and the hand disappeared.

"It's going to be with Mr. Shadow," Jimmy said, his eyes fixed on it.

"Naw, naw," Leroy gasped. He turned, pushed Wally aside, and darted through the screen door out into the night.

22

"Curtis! Wake up! Goddam you, wake up!"

Leroy shook the screen in the solitary window of Curtis Poke's room.

"Let me fucking in. It's me. Leroy."

Bewildered, Curtis was sitting up in his bed. He blinked at the face in the window. "Whatchew doing?"

This time Leroy didn't say a word. He had managed to pull the screen open, and slid through the window, tumbling into the bed next to Curtis. He righted himself and looked into Curtis's face. "Get over there."

"Where?"

"Right there," Leroy said. He was pointing to the middle of the room.

"What for?"

"Just do what I tell you," Leroy commanded frantically.

Curtis got up and walked to the spot that Leroy had indicated. "Now turn around, so's you's facing away. Look at that closet over yonder. Go on and do it!"

"What the hell—"

"Do it!"

And Curtis turned so that his back was to Leroy. The younger boy reached up and turned on the light by the bed. He watched as Curtis's shadow was cast up against the closet wall. Leroy heaved a sigh of relief.

"I had to make sure you wasn't one of them."

"One of what?" Curtis looked around.

"Them whatmajiggies." Leroy said. "It done got Jesse. And Opal. And Jimmy. And Melinda. And who knows who else."

"What you talking about?"

"That thing." And Leroy caught sight of the book, its cover facing up. It was resting on the nightstand. He went to touch it, but pulled his hand back. "That right there."

"You lost your fucking mind?"

"Naw. It got loose from that story, and we got to find a way of putting it back."

"Leroy, you plumb—"

Curtis's face had gone rigid with attention. From somewhere outside, he heard the sound of a car engine. It was a sound he had heard a hundred times before. The sound of the souped-up Cleveland 351. A year ago, he had helped put it into Jesse's black Cougar.

It was coming down Sunshine Lane, the dirt road that ran in front of Curtis's folks' trailer.

"You hear that?"

Leroy nodded.

The car was in front of the trailer now. The engine cut off. The two boys heard a door slam.

"We gotta get out of here," Leroy said.

"It's Jesse."

"It ain't Jesse no more."

But Curtis didn't believe this for a minute. "He must've lived through it, when he fell."

"You crazy?"

Curtis was going to the door of his room. Leroy ran after him and grabbed his arm. "I done told you: It ain't Jesse now."

"You're wrong. It couldn't have gotten him. Jesse wouldn't let it."

The front door of the trailer creaked on its hinges. "Curtis?" The voice was Jesse's.

"See. I done told you."

Leroy went wild. He slammed himself against the door, to keep Curtis from opening it.

"You was suppose to come with me, Curtis," the voice called. "I done told you to. Why didn't you come with me?"

"I was scared, Jesse. I'm sorry."

"I tried to come back for you. I wasn't gonna let them assholes hurt you none, Curtis. You shoulda knowed that."

"I did," Curtis yelled. He reached down for the doorknob, but Leroy knocked his hand away.

"You ain't opening this door," the younger boy hissed.

Curtis took Leroy by the arm and pulled him away, then set his hand on the doorknob again. Leroy desperately tried to peel Curtis's fingers off, but the older boy was too strong. He pulled the door open.

"Jesse?"

Leroy was backing his way toward the window.

"That you, Jesse?" Curtis called out again.

He looked down. There was something black at his feet. Curtis blinked, then looked to see where it went. It stretched back to the living room. It was breathing, it looked like, lifting up and down. Out of the blackness a slit opened, and a pair of eyes gleamed, then a hand began to pull itself free from the pitchlike ooze, reaching up toward Curtis. The hand was a boy's hand.

It was fiery red and blistered all over. It had been severed at the wrist.

The fingers were clutching a knot of pale blond hair. It was the same color Opal's had been.

But it was the eyes that caused Curtis to wheel and stagger back with horror.

They were Jesse's.

A tongue began to protrude from between the two eyes.

Curtis shrieked, slammed the door shut, and locked it.

"I done told you," Leroy said. He was already halfway out the window.

Curtis reeled for a second, as if his knees were about to give out. Leroy shouted at him to move his ass.

It was seeping beneath the door now.

"It's just gonna be me and you, Curtis. Forever."

Curtis took two steps back, then spun around. He grabbed

his blue jeans without putting them on, and jumped up onto
the bed.

"Grab that book, Curtis. We may need it."

Curtis did, and was through the window before Leroy tumbled to the ground.

23

Fifteen minutes later, Leroy finished hot-wiring Mr. Proopes's
'76 Cadillac. It was too risky, he told Curtis, trying to get back
to Wally's station wagon. Besides, nobody would be expecting
them to be in Mr. Proopes's car, anyhow.

"Where we goin' to?"

"A telephone."

Leroy drove. They headed to the outskirts of Mt. Jephtha,
to Bobby Macon's Texaco. Leroy's momma had gone out for
a couple of months with one of the mechanics who used to
work there, Phil, and Phil had taken a liking to Leroy. He
would bring him up to the station and show him how to work
things there. And, as usual, Leroy still remembered everything
he had been taught.

"You ain't got any money?" Leroy asked Curtis.

Curtis, his face still, his mouth slack, shook his head no. He
was staring down at his copy of *The Shadowstealer*, his gaze
focused on the gleaming eyeball. "It's real, ain't it?"

"Course it is, I done told you."

Leroy parked to the side of the station. He found the spare
key under a brick, where it was always hidden—Phil had forgotten his key one morning when he brought Leroy up to the
station with him. Inside, Leroy went to the cash register. The
bills had been removed, as they always were at night. But there
was a roll of quarters left. Leroy got the roll out and slapped it
on the edge of the counter, breaking it in two. He shelled out a
handful of quarters and went over to the pay phone by the rest
rooms. "Why don't you just use their phone?" Curtis asked.

"They got it fixed so it don't call out long distance," Leroy
explained. He put a quarter in, dialed the operator, and said
he wanted to make a call out to Hollywood, California. "This
here's an emergency," Leroy added solemnly. The operator

told him to insert three dollars and Leroy slipped twelve quarters into the slot.

He stared down at the piece of paper that he had gotten from Wally. When the hotel receptionist answered, he asked for Room 423.

Matt answered on the first ring, his voice urgent.

"You probably don't remember who I am. But I'm Leroy. I know your boy, Peter. He comes to the trailer park where I live. We play horseshoes sometimes. I know Tommy real good.

"Why I'm calling you is this," Leroy said. "You gotta come back. Tonight." The boy took a deep breath, then glanced over at Curtis, who was still staring into the cover of Matt's novel. "It got loose, that thing you done wrote about. It got loose and you got to put it back, 'fore it's too late."

There was a moment of stunned silence on the other end of the line.

"Is this a joke?"

"I wisht it was a joke, but it ain't," Leroy said. "So you come back. You hear what I'm saying?"

Leroy hung up the phone and turned back to Curtis. "I done the best I could," Leroy said.

"Is he coming back?"

"I dunno."

"What're we goin' to do?"

"Figure out some way to kill it, I reckon."

"How?"

"Dunno yet. I got to think." Then he looked over at Curtis. And the same thing occurred to him that had occurred to Matilda earlier. "You done read that book. They musta killed it somehow. Say! How they kill it in that book he wrote?"

Curtis blinked. He looked into Leroy's fiercely determined eyes for a moment, then turned around. "I don't know. I never did finish the last two pages."

"Well, shit, go on and read it."

"I ain't sure I want to."

"You got to. It'd take me all year to read them two pages. Go on, Curtis."

The older boy gingerly opened the book, as if, somewhere within its pages, a booby trap had been hidden, and he was afraid of setting it off. He turned to the very end.

Leroy sat on the counter and waited.

Curtis summed up a little. The hero—a man not unlike Tommy Buford—was perched up on this old water tower. It was the middle of the night. Throughout the town, the Shadowstealer had picked off one victim after another, creeping up on them, chasing them down, exhausting them until each one of them had finally turned and looked into its shadow eyes. A little before, this writer guy—who was a lot like Matt—had been gotten by it, but only after he had told his friend, the Tommy dude, that maybe there was a way of getting rid of it. "I make up another story. One where it never existed. You got to tell it, and maybe, just maybe it will keep it from ever having been."

"Did it work?" Leroy asked.

"I told you, I ain't finished it yet."

"Go on and read."

Curtis opened to the final page.

The night wind was cool on top of the tower. In his hand he held the gun. But what gun could kill a shadow?

It was coming up the ladder.

He went on with the story, desperately trying to get the words out before he felt it, the tingling that he knew was coming.

He stopped.

He heard the creaking of the platform right behind him, then felt the cold breath on his neck.

The tingling had begun.

Where was he? He had forgotten his place in the story. He tried to recall it, but it had vanished from his memory.

All around the moonlight had vanished beneath its veil of darkness.

The tingling dropped down his spine.

He shivered and put his finger through the trigger of the gun.

This is only the beginning, he knew. It would go on and on, as the story of what had happened spread. Even to warn others was impossible, as he had long ago realized. To warn of the Shadowstealer it is necessary to tell its story.

And that was all it needed.

A story. A whisper. And slowly, little by little, it would come to life again.

He could feel the cold metal of the barrel against the roof of his mouth.

He felt the claw as it gripped his shoulder.

"God help us," he whispered.

There was no more he could do.

"Now," he whispered.

"Well, go on," Leroy said when Curtis looked up from the page.

"That's the end."

"Whatchew mean, that's the end?"

"That's where the book stops."

"What you talking about." Leroy jumped up from the counter where he had been perched, went over, and snatched the book out of Curtis's hands—it was the first time he had ever touched a copy of it. He blinked and moved his lips as he read the last words to himself. " 'Now,' he whispered. THE END.

"What's that mean?"

"It means, he pulled the trigger. He shot himself."

"Why'd he do that?"

" 'Cause. There wasn't nothing else he could do."

Scandalized, Leroy's face went livid. "Shit on that," he said as he flung the book into the corner. He scowled up at Curtis. "That ain't no way to end no fucking book!" He fumed and walked over and kicked the picture of Matt on the back of the cover.

Still angry, Leroy went back and slouched against the counter, breathing hard. He looked up at Curtis. "Somebody'd better tell him he's got to change that part. And change it quick."

24

Matt sat on the bed of the plush hotel room. "What the hell is going on?"

For the last half hour, he had tried calling Tommy six times. Wally three times. The Lumpkin house five times. Nobody had answered anywhere. Then, just as he was about to panic, Leroy called him.

"Who was it?" Cathy asked, aware that the call had knocked Matt for a loop. And Matt told her about the boy. "Peter used to always complain about him, saying . . . how Leroy didn't have an ounce of imagination in him." Matt looked at Cathy, then repeated what Leroy had told him.

Cathy was stunned, then said, "Come on, Matt. That's crazy."

"I know it's crazy. But if it's crazy, then why isn't anybody answering their fucking telephone?"

"Here." Cathy took the phone and began to dial the numbers. She looked at the clock and made the time adjustment: It was after four-twenty in the morning back in Mt. Jephtha. A place, as Matt pointed out, where when the phone rings in the middle of the night, it means somebody's dead.

You answer it, in other words.

Matt stood up and walked to the window. At noon tomorrow, he was to sign the contract that would turn his story into a multimillion-dollar movie. Spielberg had joked how, together, they were going to scare the shit out of every child and adult on the face of the earth. "It's going to be bigger than *E.T.* Trust me."

Just not quite as cute and winsome.

And Spielberg, with admiration in his voice, had asked, "Where'd you ever come up with an idea like that?"

"Oh, actually, it was my Aunt Hester's idea," he had replied with a laugh.

Spielberg took it as a joke.

But as Matt looked out over the huge vast darkness of LA, he found himself asking a question that he had not raised since he and Tommy had first listened to the story as boys.

Where had Aunt Hester gotten it from?

And from long ago, Tommy's words to him came back to haunt him.

"What if it's true?"

Matt turned around and looked at Cathy. She was still doggedly dialing numbers.

"Call the airport," he told her. "We're going home."

PART
SEVEN

1

It was five-thirty in the morning when Wally led a dazed Tommy Buford out to the patrol car, his wrists shackled in handcuffs, and set him in the backseat. They drove in silence to the small Mt. Jephtha jail house, where Wally pulled around the back and let Tommy out. Wally led him inside the empty jail house and locked him in one of the town's two cells. Only then did Tommy say anything. "What are you doing this for?" he asked.

"So I won't have to do nothing worse," Wally succinctly replied. And for the first and only time since they had left the trailer park, Wally looked straight into Tommy Buford's eyes. Tommy went to say something, but seeing Wally's face, he understood what he meant by "worse."

"But why me?"

"I think whatever that thing is, it's afraid of you."

"What d'you mean? How could it be afraid of me?"

" 'Cause of how close you and Matt've always been. It's afraid you'd talk Matt out of making that movie, I reckon." Wally glanced at Tommy. "It's like, the more people know about it, believe in it, the stronger it'll become."

"You fixin' to kill me?" Tommy asked. It wasn't a question he wanted to ask. But the words had come out that way.

"S'long as Matt don't come back, there ain't nothing to worry about. S'long as he goes ahead and signs that movie deal," Wally said. "That's one of the reasons I couldn't let you talk to him last night. I knew, if I did, I'd've to kill you."

"You don't mean that, Wally."

Wally was staring down at the floor. "A man will do just about anything to protect what he loves most in the world." He glanced up. "And whatever's out there knows it."

• • •

Back at his house, Wally found Melinda sitting on the top porch step. Mercifully, her back was turned to him. Wally hoped, when he spoke to her, that she wouldn't look around. He couldn't face that just yet.

He stood close to her and said, "Melinda? I want to talk to you, hon."

"About Mr. Shadow?"

"What is it he wants, exactly? You know?" Wally squatted down. "You think you can tell me something about it? Like where did he come from?"

"He came out of a story."

"You mean, the book Peter's daddy wrote?"

"No, not that story."

"Then what story, sweetheart?"

"An old, old story. Older than you are. Older than anything is," the girl said. "You see, Daddy, God forgot something. When He made the world."

Wally frowned, puzzled by his daughter's words. "What did God forget?"

"Something."

"What does this have to do with what's been going on, hon?"

"Mr. Shadow, he's been waiting a long time. Waiting for someone to come and tell his story. The old, old story. He waited for so many years, more than anyone can count, and then somebody came, and he told the story. Almost."

"You mean, Peter's daddy?"

Melinda shook her head. "Somebody else. It was long ago, and it was right here. Here in Mt. Jephtha where he told it. Up where the water tower is, only it wasn't there then. They caught him and they took him there and they burnt him all up. And all of his children were around him, and they were being chopped up and cut. And that's when he told the story he had promised never to tell." Melinda paused, then glanced halfway back over her shoulder. "I heard them, the children. I didn't want to hear them, but Mr. Shadow, he made me." She looked down at her injured hand. "Nobody wants to hear bad things, do they, Daddy?"

"No, sweetheart."

"Or see them."

"No."

"Like what I did. What Mr. Shadow made me do. To my eye. You didn't like that, did you, you or Mommy?"

"No."

"You'd like to forget, wouldn't you?"

"A course."

"You'd like to pretend it never happened."

"Yes."

Melinda was silent, then said, "That's how everybody is. They want to forget. To pretend bad things don't happen. But they do, don't they?"

"Yes."

"And that's all Mr. Shadow wants. For nobody to ever forget."

"But people have to forget."

"Why?"

"So," Wally stammered, "so they can go on living."

"What about the ones who don't go on living?"

"I don't know. You just have to go on. That's the only thing we can do."

"Could you go on living without me?"

Wally shook his head. "No, a course not."

"But you would," the girl said softly. "You and Momma both. Other mommies and daddies do."

Wally put his hands on the girl's shoulders. "You're our life, your momma's, and mine, too. There wouldn't be nothing for us without you."

Melinda rubbed her face with the back of her hand. "I want to forget sometimes, Daddy. I want to forget what I did."

"You can, hon. We can make everything okay again, the way it was."

"No, we can't. Nobody can. Not even God," Melinda whispered. "Sometimes, God forgets that, too. Like those little children Mr. Shadow made me hear. God forgot them. That's what Mr. Shadow wants. For God to remember. And us, too. He doesn't want us ever to forget again."

"All I know is, I love you. Love you more than my own life. More than anything."

"I know that, Daddy," Melinda whispered.

2

They were somewhere over Texas.

The curved horizon of the earth was just becoming visible from the window of the plane. They had left LA at five o'clock, Pacific time. Too early to notify anyone of their departure. Matt said he would call them when they were back in Georgia.

That would be fun, he thought.

"What are you going to tell them?" Cathy, very reasonably, had asked. Meaning, of course, certainly not the truth.

"I'll tell them Peter got sick." Matt then added, "You don't think I'm crazy enough to tell them the real reason, do you?" But judging from the way she had examined his face, he wasn't sure. Maybe she did think he was crazy enough.

And maybe she was right.

Matt had the stewardess bring him another double bourbon. It was his fourth.

There has to be a reasonable explanation, Cathy kept telling him. Yes, yes, Matt agreed. But what?

Matt stared out the tiny window at the reddening arc of dawn. "You know, there's something about this whole thing that kind of spooked me all along. I kept saying that it was me just being neurotic. But I never quite managed to convince myself."

"What d'you mean?"

"The success. I know it happens sometimes. First novels get bought for big bucks. Book clubs buy the rights to 'em. Even movies get made from them. Big, expensive ones. But still sometimes I'd asked myself: Why me? Or did I deserve it? And then I'd tell myself I was just being stupid. It was a damn good book. But still, there was this nagging voice that kept saying, 'It's too good to be true. Things like this don't happen. Not in real life.' And that's when I would wonder."

"Wonder what?"

"What if I was set up? I mean, what if there really was Something behind it all, Something that only used me. Used me the way God is supposed to use prophets. Only, in this case, it wasn't God talking." Matt took another big swallow of his bourbon. "Tommy asked me about it the first night, long ago, when I thought of doing a skit of Aunt Hester's story. He said, 'What if it's true? What if it can only get you if you've heard about it?' In other words, why take the chance? And why did I? It's strange, back when we were kids, I was the one who was supposed to have the wildass imagination. Tommy was supposed to have his feet on the ground. But it was odd, when it came to Aunt Hester's story, I remember trying to explain it away to Tommy, saying how Mr. Eprin had hypnotized Wiley and convinced him that his shadow had come alive. But Tommy, he always took it seriously, as if, deep down, he really believed it. But I never did. Not for a moment. Who knows, maybe my imagination led me astray. I had always loved stories so much—hearing them, making them up myself—that maybe I convinced myself too quickly that what we were hearing was merely that—a made-up story. Made-up, if not by Hester, then by somebody called Mr. Eprin, who ran a sideshow. But I never asked myself: If there really was a Mr. Eprin, why in hell would he travel around, from little town to little town, telling such a story?" Matt paused and glanced over at Cathy, to see if she was still awake. She was. "Maybe if I had been more literal-minded, less imaginative, I would have instinctively turned and run from the story, instead of jumping into it feetfirst."

"That's possible," Cathy murmured. Matt looked at her eyes. She had that frown of deep-thinking doubt that Matt, before, had always found so lovable.

"A penny for your thoughts," he asked.

"You sure you want to hear them?"

"Let me guess. You were just thinking that I'm nuts. Right?"

Cathy shook her head no, but didn't smile. "I'm just trying to make sense of everything."

"Any luck?"

"I don't know. I was just thinking about Storyworld. The place you told Peter about. Maybe there is one, only not out there, but deep inside us."

"Where?"

"The collective unconscious?" Cathy said. "I told you when I was in school, I was fascinated by Jung. Not convinced, just fascinated. And sometimes he made sense. Take a story, a real story, the kind that gets passed on from generation to generation, that burrows its way into the mind. Folktales and myths, legends and fairy tales, some of the stories from the Bible—that kind of thing. Anyway, I thought back to when I was in college, when I read C. G. Jung, and I remembered how intrigued I was by his theory of the collective unconscious. He noticed that if you look at the various myths and legends from the world over, certain patterns emerge, certain recurrent images and themes. He said that the same basic symbols also appear in dreams. Over and over. And it made him wonder, Why? And the explanation he came up with is this, more or less: Hidden in the human mind there is a kind of an attic, and it is full of symbols and images—archetypes, he calls them. They are stored away there, because they are left from the most primitive periods of the human past. But they can be brought back to life in dreams and stories. A good story— one that compels and haunts us—has its secret source down in this layer of the mind, in the collective unconscious. Take the image of the shadow. The shadow comes up in fairy tales and myths all the time. Why? Because, according to Jung, it is a symbol of something deeply buried in the realm of the unconscious—not just yours or mine, but everyone's. But we forget. We learn to think of our shadow as simply a plain old shadow. We forget the weird sense of uncanniness it must have invoked in primitive man. And in children, too. It moves when we do, it follows us, it mimics our every gesture, and yet it is something alien to us, something mocking and even threatening. Everybody knows the phrase 'So-and-so is scared of his own shadow.' Yet aren't we all? And why? Because it's a symbol of everything that is uninvited and yet within us— all the dark impulses and wishes, all the unwanted emotions, everything that we, as civilized human beings, have tried to run away from. But we can't run away from it, any more than you can run from your own shadow. You follow me?"

Matt nodded.

"And that's what I've been wondering. What if, in some way, your story—or Hester's story, or Mr. Eprin's story— what if it managed to tap into the collective unconscious, but even more powerfully and directly than other stories? What if the cover of the book, like the marquee at the carnival, gave a vivid, brutal image to something that had never been depicted, but which has nonetheless always lurked deep within us, below the level of any form of conscious representation, either in words or in pictures? I keep thinking about the ancient Hebrews, and how they prohibited giving either a name or an image to God. For them, certain things were too sacred, too taboo, too terrible, to be allowed entry into our consciousness, either by words or by visual illustration. And what if there were other things like that? Something like the thing that is at the heart of your story? The Shadowstealer? What if it was something that was never meant to be named or drawn or spoken about?" Cathy bit her lip. "I guess what I'm saying is this. Maybe you called something into existence. Invoked it, only not from Storyworld or never-never land, but up from the deepest, most terrifying layer of human unconsciousness. The thing in our nightmares that is always just behind the next door, or over our shoulder—always before it was nameless, without form, without color. What if you have somehow allowed it to surface, to come into consciousness, to be seen, and named, and spoken about? And what if that is what that boy—Leroy— meant when he called you, when he said that the thing in your book had gotten loose? Maybe what has gotten loose is something that has been buried deep in the human mind for thousands and thousands of years. Only now, it's out there."

Matt stared back out the window.

"I wish I hadn't asked."

3

"How you goin' to get in there?"

"Dunno yet."

"You don't even know that's where he is."

"Where else would Wally've put him?"

Leroy had parked Mr. Proopes's old Cadillac in the alley behind the jail house. The sun was just coming up over the top of Mt. Joab and a few pickup trucks were already stirring, but otherwise the town was still quiet. Leroy got out of the car.

"What if Wally didn't put him anywhere?" Curtis asked as he followed after Leroy.

"Whatchew mean?"

"What if he killed him?"

"Don't be talking no shit, Curtis. S'no way Wally could kill nobody. Least of all Tommy Buford." Leroy was standing under a high, small window at the back of the jail house. "Comeer and bend down. I'm goin' to get on top of you."

Curtis obliged reluctantly. Leroy clambered onto the older boy's shoulders, then told Curtis to lift up. "Can you see anything?"

"Not much. Set me down."

Back on his feet, Leroy ran back to the car, opened the trunk, and returned with Mr. Proopes's tire jack. "Lift me up again."

"Whatchew goin' to do?"

"Break out that window. Now do what I tell you."

Curtis did.

"I'll try to keep the glass from falling on you."

" 'Preciate it," Curtis grumbled, trying to keep steady, lest Leroy fall, while at the same time preparing to dodge slivers of broken glass. Leroy began to knock the glass out of the window, carefully removing all the pieces that doggedly stuck to the sill. "There. I'm goin' in. You go on 'round the front. I'll open the door for you." And Leroy heaved himself up and in.

He landed on Wally's desk, scrambled to his feet, and called out, "Tommy? It's me, Leroy." He scooted through the corridor, got to the front door, and found that it was dead-bolted. He called to Curtis. "It's locked. You stay out there and watch for Wally. Yell if you see anything."

Leroy ran to the back of the jail house, where the two tiny holding cells were.

Tommy sat up on the bunk. "Leroy?" he asked in disbelief.

"A course. Who was you expecting it to be?" The boy scowled.

"What the hell you doing?"

"Trying to get your ass out." Leroy was examining the lock on the cell door. "You think ol' Wally keeps him a spare set of keys around here?"

"I don't know."

"You ain't no help," Leroy said. "I'm going to look around. You stay put."

Leroy dashed back into Wally's office. He rummaged through every drawer, went through the filing cabinet, groped under

Wally's desk, checked out the broom closet. But there were no keys. Undaunted, Leroy searched for a screwdriver, a hammer—anything to pick or shatter the lock. "Shit," he declared, when nothing of this variety turned up. He went back to the front door and called for Curtis. "You still out there?"

"Yeah. I ain't seen nothing yet."

"Run up to the hardware store and fetch a hacksaw, a file, and a little bitty screwdriver. Bring 'em back as fast as you can."

"The hardware store ain't open yet, Leroy."

Leroy shook his head in dismay. "Sheet, Curtis, don't you know how to throw a rock through a window?"

"What if somebody sees me?"

"Then I reckon they see you. Go on now."

Back with Tommy, Leroy told him he had sent Curtis up to the hardware store to get some things. "I called out there to Hollywood. I told him to get on back quick like."

"What did you tell him?"

"What was happening. How that thing he wrote that book about had gotten loose. I said you done told me to call him."

" 'Preciate it. You done real good, Leroy."

Leroy almost smiled at the compliment, but at the last moment changed his mind. "We got to do some serious thinking 'bout this shit," he declared. "You got any ideas?"

" 'Bout what?"

"How to kill that motherfucker. I figure, you can't kill it regular like. I mean, with no gun or nothing. Ain't no point goin' shooting at a shadow. Can't break its neck. Can't run over it in no car. So I reckon we can forget about all them things."

Tommy nodded, still dazed and reeling from what had happened the night before. He stared over at Leroy, the boy's brow knitted in fiercely concentrated determination as he turned over one scheme after another. For Leroy, the situation wasn't about to overwhelm or stupify him. He wasn't going to sit idly by and wring his hands, or ask how and why the world could suddenly turn upside down. Curiosity and speculation on the unknown, they didn't interest the boy. To Leroy, it was enough to know that the world had turned upside down, and what was now important was figuring out how to turn it right side up again.

"What I been thinking is this," Leroy continued. "If a story

done set it loose, maybe another story could pen it up again?
Whatchew think?"

"I don't know."

"Maybe if we was to get him to write another ending to that
book of his. I know he's your friend and all, but just between
you and me, that ending he done wrote for it kinda sucks. That
ain't the way to end no story. Curtis done read it to me."

"Yeah," Tommy said, unable to keep from smiling. When he
had first read the final version of *The Shadowstealer*, Tommy
had raised the same point with Matt. You think folks are going
to like a book where, on the last page, the hero and the lone
survivor puts a gun into his mouth just as the thing is crawling
up behind his back, then pulls the trigger? But Matt had told
him: That's where the story led me to. There wasn't any other
way out.

Not, at that moment, a reassuring thought, Tommy reflected.

"Course," Leroy grumbled, "I don't know why he'd want
to go and write a goofy story like that no how. Sure wish he
hadn't." He sat down on the floor next to the cell and crossed
his legs. He put his head into his hands. "What don't a shadow
like?" He was staring down at his own small dim shadow,
cast by the overhead light. He moved a little to one side, then
another.

"See that?"

"See what?"

"How it moves. Kinda like it's trying to dodge the light.
See?"

"Yeah."

"I reckon that's what a shadow don't like. Light. Only it
looks like no matter how you move, where you go to, that ol'
shadow can always get away from it somehow, dodge it like."
And Leroy stood up, to demonstrate the cunning with which his
shadow always crept to the place where the light didn't shine.
"Reckon maybe if we was to trap it. Trap somewheres where
there wasn't nothing but light. Where light was all around it.
Whatchew think? You know a place like that?"

Tommy shook his head no.

"Wush we could put it inside the sun," Leroy commented.
"Reckon that would fix it."

"I just can't think of—"

"Hush up a second." Leroy scowled. His eyes got a funny

look to them. Tommy was familiar with the look. He had seen it in Matt's eyes ever since they were kids together, a look that always boded some stupendous surge of inspiration.

"I got me an idea," he whispered. "We goin' to need to steal us a fire truck."

"A fire truck?"

Leroy nodded.

"What for?"

"Never you mind," Leroy snapped. "What the hell's taking Curtis so long for anyhow?" And before Tommy could follow up his question, Leroy had dashed back to the other part of the jail house. He climbed on top of Wally's desk, stuck his head out the window, and looked down the alleyway toward the street. Just as he was about to hurl curses on Curtis's head, the other boy came racing around the corner, glancing back over his shoulder. He was carrying a bag that said "Mt. Jephtha Hardware" on it.

"'Bout time," Leroy said. "Here, hand 'em up. Anybody see you?"

"Don't think so."

"You wait in the car. I'm going to get Tommy out, then we're goin' to steal us a fire truck."

Curtis stared up at Leroy as he handed him the tools.

"You goin' to try to drown it?"

"Course not," Leroy said contemptuously. "How the fuck you going to drown a shadow, Curtis? Sometimes I wonder about you."

4

At Hartfield Airport, Matt and Cathy went to the first pay phone. They tried each of the numbers twice. "Shit, nobody sleeps after eight in the morning in Mt. Jephtha," Matt said, "except me."

It took them an hour to find their car—they got confused between the North and the South terminal. Cathy drove—Matt had downed six bourbons on the flight. "Why don't you try to go to sleep, honey," she told him. "You may need it later."

"Yeah," Matt agreed.

5

"It's him, Daddy. He came back."

The telephone was ringing. Matilda, who had fallen into a fitful sleep on the sofa, had jumped up on the second ring and had nearly answered it on reflex. But as her hand went to the receiver, she caught a glimpse of Melinda. She was standing in the doorway that led out onto the porch, her scissors clasped in her hand. A shadow mercifully covered most of her face.

Wally had come in from the kitchen and waited until the phone had stopped ringing.

"He's coming back here," Melinda said.

"Who?"

"You know. Somebody told him." Melinda stepped into the light. Wally flinched on seeing the empty socket where her eye had been.

"I didn't have nothing to do with it, hon."

"You know your daddy won't do nothing like that."

Melinda walked over and sat down on the sofa. She was staring out through the window into the woods behind the house.

"Daddy?" she whispered. "You said you loved me. More than anything in the world. Is that true?"

"Yes. Of course."

"You don't like it when I hurt myself, do you?"

"You know I don't."

"If something bad had to happen to somebody, you'd do it, wouldn't you? Even if it was real bad."

"I don't understand."

"If Mr. Shadow thought somebody shouldn't be here, you'd help him, wouldn't you?"

"What are you talking about, hon?"

"Tommy."

"What about him?"

"If Mr. Shadow didn't want him here, you'd make him go away."

Wally felt his chest tightening. "Hon, there's some things you can't ask me. Some things I can't do."

Melinda kept staring into the woods. Wally knelt down and this time he let his hand fall on his daughter's hair. He stroked it softly. "I love you, more than anything. But there're things I just ain't made to do. So please don't ask me to do 'em."

"It's not me who's asking you," she whispered.

She turned to him.

The socket was no longer empty. There was an eye in it. It wasn't Melinda's.

It gleamed.

6

"Goddammit," Leroy declared. "Why they make these here locks so hard to pick?"

He sat down, screwdriver in hand, and wiped his forehead. "How you coming?"

"Not too good." Tommy had been trying to cut through the bars with the hacksaw. In order to slip out, he figured he would have to remove two bars. So far, in forty minutes, he had gotten through half of the first one, and the hacksaw was about ready to fall apart.

Leroy looked at its condition. "That Curtis Poke, I ain't never goin' to let him steal nothing for me again." Leroy stood back up. "Reckon we gotta keep trying."

Leroy again stuck the screwdriver into the lock. He twisted and turned it. There was a click. The boy grinned—a rare thing to see on Leroy's countenance—and pulled the door of the cell open. "Shit, I done it."

"Leroy!"

It was Curtis, calling from outside. Actually, not calling, yelling.

"It's Wally! Leroy, you hear me?"

Tommy and Leroy looked at each other for a moment. "The window, quick," Leroy told him. They made a dash down the corridor into Wally's office. "You go first," Tommy told the boy.

"Uh-uh, you go. He ain't after me."

"Go ahead," Tommy said, then lifted the boy onto the desk by the back of his blue jeans. "Go on." Leroy hesitated, then clambered over the windowsill and dropped down into the alleyway. Tommy mounted the desk and was about to pull himself up when he heard a click. He looked around.

Wally was standing in the doorway. The clicking noise had come from his gun. He had just pulled the trigger back. Neither man said a word for a moment. Then, as he looked into Wally's face—he had never seen a face so ravaged by pain in his whole life—Tommy whispered, "Whatchew want me to do, Wally?"

The older man shook his head uncertainly. "I ain't sure," he said in a hoarse, stricken voice.

"What you goin' to do if I go through that window, Wally?"

Wally stared down at the gun. "What I have to."

Tommy eased back onto the desk. "What are you here for?"

"We gotta go somewheres," Wally stammered.

"Where's that?"

"Off somewheres." Wally reached to his belt and pulled off a pair of handcuffs. "Put these here on," he said and tossed them to Tommy. He caught them and put one of the cuffs around his right hand. "I'll do the other one. Turn around." And Tommy turned around. Wally pulled Tommy's left hand behind his back, and cuffed it, and snapped the handcuffs together. "You don't know how sorry I am about this," Wally whispered. "You know what I always thought about you, ever since you was a boy. I always thought you was as decent, as fine, as—" Wally's voice broke off.

And all at once Tommy understood.

Wally Clark—the man who, when Tommy was a boy, had taught him how to pitch a fast ball, how to steal second base, the man who had taken him fishing on the Osagee River and deer hunting in the woods of North Georgia—was about to take Tommy out one last time.

7

"What're they saying?" Curtis whispered.

"I think they's leaving."

"What's going on? Where they going?"

"Dunno." Leroy was on top of Curtis's shoulders. The younger boy had kept his head just below the sill of the window. "They done left. I'm goin' back in."

"What for?"

"Wush you wouldn't ask so many questions," Leroy scolded, then slid back into the window. He emerged less than three minutes later. "Here, take this." He handed a rifle down to Curtis. "And these here." Meaning four boxes of ammunition. "And this." A Magnum .357.

"Shit, what we need these for?"

" 'Cause, Wally's taking Tommy out to kill him. That's what we need 'em for."

8

Wally put Tommy next to him in the patrol car. He started it up and pulled away from the front of the jail house. "I brought something. I figured maybe it'd help." He reached under the seat and pulled out a bottle of Rebel Yell, twisted the top off, and went to hand it to Tommy.

"Kinda hard for me to drink it, with my hands behind my back, Wally."

"Yeah," Wally said with a frown. "Here." And he held it up to Tommy's mouth. "Take you a sip. Careful." And Tommy took a swallow, spilling as much on his chin as he managed to get into his mouth. Wally took out his handkerchief and wiped the whiskey off Tommy's face.

" 'Preciate it," Tommy said.

Wally took the bottle, turned it up, and swallowed for half a minute. "Shit, reckon I needed it more than you did, anyhow."

9

They were on old Highway 437.

"See now. Ain't you glad I done stole Mr. Proopes's Caddy," Leroy gloated. "Wally sure ain't expecting ol' Mr. Proopes to be following him."

"You're goin' to let 'em get away."

"Naw. Don't wanna get too close to 'em. Don't you never watch TV? See here, Curtis, if you wasn't always reading them books, you'd know something."

Curtis sighed. He looked into the backseat at the cache of firearms that Leroy had removed from the jail house. "You and Wally goin' to have a shootout?"

Leroy frowned. "I ain't got that part figured out yet."

"They're turning."

"I got eyes, Curtis."

"Must be goin' down to the river."

"Ain't no place else to go down that way," Leroy said. One of his momma's boyfriends, Uncle Kyle, had taken him fishing down on the Osagee. The dirt road the patrol car had turned onto didn't split off anywhere, but zigzagged about five miles through the woods until it came to the riverbank.

The two boys got to the turnoff. Leroy stopped the car.

"What are we goin' to do now?"

"Reckon there ain't nothing else we can do. 'Cept go down yonder." Leroy glanced into the backseat. "You'd better start loading up them guns, Curtis."

"But how you goin' to stop him? I mean, if Wally's really goin' to do what you said."

"I swear, Curtis. You have to know everything before it happens? I'll figure something out. Just don't you worry, hear? Now load 'em up."

10

"Melinda, hon. You ain't sleepy yet? Maybe if you was to try to get some sleep."

The girl shook her head no. She was sitting on the porch swing again. By now, the porch was filled with the coils and loops of cut-up newsprint. "I'm waiting for Daddy to get back."

Matilda glanced down at her watch. 9:42. "But he may not be back for a while."

"We said ten-thirty. Remember?"

"A course I remember," Matilda said. "He'll be back. You know he will. He won't let nothing bad happen to his little girl, hon. You know that, don't you? Don't you?"

Melinda nodded quietly. A smile crossed her lips. "Daddy loves me more than anything in this world."

"That's true. That's so true," Matilda whispered, choking back the tears. "Why, we wouldn't have no reason to go on living without you. Don't you know that?"

"We know that, Mommy."

Matilda crouched down in front of the girl. "Look at me, Melinda. Please."

The girl shook her head no.

"You ain't serious 'bout what you said. It don't give him much time. Something could happen. He could have a flat tire. What you done asked him to do, it ain't goin' to be easy. You know Tommy was like a son to him, back before you was born. Tommy, he ain't never hurt anybody. Never would, either. There just ain't no cause for nobody to do nothing to him. I don't even know what I'd do if I had to do what you done asked your daddy to do. And you know how much I love you, don't you?"

Melinda nodded, still without looking into Matilda's eyes. Tears were streaming down Matilda's face. She wiped them away. "What if your daddy can't do it?" she whispered.

"Then you won't have a little girl anymore, Mommy."

Matilda bit her lip to keep it from trembling. She got up, teetering. "Don't say that. Please don't say that, hon."

"What time is it?"

"Ain't that late."

"I'm thirsty. Bring me some lemonade, Momma. Please."

"Course," Matilda said, visibly heartened by the ordinariness
of the request. "I'll make us a big pitcher, hon." She hurried
into the kitchen. Everything's going to be okay, she told herself, as if somehow the lemonade were a magical elixir that
would return life to them, would summon their child back
from the crazy shadow realm into which she had descended.
Her mind raced ahead: Melinda would drink her a glass of
lemonade and she would look up at her momma and smile, the
sweet way she used to, and say, "Can I have another one?" And
Matilda would pour her out another glass, and another. And
she would forget all about what she had said would happen
at ten-thirty, what she would do to herself if her daddy didn't
come back by then, if he didn't show her the thing in the trunk
that he had promised to bring her.

Matilda dropped the bottle of grenadine as the image rose
up before her mind.

The slack mouth, blood dripping from it, the body twisted
in what would be pain if there were still life in it, and the
bullet hole an inch above the cold, unseeing, heartbroken eyes.
Tommy's eyes.

No, he wouldn't do it. He couldn't. He'd come back, but
Melinda would still be drinking the pink lemonade out on the
porch, and Matilda would run and make another pitcher for her,
and she would go on drinking and laughing, and she wouldn't
say a thing about the trunk of Wally's patrol car, and there
would be no more Mr. Shadow, and tomorrow they would ask
the name of a good doctor down in Atlanta, and they would go
down and get Melinda a glass eyeball, a pretty blue one, some
of them were so real you couldn't even tell the difference, and
lots of people had them, famous people, like Columbo.

The pitcher crashed to the floor. Matilda gave out a little
shriek.

"Melinda? What is that? What's making that noise, hon?
What's making that—"

Matilda was on the porch. Her girl had just come from the
steps that led out into the yard. She had gone down into the
basement.

In her hands was Wally's gas-powered weed-eater that Matilda had gotten him for Father's Day. She looked at the shiny whirl
and realized that it wasn't the plastic cord, but the metal blades

that you were supposed to use on the tougher weeds.

"Whatchew got that for?"

The girl carried it to the swing and sat down. She eased its head into the mound of cut-up newspaper. Matilda jumped back in horror as the mangled shreds of paper exploded at the touch of the screaming blades. "What time is it, Mommy?"

Matilda gasped, unable even to look at her watch. "I don't know."

"That's okay, Mommy. We do." Melinda smiled.

The paper continued to whirl up and scatter.

"Mr. Shadow says, Daddy better hurry."

11

They were at the river.

Wally went around and opened the door on Tommy's side. He helped him out, then glanced down at his watch.

"What you keep looking at your watch for?"

"No reason," Wally mumbled. He took another big swallow of the Rebel Yell; The bottle had only two fingers of whiskey left in it.

"Reckon this here's what you meant by 'worse,' " Tommy said.

"Yep." Wally had his head turned away. He was staring at the river.

"You goin' look me in the eye before you do it, Wally? I'd appreciate it, if you would."

"I can't. You know I can't."

"What the hell am I supposed to do, make it easy on you? Christ, Wally, you know goddam well you can't do something like this. Look . . . look down there. We goddam went fishing right there. We'd come down here on a Saturday morning, be here at sunup, and you'd tell me all them tall tales of yours. You gotta remember that shit."

"I remember it alright."

"Then what the fuck d'you think you're trying to do?"

"I ain't got a choice." And for the first time, Wally looked into Tommy's eyes. His mouth sagged open. "It ain't just goin' be her eye this time. 'Less I do what she says. She says I got to bring you back. To prove I done it. Put you in the goddam trunk of my car. And I says, 'Don't make me do it, please, hon.' I was crying, and begging. 'I'd rather blow my own brains out before I go and hurt a boy means as much to me as Tommy does. You know that, hon.' But she says, 'Mr. Shadow, he knows it, too,' and that's why I got to bring him back by ten-thirty. So he'll know he don't have to worry no more about Tommy."

Wally looked down at his watch. Tommy saw the dial, too. It was 10:05.

It would take twenty minutes, at least, to get back to Wally's house.

"I ain't never begged a man before. And I know I ain't got no right to beg nothing from you. Not this. But don't make it harder. Don't do or say nothing to make it harder. Just go on down to the edge of the river, like you was goin' fishing." Wally reached into his holster and pulled his gun out of it. "And turn your head away. Like you was looking at something in the river. And, no matter what, don't turn back around."

"You can't ask a man that. You goin' to do it, you goin' have to do it to my face, Wally."

"Alright," Wally whispered. He clutched the gun in his hand and lifted it up. The barrel was a foot away from Tommy's face. Tommy stared into its blackness.

"I loved you as much as I ever loved a man, Tommy. You know that, don't you?"

Tommy went to say, "I know it," but fear gagged him.

From behind him Tommy could hear the sound of the river, soothing and sweet, and beyond that, the morning twittering of the birds scattered around the woods. It was a sound he loved, both as a boy, when he had come here with Wally, and as a man, when he had brought his own son down to the same spot, repeating to him the same tales that he had gotten from Wally.

And all at once, Tommy understood something that had never before made sense to him. How a man could go to his death without screaming or yelling or trying to run. How a man could die without even a whimper.

Slowly Tommy turned around and walked to the edge of the river. His face to the water, he closed his eyes.

"Go on," he whispered hoarsely.

12

Leroy had pulled Mr. Proopes's old Caddy onto the shoulder of the narrow dirt road. He told Curtis to grab the rifle and follow him. Leroy took the Magnum.

"We gotta cut through these woods, so's they won't see us coming," Leroy explained. "It ain't far."

"I still wanna know what you're goin' to do," Curtis said, trying to keep up with Leroy. The younger boy turned around and said, "Keep that rifle pointed at the ground. You could trip and blow your own brains out, Curtis."

Curtis came beside Leroy and managed to stay there through the next few feet of undergrowth. "You still ain't said what we're gonna do."

"That's 'cause I don't know, Curtis."

Curtis stopped. "I thought you had some kind of plan."

"I do. It just ain't come to me yet."

Curtis hesitated, then took after Leroy. Just as he came by next to him, Leroy stuck his arm out, indicating that they had stopped. "You hear it? That's the river. They should be right down there. Behind them trees over yonder."

They could see the other bank of the river through the little grove of poplars. At this spot the river itself was shaded and calm. "Wush we was goin' swimming instead," Leroy muttered. He glanced back at Curtis and said, "Give me that rifle. You take this."

Leroy knelt down behind the largest of the poplar trees.

The patrol car was parked about ten yards from the riverbank. Wally was standing by it. He was holding his arm straight out from him, as if trying to put as much distance between himself and the gun he had clutched in his hand.

Tommy had just then turned and was making his way down to the riverbank.

"What's Tommy doing?"

"Dunno," Leroy said.

"I ain't believing this. Looks like Wally's goin'—"

"He is."

"What are you goin' to do?"

"Dunno," Leroy repeated. "I ain't never shot a man before."

"No shit."

Leroy crouched down onto his stomach. He pulled the rifle up and lodged it in the leaves. He put his eye to the sight. "I don't know where to shoot him at."

"You can't kill ol' Wally."

"You see what he's fixing to do, Curtis."

Just then Tommy said two words.

"What d'he say?"

"He said, 'Go on.' "

"This here's crazy, Leroy. He's telling Wally to shoot him."

Leroy nodded. "I heard." He kept shifting the sights of the rifle, up to Wally's head, then down to his chest, then farther down to his legs.

"You could just try to wound him."

"I done thought of that already. But Wally could still shoot Tommy if I just hit him in the leg," Leroy said. "If I do it, I gotta kill him."

Curtis backed away. "You can't."

"I fucking got to, Curtis. I can't let nobody kill Tommy." Leroy hissed. "Even if Tommy's dumb enough to let him, I ain't."

Leroy put his finger on the trigger. He slowly squeezed it, keeping the back of Wally's head in his sights.

"I ain't happy about this, Wally," Leroy whispered to himself.

He pulled the trigger. The gunshot thundered, the rifle's recoil knocking the butt sharply, painfully into Leroy's shoulder. Leroy didn't look to watch where the bullet hit. His face was buried in the leaves as soon as the shot was fired. All around, up and down the river, the sound kept echoing, over and over, repeating itself just when it seemed to fall silent, as the echo traveled down the coves and inlets of the river.

"What happened?" Leroy whispered, his face still in the leaves. His body was trembling all over.

"You got him," Curtis said, his voice numb. "You hit him right—"

"I don't wanna know where, Curtis."

"Okay." Curtis knelt down. He put his hand on Leroy's shoulder. He went to say something, to tell Leroy he had only done what somebody had to do, but Curtis couldn't get the words out. Under his hand, he felt Leroy's shoulder blade as it heaved up and down in spasms. "You're crying," Curtis said in amazement: He had never seen Leroy cry, ever.

"Fuck, yes, I'm crying, Curtis. Now go on down with Tommy. You and him, take ol' Wally and you put him somewheres . . . somewheres I don't have to look at him no more. Hear?"

"I hear, Leroy." Curtis rubbed the boy's back a few moments longer, then got up and ran down to the riverbank.

PART EIGHT

. . . .

1

"Wake up, Matt."

Cathy nudged his shoulder twice, and Matt opened his eyes. He was about to ask where they were, when he looked up and saw the porch of the Lumpkin house. "What time is it?"

"Ten-fifteen."

"You got here fast," Matt mumbled. He put his hand to his forehead and momentarily regretted five of his last six bourbons. He blinked, rubbed his eyes, shook himself, then stared at the porch. "At least the house is still here. So far, so good."

They got out and Cathy helped Matt to wind his way up the porch steps. Inside, he called out for Simmy and Peter. There was no answer. They went through the main hallway, careful to step over the circular saw and the lumber that Tommy had left there. The kitchen was empty. Again Matt called out for his son and for Simmy. Again there was not a sound coming from anywhere in the huge old house.

"They could have gone somewhere."

Matt nodded at Cathy's attempt at reassurance, then walked out on the porch.

"Peter?"

The boy was sitting on the top step. His back to him, he was looking down at the bottom of the porch stairs. Out in the yard Matt noticed Tigger. The cat was just sitting there, staring up at Peter.

"Comeer, Tigger," Peter called. "Please?"

"Son?" Matt said. He walked behind the boy and crouched down next to him. "You okay?"

"He won't come to me anymore," Peter said, without turning around. "Tigger won't come to me now."

"We tried to call you last night. Why didn't you and Simmy answer the phone?"

"He wouldn't let us," Peter said matter-of-factly. Then he returned to his complaint. "I keep calling to him. But he won't come up. And when I go to him, he runs away. Into the woods."

"Who wouldn't let you?"

"You know, Daddy," Peter told him, his tone of voice oddly mournful. "Comeer, Tigger. Please?"

Matt stood back up and looked down at Tigger. The cat's eyes were on Matt now. Normally when Matt came back after an absence of even a day, Tigger could be counted to come running to him the moment Matt uttered his name. "Tigger?" Matt called out tentatively. The cat still didn't move. His eyes fixed on Matt's face, troubled and uncertain.

"See, Daddy," Peter said sadly. "He's scared of me now."

"Scared of you?"

Peter nodded. His voice confused, hesitant, Peter turned from the yard and looked up for a moment at his father. "I'm scared of me, too," he said, then once more began to call Tigger.

"Why d'you say that, son?" Matt asked, kneeling down next to the boy.

" 'Cause."

" 'Cause what, Peter?"

"I'm scared I'll do bad things."

"What kind of bad things?"

"Things to make you sad. Like Melinda," Peter said.

"Wally's girl?"

Peter nodded, his eyes still on the cat. "And, Jimmy," he added, "I don't want to make you sad."

"What are you talking about, son?"

"He doesn't need them anymore. He's got me now," Peter said softly.

"Who does?"

"Mr. Shadow. You let him out from Storyworld. And now he's here."

Cathy, who had been standing behind Matt, reached down and put her hand on his shoulder. He looked behind at her, then said, "Where's Simmy, Peter?"

"Dunno." Peter stood up. Matt took him by his shoulders

and turned the boy around, so that he was looking into his eyes. His face was pale, his eyes dazed and numb, as if he were sleepwalking.

"Tell me what happened."

"I didn't mean to look back. I forgot. I was looking for Tigger. Under the porch and I looked back. And now Tigger won't come to me anymore."

Matt glanced at Cathy. "You still got those phone numbers? Try to go call Tommy and Wally." She was about to go back inside when Peter said, "Mr. Shadow wants you to see Melinda, Daddy. Before . . ." The boy's voice trailed off.

"Before what?"

"Before she goes away. Mr. Shadow thinks you should see."

"See what, son?"

"See what bad things can happen when daddies don't do what Mr. Shadow wants them to."

Cathy squeezed Matt's arm. "Maybe you'd better go. I'll stay here and watch Peter."

"You'd better hurry, Daddy. It's ten twenty-three."

"What does that mean, Peter?"

"It means, you only have seven minutes."

2

Matilda looked down at her watch.

It was one minute before ten-thirty. She was at the window again, anxiously scanning the street for the approach of Wally's patrol car. From behind her, the noise of the weed-eater filled the entire house, grating and terrible. She put her hands up to her ears, but it kept on. "Please, Lord, please, Lord," she whispered over and over. "Let Wally get here. Let him—"

She broke off her prayer—the machine seemed to have suddenly gotten more revved up than before—and dashed back to the porch. "Hon," she gasped, but the machine was still busily, mindlessly shredding what little was left of the newspaper.

"He's goin' to be here any minute. You ain't got to worry about that. You and Mr. Shadow, you know your daddy ain't goin' to let nothing bad happen to you. Don't you, hon? Don't you?"

The weed-eater moved back and forth, Melinda's eyes fixed on the blades.

"It's ten-thirty, Momma."

Matilda glanced at her watch. "No, it ain't. Not—" But just as she went to say "yet," the minute hand clicked to the six. She gasped and looked back up at her daughter. Every muscle in her body froze. Melinda lifted the weed-eater up, so that it was at a forty-five-degree angle to the floor. She let it slide down between her legs, until the whirling blades were only a foot or so from her face, close enough to blow her hair back around her shoulders.

Grab it from her, Matilda screamed to herself. Just reach out and snatch it away. Even if it meant wrestling with the blades.

But Matilda didn't move. Pretty little girls just don't cut themselves up with weed-eaters. Even if she did what she did with those scissors.

She looked down at her watch, then up at the girl.

It was ten-thirty, but nothing had happened. It was a bluff. That's all.

Melinda tilted her face from one side to the other, closing her eyes, letting her hair blow back, the way Matilda had seen her do with a fan on a hot day. Just a few seconds longer, and it wouldn't be ten-thirty anymore, and everything would be okay, Melinda wouldn't have hurt herself, and Wally would pull up, and Tommy would be with him, alive and well, and they would tell her that they had figured everything out, and that the nightmare was over with now, because they had taken care of everything while they were out.

Matilda held her breath. The minute hand clicked to thirty-one minutes after ten.

And nothing had happened.

It was going to be okay now. The weed-eater would be running out of gas in just a little bit, anyway, and then, even if Melinda wanted to, there would be nothing she could do to herself.

Matilda stepped within only a few feet of her girl. "Hon? Everything's fine now, ain't it? So why don't you just go on and put that ol' thing down."

"Mr. Shadow can tell time, Momma."

"A course he can."

"He knows what time it is. He's just waiting."

"For what? For your daddy, you mean?"

She shook her head. "Daddy's gone."

"Whatchew mean? Hon, whatchew—"

At that moment she heard a screeching tire over the noise of the weed-eater. It had come from the driveway. "You're wrong, hon. There he is now. He come back. Like he done promised he would. So you can go on and put that ol' thing down now. You ain't got no need for it now." And Matilda ran to the door of the kitchen and flung it open. She yelled out, "Wally, get in here quick. She's—"

But it wasn't Wally.

His mouth open, Matt had just come running into the car-port.

"It's you," Matilda whispered.

"What's wrong?"

"Everything."

"Where's Wal—"

But Matilda had already grabbed his arm and was dragging him out to the porch. "What's that noise?"

"Tell her, tell Melinda, it was just some story you done made up in your head. Tell her there ain't really no Mr. Shadow. Tell her you was just trying to scare folks, s'all." Matilda stopped, and gave out a shriek.

The girl was standing up in the middle of the porch. She was looking at them. There was a wan, almost sad smile on her face. Matt stared at the girl's right socket, and at the eye that gleamed out wickedly.

"Hon, he's goin' to tell you, there ain't no Mr. Shadow. It's just this here story he done made up, s'all. Ain't that right. Ain't it? Tell her. Go on. Tell her." Matilda was crying hysterically.

"Mr. Shadow, he doesn't need me anymore. He's got Peter now," the girl said.

Matt took a few steps toward the girl. "What do you mean, he's got Peter? Melinda?"

"He knows you won't let bad things happen to Peter," Melinda whispered. "Bad things like this."

Matilda screamed. The girl raised the blades of the weed-eater toward her face. Matt felt the blood rushing from his head. "What are you—"

"No, hon. *No*, I won't let you. I won't—" Matilda charged at her girl, grabbing with her hands at the cover right over the blades. Melinda snatched the machine up sharply, and her momma shrieked in pain as the blades sliced through her hands.

Matt shook his head in numb horror. Three fingers of Matilda's hand were gone. Blood poured out from the stumps. She grasped them, collapsed onto her knees, her face turned up at Melinda. "Oh, Jesus, no, no, hon, no!" With her bleeding hand, Matilda made one last effort to reach up, but it was too late.

"Oh, my God."

The girl remained on her feet even after she had pulled the blades away.

Of the bloodied pulp that had once been the child's face, only one thing was recognizable.

The gleaming eye that remained fixed on Matt, even as it slid down the mangled cheek.

Matilda covered her face with what was left of her hands and wept.

3

At the edge of the river, Curtis and Tommy had just finished putting Wally's body in the backseat of the patrol car.

"You coming with me, or with Tommy?"

Curtis looked up. Leroy was standing in the middle of the stand of poplar trees. He had the rifle over his shoulder.

"What you want me to do?"

"I'm goin' to be needing me some help."

Curtis glanced over at Tommy. "I'm going with Leroy."

Tommy looked at the younger boy. "I appreciate what you did."

Leroy nodded. "S'alright," he said.

"You know what you're doing?" Tommy asked. There was no challenge in the question.

"I know what I'm goin' to try to do. I'm goin' to try to kill that motherfucker. If it can be killed. Come on, Curtis. We got to get started."

"Good luck," Tommy said.

"We's goin' to need it," Leroy replied, then turned and, without waiting for Curtis to catch up with him, headed back to Mr. Proopes's Cadillac.

4

Matt had put a sheet over Melinda's body.

Five minutes earlier, he had called Dr. Lowery. Then he called Cathy at the house.

"What's Peter doing?"

"He's still just sitting there. Trying to call Tigger."

"Watch him."

"What's wrong?"

"I don't know," Matt said. But from his tone, Cathy knew better.

"What happened over there, Matt?"

"You wouldn't believe it," he whispered.

Back on the porch, Matilda was no longer crying. She was sitting in the swing, her eyes on the bloodied sheet. Matt had done his best to bandage her hand, but the blood was soaking through the towels, and dripping onto the floor at her feet.

"I kept thinking it was some story, s'all," she said. "I kept thinking that was all it was. Some made-up story. Some—" Her voice broke off. Matilda looked up at Matt. "How come you wrote it down?" she asked him, her eyes red and burning with pain. "How come you wrote something like that down for? Seeing what it was? What would make a man do something like that?"

"I didn't know," Matt whispered. "I didn't—" But his voice broke off. He turned and walked back into the house. He stood there in the middle of the kitchen, not knowing what to do next. "He doesn't need me anymore. He's got Peter." Melinda's words kept pounding in his head. "He knows you won't let bad things happen to Peter."

The phone rang.

He grabbed it. It was Cathy. Her voice hoarse, she said, "You gotta get back here. Fast. I found Simmy."

5

Cathy walked back down the hallway, to the room where she had come across Simmy.

Hester's room.

The rocking chair had been pulled up to the window. Her knees scraped the sill. She was staring through the pane at the water tower.

Cathy went over to where the old woman was sitting and asked her what was wrong.

"Forgetting's wrong," Simmy whispered back, without turning around.

"What is it wrong to forget, Simmy?"

"Evil ways. Evil deeds. Little children screaming and crying, hollering out for mercy." Simmy shook her head sadly. "So much suffering and pain. We all guilty of that ol' forgetfulness, Miss Cathy." The old woman rocked slowly back and forth. "Even God Almighty, He's guilty of it. Forgetting all them things don't nobody want to remember. Forgetting His own shadow."

Cathy sat on the bed. "What happened here, Simmy?"

"Ol' Shadowstealer come back, Miss Cathy. Come back so's there won't be no more forgetting."

Cathy stared through the window at the water tower. Was that what Hester had always kept her eye on? Cathy wondered.

"Did something happen up there? Where the water tower is?"

Simmy nodded. "Yesum. Long ago. Why, sitting here, I can just about see them, them poor little children, and all that cutting and chopping, all that hollering and crying," she whispered. "But folks, they done forgot. But they won't be forgetting no more."

Staring out through the windowpane, Cathy whispered to herself, "The Eumenides." In Greek legend, that was their sole reason for existence: to keep people from forgetting. And her talk with Matt weeks before came back to her. What would happen if human beings couldn't forget? If they had to go on living and reliving the horrors of the past? If their minds were unable to forget, even for a moment, all the suffering and pain that the world had passed through, the *lacrymae rerum*, both great and small? To feel the tears of things made us human, Cathy had told Matt long ago, the night they had watched the cat die. And that was true. But never to forget them, never to put them out of our mind, what would that make us, she wondered. Could we still go on being human, or would we turn into something else? The Eumenides never sleep.

Is that why sleep is human?

A friend had once told her that there was no biological reason for sleep. None that anyone had come across. But maybe there was another reason. Perhaps the human soul required forgetfulness in order to retain even a shred of its humanity.

"But what if it's better to forget, Simmy?" Cathy said softly. "What if we *have* to forget?"

"Can't. Ol' Shadowstealer won't let us."

In the kitchen, Cathy stood looking out the back door, shaken.

And for the first time, she faced it.

What if it was true?

What if there was something out there, something that long antedated Matt's book or Hester's story? Something that had been lurking beneath the surface of things long before the carnival had set up in the clearing where the water tower now stood, something that went back thousands and thousands of years, and which had only been glimpsed by those nameless storytellers who handed down the myths and legends of the Greeks. Something they called Eumenides—a name that didn't name, because to call it, to speak of it at all, was too frightening. Like the story Hester had vowed to take to her grave, there is a knowledge, a truth, which it is forbidden humankind even to whisper. Because there is knowledge that no human soul can long live with, and still be human.

And before her mind's eye, there flashed the black-and-white footage she had seen as a child. Men and women and children starving behind barbed wire. The heaps of pale doughlike bodies as they were bulldozed into hastily dug ditches. Human beings, screamed at to dig their own graves faster, faster. Auschwitz and

Bergen-Belsen and Treblinka. Yet even worse than the faces of
the dying were the faces of those who had to look upon them. At
some of the camps, people who lived nearby were forced to go
through them, to see what had happened. And Cathy recalled
in the footage how quickly they turned away.

Put the knowledge of all the horror of the world together
into one shadowy creature, then let it loose, with a life of its
own, and the power to force the memory of such a nightmare
upon us at every moment, waking or sleeping, the power to
fill our eyes and ears and nostrils with the stench and cries and
images of death and disease and mutilation. Make it so that we
cannot turn away, ever.

Ever.

The thought made her reel.

This Something was the Shadowstealer.

That's why there were things that even God must forget
about.

What had Simmy called it?

God's Shadow.

Cathy jumped and spun around. Jimmy Buford was standing
only a few feet behind her. Her hand on her mouth, she looked
at the boy's severed wrist. She swallowed down her nausea
and reached out for the kitchen counter, to support herself.
She struggled to say something to him, but as she looked into
his eyes, words failed.

In his left hand he was holding Tommy's chain saw.

Jimmy looked from Cathy's eyes down to his missing hand.
A troubled, mournful frown passed over the boy's face. "I lost
it. I don't remember where," he said. "I had a nightmare."

"What is that for?" Cathy said and she pointed to the chain
saw.

"For Peter."

Cathy turned and saw Matt's son in the doorway. He was
staring at the chain saw, his mouth slightly open, his eyes
vacant except for a strange sadness. He walked slowly toward
the saw.

"Peter?"

The boy took the chain saw from Jimmy. He glanced over
his shoulder and said, "Tigger knows. That's why he won't
come to me."

"Knows what?"

"It's not me anymore," Peter whispered and looked up straight into Cathy's eyes. His face was one of utter heart-break.

"Yes it is, Peter. It is you," Cathy said frantically. She went to take hold of his shoulders, but Peter took the cord of the chain saw and pulled it back, stopping just short of what was needed to turn it on.

Cathy dropped her hands and stepped back.

"What do you want us to do?"

"Daddy saw Melinda. He knows."

"What? Tell me. What does it want? Please, Peter."

"Daddy can make people believe in him. He can tell stories that do." Peter looked down at the tip of the chain saw. "That's why Daddy was born. So everybody would know, and believe. That's why they found Daddy. Up there."

"Found him?"

Peter nodded. "Up where the water tower is."

"What are you talking about, Peter?"

"Simmy knows. Mr. Shadow told her. How Daddy was born. And why," Peter said. "Daddy always knew the story. Mr. Shadow told him a long, long time ago. Before Daddy was even born. But Daddy forgot." Peter glanced down at the floor. "Forgetting's bad." He frowned, then said, "We gotta go now."

"Where?"

"Tell Daddy, Mr. Shadow wants to be a movie star. That way, he can make sure nobody ever forgets again. Anything."

Cathy took after the boy, but Peter stopped and turned around, his hand still on the cord of the chain saw. "Tell Daddy, if he doesn't do what Mr. Shadow wants, he'd better come to the water tower at twelve o'clock."

"Why? What's going to happen then?"

Peter looked at the saw. "Whatever Mr. Shadow wants."

6

Matt saw the patrol car just as he stepped into the carport of Wally Clark's house.

Tommy jumped out. "Christ, am I glad to see you," Tommy said. He was about to ask what had happened, but looking into Matt's face, he knew.

"She's dead?"

Matt nodded, his eyes dazed. "Yeah." He walked by Tommy and stared over the embankment of kudzu on the other side of the road. Looming up in the distance was the water tower.

"You were right. All along," Matt said softly. "You warned me."

Tommy came up beside Matt, still not sure what he meant.

"You said, back then, what if it's true. You told me. But I didn't listen."

"How the hell was you to know?"

Matt shook his head uncertainly. "I'm responsible for what's happening now. I brought it on everybody. I told the story."

Tommy took his friend's arm. "You go on back home. I'll take care of things here. We'll figure something out. I swear. Okay?"

At the door, Tommy glanced back. Matt was still standing there, his gaze fixed on the water tower.

7

When Matt returned to the Lumpkin house, Cathy, in near hysterics, was waiting for him on the porch. He listened, without saying a word, as she told him what had happened in the kitchen, what Peter had said, and where he told her he was going.

"The water tower?" he repeated.

It made sense, he thought. From up there, they—whoever "they" were right now—could see Matt, or anyone else, coming. There would be no way for anyone to stop Peter, if he intended to tear himself to shreds.

They waited until Tommy drove up in the patrol car. "What do you think we should do?"

"I don't know," Tommy said. "May be best if you two stay here. I'll go out and look for 'em. See if maybe I can find where they went to."

When Tommy left, Cathy said to Matt, "I forgot. There was something else. Peter told me that Simmy knew what he was talking about. The crazy things he said about you."

Matt stood up. Cathy followed him to the third floor, to Hester's room.

He stopped outside the door.

"Simmy?" Matt whispered.

She didn't turn around. The rocking kept on. Matt went into the room.

"You come to hear more of that old story, Mr. Matt?"

"Yes."

"Ain't gonna be the way it was, last time you come here to hear some spooky story," Simmy went on. "You was thinking you could take from that old story what you wisht to take. Like old Adam thinking he could have a little teeny bit of that apple. Ain't gonna be that way. See, that old crazy story, you only got this here little piece of it. But ol' Shadowstealer, he ain't goin' to rest until you done heard it all. Ain't goin' to rest until everybody done heard it all."

"I want to hear it."

"You be thinking you do now. But you's wrong. You come to the end of this here story, you's goin' to wish you was never born. Goin' to wish you'd never seen the light of the sun on them eyes of yours."

Matt sat down on the bed. Cathy sat next to him. "I have to hear it," Matt told Simmy. "I have to know."

Simmy shook her head sadly. "Once you start to know, ain't no end to it. Ain't no way for a man to unsee what he's done seen. Ol' Shadowstealer, he knows all about that."

"Then tell me."

"You want ol' Simmy's tongue to stop, you tell her. Anytime. You hear me talking?"

And Matt nodded. Rocking slowly back and forth, Simmy began, her eyes on the windowpane.

"Way back in them slave days, there was this here old black

man they used to call the Storyteller. They say, when he told one of them stories of his, you didn't hear them words he was talking, why, you could see whatever it was he was telling you about, see right there in front of you, like. Over there in Africa, his daddy and his granddaddy, they'd been storytellers, too, and their daddies and granddaddies. And each one of them, they'd pass on little by little the secret of that storytelling to their boys, and they'd make 'em promise never to tell how they done it, how they told them stories you could see. And them boys would start learning them stories sometimes 'fore they could walk good. These here stories come from the beginning of time, back when God told the First Storyteller to go to everything that was, and to listen to it tell its story. And that's what he done. He went to the trees and to the lion, and to the river, and to the mountains, and they all told him a story. He went to the Sun and the Moon and the Stars and the Darkness, and they told him a story, too. Then God said to the First Storyteller, 'You have heard the stories of all the things I have created. Tell only these stories, and men will be happy and good.' And for a hundred years this is what the First Storyteller did.

"But then one night he woke up and there was something on top of him. Something that had no face. Something that was like a shadow. And it says to him, 'There's a story you ain't heard yet.'

" 'Who are you?' the First Storyteller asks.

" 'I ain't got no name,' it says.

" 'How can that be? Everything has a name.'

"And the thing, it says back, 'I have no name because I am what was never meant to be. What God did not want in His world. And now I will tell you my story.'

"And it do. No sooner do it finish, then God, He comes to the First Storyteller and He draws His great big ol' spear of death and He says, 'I am God who made the world. I made it with a whisper from my mouth. And from that whisper I made a story. And from that story I made the world. But there were whispers I could not let slip from my lips, lessen the world perish. Stories I could not fashion from my breath, lessen the creatures of darkness eat up the children of the light. But now you have heard what I could not speak. You have listened to what even the Lord God Almighty could not hear. You know the story of What-Was-Never-Meant-To-Be. Now I must kill you, so that this story will perish from the world forever.'

" 'I have done wrong,' the Storyteller, he says. And he sits down a-weeping, his head in his hands and he trembles all with fear and shame. 'Kill me.'

"And God, He goes to hurl His spear through the Story-teller's heart, but He stops Hisself. A look of great sadness crossed His face. 'You are the best of men, but you have disobeyed me. What can I expect from others?' God thinks a little, then He says, 'I will not kill you. I will not take from the world the story of What-Was-Never-Meant-To-Be. For maybe one day I will wish to undo what I have done with the breath of my mouth. Perhaps one day I will repent of the world I have fashioned with the words of my lips. Therefore, hear me, O Storyteller! Upon your head, and the head of your children, I will set this curse: If the story is ever told again, then I will turn my back on you, and What-Was-Never-Meant-To-Be will come into the world. And in darkness the world will perish.' And then God told him how the story was to be passed on, from generation to generation. When the First Storyteller sees ol' death coming toward him, he has to go fetch his oldest son. Anybody else—friend or kin—has to go as far as they could into that jungle, where they was supposed to sit, with their hands clamped down hard over their ears, so that the wind itself couldn't carry even so much as a single whisper of the Story. 'But watch out,' God says, 'for there is one Law you must burn into the blood of your heart, and the blood of your children's hearts.'

" 'The Law is this: This here Story cannot be whispered as other stories are whispered. The last word must be the first. Backward you must tell the Story from generation to genera-tion, each dying Storyteller to his eldest child, the last word first, the first word last. Hear me and obey. For if this Story be whispered as all other stories are told—even if the whisperer sits in the deepest caverns of the most hidden desert of the earth What-Was-Never-Meant-To-Be shall be loosed upon the earth.'

"From generation to generation, for a thousand thousand years, the Storytellers obeyed the Law that God had set down to them. Then one day there came one Storyteller, mightier than all the ones who had come before him. He told stories that could heal, stories that made children dance and old women cry. Lions and eagles and antelopes all come 'round to listen to him. But one day white men from nowhere come and stole him and his family into slavery. They chained them all up inside the hole of their black ship, and he watched as one by one his brothers and sister wept and died. He watched as they was cut up and as they was boiled, and their flesh was fed to them others inside that little hole. And that was when the hatred inside of him started up a-smoldering and a-growing. And he remembers the story he had been told by his dying father. That night he whispers three words of the story, then stops hisself. For just as he let slip them three words, he could see the shadows starting up around him, like sharks that smell the taint of blood in the water. 'These here men have made the world more terrible than I could have thought. But I must still not set loose What-Was-Never-Meant-To-Be.'

"When they got that boat to Savannah, the Storyteller, he was sold at auction and was sent up to one of them plantations, but he ran away. And he takes some of them other slaves with him. And they makes it up into them mountains, where them white men could not find them. And in those caves the African hides himself for ten years, and with him was the wife he took, and them children that were born to him. And he begins telling his stories as he had done in Africa—the ones God told the First Storyteller to tell. And other slaves, who heard about his goodness and his power, ran away, too, come to him, and he took 'em in, and he was kind to all who came to him kindly. But, one day, the man whose slave he had been, and who had lost many slaves to him, summoned a slave hunter to him. This man was wicked beyond the wickedness of men. 'Find my slave, the one who tells the stories, and make an example of him. See that no slave of mine ever comes a-running to him again.'

"And the wicked slave hunter, he grins. 'I will make him wish that he had never been born, and that his children, too, had never been born. I will make him tell a story such as has never been told before,' he says and he laughs in mockery. For to this man, there was no power in any story to touch the coldness of his evil heart.

"This here wicked man took others with him and they went up into them mountains. They catches five of the old African's

children and they brings them, all chained up and weeping, to
the cave down in this ravine where the Storyteller was hold up.
And they yell, 'Come out.' And when he didn't, they began to
chop up them kids of his, a finger first, then a hand, then an
arm. And the Storyteller, he hears them a-screaming. He comes
out and begs them to spare the lives of his children. But they
carried him and them children up to this hill and they chain
him up and they laugh and mock. 'Why don't you tell us a
story while we finish up chopping on them kids of yours?'
And he watches as the slave hunters cut and hack at them
children of his. And each piece they bring to him and holds
it up to his face and they grin and asks, 'You recognize which
one this is?'

   "And the hatred in his heart was like a fire burning, and he
looks at the wicked men and he thinks, God has already turned
His back on the world. The men, they put sticks and logs
around the Storyteller and tell him that they's going to burn
him alive. He watches his oldest boy lying in his own blood,
watches as he breathes his last breath. And the Storyteller, he
says, 'Burn me, and as I burn, I will tell you a story. It is a
story I done swore to tell to the son you have just now cut into
pieces, whose handsome head you have just now held up to my
weeping eyes. But since I have no one now to tell my story
to, I will tell it to you.' They set the fire, and the Storyteller
begins to speak the words that had not been whispered since
the beginning of time.

   "He whispers the first word of the story, and the flesh of
his legs bubbles. He whispers the second word, and the fire
gnaws at the fingers of his hand. He speaks the third word
and the fire, it reaches up to his face. But still he don't stop.
Word by word, he tells the story that had not been heard since
time begun. His nostrils suck in the black smoke of his own
burning flesh. His eyeballs begin to boil, but his tongue don't
cease to speak them words. The skin peels back from his head.
His eyeballs bust. And all around, as he comes closer to the last
words of the story, the earth, it starts a-trembling. The slave
hunters, they stop and stare down at their foots. Holes are
opening up. Them cut-up pieces of them children, they begin to
slither and crawl all around them. The mouths of them severed
heads, they open wide and mocking laughter comes a-hissing
out like steam from the bowels of the earth. 'Stop him,' the

chief of the slave hunters screams. And he draws his gun and
begins to shoot into that black blaze of the old African's body.
But still the old African he's a-telling the story. The wickedest
of the slave hunters, in despair, leaps into the fire. He reaches
to the burning head, sticks his hand into the African's mouth,
and with all his might, he yanks the tongue from the African's
head. And still he hears it, the gurgling as the African comes
to the final words of the story. And with his own hand, that
slave hunter pulls up a fiery log and he pushes it deep into
the African's throat. He holds it and watches as the African's
burning mouth tries to chew down that flaming wood. But the
slave hunter, he pushes it deeper and deeper, until at last there
ain't not a sound except the crackling of the fire.

"Only the last few words was lacking. But even so, a part
of What-Was-Never-Meant-To-Be had come slipping into the
world. The slave hunter, his flesh burnt, fell back from the fire.
He watches as this here black thing come oozing out from the
burning log at the African's feet, black as tar. 'What is it?' he
says, a-gasping.

"It slithers and it coils and it lifts up and it speaks to him. 'I
am the Shadow of What-Was-Never-Meant-To-Be,' it hisses.

"And as it lifts up, he sees what was underneath the blackness of the shadow—sees what eyes were never meant to see,
and his mind, it was done swept away just as chalk is swept
from one of them blackboards. It takes holt of his foots and he
screams. He grabs at his hatchet—the one he had used to sever
the head of the African's eldest child—and with it he hacks
away his foots. But no sooner has he done his hacking, but the
thing was on his ankles. He hacks at them, but no sooner did he
see the bleeding stumps, then it rose up and was on his knees.
And he starts in a-whimpering, 'I will do what you wish. Just
let me go.'

"And the Shadow whispers to him, 'Wander with me forever.'

"And the man, he gasps, 'I will wander with you forever.'

" 'Because the story was left unfinished, I am but a shadow.
But one day you will make me one who can finish the story.
And when it is finished, I shall cease to be a shadow, and will
become All-in-all.' Then the Shadow tells the man to hack
away the rest of his legs. 'I will return for you,' it whispers.
Then the man, he watches as the Shadow opens the earth and

is sucked down into it as a black snake slithers, coil upon coil, into its hole at evening."

"Mr. Eprin," Matt said in a whisper. "He was the slave hunter. That's how he lost his legs."

Simmy nodded, the pace of her rocking easing up. "Ol' Simmy, she's tired of talking now. You come back up this evening, and if you still want to hear, she'll tell you the rest of the story. Ol' Simmy, she goin' to tell you what you ain't never thought to hear. Your momma, she didn't die in no hospital. She didn't die in no car wreck. Your daddy, neither." The old woman whispered, "You come back up tonight, you goin' learn who you be, and how you come into this old world."

"And what you come into it with."

8

Out on the back porch, Cathy sat by Matt.

"What do you make of it?"

"I don't know."

"As I listened, I kept thinking of the story of the Garden of Eden," Cathy said. "God tells the First Storyteller he can taste of every story, the same way God told Adam he could taste the fruit of every tree, except one. In both cases, what is forbidden is a certain type of knowledge. Knowledge of Good and Evil in the Bible. I always thought that was so peculiar, when I was little. Why wouldn't God want Adam and Eve to know good and evil? But listening to Simmy's story, I wondered if it didn't provide the explanation."

"How?"

"Maybe God was ashamed," Cathy said. "Ashamed because the world wasn't perfect. And because He had created a creature, Man, who was capable of seeing the imperfection. Capable of making judgment of Good and Evil." She thought a moment, then said, "Also in both stories, God's first impulse is to kill the one who's disobeyed. But He doesn't. Instead, all He does is to condemn the transgressor—man—to go on living with the forbidden knowledge. And that's true, isn't it?"

"Yes."

"And that's the whole essence of the Shadowstealer. It's everything that once we have seen, we can't unsee, no matter how much we may want to," Cathy said. "Only there is something in it that makes anything else—any forgetfulness—impossible. It's like the Furies, the Eumenides. It's obsessed with the horror, with what should never have been. It doesn't want us to forget, even for a moment, the dark underside of existence. Suffering and pain and cruelty."

"And it will keep us from forgetting it. By reenacting it. Over and over. With our children," Matt whispers.

He stood up and walked to the porch steps and stared into the woods. "Tell me again what Peter said about me. How I was born."

Cathy did.

Matt shivered, then stared down at his foot. A moment before, when he had stood up, Cathy could tell it was hurting him. "I keep seeing that preacher at the revival. Odum. I can see his face right now. The terror in it. Just because he had seen me, had looked down at my foot. My goddam foot. Why?"

Cathy walked over to Matt and put her arms around him.

"It's like something has finally caught up with me. Something I've been running from all my life. Without even knowing I was. I feel like that boy on the cover, like I've just glimpsed over my shoulder.

"I am scared," he whispered. "In the story, the Shadow says to Mr. Eprin, he has to make someone who can finish the story. Who did he mean?"

"I don't know," Cathy whispered.

He looked at her. "What was the Story? The one that the old African tried to tell? The one that came from the beginning of time?"

Again she shook her head.

"It wasn't the story of the Shadowstealer," Matt whispered, speaking more to himself than to Cathy. "Because it is only the shadow of this other thing, What-Was-Never-Meant-To-Be. But what is it? What was never meant to be? And what is *its* story?"

Cathy got that look in her eyes that showed something deep going on. "I keep thinking of something Simmy said that struck. She said God was guilty of forgetting His own shadow. Isn't that a strange thing to say? And I kept wondering what it means. What would God's Shadow be?" She looked at Matt. "Do you think you could make a story from that?"

9

Like any other little town in North Georgia, Mt. Jephtha did not have a proper fire department. Instead, there was one old fire engine. It was kept behind the town's small courthouse, and whenever there was occasion to use it, it was manned by a small force of volunteer firemen. Tommy Buford was one of them. Leroy had gotten his first taste of the joy of fire trucks one Saturday when Tommy Buford had brought Jimmy and Leroy down to the truck. They had washed and polished it, and then Tommy had taken them for a ride in it. Leroy had sat on Tommy's lap and carefully learned the fine points of driving a fire engine. While Jimmy had yawned and looked bored, Leroy had asked Tommy how everything on the truck worked, and then stored away the information in his memory, for safekeeping. One day, he vowed, he would drive the rig by himself.

That day had come.

"What are we goin' to do with a fire engine?" Curtis asked.

"Wush you'd have a little faith in me, Curtis," Leroy said as the two boys got out of Mr. Proopes's hijacked Caddy. Leroy had considered telling Curtis his plan—Tommy, too. But he had held back. In part, this was due to Leroy's naturally closemouthed nature. But there was something else. In truth, he wasn't entirely sure himself that the idea wasn't half-crazy, and was afraid that both Curtis and Tommy would look at him, declaring Leroy must have lost his mind.

After all, Leroy's plan did have one big drawback to it.

One little fuckup and Leroy would blow himself, and Curtis, and anybody else in a hundred-yard radius, to kingdom come.

Leroy was busily hot-wiring the fire truck as Curtis watched.

"Crawl underneath, Curtis, and be draining the water tanks while I do this."

"How?"

"You'll see it. There's this little cap. Twist it off and the water'll come out. It ain't hard, Curtis."

"What'd you want to drain it for?"

"So I can put something else in it."

"What?"

"Just do what I tell you." And Curtis did. Leroy had connected the right wires by the time Curtis found the drain cap.

"It's draining," Curtis declared. "Now what?"

Leroy glanced away. He wanted to say it as casually as possible. "We need to go to a gas station."

10

Tommy had driven up the little access road that led to the old water tower. He had gotten out of his truck and looked around. But, just as he was afraid of, there was no sign of either Jimmy or Peter.

He stared at the woods. If they were back there, it would be impossible to find them. As if finding them even mattered.

Still, on the way back to the Lumpkin house, Tommy checked a few more places where he thought the boys could be, but without any luck.

It was one-thirty when he got to the Lumpkin house. Matt told him what he had heard in Hester's room, and then all three of them sat on the porch. Tommy, for the first time, told of what had happened in the past days, of how Jimmy severed his hand, how Wally came and locked him up in jail. "That thing was afraid I'd try to warn you, to stop you from going ahead with that movie. I guess, on account of how the more people who see, the stronger it'll be." Then Tommy narrated what had happened down by the river, and how Leroy had saved his life. "I reckon that's about the hardest thing anyone's ever been called upon to do. I knew he was fond of ol' Wally. I know it wasn't easy on him. But he done it, anyhow."

Matt listened to the story, then got up and walked to the railing. "How do you make a choice like that?"

"I don't know."

After a minute of brooding silence, Tommy stood up. "Maybe there ain't anything I can do. But at least I got to feel like I'm trying. Even if it's just looking for our two boys."

11

It was six o'clock.

On further consideration, Leroy had decided to leave the fire truck behind the courthouse. It was Curtis who pointed out that if Leroy came driving it into a gas station, suspicion might be aroused. And Leroy reluctantly conceded this was true.

"Reckon we best leave it till it gets dark," he told Curtis, and together the two boys got into Mr. Proopes's Cadillac, and drove to the water tower.

This, too, was part of Leroy's plan.

"What are we doing here?"

"We got to figure out some way to empty it."

"Empty it?" Curtis was about to ask, "What for?" but by this point, he was beginning to see that this was pointless. Leroy wasn't going to let him in on anything until the last moment. And no telling when that would be.

Leroy walked around to the two big pipes that descended from the water tank. One of them had a big rusted valve wheel attached to the side. Leroy tried to twist it around, but it wouldn't budge. "You give a try, Curtis." Curtis tried, but the result was the same.

"Shit, now what?"

"Reckon we goin' to have to use Mr. Proopes's tire jack again." Curtis went to the trunk of the car and returned with it.

Together the two boys took turns slamming the metal. "Goddammit, move you motherfucker," Leroy hissed, then gave it an enormous whack. It creaked.

"Here, let me," Curtis said and took the jack. Four more whacks and they were able to turn the wheel.

Leroy put his ear against it. "I hear something. It must be draining. I'm going up and see."

Curtis followed after Leroy up the ladder to the top of the platform.

He opened the door and peered inside.

"It's hard to tell right yet."

Curtis slipped off his belt and hung it over the side of the doorway.

"Whatchew doing that for?"

"I'm setting it at the water level. That way we can tell if it's emptying or not."

"That's pretty smart, Curtis," Leroy said. He walked over to the railing and looked down into the field. "Should be getting dark soon."

"Yeah."

"Reckon that's when it'll come back out," Leroy said. "This here's where I saw it first. Didn't look like nothing at first but a great big ol' long shadow. Except it was going the wrong way. I knowed something wasn't right, when I seen it."

Curtis sat down and stuck his legs over the edge of the platform.

"What's goin' to happen to everybody? I mean, if we can't kill it?"

"Dunno. Don't much care to think about it myself." Leroy glanced down at Curtis. And out of the clear blue sky, he said, "What's it like when you read, Curtis?"

"What d'you mean?"

"What it feel like?"

"You can read, Leroy. You go to school. You gotta be able to read."

"A course I can read. Words and shit. But I seen you reading, it ain't the same. I watched your eyes. It's like you're watching a picture show."

"I reckon. When I read that book, *The Shadowstealer*, I could see people's faces and I could see the woods. I could see 'em running down these dark paths, with the moon overhead, and I could see it coming up behind them, reaching its claws out."

"Wonder if I could ever do that. Read that away."

"Maybe."

"Dunno. Something about it seems kinda wrong to me. When I was little, and I made up a story, I got whupped." Leroy turned back around and checked the water level. He nodded. "It's draining fine."

• • •

Back down at the base of the tower, Curtis said, "Now what?"

"Wait till it gets dark. Won't be much longer."

Curtis, too, scanned the horizon over the woods. There was maybe another forty minutes of light. "You know, that ol' thing, it's probably goin' to be comin' after us, Curtis. Least, me."

"Yeah," Curtis said and quickly looked down at the ground.

"What're we goin' to do if it gets holt of one of us?"

"I don't know."

"We gotta watch out for it. If it gets behind me, you tell me real quick. I'll do the same if it comes up behind you. Deal?"

"Sure."

Leroy sighed. "This here, it's gonna be a long night, Curtis."

The two boys were just about to turn from the access road back onto the highway when they saw Tommy. Both cars stopped.

"You been back to the water tower?" Tommy asked.

Leroy nodded yes.

"You didn't see Jimmy and Peter, did you?"

"Naw. Wasn't nobody back there. Except us."

"They told Matt he was supposed to come there right at midnight."

"What for?"

Tommy looked away. "Peter said that if Matt hasn't given the go-ahead on that movie, then he's goin' to do something to hisself."

The two boys understood. Leroy looked back over the trees at the tower. "You sure it's goin' to be right at midnight?"

"Yeah."

"Okay. I'll be ready."

12

It was just getting dark.

Cathy walked into Matt's bedroom. He had stretched out nearly an hour before, sick with exhaustion. But as she looked at him, she saw his eyes were open.

"Frank's been calling. He knows something's wrong, he just doesn't know what or how bad. I tried to do my best, but I don't know what to say." Cathy leaned over and stroked Matt's hair. "Did you sleep any?"

"No."

"Tommy called, too. He's been looking all over, but he can't find them. He thinks they're probably in the woods."

Cathy turned away and stared at the window. She got up and walked over to it. The backyard was thick with the shadows. She looked at each of them in turn, wondering.

Matt sat up on the edge of the bed. "I have to do something."

"What?"

"I been lying here, thinking of what you said. About God's Shadow. But I just can't make anything out of it. What would it mean?"

"I guess it could be everything that's wrong with the world. All that isn't good. Darkness and pain."

Matt nodded. "All I can think of right now is my own goddam book, and how I ended it." Matt looked up at Cathy. "When I wrote it, I could almost see Tommy up there on the water tower, waiting for the thing to come up the ladder, his gun in his hand. It's scary. Maybe I didn't really make it up. Maybe I only wrote down what would happen. What is going to happen."

"Don't think that way, Matt. You can't."

"What can I do? All my life I've lived in my own little dream world. I made up stories. At every point, I tried my damnedest to outwit reality. And I thought I had done it. I thought my make-believe world could give me whatever I wanted. Money and fame. And even love. It was crazy. That world doesn't exist. It's empty." He stopped and looked at her.

"And yet it's not empty. Not anymore. Because somehow, in my little imaginary world, I stepped over a boundary. One I didn't even know was there. And I brought this thing back with me. The thing that's waiting out there. That has our children, and won't give them back to us. And I was the one who did it. I brought it to life. I fed it. I nourished it. And now, it has the whole world before it."

Cathy's face was turned away. "You have to do something, Matt. You have to stop it." She paused, then said softly, "You can't let it get any stronger."

"But it wants to be a movie star," Matt said, repeating his son's words to Cathy, his voice full of the bitter mockery of it. He pressed his hands hard against his temples, as if the very craziness of his words might be enough to burst a blood vessel in his brain. "A goddam movie star."

"You can't let it become one."

"It has my child."

Cathy looked away. "If you do what it wants you to, it will have everyone's child."

"I can't make a decision like that. I saw Wally's girl. I saw what she did to herself. There has to be another way."

"But what if there isn't, Matt?"

"I don't know."

Cathy turned Matt's face to her. "Listen to me. Whatever it is, it only knows how to hate, how to destroy. It only knows bitterness, and only sees the horror and the suffering of the world. It wants to cast everything into darkness, Matt. Do you understand that?"

"Yes."

"We can't let it."

Matt was silent. He got up from the bed and walked to the window. "It's dark," he said softly, then he turned to Cathy. "It's time."

13

Simmy had not moved from the window.

"That you?" she whispered as they opened the door.

"Yes."

"Reckon you come to hear the rest of that old story," the old woman said, her eyes on the windowpane. She was rocking slowly back and forth.

"It's a story about this preacher," she whispered. "You seen him once yourself, long time ago. Seen him up in front of all them people, inside that ol' tent he used to pitch by the roadside. You seen his arm a-burning. You seen his eyes, and how they got, when he looked down at your poor ol' crippled up foot."

"Odum," Matt said.

"That was his name. And back long time ago, he used to go 'round, preaching and casting out demons. He had him a wife and she was a good woman. Her name was Agnes. And folks come from miles and miles around to hear Preacher Odum do his preaching.

"But one evening, Odum was holding this revival not far from Mt. Jephtha. He was in the midst of his preaching about hellfire when this here thirteen-year-old girl stood up in the front row and yelled out, 'I'm a sinner bound to hell. Save me from them flames, Preacher Odum.' Then she falls down and sets to crying. Some of them ladies in the seats next to her, they tries to touch her, but she pushes them away. 'Can't nobody touch me 'cept Preacher Odum,' that girl hollers out. And Odum, he comes down from the platform and he looks at the girl. And she stares up at him and whispers, 'I'm carrying the fires of hell inside of me.'

"That's when one of them white ladies next to the girl looks down and says, 'Why, look at her belly. She's all swolled up.'

" 'Whose child is it?' Odum, he asks.

"The girl, she shakes her head sad as sad can be. 'I can't say. I can't say to nobody 'cept you.'

"Odum's wife helps the girl to her feet and Odum tells her to take that poor child to their trailer around the back of the tent. And he says a prayer for her in front of all them people at the revival.

"Agnes puts the girl in bed, then asks her what her name is, and whereabouts she's come from, but the girl, she don't answer. Instead, she looks up and says, clutching hold of that sheet and gasping, 'It's coming out tonight.'

" 'What is?'

" 'What's inside me,' she goes on.

" 'Who is the father?' the preacher's wife asks.

"The girl shook her head, her eyes flashing wild. 'My daddy and that other one, they done put it inside a me.'

" 'You mean, your Daddy and some other men, they raped you?'

"She shook her head no. 'That ain't it. It was worser.'

" 'Worser?' Agnes says.

" 'Bring me the preacher. He's the only one I can tell it to.'

"And that's when Agnes, she runs and gets Preacher Odum. And he comes in and he sits down and the girl she looks up at him, spittle running down her chin, and he says, 'Tell me what they done to you, your daddy and this other man.'

"The girl stares up at Odum, these black circles under them fevered eyes a-glistening. 'They put this thing inside me. This thing that was never meant to be,' and her voice was like the scraping of fingernails.

"And he asks, 'What thing?'

"And she says—"

" 'He called it the Shadowstealer.' "

Cathy jumped and looked at Matt. His eyes had a trancelike look to them. He stood up and walked to where Simmy was still rocking, his eyes fixed on the water tower above the woods, and as he walked he went on with the story, taking it up just as Simmy had left off.

Cathy eased herself against the headboard and listened as Matt spoke.

"Who called it that?"

"Mr. Eprin, he did," the girl told him.

"Who's Mr. Eprin?" Odum asked.

"He was the one who come to my daddy. He come and told my daddy how they could make 'em one. Mr. Eprin, he told my daddy how he had been around looking for a man who hated

God—hated God more than anything in this world."

"Hated God?" Agnes repeated, clasping her hand over her mouth at the very thought of the blasphemy.

"A man's got to come to hate God," the girl whispered. "He's got to make someplace where even God don't want to look. Just one little room, maybe, that's all. And in that room, that man's got to do something so terrible that it'll make even God turn away. That way, he can make something that God don't know is being made."

"That crazy talk. Ain't no way God don't see everything. You know that."

"I seen what God ain't seen," the girl whispered. "My daddy and Mr. Eprin, they done showed it to me."

"Seen what?"

"This room. We had us an attic where we used to live. And there was this little room up there in that attic. That's where they done it. Them things God couldn't look at."

"But why'd your daddy come to hate the Lord?" Odum asked.

" 'Cause the Lord, He done broke my daddy's heart." And the girl began the story. "Up in the mountains, where we come from, my daddy, he was a preacher. Every night he used to read to us from this big ol' family Bible. We'd sit around the fireplace and he'd read. He loved that book. He treated it like it was alive, like it had feelings. We couldn't say nothing foolish in front of it, or nothing angry, or scornful. The church where my daddy preached, it was real little. Folks called us serpent-handlers. 'Ye shall take up serpents,' the Bible says, and my daddy, he believed it. Them that had been elected to mercy could take 'em up and not be bit. Them that had been elected to hellfire would feel them fangs," the girl explained. It was an idea that both Odum and Agnes recognized. Predestination, the belief that before God lay the foundations of the universe He had already chosen the few that would know Grace. All the rest of humanity had received the sentence of eternal doom even before God whispered, 'Let there be light.'

"My daddy, he would stand up in front of the congregation. You looked into his face and you knew he wasn't afraid. He'd have a whole box full of them snakes, right there in front of him, and he'd reach inside and pull out two of the biggest of 'em, and he'd hold 'em up so's everybody could get a good

look. And they'd be writhing and squirming and hissing, but Daddy, he didn't even seem to notice 'em. He'd shout out, 'Halleluah, praise the Lord.' And then he'd boast and say, 'To them that the Lord's elected, no fang can bite, no fire can burn.'

"Sometimes Momma, she'd warn him. She'd say, 'You're tempting the Lord.'

"But Daddy, he'd just laugh: 'The Lord, He ain't no Indian giver. He don't take away what He's done given.' And then he'd send my two brothers out to the swamp, telling them to come home with the biggest moccasins and copperheads they could get hold of, that the ones they come back with last time wasn't near big enough. 'We got to show the power of the Lord to folks.' "

The girl stopped—a shudder passed over her fragile shoulders—and looked over at Agnes. "Then one night my brother, Azariah, he comes back with a bag. And I seen something wiggling inside it. I could tell it was one of them snakes, only bigger than anything I'd ever seen. 'I caught it myself,' Azariah told Daddy. 'It's nearly twelve foot long.'

"And Daddy, he tells Azariah, 'You done good, boy.' And next Sunday he takes that snake—he called it Lucifer's Staff—and he tells the congregation that he's brung something special. And he lets that big ol' copperhead out of that bag. And everybody lets out a cry, 'cause they ain't never seen a snake so big before. And Daddy, he lets out a laugh and says, 'This here's Lucifer's Staff.' And he reaches down to take it up. That's when the biting starts," the girl whispered.

"I can still see it, the way it lit into Daddy, into his arms. It'd take hold and he'd pull it off and then it'd take hold somewheres else. And Azariah and Luke—he was only nine—come running up and try to pull that big ol' copperhead off their daddy, and it starts biting them, too. And they's screaming. I seen it, sticking them fangs right into Azariah's face. Somebody come up with an ax and starts hacking at that copperhead, and they kill it. They take Daddy and the two boys back home, and Daddy, he won't hear of sending for no doctor. Azariah and Luke, they die near to morning. And Daddy, he's close to death. And he's talking crazy. So crazy. The poison's racing through his head, and he's seeing things. Seeing hellfire, and seeing them snake mouths, wide*

*and gaping, and them big fangs dripping poison all around
him, and he whispers, 'I'm inside the jaws of hell.' It goes
on a week like that, but Daddy, he don't die. A month after
we buried them two boys, Momma dies of a broken heart—she
loved them boys of hers. And Daddy, he can get around now,
but I seen in his eyes something that made me scared inside,
seen that something had happened to his mind.*

*"It was just me and Daddy left now. And one night he calls
me into the parlor, where he used to read the Bible, and he's
holding it and staring down into it. And I was surprised, 'cause
he ain't read from it since what happened. His eyes, they were
dancing with the craziness. He opens that Bible and he pulls
out the first page of it, and drops it into the fire in the
fireplace. And all night long he sits there, burning it, burning
that Bible, page by page, all night long, pulling out page after
page, and dropping it into the fire. 'What you doing, Daddy?'
I asked him.*

*" 'I seen it,' he says, 'how from all eternity He's done
mocked me. Mocked one that's been faithful to Him. He ain't
mocking me no more.' From that night, my daddy, he swore
that he would get back at the Lord, for what He done to him.
Toward morning, he went out and he went to where he knew
that old snake had been buried, and he digs it out, piece by
piece, and he carries all them pieces back to the house with
him. And he sets them all in a big old jar and put it where
the Bible used to be. And each night he goes and he stares
at them snake eyes. And one night I wake and I hear him
talking. And he's talking to it, to that snake. And he's saying,
'Who made this here world? Who made it way it is? Who
made them crippled children, them lame, them blind, who
made them lepers, who made them retards, who made them
diseases and afflictions? Who made them orphans, who made
all them poor, dying heathen children? Who sends all them lost
souls to an eternity of fire? When God made light, He made
the first shadow. God said the light was good, but He didn't
say nothing about that shadow. He wanted to forget about that
shadow. But it don't go away.' "*

*The girl paused a moment, and pushed her limp, dirty hair
out of her eyes. "That was the night Mr. Eprin come up the
road. It was dark, but I heard him. Heard them wheels just
a-clattering, fast as he could be. And I looked out and I seen*

him, a-crouched down in that wagon of his. On account of how he didn't have no legs. And he comes up to the porch and he says, 'Howdy.'

" 'Whatchew looking for?' I asked him, 'cause I knowed something wasn't right.

"And he grins and says, 'I'm looking for a man ain't got a speck of the love of the Lord inside a him.' And that's when my daddy come to the door, and Mr. Eprin, he grins up at him and says, 'You that preacher what hates God, ain't you?' And my daddy, he nods. And Mr. Eprin, he says, 'You hate Him more than you love . . . say . . . this girl of yours?' And Daddy, he looks at me with them crazy eyes and he nods, and I feel a shiver go all up and down me, 'cause Mr. Eprin, he's grinning. Then he says, 'We gonna need us a room.' And my daddy asks, 'What for?' And Mr. Eprin says, 'We gonna make what ol' God A-mighty never wanted in this world of his. We gonna make what was never meant to be.' "

The girl stopped. Agnes squeezed Odum's shoulder. He told the girl to go on. "That's when they commenced to make that little room, the one up in the attic. My daddy, he kept it locked good. But I was too scared to want to see what he was doing up there. Each night Mr. Eprin would come by and him and my daddy, they'd go off somewheres, and when it was close to morning, my daddy, he'd come back with some ol' bag, and that bag would have something inside it, only I wouldn't know what. Sometimes it wiggled, sometimes it didn't move none. And he carried it up to that little room, that room he was fixing, making it a place even the Lord wouldn't look inside of. And then one night, he wakes me up, and I look in his eyes and I see the craziness. Then I see how he's tied me up, with rope around my wrists and ankles. And I say, 'What are you doing?'

"And he says, 'I'm taking you to the attic.' "

The girl shivered. "He took me up there. To that room. I ain't never seen nothing like that. And that's when I seen Mr. Eprin over in a corner, a-grinning. 'We done made us a place where even God don't want to look.' And I seen them things all around me. My daddy done nailed and hung them all over the walls of them room. I seen the snake heads, moccasins and rattlers. I seen salamanders and big toads nailed up. But I seen skeletons, some small, like a baby, some middle size, like

a child's. But everyone of them had something wrong about
'em, something twisted, or not made right.

" 'I dug 'em up myself,' he told me. 'See this one here,'
he says, and he points to one of them. 'This here was that
Sawyer baby. See how twisted his bones are. He come like
that from his momma's belly. He didn't live but two weeks,
then died. Wasn't nothing in them two weeks but pain and
affliction. I dug him myself. This here, you remember her?'
And he shows me another one. 'It was the Watkins's girl.
The one got drowned, when the ice broke while she was
crossing the river. Her momma watched her, saw her little
face pressed up against that ice, turning blue.' And there
was others, too, all mangled up or deformed. He had done
gone 'round and dug up every little boy or girl that had
done been misborn or killed somehow. And he had hung
'em up along them walls, in between the snakes. And he
had taped him up some pictures, too, pictures of children with
whatall wrong with 'em—some without faces, only mouths,
some looked like frogs. He got all them pictures out of books
and magazines.

"And Mr. Eprin, he says, 'This here room, it was meant to
keep God out. 'Cause He don't want to look at them things.
He don't want to be reminded of 'em. We done made us a
tabernacle of darkness. We done gathered together all them
shadowy misbegottens, them half-made things, whatall was
never meant to be.' He whispers to me, 'You know why I
done made it so dark? 'Cause in a room so dark, things can
happen, a man can do things he can't do nowhere else. Things
like you ain't dreamed.' Then he laughs, and says, 'Things
ol' God ain't even dreamed of.' Then Mr. Eprin says to my
daddy, 'You want to show it to her?' And my daddy, he nods
and then goes over and he lifts up this quilt he had set on
it—it was in the middle of that room. At first, when I seen
it, I just thought it was some old box. But it wasn't. And he
pulls me over to where it was and I look down at it." The girl
whispered, her eyes growing more frightened as she went on.
"It was a child's coffin. It was my brother, Azariah's coffin.
He dug it up. Only, when I looked inside it, I seen it wasn't
Azariah.

"I can still see it, what was inside that ol' coffin. It was
this thing. It had a head, and arms, and legs, and a body.

*It had hands and wrists and feet. Only wasn't none of it
that belonged together. All them parts, they come from somewheres else, cut off, or chopped off. That right hand, it was
Azariah's. Only the wrist it went on, it come from part of
that big ol' snake. Whilst the arm, it belonged to this dead
boy Daddy dug up—his own daddy had killed him. My daddy,
he points to them other pieces—them eyeballs, them ears, feet
and leg parts—and he says how Mr. Eprin brung him these. It
was kinda like one of them old crazy quilts my grandmomma
used to make, only them pieces was from bodies," the girl
said. She stopped and swallowed hard. "And then Daddy
gets this look in his eyes and he points right between the
legs of that thing he'd made. Sticking up right between them
dead legs was the head of that old snake—the one Daddy
kept in the glass jar. 'What that remind you of,' he whispers to me. And a course, I know, but I don't say nothing.*

"Instead I say, 'What you done made this for?'

*"And he says, 'Things can happen in that coffin can't hap-
pen no place else.'*

*"And Mr. Eprin, he slides closer in that wagon of his and
he lifts up this mason jar. He takes the top of it off and I says,
'Whatchew doing?'*

*"And he says, 'Why, it's got everything it needs. Except a
shadow. And that's what I'm going to give it.' Then he pours
that jar into the coffin."*

*The girl shook her head. "It was black as pitch, what he
poured in. Only it was alive, too. And I looked down and I
seen it was making all them pieces come alive, too. Them
eyeballs was stirring, looking around. Looking up at me. And
the mouth, it twisted like. 'See there,' my daddy whispers, and
points down to that ol' snake head. And I seen that tongue,
it was a-darting in and out of the mouth of that dead snake.
Then that mouth opened up and I seen whatall commenced
to dribbling out, maggots and tadpoles and these here little
worms . . ."*

"That's craziness," Odum suddenly said.

*But the girl only nodded. Her eyes numb with the horror
of it, she whispered, "That's when they put me in that coffin.
Then put the lid down on top of it. That night, something
come sneaking into the world, something God never meant*

to be." Then the girl felt her belly and said, "And tonight it's coming out."

Odum and his wife left the girl. "I ain't never heard the like," Agnes said, her pale face. "Why, she must be crazy. Imagining all them things."

"Some demon come to her. Got holta her," Odum whispered.

"What we going to do?"

"Pray."

The girl was right.

At two o'clock that morning Agnes was awakened by a scream. She rushed into the room where they had put the girl. "It's coming out," she gasped.

Agnes had tended over births before. But never anything like she witnessed that night.

In a daze of horrified anticipation, she watched as the child emerged.

The head was normal.

Its arms, its chest, were normal.

The girl kept crying, "What's it look like?"

"It looks fine," Agnes said. The lower part of the child's body emerged. Again, there was not a sign of anything hideous or deformed.

It's just a baby, Agnes thought to herself with relief. It must have been as Agnes had supposed. The girl's story, it had been the work of a crazed, no doubt guilt-ridden, imagination. Her baby, it could have come from the normal perils of adolescent temptation. Only the girl, in an effort to rid herself of the guilt, had concocted her story. Perhaps intertwined in it were shreds of truth. Maybe her daddy, enflamed by despair and madness, had actually locked his daughter inside a coffin, perhaps he had even filled it with all manner of vileness, but only in order to punish the girl for her transgression.

Agnes's eyes were fixed on the child's legs.

They, too, were normal.

The girl gasped, "It's some trick. Some—"

"Hon, there ain't nothing wrong with this child. Nothing at—" Agnes stopped.

"Lord Jesus," the girl screamed. "There's something else coming out."

Agnes, her head awhirl, stared at the child's right foot.

Stared at what had hold of it. At what was reaching out from the girl's insides.

Agnes shrieked. Odum rushed into the room and saw it.

It was a claw. Gnarled and slimy. It held in its clutches the foot of the child.

"Don't let it come out!" the girl cried.

Odum picked up a knife, the one that Agnes had brought in to cut the umbilical cord. He took it and began to sever the arm of what was reaching out.

He cut through it, but the claw still did not release its grip on the child's foot. Odum tore at it, pulled it loose, then flung it to the floor. To his horror, he watched as the claw came to life, scurrying back and forth across the floor like some kind of hideous animal.

The girl was shrieking in agony now.

What was left inside was tearing its way loose.

Neither Odum nor Agnes moved. They watched as the thing ripped itself free and oozed down onto the floor. Oozed as if it had been a mass of molten tar. Only the surface of it was crawling, squirming with vileness—tiny eyeballs glared, fingers twitched, tiny snake tails whizzed crazily, fangs protruded.

"God Almighty."

The girl, as her life drained out of her, lifted her head, her terrified eyes fixed on the thing that had oozed out from her, then collapsed back.

Agnes watched the thing on the floor as part of it stretched out a kind of arm. The oozing arm reached the dismembered claw and attached itself to it, then began to drag the whole mass across toward the open door.

"It's getting away," Agnes gasped.

But Odum was motionless, his eyes fixed on the monstrosity.

It had become elongated. It twisted, then rolled over, showing now only a black, featureless surface, like a slick of oil. It slithered to the door and vanished.

Agnes was still holding the child. She looked back at the girl. Her mouth was distended in lifelessness.

"She's dead," Agnes whispered, then looked at her husband's face. His eyes were on the child she was holding.

Agnes, too, looked down at the baby. "There ain't nothing wrong with him. Wrong atall. 'Cept for his foot. Where that thing took hold of his foot," Agnes whispered.

Odum stared long and hard at the child's mangled foot. "He ain't," Odum said. "He ain't right."

"But just look at him."

"I don't care. You seen what come out with him." And Odum walked to the door of the trailer and stared into the woods around them.

"Something come into the world tonight," he whispered.

Three nights after the girl was buried, Agnes woke up toward morning—after fitful, dream-filled sleep—she looked over and saw that her husband was not in bed. She got up and looked around, then went to the room where she had put the baby. It was gone. "Oh, my Lord," she whispered.

She hurried outside and called her husband's name. She looked around—there were a few streaks of light over the top of the woods behind the trailer—but she didn't see a trace of Odum anywhere. She clutched her arms against her nightgown—there was a chill in the wind—and tiptoed over to the edge of the clearing, to the point where the North Georgia woods began. She heard something. The sound of a man's footsteps, magnified by the crackling of the underbrush. She moved back and squinted. "Hon, that you?"

The footsteps stopped.

"Hon?"

Then she saw him. It was Odum. "What you doing back there?" she said, then hurriedly added, "The baby's gone."

Odum came closer, close enough for Agnes to see what he was holding in his hand. It was a shovel.

"What you got there?" she asked, although she knew perfectly well what the thing in his hand was. "What you been doing?"

"I done buried it," Odum said.

"Buried what?"

"What come from that girl," he told his wife.

Agnes gasped. "What you saying?"

"It must've died in the night. It was dead when I woke up," Odum said. But his face, it was turned away from Agnes, so as not to meet her eyes.

"Dead?" Agnes repeated. "But he was fine when I put him to sleep earlier. How could it up and die so quick?"

" 'Cause it wasn't never meant to be alive," Odum said.

Agnes stared at her husband in horror, then whispered, "What you talking about?"

"I done the only thing I could with it."

That was when Agnes heard the sound. It was coming from back in the darkness of the wood. It was a strangely muffled cry. She grabbed hold of Odum's arm. "What's that? You hear that?"

Odum looked around, back into the woods, but said nothing.

"You done buried it alive," Agnes gasped.

"It wasn't never meant to be," Odum said.

"Hon, we got to save it."

This time Odum clutched on to his wife's arm, so tight that she gave out a little scream. "Ain't nothing to save," he hissed. "You forget that ever was, you hear?"

But Agnes's eyes frantically searched the darkness. She shook her head. "We can't leave it to die."

"We ain't leaving it to die," Odum whispered, his voice hoarse. "We's just leaving it."

"I can't. I can't." Agnes sobbed and broke away from her husband's grasp. She ran into the woods, stumbling over a vine-covered log. "Where'd you put him?" She looked around, but the floor of the woods was too thickly entangled with weeds and underbrush to make out any possible burial place. She heard another cry, jerked around, and ran in the direction she thought the sound had been coming from. She stopped, and again she heard the cry, only this time coming from the opposite direction. She ran and collapsed onto her knees. She pulled up some of the ground crawlers, but there was nothing underneath. It was hopeless.

"Leave it be. I done put back into darkness what was meant to stay in darkness."

He turned and walked back to the trailer.

Hester's room was pitch-black, except for the moonlight that fell across Matt's face. He turned from the window.

"He did bury me alive. That's how he knew who I was. Because of what it did to my foot. That thing that came into the world with me."

And Simmy nodded.

"Who found me?" he asked her.

There was not a sound, except for the soft creak-creak of the rocking chair. Cathy stood up and went over to Matt. She took his hand into hers and could feel the clammy dampness of his palm.

"Aunt Hester, she woke up that night, and she starts to raise hell. She wakes me and Leon up and she says she's hearing this here baby cry. Leon and me, we looks at each other, and we don't know what to think, 'cause we know Hester ain't heard much of nothing goin' on thirty years. She puts on her housecoat and she goes out there onto the back porch, and she looked into them woods behind the house. 'Don't you hear it a-crying?' she says. But me and Leon, we don't hear a thing. And Hester takes off out into them woods. Me and Leon, we try to follow her best we can.

"We come to that little clearing. You know the one. Where they put up that ol' water tower. And that's when I hear it, too. This little soft crying. And Leon, he hears it. And Aunt Hester, she's already down on her knees, digging into the ground with her hands. 'Quick, Leon,' she yells back. And Leon, he goes over and him and me, we both start clearing away the dirt. And that's when we seen this here box, and inside this box we done found this little child. As pretty and sweet a baby as you ever did see.

"And Leon says, 'Who could've done this?' And we take that baby back, and Leon says, 'This child's been saved for something. Like Moses in the bullrushes.'

"And Hester, she thinks the same thing. 'It's a miracle,' she tells Leon. And ol' Simmy, she believed it, too. Believed that little child has been spared for something. Only we didn't know what it could be.

"We raised that child as if it was our own. And it grow to be sweet and bright as it could be. Wasn't a trace of meanness in it, and each day as it got to be prettier and sweeter, Leon says to me, 'We done right, Simmy. The Lord guided Hester to that boy.' And that's how come Leon was always saying how you was touched by the hand of Fate, and how you was destined for something."

"I see," Matt whispered.

Cathy felt him remove his hand from hers. He stood up and walked from the room. Cathy waited a moment, letting the full horror of the story, with all its implications, sink into her. Then she followed him.

He was standing in the hallway, his arms limp by his side, his eyes vacant. "I was all wrong, wasn't I? I didn't create Mr. Eprin. He created me. 'Touched by the hand of Fate.' "

And then Matt began to walk down toward the staircase.

"Where are you going?" Cathy asked. "Matt?"

He didn't turn to look at her. "Back to where they found me." He hesitated, then whispered, "I understand now why God wanted to forget."

14

They were at Bobby Macon's Texaco again.

Leroy retrieved the key he had used the night before and let himself into the station. Curtis was standing outside by the fire truck. Leroy found the switch that turned the pumps on, then hurried back outside.

Curtis twisted off the gas cap of the truck, and began to pump unleaded into it. That was when he saw that Leroy was unhooking the pump that said regular.

"Whatchew doing, Leroy?"

But the boy didn't answer. He stretched the hose as far as it would go; he was taking it around to the other side of the fire engine. "It's only got one tank, Leroy."

"No, it don't."

Curtis put his nozzle on automatic and walked around to where Leroy was standing. "What the hell are you doing? That's where you're supposed to put the water in. Leroy, you listening to me? That's where the water goes that the firemen spray out of their hoses."

Leroy glanced up with a daunting scowl. "Don't you think I know that, Curtis? I ain't no goofball."

"Then what are you putting gasoline in there for?"

"So I can pump it back out again."

"Pump it out where?"

"Where you think, Curtis? I swear sometimes I don't know about you."

"Shit, you ain't serious," Curtis said with a gasp. "You can't be."

"Course I'm serious."

"That's why you wanted to drain the old water tower. So
you could pump this here gasoline into it. Ain't that right?"

"That's right?"

"Hell, Leroy, you could blow us both up."

"I done thought of it."

"What for?"

"I'm goin' to trap it, that shadow thing. Trap it inside
that water tower. See here, Curtis, this is how I figured it.
That ol' shadow, it needs something. It needs darkness. Can't
be no shadow without darkness. So I'm going to drown it,
kinda."

"In gasoline?"

"No, stupid. In light. I figured, if I can keep it trapped inside
of a big ol' fire, maybe it'll kinda suffocate on the light. 'Cause
inside that ol' tank, once it starts to go, there won't be nothing
but light all around it. You see what I'm saying? I hoping it
breathes on the darkness, kinda like, and if there ain't no
darkness around, then maybe it'll up and die."

"You think it will work?"

"I'm hoping it will. Ain't never killed no shadow before,
Curtis. Reckon nobody has." Leroy sighed, looking back down
at the nozzle in his hand. "A course, the way I figure it,
big problem's goin' to be you and me not getting blowed
up first."

"Yeah."

15

It was after ten o'clock when Matt pulled onto the dirt access
road that wound through the woods up toward the water tower.

He had gone only a mile when he stopped his car. He
turned off the engine and, the windows rolled down, he listened. It was crazy, he thought, but what he heard was unmis-
takable.

It was the music of a merry-go-round.

He pulled the car onto the shoulder of the road and got out.
Again he listened. The music still droned on.

Slowly he walked up the sloping hill. He stopped, right as he came to the first clear view of the field around the water tower.

His mouth open, he stared at it in disbelief. I'm losing my mind, he thought.

Around the base of the water tower, a sleazy, threadbare carnival had been set up. A merry-go-round, emptily spinning, was flanked by a row of tents. Each of them had a cheaply painted marquee in front of them.

The merry-go-round came to a halt. No one got off. No one got on. It waited a half minute, and then, creak by creak, it slowly began to move, the music starting up all over again.

The carnival, as far as Matt could see, was empty. No one, nothing—except the merry-go-round—stirred beneath the sliver of moon directly over the tower.

Everything was exactly as he had pictured it. Exactly as he had described in *The Shadowstealer*.

Matt walked toward it slowly.

There, at the far side, was the marquee he knew would be there.

It showed a terrified boy running through the woods, his head turned to glance behind him, his eyes bulging from his head, the shadow right on his heels. As Matt walked closer, he saw the claws, and at last, the single gleaming eyeball.

At the top of the painting were the words "THE SHADOW-STEALER."

The carnival had come back. It had returned to the same spot where it had set up nearly a century before. The same spot where, long before that, Mr. Eprin had brought the old African. It was here the Storyteller had watched as his children were defiled and chopped to pieces before his weeping eyes. Here that the old African had been burnt to death, while the brutal men around him had mocked and tormented him. Mocked him into speaking the Story that had been forbidden since the beginning of the world. Here that the Shadow of What-Was-Never-Meant-To-Be had risen out of the earth.

Matt stood in front of the tent that Hester and Wiley had peered into. He lifted back the flap and walked inside.

The kerosene lamp was suspended above the solitary table in the middle of the tent. For a floor, sawdust had been scattered.

"Where are you?" Matt called out.

And from a corner of the dim tent, another flap opened out. The old wheels squeaked. The face came first, then a hand reaching down into the sawdust to pull the wagon along.

"Why, looky who's here?" Mr. Eprin grinned. "If it ain't little Matthew." Mr. Eprin pushed and pulled himself closer to Matt. "I been looking forward to meeting you. Wanted to thank you for all you done for us. Time was, me and my Shadowstealer, why, we weren't nothing but a little carnival sideshow. And wasn't even much of a carnival at that. But we ain't no more." And Mr. Eprin's pointed teeth gleamed in the light of the kerosene lamp. "No, sir, you done made us famous. And we's goin' get famous-er, ain't that so?"

"Not if I can help it."

Mr. Eprin's grin did not show a trace of sag. "How you goin' to help it? My shadow, it done got your boy. You can always count on them little boys and little girls to go looking back at their shadows. Why, sometimes they run and run, sometimes they hide their eyes, go nearly all night long, trying to keep from looking back over their shoulders. But they always do, I found. Way yours done. Them others, too."

"I think I know the story. The one that God forbade anyone to repeat."

Mr. Eprin eyed him suspiciously. "You want to tell me what it's about?"

"It's about a shadow."

"Whose shadow?" Mr. Eprin grinned.

"God's. It's about God's Shadow."

Mr. Eprin eased closer to Matt. "I was right. I knowed all along you'd be the one to tell it."

"The thing that was never meant to be, it was God's Shadow. Wasn't it?"

And again Mr. Eprin nodded.

"And so the Shadowstealer is only the shadow of a shadow."

"Yes. But one that's getting stronger and stronger every day, every night. The more folks believe in him, the more realer he becomes. Why, it's almost fat now. I seen him a while back, with that boy of yours. You remember that boy of yours, don't you?"

"Yes," Matt said softly.

"See here," Mr. Eprin said, "all it wants is for everybody to know the Story—the Story that God never meant nobody to hear. The Story that ain't never whispered through to the end, not since time begun. The Story of What-Was-Never-Meant-To-Be."

"The Story you stopped the old African from telling."

Mr. Eprin nodded. "And which I done been wandering ever since, so's it could be finished. Wandered till I come across a little girl whose brother was done git by the Shadowstealer, wandered till I found a man what hated God, wandered till I found a preacher what was afraid of the Fires Everlasting, wandered till I found a boy who loved them stories, but loved best the story this here old crazy woman done told up in her bedroom." Mr. Eprin looked into Matt's eyes. "And that old, old story, you ain't just going to whisper it. No, you gonna write it down, and you gonna send out there to Hollywood, and you tell 'em, put this here story in that ol' movie. Right there near the end. The Story of what God didn't want in his world. The Story of what God don't even want to remember."

"And if I don't?"

"Your boy will be waiting for you up at that ol' water tower," Mr. Eprin said.

"If I tell the Story, then I ask one thing. And only one thing."

Mr. Eprin waited.

"Before I die, I want to have my shadow back."

"Your shadow?"

"The one I was born with. The one that held me by my foot as I came out of the womb."

Mr. Eprin grinned as he pushed himself back into darkness. "Why, I can't," he said. "I can't give you what always been yours."

16

Matt let the flap of the tent drop behind him. He stared up at the water tower.

"Where the hell this come from?"

Startled, Matt turned and stared at the boy. He was scowling up at the painting over the tent. "Looks just like that book cover, don't it?"

"Leroy?"

The boy glanced at Matt and nodded. He jerked his head back toward the access road. "Curtis Poke's with me. He's back there with the fire truck."

"Fire truck?"

"I got me a plan," Leroy said. "Hope you got one, too."

"Maybe."

"Sure hope one of them works." Leroy turned to go back toward the road, but stopped. "You mind telling me, where'd all this here shit come from?"

"Storyworld," Matt whispered.

Stone-faced, Leroy nodded. "I figured it was something like that."

Leroy and Matt walked together in silence back down the access road to where the fire truck was parked.

"That took guts, what you did this morning, saving Tommy's life," Matt said to the boy.

"I know." Leroy glanced away.

Matt stopped. "I know it's not easy for you to talk about. But I need to make a decision like the one you made, and I want you to help me do it."

Surprised, Leroy asked, "Want me to help you?"

"I want you to tell me how you did it."

The boy thought a moment. "I reckon I knew something had to be done. And there wasn't nobody else around to do it. So I done it." Leroy looked up at Matt. "That enough?"

Matt thought a moment, then said, "I think so."

They walked on a little farther.

"Listen."

Leroy stopped. "To what?"

"It's gone. The music."

The boy turned and stared up the slope of the road. He listened, too. There was not a sound. "Maybe that merry-go-round just stopped for a bit."

Matt turned and walked back up to the top of the hill. He stared into the clearing beneath the water tower.

It was empty now.

There was not a trace of the merry-go-round or the sideshow.

Not a trace of Mr. Eprin or his wagon. Leroy came up next to Matt. "Where it go to?"

"I don't know. Maybe it's always been there. Maybe it only lets you see it when it wants you to."

"I reckon," Leroy said with a frown.

"You saw it, too, didn't you?"

"Yeah. I seen it alright."

Matt sighed. "I was hoping maybe it was just me."

"Naw, it ain't just you. It's everything. Like there ain't nothing that's the way it's supposed to be no more."

Back at the fire truck, Matt told the two boys that he had to go somewhere. "I'll be back before twelve. There's something I got to do."

17

When Matt got back to the house, Tommy was just about to drive off. "I was just gonna go looking for you."

Cathy was on the porch. As Matt hurried up the steps, she took hold of his arm. "What are you doing?"

"What I have to."

Matt disappeared into the house. Tommy came up on the porch.

"What's he doing?"

"I don't know."

Cathy went inside. The room to the library was closed. But she could hear Matt talking. He was on the phone. She walked back onto the porch.

"He's calling somebody."

Less than five minutes later, Matt stepped back outside. His face was ashen.

"Matt?"

"I just called Frank. There's not going to be a movie. There's not going to be any more printings of the book."

"What did you tell him?"

"I told him," Matt stammered, "I said I plagiarized the whole thing. And that a lawsuit was pending." Matt shrugged.

Just then Cathy noticed Simmy. She was leaning against the banister. All three of them hurried inside.

"Simmy?"

"I come to tell y'all," she whispered. "It's scared. I feel it. It's scared a something. Don't know what. That ol' thing, it's mighty worried 'bout something."

Cathy and Tommy looked at each other, then hurried out to the car.

18

Leroy drove the fire truck to the end of the access road, right at the base of the water tower. "I sure hope that hose is long enough."

He hopped out, and with Curtis's help, he unfastened the hose and lay it on the ground. "We gotta turn that valve back off." Together the two boys went over to the outflow pipe and closed the valve as tight as they could. "I think that oughtta do it."

"Now what?"

"Now I climb up yonder," Leroy said, glancing to the top of the water tower. "With that hose. If I can."

Curtis looked at Leroy. "I'd better do it. I'm bigger."

"Okay. I'll come up behind you, holding it."

They went to the metal ladder and Curtis mounted the first few rungs. Leroy dragged the hose over and handed it up to Curtis.

"Shit, it's heavy as fuck."

"Yeah," Curtis said as he took it from the other boy. He set the nozzle over his shoulder, holding it with one hand, while he climbed with the other.

"Don't you fall on me now, hear?"

"I'll try not to, Leroy."

Leroy took hold of his part of the hose and slowly the two boys began to climb the ladder. "Take your time," Leroy advised, and Curtis did.

Halfway up, Leroy glanced down at the base of the tower. "Shit," he mumbled.

"Whatchew say?"

"Nothing," and again they continued up the ladder.

"Is it gonna stretch that far?"

"I dunno," Leroy said, looking back at the remaining coil of hose that still lay slack by the fire engine. "I might have to move the truck closer."

Five rungs from the top, Leroy checked again. "It ain't gonna make it. Ain't long enough. Shit."

"We gotta try."

Moments later, Curtis mounted the platform. He put his foot on the hose and helped Leroy up. Together they stretched as tight as they could. They were about five or six feet short of the metal door into the tank.

"Godfuckingdam," Leroy hissed.

"I guess you'll have to go back down and move the truck."

"I reckon so. I should've thought about it before." Leroy stared down the ladder.

"I'll yell down when I get it to reach inside the tank. Then you can turn the pumps on."

Leroy backed down the ladder carefully. At the bottom, he yelled up. "You got holt of it good?"

"Yeah," Curtis shouted.

Leroy jumped into the fire truck, started it up, and backed it toward the concrete slabs at the base of the tower. He smacked into one and stopped. He leaned out the window and called up, "How's that?"

There was no answer.

"Curtis? You still up there?"

Still there was no response. Leroy poked his head all the way out the window and strained to look up. But he was directly under the platform and could not see a sign of the other boy. "Curtis?" he yelled out again, even louder. He waited, then looked around him at the woods at the edge of the clearing. He shivered. Shadows were everywhere.

He got out of the cab of the truck and hurried to a point where he could see most of the platform.

There was no Curtis.

"Goddammit, where'd you go to?"

Then he saw the hose moving.

A second later, Curtis shouted, "I got it in. Turn the pumps on."

"You done scared the shit out of me. Answer me when I call you from now on."

"I didn't hear you. I was leaning inside the tank, to see if the water was gone."

Satisfied with the explanation, Leroy ran back to the pump box. He looked at the controls, found the switch, and went to turn it on. He stopped. If the thing was going to blow, it would probably do it the moment he clicked the switch. There could be a spark. After all, fire trucks were designed to pump water, not gas. Still, Leroy knew they had come too far for him to chicken out now.

He closed his eyes.

He flicked the switch. He waited and realized that he hadn't blown up yet.

"Goddam," he said, grinning. "I done it."

He was about to call up to Curtis, but he stopped.

On the back of his neck, he had felt a tingling. *"CURTIS!"*

It was what, in Curtis's reading, was always called a blood-curdling scream. The boy was trying to keep the hose from flying every which way as the gasoline poured into the empty tank of the water tower. Holding the hose in place over the bottom of the door, he turned as far around as he could and yelled back, "What is it, Leroy?"

"It's got me!"

"What got—" Curtis started to call back. But all at once he understood. "Turn the pumps off," he shouted. "Hear me?"

Curtis waited, then carried the still trickling hose over to the railing. He stared down at the other boy and at the shadow behind him.

Leroy's shadow and that of the water tower made a uneven V shape, one shadow arm being much longer than the other.

Leroy's shadow was longer.

"Turn around," Curtis shouted down to the other boy. Curtis watched as Leroy's shadow slowly swiveled behind him. Only it didn't move the way something rigid might move, each part moving equally. Instead, there was a noticeable lag at the far end of it, as if the shadow were made of something heavy and not easy to move. Curtis squeezed the railing as he watched Leroy's shadow swirl first one way, then another, like the tail of a huge black snake.

"You see it?" Leroy yelled.

"I see it," Curtis said.

"I ain't gonna look back at it," Leroy shouted.

"Don't," Curtis whispered. Then he yelled so that Leroy could hear him, "Turn the pumps back on."

Keeping his eyes rigidly straight, Leroy walked slowly back to the fire engine and turned the pump on again. The tingling was all up and down his spine now. He wanted to swat at it, but he couldn't take the chance. Even an accidental glimpse of the shadow thing, and Leroy knew it would be all over for him.

He had to make it until morning.

It was easy, he told himself. He only needed to remember one thing.

No matter what, he couldn't look back. Not for anything.

He stepped straight back from the pump and then he heard a voice. It was coming right behind him. So close that she couldn't have been more than two feet away.

"I'll tell you that story, Leroy. The one about The Saddest Song."

Every muscle in the boy's body froze.

"It's me, Opal."

"Naw," Leroy whispered. "Naw, it ain't. I know who it is. It's a trick."

"Look around and see if it ain't me," the voice said. And Leroy had to admit, it did sound like his sister. What if it was her. What if it had all been a nightmare, one long goofy nightmare, and she had come out to wake him up, he wondered.

"That's right," the voice said. "That's all it is, Leroy. Just an ol' nightmare. I come to take you back to the trailer."

"Naw, you ain't fooling me."

"I'll tell you about that big ol' house we're going to have up in Nashville, and about the bowling alley, and the rink. All you got to do is turn around."

"Uh-uh. I ain't. I ain't turning around for nothing." And he closed his eyes and clamped his hands to his ears, he began to sing his favorite song in the world, "Love Me Tender."

And that's when he felt it on his shoulder.

The claw.

His eyes popped open. His neck muscles tensed. He was in a heartbeat of looking down at his shoulder, looking down at the thing. But he caught himself. His eyes riveted to the fire

engine, he gasped, "You ain't goin' to get me, you motherfucker. You can get all them others, but you ain't getting
Leroy!"

He reached over and grabbed at the thing on his shoulder,
keeping his eyes straight ahead of him.

At the touch of it, he let go.

It was cold and oozy, like something nasty at the bottom of
a lake.

He looked up at the platform. Just keep looking up yonder,
Leroy told himself. He could make it. He knew he could.

Curtis waited for the last of the gasoline to trickle from
the hose.

He stared into the dark tank.

Of course, the gasoline hadn't come up nearly as far as the
water had. But there was enough. Besides, the fumes were
filling the cavernous upper regions of the water tower. All
it needed was a spark, and the whole structure would blow
sky-high.

He went to close the door, but stopped. What if the metal of
the door scraped too sharply against the metal of the tower?

A single spark and that would be all she wrote for Curtis.

He decided to leave the door where it was. He carried
the hose to the railing. "I'm going to drop it down. Watch
out."

Curtis let the hose fall under the side of the tower.

"You got to get out of here, Curtis," Leroy yelled up. " 'Fore
it's too late."

Descending in record speed, Curtis, back on the ground,
turned and looked at Leroy. "Shit, Leroy, what are we goin'
to do?"

"Dunno yet."

Curtis glanced back up at the tower. The plan had been
to lure the shadow thing inside the tank, once it was full
of gasoline. To close the metal door and try to trap it there.
Then, using the rifle, to shoot at the tank from the edge of
the clearing. Maybe not the first shot, but one of the shots
would do the trick, transforming the water tower into a fireball
and, it was hoped, depriving the thing within of the darkness
indispensable to its survival. But now, Curtis realized, it wasn't
going to be that easy.

It had got Leroy, and it obviously didn't want to let him go.

"Just let me think a little bit," Leroy said.

Curtis nodded, his eyes fixed on the coiling shadow behind the other boy.

"We can still do it."

"Whatchew mean?" Curtis asked.

Leroy's face was rigidly fixed on Curtis's. "Only thing is, I gotta take it up there with me. Up yonder."

"Then what?"

"I ain't sure yet. Reckon, we'll just have to see."

"But how you goin' to get it inside the tank?"

"Reckon I'll have to get in there myself."

"That's crazy. Them fumes, you couldn't take 'em for longer than a minute or two," Curtis said. " 'Sides, even if you could, what if it still don't let go of you?"

Leroy didn't blink. "Then I reckon we ain't got much choice. You and me both."

"What are you talking about?"

"Hell, Curtis, even you can hit something big as that ol' water tower with a rifle."

"Naw, Leroy. You're crazy. I ain't doing that. I ain't doing nothing like that."

"Look behind me, goddammit!"

Curtis was trying not to, but again his eyes fell to the undulating ooze of shadow that stretched behind Leroy.

"If I gotta die, Curtis, I am taking this here motherfucker with me when I do. The rifle's in the truck. You get and you take it over yonder, as far away as you can git and still hit that ol' water tower."

"I told you, I ain't gonna do it, Leroy. You're my goddam friend."

"Whatchew think Wally was to me, Curtis?" Leroy said, his eyes bursting with anger. "I done it 'cause there wasn't nothing else to do. And this here, it's the same thing. So go on." Leroy began moving toward the ladder. He stopped at the foot of it, not daring to look back at Curtis, and stood absolutely rigid, "Go on, Curtis. I mean it now."

Eyes on the shadow, Curtis stepped backward to the cab of the fire engine.

Curtis watched as Leroy started up the ladder, then he grabbed the rifle and ran to the edge of the clearing.

● ● ●

Leroy clutched the metal poles of the ladder. He was only ten or so rungs from the platform.

He had closed his eyes.

When he was little, there was an old couple in the trailer park who used to take him and Opal with them to the First Baptist Church of Mt. Jephtha. The man would come by to pick them up on a Sunday morning and would stand at the door of the trailer and try his best to pretend like he wasn't looking inside, on account of the mess the trailer was, and also because Leroy's momma was usually still in her bathrobe and was having breakfast with one of Leroy's temporary uncles. Leroy's momma would always try to make everything seem right, introducing the man sitting at the table in his underwear as her cousin and the old man would say, "Pleased to meet you." They were what was good people, the old man and his wife.

They felt sorry for Leroy, because of the way he was being brought up.

And Leroy hated them for it.

And he hated his momma for his having to hate them when they were only trying, in their own way, to be nice to him and to his sister, Opal.

He also hated the little man who taught them Sunday school. The man told Leroy and the others stories from the Bible. Most of them, in Leroy's opinion, were goofy as hell.

But there was one he liked.

It was the story of David and Goliath.

And Leroy, as he listened to the story, knew damn well he'd have thought of the slingshot, too. And he couldn't help feeling a little resentful that all this fuss was made over a boy who had only thought of something that Leroy would have thought of, too.

Leroy opened his eyes.

He glanced down at the dark ground far below him. A night breeze chilled the sweat on his face.

He didn't believe in heaven, though he figured something would have to go on afterward. Only it probably wasn't like people thought.

Who knows? One of the papers his momma bought at the grocery store once had an article about how Elvis had been picked up in a UFO and was being given a grand tour of the whole universe from one end to another, going to every planet and visiting with everybody who was anywhere. Leroy thought that would be nice, to be on a flying saucer with Elvis, and to travel around.

Maybe there was a planet where nothing goofy ever happened, and people had sense, the way Leroy did. He and Elvis would probably like it there, and maybe they'd stay.

Leroy looked up at the remaining rungs, and debated about whether or not he should pray. He had done it once or twice aloud, with the old people in the trailer park. It was their idea. "Pray for your momma, hon," they told him. And he did. Though not the way they wanted him to. "I hope Momma wins the McDonald's Sweepstakes," he had asked Jesus.

She didn't.

Leroy sighed. "Okay, Jesus, I'm giving you one more chance. Kill that motherfucker. Kill him dead." He thought a moment more, then said, "Amen."

Then he again felt the tingling on the back of his neck, and began climbing the rest of the way.

Curtis crouched down at the edge of the woods. He lay flat on his stomach and set the rifle so that its sights were fixed on the bottom of the water tower.

Leroy was almost at the top.

That was when he noticed something.

A shadow on the platform. Then another.

Somebody was already up there. Must have been hidden on the other side of the tower the whole time Curtis had been filling the tank with gasoline. Or maybe they had gotten up there some other way—

He lifted himself up a few inches and shouted, "Leroy, watch out!"

But the boy couldn't hear him.

Curtis was about to get back up on his feet when suddenly he stopped.

Somebody was behind him.

Curtis froze.

"I come back for you, Curtis."

Then he felt his back being straddled. He knew whose voice it was.

"Feels good, don't it?"

And Curtis felt the strong hands as they rubbed up and down, from the back of his neck to the base of his spine. And then Jesse said again, "I come back for you."

"Naw," Curtis whispered. "It ain't you."

"Look."

And Curtis twisted around.

Jesse's body was on him, just as it had been out in the hay barn that night. His chest glistened the same way in the moonlight, his arms and shoulders taut and muscular. Only his face was in shadow.

His fingers caressed Curtis's stomach through his T-shirt. "Just goin' to be you and me from now on. Won't be nobody to say nothing 'bout us, nobody to call us nothing, neither."

Jesse's hands reached down lower. He brought his face toward Curtis.

The moonlight fell across the empty sockets.

A trickle of something oozed down his cheeks from the two holes.

All at once, the trickle became a downpour.

Leroy heard the echo of the shriek just as he was about to climb onto the platform.

He twisted his neck around, got a few inches, then remembered, gasping, "Oh, shit." He shut his eyes and his left hand lost hold of the railing.

His right hand slid down, but as he dropped all he thought was, Don't look. Don't look back.

His knee slammed against a rung, painfully breaking his slide for a second, enough for him to open his eyes again, grasping desperately for the rung overhead. He caught it, and panting hard, he lifted himself up so that he was again standing on the ladder. He waited to see if anything would happen, still not sure whether, in his half second of forgetfulness, he had actually looked back at the thing or not.

But nothing happened.

Only the tingling went on.

He was okay.

He glanced up and climbed the remaining rungs. His hand reached to take hold of the metal post of the railing. He lifted himself on the platform itself, then stopped and stared at the shadow that fell across the wooden planks right in front of him.

Startled, he looked up to his left and saw them.

"Mother*fucker*," he whispered.

19

They had heard the shriek, too.

Matt was already out of the car. Tommy and Cathy were following close behind him.

"What was that?"

"I don't know."

"Look." It was Cathy who noticed the three dark figures on the platform of the water tower. "Who is it?"

Tommy stopped and stared at them. "Our boys. Leroy's with 'em."

"What are they doing?"

Suddenly all three of them froze. From high up on the tower, a sound cut piercingly through the still night. It was the sound of a chain saw starting up.

But Tommy wasn't looking at the tower anymore. "Over there. See?"

He ran to the edge of the clearing.

"Jesus Christ," he gasped, staggering backward. Matt was alongside of him. He turned and stopped Cathy.

There, in the undergrowth, lit in a few patches by the moonlight, they watched the black oozing thing as it engulfed Curtis's writhing arm.

Tommy aimed his .22 and fired five shots in it. The bullets hit it with a dull plunk, as if he had been firing into quicksand. It twitched and squirmed, parts of it rising up like pseudopods, transforming into shadowlike hands, then dissolving shape again. A shadow face suddenly formed, the mouth opening, then folding back over it seamlessly. The shapes and forms changed rapidly, endlessly. Long ago, on TV, Matt had seen a man who could make anything out of the shadow of his hands. Set against a strong light, he would transform his shadow fingers into giraffes and monkeys and famous people, each new silhouette immediately disappearing into the next. What

he saw now was like a horrifying three-dimensional parody of
the man's act, the pure image of chaos and dissolution, a realm
in which nothing and something were indistinguishable.

"Look. There."

Tommy was pointing to a thin thread of blackness that led
from the thing in front of them across the moonlit field and
up the ladder of the water tower.

Curtis's fingers wiggled, then were sucked into the dark boiling mass. The thread of shadow abruptly thickened, undulating
back and forth across the field. It was as if the thing in the
undergrowth was being pulled by the thread of shadow back
across the field, to the water tower.

"Oh, Christ," Matt whispered. "It's up there, too, on the
tower. They're connected."

An image from a high school biology course rose up in Matt's
mind. That of an amoeba reproducing itself. A pseudopod would
stretch and stretch from the original cell. At a certain distance,
it would draw out some of the material of the old cell, grow
larger and larger, until finally it would split away entirely. This
was how this was doing, only in reverse, and without there ever
being a final rupture.

The thread grew fatter as the squirming blob was pulled back
toward the tower.

At the base, it began to be drawn upward by a strand of
blackness. When Peter was five, Matt had given him some
Silly Putty, though he had ended up playing with it as much
as the boy. It fascinated him to watch how, when you stretched
out a long, attenuated piece of it, then dropped it, the extended
piece would be slowly pulled back up into the main knot of
it.

That was what was happening now.

The blob of writhing shadow that only a minute before
had engulfed Curtis was now oozing backward up onto the
platform of the tower.

And Matt recalled Mr. Eprin's word, how it was getting
fatter, and realer.

"I'm going up there," Matt said.

"No, that's crazy."

Matt ran to the spot where Curtis had been. He picked up
the rifle. "Here, take it."

"What am I supposed to do with it, Matt?"

"I don't know yet. Just keep it."

"Matt?" Cathy grabbed hold of him. "You sure?"

He nodded. "I'm sure." He kissed her, then turned and ran toward the tower.

20

"Go on back. Don't come up here!"

Matt was ten rungs from the platform. He had stopped. His bad foot was in unbearable pain. He looked up. Leroy had been yelling at him since he began to climb the ladder, but only now had he been able to hear the boy's words over the noise of the chain saw.

"That motherfucker, it got me. I ain't turned 'round yet. But it's got aholta me."

"What about Peter and Jimmy?"

"They's acting goofy as shit."

Ignoring Leroy's advice, Matt painfully worked his way up the rest of the ladder, then clambered onto the platform.

The noise of the chain saw had stopped seconds before.

Peter was holding it. He set it down on Jimmy's shoulder, so that the saw blades were lying next to his neck.

"Mr. Shadow wants to know why you've been bad," Jimmy asked.

"I—"

Then before Matt could say another word, Peter pulled the cord of the chain saw. Matt staggered back against the railing as the blades began spinning. The chain saw ripped into Jimmy's neck, blood splattering against the side of the tower.

"Christ, no!"

The boy's head tumbled down his chest into his lap, then rolled from the tower.

Leroy reached out and clutched Matt's arm. Speechless, they watched as Jimmy's body sagged backward against Peter's legs. Blood spurted from the severed carotid, all over Peter.

The boy lifted the chain saw up.

"Son," Matt gasped, his fingers gripping the railing in a desperate effort to keep from passing out. "Don't."

"I have to," Peter said softly. "You made Mr. Shadow

unhappy. And now he's going to make you unhappy."

"*Nooo!*" Matt screamed. "I'll do whatever he wants. I swear to fucking God I will."

"He wants everybody to believe in him. That's all. But you don't want them to. You want them to forget about him, the way they forget about all the bad things. But you won't forget about this," Peter said. The chain saw was only inches in front of his face. "You'll remember, when it's Mommy's turn. You'll do right then, won't you?"

Peter began to pull the chain saw slowly toward his face.

"*No, Goddammit, noooo!*"

Suddenly, from behind Matt's back, there was an explosion. Peter's arm flew back, the chain saw dropped, hit Jimmy's lifeless body, cutting into it. Both the saw and the body thrashed crazily for a few horrible moments, then, together, they spun off over the edge of the platform.

Peter looked down at his arm.

It was bleeding from the bullet wound.

Matt turned and saw Tommy. He was holding the rifle. But his eyes were on the place where, seconds before, the body of his son had been. His face white, he took a step toward it, then shook his head. "Uh-uh," he whispered.

"I couldn't do anything," Matt said.

"Y'all gotta get off a here," Leroy shouted at them. "Quick."

Matt snatched Peter into his arms and held him. "It's gonna be okay," he whispered, although he wasn't sure whether he was telling this to his son or to himself.

Peter's body was limp, even lifeless. "I'm having a bad dream. I can't find Tigger. I want to wake up, Daddy. Wake me up, please," the boy mumbled, just as a child mumbles in his sleep.

"I will," Matt said, then took his son over to the ladder. He looked at the ground. How was he going to carry Peter down? "You gotta get down the ladder, son. You gotta make it."

"I call to him, but he won't come to me anymore," the boy went on, his eyes gazed numbly into the distant woods.

There was no way Peter was going to make it. No way that Matt could trust himself to carry the boy down. He looked at Tommy.

Tommy hadn't moved. Matt went to him and took hold of his arm. "Tommy. You got to help me. Help me get Peter down."

Tommy looked into Matt's eyes and nodded. Then he stared back down where Jimmy had been.

"I'm so sorry. Sorry for them things I used to think. You don't know how sorry I—" His voice broke off.

Matt turned Tommy away. "I can't get Peter down myself. Christ, I'm not sure I can even get myself down. But you can. You're the only one of us who can do it. You have to."

Tommy nodded, unable to say a word.

"You take him back to the car, Tommy. You listening?"

Tommy nodded.

Matt put Peter into Tommy's hands. "I'll do it, Matt," he said.

Tommy put his arm around Peter's waist and pulled the boy close to him. "Can you hold on to me?"

Peter nodded. "Uh-huh."

Matt watched as Tommy began down the ladder, using only his right hand to hold on with, while his left hand clutched tight to Peter's waist.

"You go on with him," Leroy said, "and take this with you."

Matt stared at the rifle Leroy was holding out to him. "What am I supposed to do with it?"

"What I'd do, if I could," Leroy replied.

"No."

"You got to. You or Tommy, either one. Don't matter who does it. A couple of shots and this whole thing's goin' to blow sky-high. And maybe it'll take this motherfucker behind me with it."

Matt stared at Leroy's shadow. The entire mass of black ooze had compressed itself to what anyone looking at it would have figured to be Leroy's normal shadow. The only difference was that it was much darker than the surrounding shadows, and, of course, the fact that it moved directly behind Leroy instead of following the path of the moonlight.

Leroy walked to the door of the tank. He stuck his head inside. The fumes were so powerful that he had to turn away. "I'll wait until you're down there. You can see when I go inside. That's when you gotta do it. You listening to me?"

Matt was staring at the shadow.

"I've come to tell the story," he whispered.

Leroy scowled. "What you saying?" He looked into Matt's face. His eyes were not on Leroy. They were on Leroy's shadow. On what was hidden beneath his shadow.

"Who you talking to?" Leroy asked, though he already knew.

"Leave him. Come to me," Matt whispered. "Come to me and I will tell the Story of What-Was-Never-Meant-To-Be."

Suddenly the tingling stopped on the back of Leroy's neck. "You're calling it to you," Leroy gasped. He shivered as the thing ebbed down his spine. He looked down at his feet as he watched as it oozed toward Matt's shadow. It was cast to his right side, rising diagonally across the side of the water tower. The Shadowstealer slowly filled it, just as in Hester's story, it had filled Wiley's shadow so long ago, creeping up the side of the water tower until every inch of Matt's normal shadow had turned pitch-black. Then slowly it began to ooze down from the surface of the water tower to the platform, until, finally, it was gathered directly behind Matt's back.

"Go on, Leroy. Get off of here."

"Whatchew goin' to do."

"I'm goin' to do what I'm good at. I goin' to tell it a story."

"A story?"

"Go on. And take this." Matt handed Leroy the rifle. "Don't let them see you, Leroy. You understand? They'll try to stop you. You're the only one I can trust."

Leroy glared up at him. "You shouldn't a done it," Leroy said. "You's important. I ain't. Who's goin' to fucking miss ol' Leroy?"

"I would have."

"Shit," the boy said. He went to the ladder, then stopped. Matt called to him to come back. Matt stuck his hand out.

"Same deal. When you see me go through the door, you shoot, same as I'd have done for you."

Leroy frowned. "Naw. You wouldn't't've. But I will." Leroy put his hand out and they shook, then the boy turned and began down the ladder.

Matt stared out over the railing and waited until he saw Leroy running across the moonlit clearing. He kept his word. He had headed in the opposite direction from the access road.

He saw the barrel of the rifle gleam in the moonlight as Leroy crouched down.

Slowly he turned back to the door of the tank, careful to keep his body and his head aligned so that he would not accidentally glimpse what was behind him.

"I will tell the story I was born to tell," Matt said aloud. "The story you have waited so long to hear. The story that God's Shadow spoke to the First Storyteller at the beginning of time. The story that long ago, at this very place, the old African spoke as he was dying, and as he watched his children die."

He closed his eyes. *"Veni, Creator Spiritus,"* he whispered. The tingling swept up and down his spine as he began:

"Once there was nothing but the Lord. And the Lord God thought to himself, I will make me a world. And he set up the earth, and above it, he put the moon and the stars. But this was still not enough light to please him. And so he set in its place the sun. For of all things He had made, there was nothing more pleasing to God than light.

"And God wandered through the dazzling brightness of the world and he was greatly pleased. For he had created nothing but what was good and wholesome.

"At evening as He went to rest among a grove of trees, He turned and glimpsed something that was following Him. He stopped and said, 'Who are you?' For behind Him there stretched a great swath of darkness. 'I know nothing of what you are. Surely I did not make you with the breath of my mouth.'

" 'That is true. And yet I am.'

" 'How did you come into the world, if I did not create you?' God said, growing angry.

" 'Did you not know that when you made light, that you, too, would cast a shadow?'

" 'But I did not intend you to be part of the world I have made.'

" 'Yet I am here,' God's Shadow replied.

"And God grew vexed and repented Him of the world He had breathed into being with the breath of His mouth. For he had not considered that by making light He too would cast a shadow.

"All night long God wandered, and all the creatures that God had made trembled and were afraid and they whispered to themselves, 'Lord God is no longer pleased with what He has made. Surely He will wipe it away in the sweep of His hand, and darkness will again be All-in-all.'

"Toward morning God spoke to His Shadow. 'I have decided this: From this day forward, I will have no Shadow about me. No one shall ever speak of you, or look upon you. From this day forward, you shall wander nameless, and all creatures will be forbidden even to whisper of you, or to glance with their eyes upon you. If any creature ever disobeys my Law, then I will undo what I have done. I will abandon the world and leave it to my Shadow, and darkness will become All-in-all.'

"All the creatures that God had created quickly obeyed. For they were grateful that God had made them, and given them light. And soon they forgot all about the Shadow that God had forbidden them to look upon or whisper of.

"But God's Shadow thought to himself, God has declared I did not exist. And wherever I wander, all creatures I come across avert their eyes from me, for they are docile and stupid and timorous, and wish to flatter the God whom they fear.

"But there is one creature whose eyes I watch carefully when he comes close to God. The eyes of man I watch. For sometimes I have caught those eyes painfully struggling not to look upon me. Tonight I will go to the wisest of men, the Storyteller, and I will sit down upon him in his sleep, and I will become the First Nightmare. For even man's fear cannot overcome his wish to know.

"And that is what he did. He went to the First Storyteller and told him his story. And Lord God, upon discovering man's disobedience, grew angry, and set His curse upon the Storyteller and upon all of his descendants. Forever they must pass the story on, but never must they speak it as other stories are spoken.

"God's Shadow was pleased with the curse. For he knew that one day, the story would be told as other stories are told, aloud and with the words going from the beginning to the end, and that God would abandon the world, and all the creatures within it, to him.

"Long he waited, and watched with joy as the Last Storyteller suffered torments as no other man had suffered them. Joyous was his heart as he listened to the story of God's Shadow unfold. 'Soon all creatures will know that God, too, has a shadow, and that I am that shadow. Soon I alone will rule all of creation.' But as the last words were about to be spoken, God came upon His Shadow, and He said to him—"

Matt stopped and opened his eyes. He heard a strange, eerie squeal coming from the thing within his shadow. A squeal of hideous, terrible anticipation. He knew it was here that the old African's story had ended. He took a deep breath and again closed his eyes.

"For when God heard the last words were about to be spoken, because of the agony that the good man was suffering, and because of the agony that his innocent children had suffered, He stared down at the world He created, and He saw before Him, all at once, all the evil and all the pain and all the suffering that had come into the world since He had whispered, 'Let there be light.' And He turned to His Shadow, the Shadow that He had long forbidden any of His creatures even to whisper of. 'I am God who made light,' He said. 'But in making light, I forgot that I too was condemned to cast a shadow. From all eternity I have pretended that I alone cast no shadow. But no longer will I pretend this, O my Shadow. For I have learned that this is the price of light. That shadows must be cast. And that even God must cast one.

" 'This I offer you. I will forgive you for your existence. But you in turn must forgive me mine.'

"And God's Shadow, when he heard God Almighty asking for forgiveness, trembled. For he saw tears in the eyes of the Most High God, the God who had made all that is, who had sent the light in the heavens and laid the foundations of the earth.

"And in a hoarse whisper, God's Shadow fell upon his face and said—"

Matt swallowed hard. " 'Thy will be done.' "

On the back of his neck, the tingling suddenly stopped. And speaking to the thing that had crept inside his own shadow, Matt said, "So, too, you must forgive us. You must forgive us for our forgetfulness. We must forgive you for your remembering."

Then Matt turned and stared into his shadow.

"Together we came into the world. Together we will leave it."

The blackness squirmed and writhed before him. And a sound came from it, a low, agonized squeal.

It was afraid.

Matt could feel it as it unloosed itself from his spine and from his ankles.

It was trying to get away.

Matt stared at it as it undulated and oozed toward the edge of the platform. He reached down and grabbed at it.

"Matt?"

It was Tommy. He was standing at the top of the ladder. He ran to where Matt was struggling with the thing. "Get off of here," Matt shouted. "Quick."

Tommy looked at the thing as it began to seep and drip down the side of the tower.

He got on his stomach and reached down and grabbed it in his hands and hauled it back up.

"We got to get it inside."

Together they snatched it from the platform, as it writhered crazily. "Don't look at it," Matt said. But Tommy already had. Two eyes opened up out of the mass and stared into Tommy's face. A mouth gaped wide and a tongue oozed out of it. The squeals went on, louder and more horrifyingly frantic.

They pushed it through the opening into the tank.

"Close the door," Tommy yelled.

Matt tried, but the metal door didn't budge. It was stuck. "You gotta do it. I can't."

Tommy pushed against the door with all his might. But it wouldn't close.

"Christ."

From the opening, Matt watched a black tentacle as it squirmed up over the ledge.

"It's coming back out. We gotta get it closed."

"You go on. I can do it."

"No."

"Go on, goddammit," Tommy screamed.

"No." This time both men pushed against the door with everything they had. There was a sharp creak and it snapped shut.

Matt hurried toward the ladder. Tommy followed him. He knew that Leroy must have been watching everything. He hadn't shot yet, but Matt knew that the boy would if he felt he had to. A single shot, through the tank, and the water tower—and anyone near it—would be gone.

Matt was a third of the way down the ladder—there was about fifteen feet now between him and the ground—when Tommy stopped.

"You hear that?"

"What?" Matt heard nothing: He was breathing too hard.

"The hinges. It's pushing that door open."

"You sure?"

And this time Matt heard it, too.

"I'm going back up."

"No," Matt yelled, then reached up for the rung above when suddenly his hand slipped. He lost his balance, swayed, struggled to keep hold with his remaining hand, but as he spun and tumbled against the ladder, his wrist twisted sharply, and he let go.

His right leg was straight when it hit the ground. The bone snapped at once. Matt collapsed onto his face, jerking and rolling in pain. Still, he managed to call out for Tommy. He lifted his head and watched as his friend disappeared over the top of the ladder.

"Tommy!"

There was a hand on Matt's shoulder. It was Leroy. "Come on, get up. You gotta get out a here." With Leroy's help and support, Matt managed to get onto his good leg. "Oh, Jesus," he whispered. "We gotta save Tommy." The pain was horrible, but Matt still managed to get to the base of the ladder. He put his hands on to the highest rung he could reach, and struggled to pull himself up. "Tommy," he screamed. He made it to the third rung when again he collapsed, the pain so intense that for a moment he was on the verge of losing consciousness.

"Come on. Ain't nothing you can do."

And Leroy dragged Matt limping from the base of the tower.

21

The door was open only a few inches. A single black arm, dripping like hot tar, was emerging from it, and inside, the whole mass of it was struggling to push the door farther open.

He ran to it and was about to try to knock the door shut when suddenly a hand squirmed loose from the black muck. Tommy stared at it. It was still blistered and fiery red. Just as it had been on the day his son had stuck it into Simmy's skillet.

He stared at it in a shock of horror.

Stared just long enough for another tentacle to shoot out from the narrow opening and grab Tommy on the back of his neck.

22

Leroy had gotten Matt back to the edge of the clearing. Cathy was there with Peter. "Where's Tommy?"

"He's still up there."

"What are you going to do?"

Leroy had the rifle slung over his back. "I can still hit the tank from here," he said. He looked at Matt. Both of them were panting, from exhaustion, from fear, from confusion.

The boy unslung the rifle and held it. "Somebody got to do it. We can't let it loose again."

"I know."

Leroy stared down at the gun. "I just ain't sure . . . I don't know if I can do it again. I done it once already." He looked at Matt. "When you was up there, I had my finger on the trigger. I kept telling myself to squeeze, but I couldn't. I just couldn't do it," the boy said. Then he looked back at the tower. "But somebody's got to."

Matt took the rifle from Leroy's hands.

"Matt, what are you doing?" Cathy asked.

"What Tommy would want me to do," he said. Leroy helped him to get flat on his stomach. Matt closed one eye and squinted the other through the sights.

He put his finger on the trigger.

"Christ," he whispered.

23

On the tower, Tommy struggled to pull the thing from him, as coil after coil was dropping through the opening on to the platform. "Christ," he gasped. "Shoot now," he was yelling. "Shoot the goddam tower now!"

Then the idea struck him.

"You fucker. I'm goin' to kill you," he hissed.

He yanked the metal door back with all his might. He got up on the ledge of the door. He turned and as he began to slide down the side of the tank, the coils began to be pulled back inside. He grabbed them, reached up, and managed to pull the door shut.

It was pitch-black.

He was sliding down into the gasoline.

The fumes were overwhelming. He held his breath. He groped into the pocket of the shirt and pulled out his Bic lighter.

He held it up.

Then flicked it.

24

"Oh, my God."

Cathy turned away as the water tower exploded into a blaze of light and fire. She hid Peter's head in her lap.

Matt, still lying on the ground, watched as shreds and pieces of the tower flew up into the night air. His finger was on the trigger of the rifle.

He had managed to pull it back halfway.

For a full two minutes no one said a word.

Leroy sat down on the ground next to Matt. He looked into Matt's eyes hard and scrutinizing. "Is it gone?"

Matt stared at the flaming debris as it fell and scattered over the clearing.

"I don't know if it can ever be gone."

Leroy obviously didn't care much for this answer. He stared down at the ground for a moment, then looked up. "You ain't goin' write no more stories 'bout it, though."

"No."

Leroy helped Matt to his feet. Matt was still staring at the water tower. Leroy knew what he was thinking.

"Somebody had to do it," Leroy told him. "You know that much, don't you?"

"I know that much."

Cathy lay Peter in the backseat of the car and walked over to where Matt was leaning against the hood.

Leroy nodded at her. They had never met until a few minutes before.

"You think it'd be okay if I stayed with you tonight? No telling when my momma's coming home."

Cathy smiled. "Sure."

" 'Preciate it," Leroy said.

EPILOGUE

....

1

A year had passed.

It was three-thirty on a Friday afternoon. Matt Hardison was sitting behind his desk at Wally Clark Memorial Middle School. He was grading papers when Leroy walked into the room.

Matt looked up and grinned.

"Want to do some reading?" Leroy asked him. "I done brung my book."

Matt said sure, and Leroy pulled up his chair next to Matt's desk. He sat down in it and with the utmost seriousness of countenance, he opened his copy of *Freddie Goes to Florida*. Inside, written in Matt's handwriting, were the words, "To my good friend and favorite eighth-grader, Leroy Cates."

Leroy squirmed for a moment, cleared his throat, and then slowly read:

" 'Mrs. Wiggins was a character. That means that when she did anything, she always did it in a little different way than anyone else would have done. And she did a good many things that nobody else would ever have thought of.' "

Leroy set the book down and stared at Matt. "Ain't that what you said I was? A character?"

"Yes, Leroy. I think I did say that."

The boy again looked over the paragraph, a glimpse of a glimmer of a smile crossing his lips. "I reckon that's so. I don't do much of anything way other folks do." Leroy thought for a moment, then said, "This here kind of book I like. I like them stories that are true-to-life and make good sense." And looking back down at the page, Leroy again cleared his throat and resumed telling how Freddie the Pig, Jinx the Cat, Mrs.

Wiggins the Horse, and Alice the Duck all decided to make their true-to-life trip down to Florida one cold winter.

It was after four-thirty when Leroy stopped reading.

"I done pretty good."

"Yep, Leroy. You done real good," Matt said, although he noticed that it hadn't really been a question.

Leroy was about to leave the room when he stopped and turned back to Matt. "I'll have that radio ready for you next Monday. It's goin' be six bucks," Leroy stated. "You got it?"

"I got it."

"Need to save up. College's expensive. Ain't that right?"

Matt grinned. "That's right."

2

Back at the Lumpkin house, Matt found Cathy in her study. She was editing an article for an Atlanta magazine.

They kissed. "How'd it go today?"

"Not bad."

Tigger glanced up from the stack of corrected pages that Cathy had set on the left-hand corner of the desk.

"What you say, Tigger?"

"Oh, Daddy, this guy Mommy's helping edit, he can't write near as good as you. He sucks."

"Oh, really," Matt said, with an impatient glance at Cathy's lips. "Well, Tigger, you know your daddy doesn't write anymore."

"That's such a shame, Daddy, you so talented. You could write stories about Tigger the Talking Cat."

"No, I couldn't, Tigger."

And Matt got up and left the room.

"You really put your foot in it this time, Tigger," Cathy said.

3

Simmy was out in the kitchen cooking.

A year earlier, the night that Tommy died, they had come back to the house and had found Simmy on the floor by the staircase. She had had a stroke. It had left her without speech, lying motionless in her bedroom. After two months, Matt and Cathy had decided that there wasn't much hope left. Then one morning, Matt went in and found Tigger in the bed with Simmy.

She spoke something. At first, it was just a cluster of meaningless sounds, but at least, it was an effort. She lifted a weak hand, as if to shoo Tigger off the bed, but the wrist gave out. She arched an eyebrow, tried again to speak, and this time Matt understood. She was trying to say, "Worthless ol' cat."

A month later, she was saying it.

"Where's Peter?" Matt asked her.

"He's 'round back."

Matt went down the steps from the back porch into the yard.

He found his son sitting by himself, right at the entry point to the crawlspace beneath the porch.

"Something wrong?"

The boy shrugged, without looking at his father.

"You want to tell me about it?"

"Why do bad things happen?" Peter asked. "Like what happened to Uncle Tommy, and to Jimmy?"

Matt turned away from his son's imploring eyes. It wasn't his favorite question. "I can't say I know, son. I'd be lying if I did."

"Does God even care about us?"

Matt was stumped. He turned to his son, his eyes full of the first hint of metaphysical doubt that he had always found so touching in children. Before.

"I'm sure he does. Maybe we just expect too much."

"I wish I was God."

"Why do you say that?"

" 'Cause. I'd make sure nothing bad ever happened."

"How?"

"Dunno. Guess, I'd make everybody do what I told 'em to do."

"Maybe that's why you're not God, son." Matt smiled. "Maybe He can't do that. Or won't let Himself, even if He could."

"Yeah." But Peter's eyes were still unconvinced.

You can't learn everything all at once, Matt reflected. He patted his son on the head and went back inside.

4

It was after ten.

Matt and Cathy were in bed reading—Tigger was on his usual pillow—when Peter walked in and, without asking for an invitation, hopped up with them. He stroked Tigger's chin.

"Remember when you used to tell me stories? Before I went to bed. The ones about Tigger?"

Matt glanced up from his book—it was a history of the Civil War. He nodded, then went back to his reading. "I remember."

"Why don't you anymore?"

"Dunno. I guess I don't like telling stories so much now."

"Because of what happened?" Peter asked.

"Probably."

"I miss 'em. They were good," Peter told him. "I like the one you told about how Tigger got locked inside the pyramid and the mummy started chasing him around. I'd like to hear that one again."

Cathy smiled. "I kinda like to hear that one myself."

"No," Matt said firmly.

"Please!"

"Come on, Matt. Be a sport," Cathy said. But Matt's eyes did not move from the book he was holding.

"I don't tell stories anymore. Okay?"

"Okay." And Peter wearily got up from the bed. He glanced over his shoulder and said, "Come on, Tigger. Reckon you won't have any adventures tonight."

When the boy left, Cathy looked at Matt. "Would it really

hurt? I mean, one little Tigger story? Lord, you haven't even talked like Tigger in a year, honey. Peter and I, we've had to do all his talking for him. And we're not nearly as good as you are."

Matt sighed. "Maybe one day. Just not now."

5

When Cathy woke up, Matt was not beside her.

She looked at the clock by the bed. It was after four in the morning.

"Lord," Cathy whispered. She got up and slipped on her nightgown.

She stopped by the window and stared into the backyard. As always, it was full of shadows. Shadows that never again could look quite as innocent as they once had.

Out in the hallway, she called Matt's name. But there was no answer.

She went to each room, but it was empty.

At last, she turned to the door that led up to the attic.

Somebody was up there.

"Matt?" she called out in disbelief. How long had it been? A year. Not once during that time had Matt even set foot up in that room. Not once had he cast a glance at the screen of his computer.

Why would he be up there now?

On tiptoe she went up the dark and narrow attic stairway. She heard the computer keys. They were fluttering at a hundred miles a minute.

She quietly pushed open the door.

No light was on. There was only the little yellow letters glowing on the monitor screen.

"Matt?"

He jumped and swiveled around in his chair. "Christ, you scared the shit out of me."

"What are you doing?"

He looked back at the screen. "Nothing."

"You're writing something, aren't you?"

"No. I'm not doing anything."

"Yes, you are."

"Okay, I'm balancing my checkbook."

Cathy laughed. "You've never balanced a checkbook in your life." She walked over to where Matt was sitting. She stared down at the screen and read aloud the sentence beneath the words "CHAPTER ONE."

" 'When Tommy first looked at me, with my crippled foot, I knew that there would never be any love between us. I was wrong.' "

She put her hands on Matt's shoulder. "You're writing about Tommy, aren't you?"

"It's not a story. It's . . . true-to-life."

Cathy smiled and eased herself into his lap. She put her hands on the keyboard and typed.

"I love you very much."

He hesitated, then typed. " 'Preciate it."

6

"Where you taking me?"

They were at the end of the hallway on the third floor. It was after five in the morning. Cathy and Matt had decided not to go back to sleep, but instead they had opened a bottle of champagne. It, along with five other cases, had been left over from the party they were planning to have on their triumphant return from California one year before.

"I haven't been up here since I was a boy."

And taking Cathy's hand, Matt led her up the stairway. They both stopped and giggled when their heads bumped against the ceiling. It was old Great-grandpa Leon's stairway that led nowhere.

They sat down and Matt uncorked the bottle of champagne.

He stared up, shook his head, and grinned.

"Tommy and I used to sit up here and wonder why in hell it didn't go anyplace."

"Did you ever figure it out?"

"I think I said, 'Maybe it did go someplace. Maybe it went up to Storyworld.' And I remember, Tommy shook his head and gave me that look he always gave me. 'Lord, Matt, ain't you got eyes? It goes up to the ceiling, s'all.' " Matt sipped the champagne. "Who knows"—he smiled—"maybe we were both right."